THE SIPHONING
BOOK 1 OF THE REDEMPTION SERIES

D.T. Stubblefield

The Siphoning

Text © D.T. Stubblefield, 2023

ISBN 979-8-9878489-1-3

Cover by BEAUTeBOOK

Cover illustration by illustrate_vnzl

Also available in eBook.

PART I

CHAPTER 1

Drakon heaved himself through the open third-story window. His black cloak flowed about him, concealing him in shadow. His muscles quivered from the rapid ascent. Below, the clamp of boots and a muttered conversation passed beneath the window and then receded.

Another close call.

This made the fourth such encounter of the night. He lived by a rule: two close calls and he would abort a mission. Each time he ignored this simple rule, something untoward happened. His survival instincts screamed for him to turn back and return another night but time was short, and he was dangerously close to missing his deadline. The manor grounds were an ant colony of activity, and it took him longer than expected to make it this far. Seconds dripped by, increasing his chances of being discovered.

Discovery meant death.

Silently, he settled into the wooden floorboards. No groan of protest announced his entry. Crouching, Drakon pulled the cowl of his cloak lower and drifted wraith-like into the chamber. A breeze swept inward. The cool, crisp air did nothing to purify the overwhelming stench of incense hanging in the bedchamber.

A light orb floated overhead, casting the chamber in a warm yellow glow, elongating the shadows in which

Drakon hid. Art canvases of all sizes hung on the stone walls, ornate furniture adorned every square inch, and a massive four-poster bed overflowing with furs stood at the chamber's center.

Drakon curled his lip in disdain. The warden's blatant show of wealth was in contrast to the poverty of the people he lorded over. Another warden charged with the well-being of commoners lining his pockets from the people's labor. He hadn't expected much humility from a noble, and even less from a mage such as the Jenna City Warden.

Drakon's orders from the king were clear. The warden was to appear to have died of natural causes. Drakon wasn't privy to the transgression the man committed to garner himself a spot on the king's kill list. The reason was inconsequential. He didn't care, nor did he mete out judgments. The Royal Council dealt with such things. He was but the gnarled hand of death employed to dole out the punishment. Drakon recalled the death and poverty he witnessed while traversing the Commoner District of the city and grimaced. He would enjoy killing this warden.

The bedchamber was empty, as Drakon knew it would be. He committed his mark's routine to memory. The warden was middle-aged, but his habit of nightly drinking and debauchery was legendary throughout the Kingdom of Somorrah.

Drakon's gaze searched the chamber for the warden's favorite vice. *There.* A pitcher and glass sat on a table next to the bed; remnants of red wine stained the bottom of the glass. Drakon removed a vial from his cloak. A colorless, odorless liquid sloshed within its clear container. He would add one drop into the glass, and the deed would be done.

He would send word of the mission's completion to the king. Afterward, he might take an overdue leave of absence.

He moved toward the table. Laughter and shuffling footsteps from outside the closed door froze him halfway across the chamber. The doorknob turned, and the door banged open. Drakon threw himself into the shadows of a wardrobe. Sounds of merriment drifted into the room and then were muted as the door snicked shut.

The warden was early. Drakon hadn't expected him until nearer to dawn. He cursed inwardly. He couldn't wait in the shadows until the man passed out. The king made his instructions all too clear. The warden was to die before sunrise. Drakon gritted his teeth. He would have to improvise. He hated improvising. It reduced his chances of an undetected escape, but what other choice was there?

He pocketed the vial and pressed against the wardrobe. The warden, red-faced and inebriated, stumbled on unsteady legs toward the bed, hauling a struggling woman behind him. He was small and slender, manual labor having never sculpted the muscles of his body. Like all wardens, he was also a magical mage. The man's diminutive physique was no indication of his power.

Alabaster skin inked with tattoos peeked from the warden's robes, testaments of his magical aptitude. Only his face was unmarred. Each tattoo was a rune etched to guard the warden against the harmful effects of drawing the goddess's power. Such power came with a price, and the wardens protected themselves with the tattoos.

The warden's hair was a dirty blond, and his skin was pale but not an unearthly translucent. A mage's hair, eyes, and skin lightened with their growth in magic. This mage wasn't as strong as the others Drakon killed. His tongue prodded a void a molar once occupied as a reminder of past battles against magical enemies. *Thank the goddess for small mercies.*

A sob drew his attention to the woman the warden dragged in tow. She was waif-like. Oily black hair concealed her face, and her chestnut skin identified her as a commoner. Her threadbare dress was torn at the neck and thin enough to see through. She was probably a slave. He resigned himself to the possibility of collateral. From the look of her, death would be preferable to her current lot in life. He could give her that escape, at least.

The warden yanked the woman forward. She struggled all the more, whimpering and pleading for release. The warden cursed and slapped her hard enough to snap her head back. The blow whipped her face toward Drakon and freed it from its curtain of dirty hair.

Drakon's eyes flared. A face smooth with youth was decorated with black and blue bruises and a split lip. Terror-filled eyes glistened with tears and, more disturbing, resignation. This was no woman as he initially believed. It was a young girl.

The warden slapped the girl again. The crack ricocheted off the walls, and she slumped dazed into the warden's arms. Having subdued her struggles, the man dragged her to the bed and flung her across it. She curled into a tight ball and whimpered. The warden grabbed her thin ankle and yanked her toward the edge of the bed.

"Quit your yammering!" He climbed atop her, clasping her wrists in one hand. "You should be honored that I would bring a smut like you to my bed!"

Blood pounded in Drakon's ears. Unbidden, dark memories rushed to the surface of his mind.

A slave child. Powerless. Drakon blinked and shook his head, trying to dislodge the memory. Nausea rolled through him. His blood heated in his veins.

Hay scratching tender skin.

Powerless.

With effort, he forced the memories back, slamming the door on their mental prison. Yet, the rage left in their wake had Drakon darting silently from the shadows and toward the warden, who tore at the girl's clothing, before he realized he was moving.

The warden stiffened with awareness, some part of his inebriated psyche realizing they were not alone.

Too late. Drakon's blade slipped in the hollow at the base of the man's skull. The body jerked. Drakon twisted, severing the spine, and yanked the dagger free. The body slumped forward. Blood gushed from the wound, coating the bed and the startled girl beneath. He pushed the body aside and freed her.

Wide, oddly ancient eyes—much too knowing for a child—peered back at him from a tear-streaked face mottled with bruises. She sucked in a deep breath, a preamble to a scream. His hand clamped over her mouth.

"Do. Not. Scream. I won't harm you, but you will remain silent." He stared into her shining, unblinking eyes.

"Nod if you understand."

She nodded slowly, and he peeled his hand away, ready to place it back. She didn't scream but sat up and eyed him with caution. He grabbed an unsoiled coverlet from the bed and tossed it at her.

"Cover yourself and get out of here. Tell no one of what you've seen."

Even as he uttered the command, he knew he was being a fool. The only way to ensure her silence was to kill her, but he couldn't bring himself to kill an innocent. No doubt, her short life was filled with atrocities for which this night was but a culmination. Her petite frame trembled beneath the coverlet.

No. Drakon was not so far gone that he would kill a slave girl. His soul was black and withered, but he had not delivered it to the pits of Targarius. *Not yet.*

The girl's throat worked. "Th–thank you." Her voice was an unsteady whisper in the quiet chamber.

He cleared his throat. Her thanks unsettled him for reasons he didn't want to acknowledge. He turned, focusing on the warden, and grimaced at the mess he had made. Blood soaked the bed beneath the corpse and pooled on the floor. A frozen mask of surprise rested on the man's face. His pale-blue eyes locked on the nothingness of death. Already pale skin drained of its color as blood leaked from the body.

Drakon took in the tattooed runes on the warden's skin. All that power and useless against a simple dagger. In the mage's assurance in his magical superiority, he never suspected or spelled against nonmagical attacks. It was the way of nobles—arrogance above intellect.

Drakon sighed. The man's death would never pass for natural causes. His moment of untethered emotion destroyed weeks of planning. The outburst he exhibited was out of character. His lapse of control annoyed him, but he couldn't dwell on it. He had to plan his next steps, or they would be his last.

There was only one recourse left to him. He would re-move himself from the city before the warden's body was discovered. But before he fled, he would retrieve the other reason he was eager for this mission. He bent over the body, rummaging through the folds of the robes.

"Where is it?"

He rolled the corpse on its stomach and patted it down. He cursed. *Nothing.*

The warden always carried an object of power when he visited Sura City. Indeed, this mission excited Drakon for this reason. Desire to own such an object clouded his logic. In hindsight, it went to reason the warden would travel to court with additional protection. Nobles and commoners alike distrusted the king and the royal mage. The Jenna Warden would've been a fool not to travel with safeguards. However, the man wouldn't carry such items in his dwell-ing. He should have understood this sooner.

Drakon stood with a grunt of frustration, wiped his blade on his leathers, and returned it to its sheath. If the mission went according to plan, he would've had time to search the chamber. As it were, he would be leaving with-out his prize.

He spared a glance at the girl. Shock had yet to release her from its grasp. If the warden's guards found her, they would sacrifice her in Drakon's stead. He hoped she didn't waste his gift of mercy. She would live or die by her action or inaction alone.

He sprinted to the window and glanced out. No sentries stood guard or moved across the grounds. That was good, and no one would enter the warden's chamber until the maid arrived for the morning cleaning. Drakon would be long gone by then. As if summoned by the thought, a creak sounded from the door.

"Rainore? What the devil is taking so long? Finish with the—"

A slender man, clad in nothing more than skin and his mage tattoos, stopped mid-stride into the room. His pale-blue eyes locked on Drakon's cloaked figure, widened, and then flicked to the body cradled in a crimson stain on the bed.

He screamed.

ॐ

Mages were the only wielders of magic in the Kingdom. This was law. Yet, the force Drakon summoned was as effective as any mage spell.

Drakon directed his power around the mage's neck with a raised hand. A force clamped down on the man like the jaws of a hungry stray dog. The shriek was crushed, silencing the mage and sealing off any spells he might utter.

A panicked gurgle slipped through the man's trembling lips, and his pale eyes bulged. He clawed at his neck, struggling to suck in air that wouldn't pass Drakon's magical hold.

Drakon closed his outstretched hand into a fist. The man's throat crumpled with an audible crunch. Drakon released his hold, and the body collapsed to the floor.

Fatigue washed over Drakon, the cost of using his hidden gift. He sagged against the wall and dragged in a steadying breath, pushing past the weakness. This drain to his strength was one reason he sought an object of power from the warden. One could never have enough power.

Controlling his breathing, he listened. The music downstairs had ceased. A murmur of concerned voices rose in its place. Footsteps thundered up the stairs. He propelled across the chamber and latched the door closed.

Moments later, the doorknob turned. "Warden? You all right in there?" a voice asked from the other side of the door.

When there was no answer, a more forceful knock came and then muffled whispers. A body slammed into the door from the other side. The wood shuttered in the frame. That hadn't taken long. The door wouldn't withstand much more. Sooner or later, either force or spell would open it. He wouldn't be there when it did.

He strode back to the window and peered out across the grounds. Armed men raced toward the manor from the perimeter wall and gatehouse. He cursed and ducked back into the chamber. He would be spotted and shot through with arrows before he reached the ground. His other option was to fight his way through the crowd at the door with only a blade. He didn't like either option. His magic might work against one or two unsuspecting mages, but it wouldn't stand against a mob of them. After the element of surprise wore off, it would be their magic against his physical skills, in which case his survival odds dropped drastically.

He could've used an object of power right about now.

"My Lord?"

The girl's voice broke through his thoughts. He had forgotten about her in all the excitement. She stood beside the bed, the coverlet wrapped about her in a makeshift toga. Large, oddly assessing eyes stared at him. Her gaze stared into his being as if she scanned the inner-most workings of his character. *Peculiar child.* He shook the eerie feeling away.

"I'm no one's master," he said, only loud enough to be heard above the banging. She shrank into herself at his words. He didn't have time for this. She should have left when he instructed her to.

He moved closer. "Speak your mind. I don't have time to pry the words from you."

Small hands twisted in her covering. Her eyes flicked to the rattling door and back to Drakon. "I know another way out."

He lifted a brow and scanned the room for a door or opening he overlooked. "Where is it?"

"I'll show you, but in return, you must promise to take me with you." Her determined eyes met his and held.

This waif witnessed him dispatch two mages, they were moments away from death, and she had the gumption to give him an ultimatum? He let out a huff of approval. He respected her audacity.

The pummeling of the door stopped, and chanting began. The mages had arrived. It would seem he would have a traveling partner.

He nodded. "You have my word. I'll see you out of the city, but we won't be waiting until morning. We leave *tonight*." He emphasized the last word so there was no misunderstanding.

To the people of Somorrah, torture and death were preferable to venturing outside a city or Waystation during the night. Her face went ashen. She understood the risk.

The chanting increased to a crescendo. Conjured magic

vibrated the heavy door.

"Decide quickly, girl!"

She blinked out of her stupor—her present danger seeming to outweigh her fear of possible tribulations she might face outside the city.

"This way." She raced to the wardrobe, flung open the doors, and disappeared inside.

Did the girl think to hide inside the furnishing? The royal mage provided him with the schematics for the manor. Nolan would've been aware of any hidden passages, and he hadn't shared any such details with Drakon.

Drakon pinched the bridge of his nose. He had allowed himself to believe she knew another way from the chamber. Resigned, he withdrew his dagger. He would fight. Capture was not an option.

The girl's head peeked from the open door. She waved him forward. "What are you waiting for? Hurry. Follow me."

She vanished back inside before Drakon could reply. The grinding of stone sounded, and a dusty odor, akin to a tomb being open, tickled his nose. He followed and ducked in after her, pulling the door closed behind him.

Pushed to one side, a handful of mage robes hung, and the back of the wardrobe opened to yawning darkness. He scowled as unease stirred in his belly. Nolan had to know about this secret entrance. The royal mage was no fool. He would've understood withholding such vital information would lower Drakon's chances of escape.

It would appear the Jenna Warden's death wasn't the only planned assassination of the night.

A flame flickered to life. The soft glow danced on the

walls of a narrow stairwell. Drakon stepped inside.

"Here." The girl shoved a torch at him.

She reached up and pulled a lever hidden between the brick-and-mortar. The false wall slid back into place. She held out a small hand for the torch, and Drakon returned it. He would need his hands unencumbered should they come upon any guards or mages in the tight passage.

She scampered down the stairs, her bare feet quick and silent against the stone. "These are the servant passages. They run throughout the house. Master Rainore doesn't," she stopped and corrected herself, "he didn't like us slaves wandering the main corridors."

Drakon grunted. The warden might not have allowed slaves in his halls, but he had no problem with them filling his bed. The hypocrite. It was all the same with nobles. They abused the commoner women and employed magic to ensure no whelps spawned from the unions. It made him wonder about his conception. The only mixed blood...

"You're the king's royal assassin."

He focused on his tiny guide. The girl stared over her shoulder at him, her eyes twinkling in the torchlight.

Although his face was hidden in the shadows of his hood, the skin of his hands was exposed. His mocha skin was an oddity compared to the alabaster of the nobles and the contrasting browns of commoner skin.

"They say you're an evil spirit and the goddess cursed you from the womb."

He scoffed. Nobles and commoners alike whispered tales about him. He did nothing to dissuade them. Their belief he was more than a man demonstrated their simplemindedness. They would rather believe a lie than acknowledge the fact noblemen hated every aspect of commoners, except the women.

"None of what they say concerns me. Your immediate concern should be our capture and painful deaths at the hands of the wardens guards and fellow mages."

Her large eyes widened in the dim light, and she quickened her pace. They moved in silence, steadily heading downward. Drakon readied his blade and listened for sounds of pursuit but heard nothing. If they were being followed, their pursuers wouldn't know the exact route they took. He hoped that would buy them more time to escape.

The narrow passage walls scrubbed his broad shoulders as they marched along, and the low ceiling grazed his head. Fending off any attacks in the tight space would be disastrous. The only positive in this situation was he had seen the guards' weapons. They carried long swords. In a frontal assault, they would have difficulty maneuvering. Only one man would be able to attack at a time. He would need to get in close with his dagger for his kills, but he had no problem with hand-to-hand combat.

Shouts and the sound of pounding feet along corridors seeped through the passage walls. Every guard and mage in the manor would be on the lookout. He peered into the inky blackness at his rear for any sign of movement.

"Do the warden's guards know of these passages?"

"Yes. The entrances are easy enough to find if one knows where to look." She shrugged her thin shoulders. "I assume guards and mages would know their locations."

As if on cue, the grinding of an unseen wall sliding open echoed through the passage. Ordered shouts filled the space. Drakon muttered an oath. *This night gets better and better*. He turned to spur the girl forward, but she was already racing away, the light of her torch fading with her retreat.

After a few hurried moments, they skidded to an abrupt halt at the end of the passage. The girl hung the torch on the wall, stood on tiptoes, and yanked down a handle. She started to reach for the door.

"Wait," Drakon said, "I'll go first."

Dagger in hand, he stepped around her and gripped the door handle. The door flew from his grasp, and a surprised guard gaped at him. The man recovered in an instant, bearing his sword and thrusting it toward Drakon's midsection.

In a moment of instinct, Drakon flattened himself against the wall. The thrust sliced through the folds of his cloak. Drakon pinned the outstretched bicep to the wall. He drove his blade into the man's exposed neck and sliced it across in one fluid motion. The guard collapsed backward onto the floor of the kitchen beyond.

Drakon waved the girl forward. "Out! Now!" She stared at him, eyes unblinking, fingers touching parted lips. "Now!" he said with more urgency.

She blinked, freeing herself from her temporary paralysis, and skirted the body and the spreading pool of crimson. Drakon latched the door behind them. It wasn't much, but the locked door would hinder any pursuers for a minute at least. He would take what he could get.

A wooden table and four chairs ate up much of the space in the kitchen. A knife and chopped vegetables lay abandoned on the table. The servants must have been vacated in a hurry. The girl scampered around the table, grabbing fistfuls of food and stuffing them within the folds of her clothing as she hurried to the door.

"This way leads to the west wall." She opened the door and peered outside. "I don't see anyone. We should leave now while no one is around."

Drakon moved to follow, but two armed guards rushed through a doorway leading to the dining area, cutting off his route. The first man slid on the widening pool of blood. His arms pinwheeled before he went heels up. His skull met the stone floor with a sickening thud. His body went limp. Seeing his downed comrade, the second guard skirted the blood more carefully and drew his sword.

With a battle cry, he charged at Drakon.

At the last moment, Drakon twisted inside the swing, catching his attacker's wrist in his grip. He drove his knee up into the extended elbow. The man let out an ear-piercing scream as bone snapped. Drakon silenced him with his dagger and let the body slump to the floor with the others.

The door to the servants' passages banged behind him. Drakon's gaze flicked upward, and he sighed. *Goddess save him.* The door rattled and bowed outward from the blows. It would not hold his pursuers for long, and then he would be overrun. A massive cabinet stood to the right of the door. He dashed over to it and shoved. It crashed to the floor. Dishes and serving platters flew from its innards and shattered into shards, but the door was blocked.

So much for a stealthy escape, he lamented. This mission had officially devolved into a debacle.

He sprinted to the open door and the girl. A quick glance outside revealed the deserted manor grounds. He nodded toward the perimeter wall.

"Run straight for the wall. Don't look back and don't get

caught."

He had given his word he would help her escape but not at the cost of his own capture and death. If she wanted to live, she would keep up. He sprang from the door and raced across the yard, his long legs devouring the distance between the house and the wall.

He didn't slow or look back, the girl's shallow breaths the only indication she followed close behind. Shouts rang out behind them. They were spotted. He angled for a cluster of trees in front of the wall, skidded to a stop, and knelt to remove branches and debris from the base of a tree.

The girl stopped beside him and began to bounce from foot to foot. She dragged a trembling hand through her dirty hair and spared a glance toward the shouts and pursuit, which grew louder with every moment.

"Please hurry. They're coming!"

Drakon yanked a sack from its hiding place, opened it, and freed a four-pronged hook with a rope attached. He stood, hurled it over the wall, and tugged until the hook caught and the rope went taut.

"Climb. The wall is over eight feet high. Roll into the landing, so you don't break your neck on impact."

Her eyes were bright with fear, but she needed no further instruction. She grabbed the rope from his grasp and shimmied up the wall. At the top, she glanced back for a moment before she leaped from view. With any luck, Drakon wouldn't find her in a broken heap on the other side.

The sounds of the nearing guards grabbed Drakon's attention. He could make out faces, but they wouldn't be able to identify him with his face hidden within the shadows of his hood. He grabbed the rope, making quick work of the climb. He straddled the wall and dropped down, following his own advice and rolling into the landing. Drakon stood, repositioned his hood, and dusted the dirt from his cloak.

A "psst" from a nearby bush drew his attention. The girl stood from where she was crouched behind the shrubbery. Her hair was mussed, and her makeshift dress was decorated with dirt and leaves, but she appeared uninjured. He inclined his head to her. She might live through this night after all.

CHAPTER 2

Beyond the warden's barricaded stronghold, the Noble District of Jenna City slept on. The panic and clamor associated with the murder had yet to spill out into the quiet. The tidy streets lined with ornate homes and posts lit with soft yellow orb light were free of curious eyes.

Drakon jogged toward the nearest alleyway. *Silent it might be, but the alarm would—*

A siren blared from somewhere on the manor grounds, interrupting his thoughts. The shrill sound pierced the night like a banshee announcing imminent death. Moments later, an answering siren echoed to the east. More sirens joined the chorus from the south and north. Lights began to glow within the houses like stoked embers. The city awakened.

"Move, now, before we're seen."

He slipped into the cover of the alleyway. The girl crouched beside him, her breathing shallow but quiet. They hurried to the opposite alley mouth. The street was empty. No nobles ventured from their homes, but they soon would. It would be a matter of time before the roads were crawling with the city's noble inhabitants. He dashed across the lane and ducked into another backstreet.

Drakon and his ward moved in this manner, without seeing guard or mage, for long minutes. Tension drained from him with the distance he placed between himself and the manor. Their pursuers were likely establishing a blockade at Jenna's gates. They would organize a checkpoint to apprehend him and the girl as they tried to leave in the morning. It was a logical strategic response. There was only one entrance into Jenna, and no one would expect them to flee tonight.

However, Drakon wouldn't be leaving the city through the well-known access point. He would be long gone by morning and halfway to his destination before the search migrated outside Jenna.

He rested against the chilled stone of a building, concealed within its shadows. His lungs burned, and the muscles of his legs quivered at the pace of his continuous jog. It had been years since more than a short trot was required for his work. Such was the benefit of well-laid planning. One had the luxury of slipping out unnoticed and unhurried. He berated himself again for dispatching the warden contrary to his orders.

Beside him, the girl was bent at the waist, her hands on her knees, sucking in gulps of air. He hadn't slowed his stride for her, and she kept pace without a word of complaint. It was commendable.

He gestured to a rickety wooden bridge, which stretched over a small canal, separating the lit, pristine streets of the Noble District from the darkened, debris-laden roads of the Commoner District slum. Their escape would be concealed in the unlit, tight walkways and the closely packed shanties.

"We're almost to the Commoner District. Once we're there, our progress will be harder to track and less encumbered."

In the distance, Jenna's outer wall towered over the uneven, slanted roofs of the commoner shacks like a beacon of hope. *Just a little farther.* Mages rarely crossed into the Commoner District, and the commoners continuously built new structures to accommodate their growing population. They could disappear.

The echo of boots sounded on the street. Three men approached, peering into alleys as they passed. Their dark skin and hair glistened in the torchlight brightening their path.

Drakon retreated deeper into the shadows, wrapped his cloak snugly about himself, and flattened against the building. The light peeled back the darkness of the alley like a coverlet, stopping inches from his hiding place.

A guard separated from the group to squint into the blackness. His hand hovered over the hilt of his sword. Drakon eased his blade free. His muscles coiled, preparing to strike if the man took another step.

An exasperated sigh came from the street. "Hurry it up, Grandor! We're wasting time," another of the guards said. "There's no way they would head deeper into the city. It doesn't make sense. We should be searching near the gates." He waved a hand at the empty road. "No one's out here. The commander sent us out here because he doesn't like you."

This drew a groan from the guard nearest Drakon. "Not that again." His hand dropped from his sword, and he rejoined his companions. "Should we search the Commoner District?"

The man who spoke earlier glanced at the bridge and

scoffed. "And waste the whole night in there? As I said, no one's going to head deeper into the city. We'll tell the commander we searched it."

The other two guards assented, and the group moved off, heading toward the gates. Drakon stayed unmoving until their footsteps retreated along with the torchlight. He let out a breath he hadn't realized he was holding, replaced his dagger, and inched back to the alley mouth. He peered into the road. There was no sign of the men.

"Let's move before anyone else passes through the area."

Silence at his rear caused him to turn. The girl was nowhere in sight. Before he could contemplate her absence, a scream came from the street behind him. Drakon gave a weary exhale and scrubbed a hand down his face. Perhaps the child was more trouble than she was worth. Still, he backtracked for a closer inspection of the situation.

A barrel-chested guard held the kicking, screaming girl aloft in meaty arms. Her twiggy limbs flailed in a wild attempt at escape.

"Stop squirming, chit!" He cuffed her head. Her scream morphed into a dazed groan, and she ceased her struggles.

He leaned down to speak in her ear. "That's better. Now, where's the man you were with? I know he's got to be around here somewhere."

She started to shake her head, but his arms tightened around her waist, eliciting a yipe of pain. "Don't lie to me. You fled the warden's manor with someone. Tell me the truth, or I'll make you tell me. Do yourself a favor and choose the easy option."

Drakon gritted his teeth. This was a complication he

didn't need. He should turn and leave. He could make it through the Commoner District faster and be out of the city in a matter of minutes.

But he couldn't abandon her. For one, she had seen his face. She wouldn't withstand an interrogation from the mages, and two, he had given his word to see her safely from Jenna. The dull sound of a fist meeting flesh and the girl's cry steeled his resolve.

He stepped into the roadway, sweeping back his hood and revealing himself. The man glanced up from his abuse and took in Drakon's visage. His eyes flared with recognition and then fear.

Drakon allowed a corner of his mouth to lift with amusement. "Release the girl, and I promise you a swift death," he said.

The guard, muttering incoherently, shoved the girl away. She sprawled on the ground and scuttled away on her hands and knees. The man scampered back, fumbling for his sword, his hands clumsy with panic.

Drakon threw his dagger with a whip of his hand. It flew end over end, striking the stunned man in the chest. The guard glanced down in confusion at the blade protruding from him. Drakon crossed the distance before the man could react. In a whirl of cloak, he front kicked the blade hilt deep into the man's heart.

The guard dropped to his knees with a wheeze, his arms limp at his sides and his eyes wide. Drakon approached, planted a foot on his chest, and yanked free his blade, allowing the man to flop to the street. With an efficient movement, he bent and ran the weapon across the man's throat, ending his life. Drakon straightened and replaced his hood.

He flicked the blood from his dagger and sheathed it.

He turned and strode past the wide-eyed girl. A few moments later, her hurried footsteps followed.

"Thank you," she said to his retreating back.

He nodded in response and led them back through the alley, across the street, over the bridge, and into the Commoner District. They fled unobstructed through the tight maze of dilapidated buildings and crumbling walkways. A few bedraggled inhabitants shuffled along the moonlit roads on their way to goddess knew where. Emaciated cats and dogs rummaged through piles of rubbish, not bothering to look up as they passed.

Before long, Drakon was staring at the outer wall. He moved forward and ran a hand against the vine-laden barricade, searching. The opening he sought was impossible to detect unless one knew where to look. *Ah ha, there it was:* a door's outline.

He probed lower still and detected the keyhole indentation. He pulled a key from his cloak. The moonlight glimmered across the metal like ripples along the surface of water. He pushed it in and twisted. The time-rusted tumblers turned with effort, and he pocketed the key.

He turned to the girl and noticed her trembling. She feared what lay outside the city walls, as any wise person would, but she had no other options. There was nothing but death here for her. Sooner or later, she would be apprehended, tortured for information, and executed for her nonexistent role in the warden's murder.

"Pick your danger, girl, and do so quickly. You can stay here and be captured, and you will be found soon enough, or you can come with me and take a chance on the night."

"I'll die out there if I go with you, and so will you."

"I won't lie to you. You might still die tonight, but I will try my best to ensure you don't."

The words shocked Drakon when he realized they were true. He would protect her until he could get her to relative safety.

She stepped away from him, shaking her head, her eyes overbright with growing terror. "It's not safe. W–we can hide 'til morning."

He should've known this would happen. He couldn't begrudge this child her fear. Fear could decimate even the most well-made intentions. He understood her reservations, but he wouldn't let them stop him.

He gave what he hoped was a reassuring smile. "You're right. We'll hide out and wait until morning." He made to move past her.

She released a breath, her shoulders sagging in relief. She wasn't prepared when Drakon's hand shot out toward her. He applied pressure to two points above her collarbone. Her eyes widened for a split-second before they rolled upward, and she collapsed.

Drakon caught her slight weight before she hit the ground and slung her over his shoulder. A fleeting discomfort settled over him at her proximity, but he pushed past it. She wouldn't be unconscious for long. It would be better for them both if they were at his camp before she awoke.

He shouldered open the door and slipped out into the night. The door fell back into place with a clang that echoed into the distance. A chill kissed the nape of his neck. The night was as still as a tomb, and a cool breeze ruffled his hood. The surrounding forest cast menacing shadows like fingers stretching and snaking out to grab them.

From afar, a wail rose, traveling on the wind like a messenger of death. Guttural huffs and whines answered. Drakon tightened his grip on the girl and raced into the trees.

ॐ

To stop was to die.

Drakon crashed through the forest, leaping over foliage and ducking low hanging branches. Fear threatened to paralyze him, amplified by each huff and grunt hounding him. Rustling underbrush kept pace with him. Pale blurs darted in and out of the shadows and thundered overhead among the trees.

His fatigued legs screamed in protest. Sweat beaded along his forehead.

To stop was to die.

The forests of Somorrah were once safe places, plentiful with wildlife. But now, no animals lived outside the warded cities and Waystations, consumed by the creatures pursuing him.

Moonlight trickled through the dense canopy to the forest floor, illuminating the way. Drakon kept his eyes steady on the path. The girl's weight lay as heavy as lead across his shoulder, setting a blaze of fire down the muscle.

To stop was to die.

Safety was within reach. His camp wasn't much farther. The beasts wouldn't attack him. *He hoped.* He had no such illusions about the girl, but they wouldn't be getting her either.

Deafening wails and shrieks swirled around him.

Branches shook. Leaves rained down as heavy bodies leaped from tree to tree. Drakon pushed his legs harder, moving faster. He couldn't outrun them.

As if conjured, one of the creatures dropped from the trees a few strides ahead. Drakon skidded to a stop to avoid running headlong into the beast. It rose from its crouched position to a staggering height. Muscles in its massive hind legs twitched. It rocked forward on taloned feet, primed to pounce.

Moonbeams streamed across its milky skin. The flattened mass of flesh of its head connected to a short neck as thick as Drakon's thigh. Elongated dagger-like vertebrae jutted from its back and down to a stubby tail. A translucent membrane of flesh fused over the spine in a dorsal sail. Lumbering arms hung nearly to the ground, and taloned hands dangled at its sides. Its two sets of eyes, two on either side of its head, shone as if backlit with brimstone.

It watched Drakon. Thin lips peeled back in a hiss, revealing a double row of jagged teeth. Tendrils of roped saliva dripped from its mouth, pattering the ground.

The creatures were called wailers after their mournful cries, which could elicit a shudder from the most formidable warrior. Standing face to face with one of the monsters, Drakon could decipher nothing melancholy about this denizen of death.

The night breeze chilled his sweat-dampened skin, and he tightened his hold on the girl. A scan of the area revealed pale forms materializing from the darkness. At least a dozen were visible. No doubt more were hidden from view.

Another hiss came from the wailer blocking his path. Drakon took a controlling breath. The adrenaline spiking his blood and knotting his gut became bearable. His flight or fight response warred for control of his body. Yet, his mind reasoned they hadn't attacked him. They wanted something. He wasn't so horror-struck he didn't know what they desired.

The beast gestured to the girl slung over Drakon's shoulder. It huffed what he could only assume was a demand. The communication, rudimentary as it was, was unexpected. The Gathi believed wailers unthinking creatures. He didn't find the discovery to the contrary encouraging. Mindless beasts were dangerous but easily outsmarted. Intelligent beasts were potentially detrimental to the safety of the Kingdom.

The wailer hissed its impatience. It took a step forward, its statement clear. It demanded the girl as toll. Self-preservation screamed for him to surrender the child and not look back. However, it would've been more merciful to have killed her than to feed her to these abominations. He also promised her protection. Even an assassin honored his word. He didn't give it often.

Drakon took a measured step back. It had been some time since his last use of power. He might have another surge in him. He willed the energy to gather and swell, shaping an orb within himself.

Drakon met the monstrosity's cold glare. He shook his head in defiance. "I won't be feeding you this night."

Although the wailer didn't speak his language, the beast was astute enough to read Drakon's retreat as refusal. It threw back its head and roared in a fury, the sound scraping his eardrums like a dull knife against rawhide.

Over his shoulder, the girl jerked awake. She scanned

her surroundings. Her body tensed as she noticed the creatures lurking around them. The scream she issued rivaled the wailers.

Her screech was like a dinner bell, causing pale bodies to converge on them, surging from the shadows. Drakon released the power orb he prepared. The force crashed over the charging wailers like a wave against a rock, hurtling them into trees and underbrush. Adrenaline and terror wrestled with the customary fatigue following the use of his power. Drakon fought against the shroud of unconsciousness dancing in his peripheral. If he fell, it would be the end of him and the girl.

A jab to his ribs focused his attention on the child. She floundered on his shoulder like a beached fish. He gripped her tighter and broke into a sprint.

Spiny branches clawed and clutched at him as he tore past. He barreled on with no regard to the stings lashing his body. Deafening howls and the pounding of renewed pursuit shook the earth beneath his feet. A grunt came from close behind. Instincts drew Drakon's gaze over his shoulder. Outstretched talons reached inches from the girl's face. He twisted away, never slowing his pace. Momentum carried the creature past and into the brambles in a tangle of limbs, snapped twigs, and agonized shrieks.

The trees thinned, and a valley came into view. Drakon could make out his camp nestled at the bottom of the hill against an overhang of rock. Relief flooded him. They were going to make it.

A violent jerk halted his forward dash, nearly yanking him from his feet. The girl cried out as she was lifted from his shoulder. Drakon clamped a forearm across her legs, freeing his dagger as he whirled around. A beast hung from a branch, a taloned hand fisting the girl's ebony locks. It flexed its arm to yank. Drakon swung his blade in an upward arch, slicing through the curtain of her hair. Then they were free and running again.

The wailer screamed in frustration. Drakon didn't look back. Instead, he bore down, his legs eating up the distance toward his camp.

Just a bit farther.

He crossed into the haven of his encampment. Moments later, an explosion sparked with an impact. Drakon spun back in time to see a wailer hurtling. It landed with a heavy thud, motionless in the grass. Smoke rose in long wisps from its scorched and blackened skin.

The remaining creatures prowled the perimeter, not daring to venture closer but not straying too far away. They eyed Drakon with wary amber eyes. These weren't the unthinking beasts he believed them to be. That knowledge sent a chill of unease through him.

A nicker drew his attention. Drakon's horse pawed at the dirt with restless energy. Thank the goddess, he tied and hooded the animal before his trek into Jenna. Had he not, the sight of the circling wailers might have sent it running from the safety of the ward.

He strode to the cold fire ring and deposited the girl on the ground.

"Don't move."

He needed not issue the command. The girl sat motionless, her eyes squeezed shut and her face wet with tears. A tight nod was the only sign she heard him. She drew her knobby knees to her chest and buried her head in them. He contemplated if he ought to say something to ease her fear but found no words. Instead, he continued to his horse.

Wailers paced him along their side of the ward, but he ignored them. They couldn't cross the enchantment. He paid a small fortune to guarantee it. Drakon stroked the horse's mane, whispering shushing sounds until the animal calmed. He dug inside the saddlebag hung across its flank and removed flint and steel. With a pat on his steed's neck, he returned to the fire ring and lit the kindling he gathered during the day. Flames sprung forth. Crackles and pops of the fire joined with the continuous hisses and grunts of their stalkers.

"You used magic." The girl's soft voice was raw from screaming, but the accusation was explicit.

"Commoners aren't supposed to use magic."

It was true. Mages supplied charms and trinkets to merchants and servants to ease chores or to heal minor sicknesses. For a commoner to employ real magic... It was forbidden. The nobles denied commoners access to that sufficient weapon.

Drakon glared at her until her oddly mature eyes shifted from him to the creatures pacing outside the ward. Firelight danced across her tear-streaked face, creating shimmering rivulets on her cheeks. Her hair was shorn unevenly above her ears due to his efforts to release her. She didn't seem to notice, however. She looked small and frightened. Even so, Drakon wouldn't be revealing the power he wielded was his own, and not the magic known to the nobles.

"Don't speak on things of no concern to you. Your concerns should be for your continued survival through the night, not how I decide to save you."

He stood abruptly, strode to his mount, and replaced the flint and steel. He unstrapped his sleeping mat from the saddlebag, returned, and dropped it at her feet.

"Here. Try to get some sleep."

She nodded but continued to stare up at him with expectant eyes. He turned away and settled down beside the fire. She rubbed her thin arms and glanced again at the prowling, watchful beasts. She shuddered and scooted closer to the warmth.

"The ward will hold, right?"

"It will hold." He shrugged out of his cloak, balled it into a makeshift pillow, and lay back in the grass. "Now sleep. We head out at first light. I'll drop you off at the closest Waystation. It's no more than a half-day ride. The Jenna guards and mages will waste that much time before discovering we're no longer in the city."

The girl didn't speak, but he heard the rustling of the sleeping mat as she climbed inside. He closed his eyes, feeling the aches adrenaline had numbed. Perhaps, he would have time to visit a merchant for healing salve before leaving the Waystation.

"Thank you again. For everything."

The gratitude was whispered, but Drakon heard it, nonetheless. He remained silent for a long while and then said, "You're welcome."

CHAPTER 3

The Waystation ramparts stretched to the heavens, proclaiming sanctuary for those seeking refuge. Drakon guided his mount against the current of people gushing from the open gates and toward the protection the stronghold promised. The travelers would begin their journeys anew until night once again chased them behind the warded walls of another Waystation or city.

The overpowering stench of unwashed bodies, urine, and excrement permeated the air. Drakon spat, clearing the acrid taste from the back of his throat, and weaved through numerous piles of rubbish and manure littering the muddy street. To his right, a pack of emaciated dogs fought over meager scraps in a gully.

Drakon curled his lip. Goddess, he hated Waystations. Too many people and animals in too small a place. Jurisdiction over the Waystations fell to the wardens, but most of them neglected to enforce measures of sanitary living conditions. As a result, waste from both the Gathi and their livestock was left to ferment in the sun. Disease ran rampant. Drakon's boot squished in a puddle, splashing rank liquid on his leathers. He swore.

He loathed these places.

"This place reeks." The girl's muffled voice traveled down from her seat atop the horse.

Drakon glanced up at her. She was swaddled in his spare cloak to shield herself from prying eyes. She clutched it against her nose and mouth. Her wide eyes took in her surroundings. As a house slave, she likely wouldn't have ventured to a Waystation, or outside Jenna for that matter.

"Breathe through your mouth. It helps, somewhat."

Drakon navigated through the throng. Journeyers brushed past and against him. He gritted his teeth against the distress and anxiety building with each unintentional invasion. His cloak and raised hood muted much of the contact, but Drakon found himself perspiring beneath his clothing, his heart increasing its pace. With the size of the crowd, he would have to push through his aversion. Once he completed this bit of business, he could be gone from this place.

Vendor stalls crammed both sides of the narrow street. Warring smells of baked goods, spices, and perfumes mingled with the Waystation's rancid stench. His stomach flopped. He would do better to mind his own advice. He breathed through his mouth and hurried along the road.

Commoner merchants shouted at passersby to come closer and try their "one-of-a-kind" magical salves and trinkets or to sample the goods they sold. Such was the way of Waystations. Nobles supplied merchants with minor enchantments for a majority percentage of the profit. It was robbery.

A merchant fell into step with Drakon. He eyed the man from beneath his hood. The merchant wore tattered robes. His chocolate skin was signed with lines, and thinning gray hair was tied back at his neck.

"I'm not interested," Drakon said, not breaking his stride.

The man ignored him, opening a small jar and thrusting it under Drakon's nose. "This salve reverses the effects of time. It was made by one of the strongest mages in Somorrah." He dug out a yellow glob with an index finger and smeared it onto the leathery skin of his face.

The deep lines marring his face dissolved as the flesh tightened. Age spots pockmarking his visage vanished. His thin lips and cheeks plumped with youth. He smiled at Drakon, showcasing blackened, crumbling teeth and brown gums. A pity the ointment didn't remedy dental rot.

"With this, there's no need to hide under a hood."

Drakon stopped and faced the merchant, allowing the man a glance at his scowling face. The smile fell from the man's youthful facade. His lips moved, but no words came out.

"Take your salve and move on."

The man nodded, his gray ponytail flopping at his neck. Drakon resumed his amble and turned off the busy street, guiding his mount along the empty alleyway. He stopped before reaching the lane beyond.

Across the road, a small two-story building with a hanging sign in chipped white paint read, "Willowing Way Inn."

He glanced up at the girl. "This is where we part ways."

Her gaze shifted to the building, and then she slid down to stand beside the horse. The cloak engulfed her and pooled at her feet.

"The owner's name is Angus. Give him this," he dug out a note he wrote that morning and handed it to her. "He owes me a debt and will take you in, no questions asked."

The girl crushed the slip of paper to her chest and stared up at him, not moving toward the building. Her brown eyes shone with emotion and once again with an unsettling assessing calculation, making Drakon uncomfortable and long to conclude this unpleasant business.

She stepped forward, arms stretched as if to embrace him. With a swift movement, Drakon retreated from the attempted contact. Escaping from Jenna with her thrown over his shoulder had been tolerable. He had been more concerned about being killed and then devoured. However, this gesture, made in kindness—stirred up panic he hadn't experience in years.

Thin arms dropped to her sides. She gave Drakon a sad smile. "You never asked me my name. You know that?"

"I do, and it's of little consequence."

She nodded thoughtfully. "In any case, thank you again for helping me. No matter what people say, you're a good person."

The lift of Drakon's brows was the only hint of shock evident on his stoic face. "For your sake, I hope you become a better judge of character, or you'll end up back in servitude or dead."

Her eyes widened, but he continued. "In Somorrah, only the power you possess and wield over another is relevant. As a commoner, you do not possess magic, which makes you innately weaker. Prey for the nobles to do what they will with you. The slave brands you no doubt have on your wrists are a reminder of this fact. Yet, you can gain intellect and physical strength to equip yourself against those who will undoubtedly attempt to victimize you. Trust no one. Do you understand?"

She worried her bottom lip with her teeth but nodded.

"Good. Give Angus the note, keep your head down, and

you can live a decent life."

The girl turned and hurried across the street to the inn, disappearing through the door without a backward glance.

Her continued survival was up to her. Drakon did what he could for her. Now, he needed to see to his own skin. He sighed and swung up into the saddle. He urged his mount in the opposite direction and turned his attention to the business at hand: contacting the king.

King Ewen would've undoubtedly heard varying versions of the events of last night. Drakon would fill in the details of the botched assassination. He had no doubt Ewen would demand an explanation. Drakon's recount would be a concoction of truth and fabrication. He would omit his saving the girl. The omission might be the only thing to keep him from the noose. He rubbed his neck at the thought.

He wouldn't let that happen. He would control the narrative, and he had killed all who could contradict his version of the truth. There would be no fallout from last night.

෴

The Waystation temple rose above the brick-and-mortar buildings. Unlike its surroundings, which were neglected and in disrepair, the temple displayed ornate wealth. Marble statues of the beautiful Goddess Melika guarded a sizable golden door. Massive pillars encircled the structure and supported a domed roof.

Drakon swung down from his horse and secured it to the hitching. He took the steps two at a time and banged a fist against the door. Shuffling came from inside.

The door groaned open. A face as white as marble with

frosty eyes glared out from the slit. Purple mage robes hung loosely from the man's small frame. Moonbeam-colored hair sat in a knot atop the mage's head, and tattoos covered his hands and arms but not yet his face.

He narrowed his eyes. "How dare you come here? No smuts are allowed in the temple! If you have an offering, leave it at the door like all the others." His gaze flicked past Drakon to the busy street and back.

"Be gone before someone sees you," he shooed Drakon with a dainty flick of his wrist and moved to shut the door.

Drakon shoved a boot between the door and the jam, preventing the mage from slamming the door in his face. Aware he was drawing a small crowd of onlookers, he removed his hood. He leveled a cool glare at the nobleman.

"You will let me enter or answer to the king as to why you turned away a servant on a royal errand."

The mage licked thin lips and gave Drakon a once over, taking in the unique skin, intense hazel eyes, and brown hair, all indications of his mixed blood and identity.

Drakon leaned closer to whisper conspiratorially. "We both know you must already be on someone's piss list to be assigned to a Waystation temple. Do yourself a favor and get out of my way."

The man trembled. Whether from fear or anger, Drakon didn't care. The subtle movement of the mage's mouth spurred Drakon from his thoughts. His hand shot around the nobleman's throat and squeezed off the words of an incantation.

He tsked. "You wouldn't be trying to spell me, would you?" Drakon lifted the mage with ease and walked him back into the temple and away from curious eyes. "Because that would be a grave mistake on your part."

The man pried at Drakon's grip, his wild eyes bulging. His slipper-covered feet kicked. He shook his head and tried to speak, but only a choked gasp slipped through his gaping mouth.

"I will let you speak, but if you attempt to spell me again, I will kill you. Do you understand?"

The mage nodded, and Drakon loosened his hold enough for the man to speak but didn't release him.

His captive sucked in a breath. "I wasn't casting on you. It was but a spell of protection for my safety! I meant no harm."

It was a lie, but Drakon lowered the nobleman and released his hold. "Of course, you weren't because I could kill you in the time it would take to finish the spell."

The mage rubbed his neck and scowled at Drakon. "I'll report you to the king! You have my word! I'll see you beaten raw for laying your filthy hands on me!" He all but foamed at the mouth with indignation.

Drakon pushed the heavy door closed. "You do that."

His eyes adjusted to the soft light. Orb light hung fixed to the ceiling, and four corridors split from the entryway. Beneath him, a mural depicting Melika and the Gathi's legendary battle against the monstrous Lim covered the floor. No temple would be complete without such an exhibition. It was the nobles' constant reminder to commoners that Melika anointed them as the Kingdom's defenders and created the Glens as a barrier against further attacks.

No doubt the nobles shaped history to explain away commoner servitude and their hoarding of magic. The Glens was more prison than a refuge. He didn't know what the Lim were or had been, but they couldn't be much worse than the nobles and wailers.

A rustle of robes snared his attention, and he turned back to the mage. The nobleman lingered near the door, righting his robes, and glaring at Drakon. It reminded Drakon he wasn't welcomed and shouldn't tarry.

"I need access to your veil. Now."

The mage's jaw clenched at the command, but he didn't offer a retort. He summoned an orb light. It rose to hover above them. The mage turned in a flutter of fabric and hurried down a corridor, his magical light source and Drakon in tow. Drakon logged each turn to memory.

At the end of a long hallway, they entered a small chamber. Unlit candles lined the floor. A thick blanket of wax covered the perimeter, and a lone candle burned on an oblong, stone table, the single furnishing in the room. A haze of smoke lingered in the air and stung Drakon's eyes. He marveled at the waste of it all. Mages could conjure orb light, yet they insisted on the use of candles for their rituals. Commoner homes went dark after sunset so mages could have their traditions.

Wasteful curs. The lot of them.

The mage motioned toward a curtained doorway set in the opposite wall.

"The veil is through there. Once the king's business is concluded, I want you gone. I'll send someone to show you out the back entrance."

Without another word, he left Drakon alone in the chamber, taking the orb light with him. Drakon stood motionless in the dim flicker of candlelight until the footsteps faded down the corridor. Only then did he stride to the table and lift the candle. Its light offered scant illumination, but it was all he had.

He moved back to the curtained doorway and pushed inside. The area beyond was a five-by-five space and as small as a cupboard. An ornate mirror covered the wall across from the door. Carved into its wooden frame was an ancient script. As a commoner, Drakon was ignorant of its meaning, but weaved within those symbols was an enchantment to allow him to speak across any distance.

A wooden stool stood inside. He dragged it before the mirror and eased down onto it. Placing the candle on the floor, he gazed into the mirror. Candlelight danced across his darkened reflection. Deep-set hazel eyes stared from a lean face. Several days of stubble spiked up like wild shortgrass from his chin and hollow cheeks. Drakon raked his overgrown mane from his eyes. It was a rare occurrence for him to look on his countenance. He didn't relish the view—

more reason to be done with this business and on his way.

He laid a palm on the cool glass. Pinpricks of energy nipped up his arm and through his body like lightning. He fought the urge to pull away and held steady. Magic radiated from the veil, snaked up his neck, and coiled at his temples. He pushed his thoughts outward toward the palace and focused on King Ewen. Slowly, Drakon's reflection misted, distorted, and vanished.

The mist cleared, and King Ewen appeared, adorned in flowing black and crimson robes, seated atop a golden, bejeweled throne. His unpigmented hair and skin gleamed in orb light. Tattoos covered the expanse of his exposed skin, including his face and the palms of his hands. All nobles were tattooed to the degree of their magical adeptness: the more tattoos, the greater the noble's connection to the goddess. Mages were the most tattooed of nobles.

Before Drakon sat the most powerful mage in the Kingdom. Ewen's colorless, emotionless eyes met Drakon's from across the veil. The alien orbs radiated the full force of Melika's power. Beside Ewen stood the second strongest mage, Nolan. He was tall for a noble and was almost as pale and tattooed as the king.

Nolan's eyes widened almost imperceptibly at Drakon's appearance. Drakon's suspicions were confirmed. Nolan expected his capture and death in Jenna. *But why?* The king wouldn't have authorized such an act. Ewen was a cruel ruler, and he governed with fear. He would've ordered Drakon's public execution. He wouldn't have foregone an opportunity to send a message to others who would dare cross him. *No,* Drakon thought, *Nolan acted alone.*

Drakon met Nolan's frosty glower and inclined his head in a silent message. *I understand where we stand.* Nolan's eyes flashed, and he bared his teeth in a scowl. Drakon let one side of his mouth tilt up in a smirk. Nolan was a threat Drakon would have to neutralize, no matter how long it took. After all, patience was a trait of an assassin.

"Do I amuse you, Deathmark?" The king's menacing voice severed Drakon and Nolan's stare-off.

"No, Your Highness. I—"

Ewen silenced him with a slash of his hand. "Save your excuses."

Drakon clenched his jaw, allowing none of the annoyance he felt to seep through his features.

"You are late, and I hate waiting."

"I ran into trouble during the mission. The Jenna Warden expected me." The lie rolled off Drakon's tongue effortlessly. "To leave with my life, I had to kill him before he could call for help. I fled and hid in the Commoner District until morning and escaped in the confusion of the search."

Nolan huffed. "Doubtful. You expect us to believe a smut overpowered a mage of Rainore's magical abilities head on? You have been successful in the past because those you kill never see you coming. Rainore wasn't the strongest mage, to say the least, but it wouldn't take much to subdue a commoner." He addressed Ewen, "Clearly, Deathmark is lying. He failed, and now unwanted suspicion is on you. The assassin should be punished for his ineptitude."

The king lifted a pale eyebrow. "Nolan does raise a good point. How were you able to get the better of Rainore? There were also reports of a second mage with a broken neck. I employ you for your cunning and stealth to dispose of my enemies. Unless I am mistaken, you possess no abilities to help you dispatch one, much less two mages in open combat."

Ewen's cold, probing gaze bore into Drakon, and Drakon kept his face clear of his raising discomfort. "Any man can be overpowered when his mind is clouded with mead. The warden was inebriated, overconfident, and slow to cast. I caught the second mage as he walked into the bedchamber unawares."

Ewen chuckled. "Truly? I'll have to keep that in mind. Tell me, how did you escape the manor? There would've been at least a score of mages in attendance. Surely, mead hadn't addled all their senses."

"I fled through the hidden slave passages to escape the house."

Nolan's lips pursed at the mention of the passages. Now, the royal mage would have to admit ignorance of the manor layout or explain why he withheld information. Neither was favorable.

"There are hidden passages, you say? Nolan, were you aware of this?"

"It is possible. Many of the warden manors have them."

"I don't recall you passing this information to Deathmark," the king said.

Nolan cleared his throat, nervous. "I assumed he already knew. This isn't the first warden he has removed. It's a common manor layout in Somorrah."

Ewen tapped a long finger against his throne in thought and nodded. "What's done is done. This isn't the first time the wardens suspected me of ordering an assassination, although none will have the courage to do anything about it."

Drakon let out a breath and relaxed on the stool.

"Now, what's this about a slave girl?" The king's question stalled Drakon.

He folded his arms, portraying a nonchalance he didn't feel. "She guided me through the corridors. In return, I promised to free her, but I killed her after we reached the Commoner District. Once the dogs are done with the body, there won't be anything left for the guards to find."

Ewen nodded in approval. "Good. I don't like loose ends."

He leaned back into his throne with a heavy sigh. "Now, on to the complicated position you've placed me in."

Drakon stiffened. "I don't understand. The mark is

dead, and no one can tie the killing to you."

"Of course, you don't understand." Ewen gave a humorless laugh. "Killing Rainore was a means to an end. Tell me, Deathmark, what happens when a warden dies of natural causes?"

Drakon frowned. *What did this have to do with anything?*

"There's a week-long mourning period. The High Priestess travels from the Temple of Melika to select the new warden with you. She presides over the funeral proceedings."

The menace in Ewen's eyes clashed with the smile spreading across his pale face. "Precisely. It is one of the few times the High Priestess and I are in proximity. She is warded in the temple with few exceptions. Your failure to kill the warden as I instructed has obliterated my only opportunity to kill her. That's where you come in."

Drakon's mask of indifference slipped. He frowned and blinked, once, twice, and a third time. Indeed, he must have misheard.

The High Priestess was the Kingdom's spiritual leader. Untouchable. Hers was the twin power to Ewen's political rule. How in Melika's name did Ewen expect him to murder the High Priestess? It was insanity.

"You cannot presume—"

Ewen slammed a fist on the arm of his throne. The sound traveled through the veil to echo off the walls of Drakon's cramped chamber.

"I can presume anything I please, and you will do well to remember as much. Obey me, or your former guardian will find himself on the executioner's block! And don't pretend you don't care. I know you visit the general from time to time. Do exactly what's asked of you this time, and all will be well."

Drakon's vision clouded, and pain shot through his biceps where his hands dug into the flesh like claws. "As you wish, Your Highness."

Ewen drew in a calming breath. When he spoke next, his voice was gentle as if speaking to a wayward child.

"Your own incompetence has placed you in this predicament. Unfortunately, it cannot be avoided, and you can only blame yourself for it. Now, come, and we will speak more on specifics."

Before Drakon could respond, Ewen uttered a chant. A ringlet of fire appeared on a wall of Drakon's chamber. It stretched, lengthening until it covered the wall. The black maw of the transportation veil gaped. Drakon hated traveling via the portals and Ewen knew it. Yet more punishment for his failure.

Ewen gave him a tight-lipped smile. "Come, Deathmark. I won't ask again."

Thoughts of refusal crossed Drakon's mind, but he pushed them away. If he managed to escape, which was unlikely, Drakon had no illusions Ewen wouldn't make good on his promise to kill his former guardian. He wouldn't risk it. He owed Umgar everything.

He stood and turned toward the portal. With one option open to him, Drakon stepped into the veil.

CHAPTER 4

The sensation of being plucked from solid ground assaulted Drakon's senses. He struggled for orientation within the void of space distortion. He gulped deep breaths, eyes squeezed tight, combating vertigo.

After a moment, he opened his eyes. His breath frosted in the frigid air. Cold settled in his bones from the temperature and from what he didn't see. He wasn't in Ewen's throne room. A pinprick of light shone like a beacon in the void. Instinctively, Drakon understood he needed to reach the prick of illumination.

In his periphery, a shade peeled from the blackness. It crept toward him with jerky movements. Drakon ran, tracking the wraith as he went and scanning the darkness for more threats. His feet sank into the unseen ground as if the terrain fought to entrap him. The shadows began to shift and roll as smaller wraiths separated from the void. They closed in around him.

Drakon was expelled into a sunbathed chamber. His boots echoed off the marble floor, anchoring him. A disbursement of air and the portal sealed behind him, trapping the wraiths stalking him. He sucked in a shaky breath.

"Trouble with the veil?" Ewen's voice drew Drakon's attention back to the present.

The king stared down at him from atop the dais. His

eyes twinkled with mirth, and the edges of his thin lips raised in a smirk. Nolan stood at the king's side, wearing an open grin. His shoulders shook in silent laughter.

Heat bloomed in Drakon's neck and traveled to his face as realization dawned. The detour in the veil was intentional. Ewen forced him to sojourn through that dark place as punishment for his performance in Jenna. Drakon pressed his lips together to keep from speaking. Anything he said in his growing anger would likely get him killed.

A door opening to the dais emitted a screech, drawing their gazes. Queen Opel glided into the room. Emerald silk robes flowed over her lithe body like poured water, managing to conceal and flaunt every inch of her slight frame. Her blond ringlets fell to her back and bounced with each step. She would've been beautiful, but her unfeeling pale eyes betrayed her soulless demeanor. She was a malevolent dove. As much as he despised her, those feelings paled in comparison to his loathing for the man accompanying her.

Prince Tobiah glared at Drakon as he trailed his mother into the room. His indigo eyes, olive skin, and dirty blond hair were testaments to his magical inferiority. Unfortunately, he compensated with brutality. Despite his lineage, the prince was inadequate, entitled, and reveled in the control he wielded over nobles and commoners alike.

All save Drakon. The title of Royal Assassin shielded Drakon from Tobiah's power trips and tantrums. Drakon's exemption to the prince's dominance and intimidation galled Tobiah. The prince made no secret his plan to execute Drakon and appoint a new Royal Assassin when he succeeded his father. Drakon planned to ensure he never assumed the throne. And there they were, at an impasse.

Queen Opel gave Ewen a chaste kiss on the cheek and seated herself on a matching throne. Tobiah bowed to his father and took up residence at her side, his glare boring into Drakon.

Opel focused on Drakon. Her face was pinched as if smelling week-old meat left to ferment in the sun. She made no secret of her distaste for his tainted bloodline. She gestured toward him. Gold bracelets adorning her wrist tinkled with the movement.

"I see your dog has returned." She sighed. "A pity."

Drakon ignored the insult, concealing the white-hot flame of humiliation torching its way through him as Nolan and Tobiah cackled. The affront was a ruse to goad him into a misstep. They played this game time and time again. She sought a reason to have him whipped for a perceived offense. He wouldn't engage.

"Deathmark is resourceful. I will give him that," Ewen said in reply. He turned to Opel, covering her hand with his own. "My love, would you excuse us? I have private matters to attend with Deathmark."

The queen's expression tightened and uncharacteristic color pinkened in her cheeks at his dismissal. Her eyes flicked to Drakon and back to Ewen. "You do remember, it was you who summoned me here to review plans for the south wing renovations? Could not your business with the smut wait?"

Ewen patted her hand and straightened, clearly done with the conversation. "It cannot, I'm afraid. I will summon for you once my business has concluded." He nodded to Tobiah. "Take him with you."

Tobiah grimaced, turning his gaze away from his

father. A weighted hush draped the throne room following Ewen's command. Then Opel stood, smoothing the silk of her robes, and gave a nod of acceptance that warred with the spasmodic tics surrounding her tight smile.

"We will leave you to your business." She stormed from the room, her son in tow. The slamming door punctuated her fury.

Drakon pitied any commoner who crossed the paths of their crushed egos. Ewen sighed and pinched the bridge of his thin nose. After a moment, he lowered his hand, and his pale stare landed on Drakon.

"Where was I? Ah, yes. I will arrange for you to travel to the Temple of Melika in Amberwell tonight. Your objective is simple. Kill the High Priestess by any means. All collateral is acceptable. Nolan will arrange a distraction to get you into the temple unseen."

Drakon schooled his expression. The High Priestess was arguably closer to the Goddess Melika than Ewen. Supposedly, Melika handpicked each High Priestess. This had been the tradition since Melika rescued the Gathi people from the Lim and erected the Glens to protect them. Rituals the High Priestess performed were said to reinforce the barrier. The Gathi nobility would call for Ewen's head if word of his plans were made public. Perhaps it should be, for Ewen must be crazed to suggest such a coup.

Drakon removed his dagger and toyed with its sharp edge, measuring his next words. "How would I kill the High Priestess? As the royal mage loves to point out, I am but a magicless smut. Stealth and blade wouldn't be enough against a powerful priestess. Assuming I manage this high feat you have set before me, what happens to the Glens?"

Drakon didn't care if Ewen and the High Priestess killed each other. However, the integrity of the barrier without the High Priestess did concern him. If the Glens fell, what horrors would invade Somorrah?

Ewen waved away his question as if the safety of the Kingdom was of little importance.

"The stability of the Glens is tied to the rites the High Priestess performs, not the woman. She can be replaced."

Ewen stood abruptly. His robes hung like expensive drapery from his slim frame. He descended the stairs to stand before Drakon. The king was not a tall man and stood a foot shorter than Drakon, but the power emanating from him gave him the air of someone twice his size.

Nolan stiffened from his place atop the dais. "Your Highness, I wouldn't advise—"

Ewen held up a hand. Nolan fell into reluctant silence. Drakon tensed but continued the casual handling of his dagger. He arched an inquiring eyebrow at Ewen.

Ewen's penetrating glare traveled Drakon's body, leaving gooseflesh in its wake. "You are the only mixed breed ever allowed to exist in Somorrah. Do you know why?"

The question startled Drakon, and he stared down at Ewen with a mixture of apprehension and curiosity. What Drakon knew of his conception was vague. An unknown nobleman had impregnated a commoner, and she had died in childbirth. Drakon was raised in slavery until a chance meeting with Umgar changed his fate. Still...his past's relevance was beyond his deduction.

"No. I don't know why I was spared," he said after a moment.

Ewen smiled, a sly, ugly movement of thin lips.

"Because I allowed it. My mercy spared you then as it does now. That is all. You live because I deem it." He let the false smile drop. "If I deem it, you can cease to exist. Do you understand?"

Pain radiated in Drakon's hand. He glanced down. His blade had sliced open his palm. Blood welled from the wound, but he welcomed the pain. It kept his mind from the burning anger twisting in his sternum. He closed his hand into a fist and replaced his dagger.

He met Ewen's colorless gaze and bit out, "Understood."

"Perfect. However, to ease your mind on why I have decided this, I will say the High Priestess is dabbling in dark magic and rites. Yearning more and more power. Such an offense to the goddess won't be condoned or tolerated. Tonight, I will ensure she will be in no position to withstand our attack. Do not worry over the details. You are useful because my enemies assume I will use magic against them or endow you with some magical trinket they can detect. Attacks from primitive means are unexpected in these civilized times and most effective, even against the High Priestess."

"Do you have a preference for the cause of death?"

Ewen scoffed. "I did with Rainore and look how that turned out. Just get it done. Nolan will handle the aftermath. Rest and refresh yourself. You will need your strength for the task ahead."

Drakon nodded. "May I have your leave?"

Ewen inclined his head, and Drakon strode from the throne room without a backward glance and pulled the door closed behind him. He let out a shaky breath. He was no follower of Melika. She had never answered any of the supplications of his youth. Unfortunately for the High Priestess, her goddess had neglected her prayers as well.

Drakon would do his duty. He would live through this mission. He was many things, a survivor being foremost.

ॐ

"The bastard would have made a formidable archmage, I am sure."

Eyebrow raised, Ewen turned to Nolan. Sunlight poured through the tall windows lining the throne room, bathing the royal mage's violet robes in a golden sheen as he stood atop the dais. His narrow gaze was fixed on the closed door Deathmark had exited as if he could see through the thick mahogany.

"That is high praise coming from one who hates him so."

Nolan's pale eyes shifted to Ewen. He folded his arms across a slender chest and huffed. "I am merely making an observation, Your Highness. The assassin is as cunning as any noble, albeit powerless. Although his blood and mind are muddied with commoner taint, trusting him would be like hugging a viper to your breast. Sooner or later, he will sink fangs into you."

Ewen emitted a noncommittal grunt. Truth lingered in the warning, but he leveled a narrowed-eyed glare at Nolan. "Do you truly believe I require protection from the likes of Deathmark? Would you have me think you are a gentle lamb only here to serve my needs and not your own agenda?"

The nobleman drew back as if struck and began to

shake his head, but Ewen continued before he could verbalize the denial. "A great leader knows anyone can become a threat, given the right circumstances and opportunity. Should I forget my grandfather held the position as royal mage before he seized control from his king?"

Nolan didn't answer, only blinked in dismay. Ewen scoffed. "Leave the assassin to me. I have complete control and power over my servant, in magic and regarding the life of his beloved general. He will do as commanded to ensure the continued health of Umgar, do not doubt it. You are more threat than the lowborn Deathmark, and we both know it."

Hands clasped tightly before him; his knuckles bleached white. Nolan pasted on a stiff smile. His gaze fluttered about the room before finally settling on Ewen. "I do not discredit your caution, Sire; however, have I not earned your trust? I have been nothing but your most devoted servant since rising to this much-esteemed position. I wish only to do your will for the Kingdom."

Ewen crossed the dais, climbed the stairs, and stopped directly before Nolan. Although the royal mage wasn't a tall man by commoner standards, Ewen still had to crane his head to meet the nobleman's pale eyes. Still yet, both understood physical stature meant little when the goddess's blessing gave Ewen the power to rule over all in the land.

Ewen lifted one side of his mouth in a knowing smirk as Nolan shifted from foot to foot beneath his scrutiny.

"Let's keep the lies at a minimum, shall we? If you do not plot to one day usurp me, you are either a coward or too lacking in magic to do so."

He rested a hand on Nolan's shoulder and felt the

muscles go taut under his palm. "It matters not which you are since both work in my favor to keep you where you belong...as my servant. Do not forget, dear Nolan."

An uneasy silence followed Ewen's words, pregnant with suppressed violence. Sparks crackled in Nolan's eyes for a moment, threatening to overcome his feigned meekness. As suddenly as it appeared, the emotion was hidden behind a bobbing Adam's Apple and rounded shoulders.

Ewen sighed. He wanted to take out his anger on someone.

"Your—"

Ewen held up a hand, stopping whatever words the royal mage intended to say. "Enough. Get in order the details for tonight's work. Do you have what is needed?"

Seemingly relieved by the subject change, Nolan gave a speedy response, "Yes, Your Highness. The High Priestess's temple is warded against magical attacks on the people and structure itself, but I believe a spell to attack the wards can damage their integrity enough for them to fail. For a short time at least."

Ewen patted Nolan's shoulder and let his hand drop. "Good. We do not require much time. Go prepare and take Archmage Fynna with you. She is the second-strongest mage in the Kingdom and comes from a loyal family. I will tolerate no mistakes this night."

"Fynna?" Nolan asked, his voice rising an octave. "I do not believe such caution is necessary. I am fully capable of managing the task alone."

Annoyance manifested as a throbbing in Ewen's temples, and he rubbed at them absently. "I do not remember asking your opinion. We take a significant risk with this scheme. Do not forget!"

His words echoed off the walls, serving as a reminder that his conversation should not carry beyond the chamber.

Taking a deep, calming breath, Ewen gathered his composure and lowered his voice. "Must I state that failure will surely begin a civil war among those who support me and those who support High Priestess Evadale? There will be but one chance to catch her unawares and strike before she realizes I sent Deathmark and retaliates. This night is more important than your pride or hatred toward the assassin. I have not forgotten Deathmark's accusation that you withheld information about the manor layout. In which case, you are as accountable for the debacle in Jenna City as he."

Ewen slapped the mage lightly on the cheek in a gesture that might have been affectionate at a glance. Bending forward, he whispered into Nolan's ear. "My tolerance for failures has expired. Succeed or if Evadale does not kill you, I will."

Leaning back, he smiled wide as he stared into the nobleman's ashen face. The royal mage managed a slow nod, and Ewen clapped the man's shoulders, his excellent mood returning.

"Smart man," he said, releasing his hold and taking a step back. "We both agree my people deserve consolidated leadership. Evadale's inability to see the need to be free of the Glens and the creatures here threatens the future I envision. She is an enemy of progress and must be treated as such."

Nolan bobbed his head. "I will gather Fynna and inform her of the plan. I support your ruling on the High Priestess. The Glens has done its job to protect us from the Lim but now feels more prison than sanctuary. Unfortunately, the High Priestess disagrees. I trust your decision to expand the Kingdom beyond the barrier."

"It is because I believe your vision aligns with my own that you continue to enjoy your status. But make no mistake, should your goals no longer align with mine, there are powerful archmages eager to take your place. Fynna being foremost."

Nolan gaped and stuttered, but Ewen turned, summoning a veil with a chant in the flick of his wrist and disappearing inside, leaving the mage to ponder his threat.

Darkness greeted him as he stepped from the portal. The faint scent of blood and smoke hovered in the room...ghosts of past offerings. With an uttered word, blue flames sprouted from the ebony candles around the room's perimeter, bathing the sacrificial chamber in soft, flickering light.

Removing his slippers, he approached the stone altar at the chamber's center, his feet barely registering the cold of the floor beneath them. Palms sweaty and hands trembling, he drew closer to the heartbeat of energy radiating from the shrine. The fluttering in his stomach and pounding of his heart were familiar companions whenever he entered this sacred place for cleansing.

Melika was a just, yet vengeful goddess, and one could never be too cautious when seeking her blessing. Any misstep or perceived offense constituted a swift death.

Such was the way of things. During his religious training, Ewen was regaled with stories of the foolish and prideful Gathi Melika struck down for entering her presence illprepared. He listened to the warnings out of habit, not true belief, until he witnessed an older cousin drained to mere dust for summoning the goddess with an unclean heart. A reverent fear was born in him that day and humbled his ambitions.

Yet, tonight he would risk death—even his soul—for an edge against the High Priestess. An additional blessing from Melika could make the difference between victory and defeat.

Ewen knelt before the altar, his thin knees knocking on the hard and unforgiving floor. He felt nothing, so set on his task; the pain was no concern. Lifting a bejeweled knife crusted with blood, he ran its blade across the palm of his left hand.

Blood welled from the cut, and Ewen held his wound out over a shallow basin, allowing it to drip inside. Closing his eyes, he called out to Melika, coaxing her essence forward. The air between him and the altar rippled like the surface of a lake in a storm, and a surge of awareness filled the chamber. Melika's benevolent presence skimmed along his body in a lover's caress.

Ewen's body filled with an indescribable lightness and clarity of mind as energy flowed through him. She was here with him. In him. He opened his eyes. White mist rose from his tattoo-runed skin to dissipate in the air. A smile lifted his lips. He was paling. The goddess accepted his offering. Her blessing was his.

She would side with him against Evadale. His victory was all but guaranteed.

CHAPTER 5

The sun painted a rosy hue across the morning sky, but its golden fingertips had yet to chase away the lingering night's chill.

Drakon stepped out into the vacant courtyard. His breath fogged in the air, and he tugged his hood over his head against the cold. Quickening his pace, he jogged toward the palace gates. If he was careful, he might be able to send word to Umgar—

The chime of a clock tower rang out in the distance, drawing his attention. Eight tolls followed, and Drakon paused mid-stride. *Was it that time already? How had he forgotten?* Cursing, he glanced at the closed gates. They were only a few yards away but might as well have been miles. He wouldn't make it out in time. The Call to Melika had begun.

Gathi nobles poured from doorways and the garden path like angry hornets from a nest to assemble at the courtyard center. An archmage dressed in flowing robes of crimson and black was the last to arrive. With white hair tied in a bun atop his head and a pale tattooed face, the nobleman resembled a living corpse as his powder blue eyes scanned the crowd. He beckoned his flock closer.

Drakon observed the gathering through his half-lowered lashes, bowing his head as was custom. The multitude formed a circle around the mage. They began a chant incomprehensible to the untrained commoner ear but with enough magic lacing the words to raise the fine hairs along Drakon's arms.

Hands linked, the men, women, and children swayed, trance-like, as their voices rose to mingle with those rising from outside the palace walls. Like steam from a kettle, an eerie mist lifted from their exposed skin.

Unease tugged at Drakon's gut, as it did each time he witnessed the Call, which was why he usually spent the ninth hour alone inside his quarters. As much as he longed for the goddess's blessing and power, something about the display unsettled him.

He dropped his gaze to the ground and waited for the minutes to pass. When the chant finally ended, he hurried to the gates, careful to avoid the glares of the passing nobility.

A guardsman spotted him as he approached and began pulling the massive doors apart. For a fleeting moment, Drakon contemplated having the man send a message to Umgar but dismissed the thought. The palace had ears. Anything he said would make it back to the king as surely as if Drakon spoke directly to the man. Better to wait and visit Umgar in person.

A movement to his right drew Drakon's notice, and he glanced over from beneath his hood. Two men wearing mage robes walked with purposeful strides toward him. It would seem Ewen wanted to give him a royal escort. He gave a long weary sigh. *Would nothing be easy this day?*

Giving the guardsman a nod of acknowledgment, he hastened outside. Sura's Noble District teemed with nobles and commoner merchants going about their daily errands, and Drakon strode forward, grateful their disdain for him caused them to split for his passing.

Ignoring their stares and occasional curses, he made his way into the Commoner District, never losing sight of his two shadows. He slipped into the flow of bodies entering the spice market.

Stall after stall lined the alleys, narrowing the walkway and creating a maze of vibrant colors, delicious smells, and a near-deafening rumble of conversations. Dried meats hung from roofs for passing shoppers' inspection, and rows of spices sat heaped in overflowing baskets. The aroma of freshly baked bread wafted in the breeze, and Drakon's stomach growled in response.

Pulling coins from a pouch, he angled toward a baker's stall. The plump black man hawking his goods frowned as Drakon approached. The merchant waddled over and placed a hand on his wide hip.

"Ya again? Ya always coming here when there are hundreds of vendors to choose from," he said. His words were gruff, but a smirk played on his round face.

Drakon leaned over the stall's counter to look at the wall of assorted goods. His stomach grumbled again, but the bustle of the market masked the sound.

"I like the bread here best," he said.

The baker sucked his teeth and waved away the words. "Psst! More like I'm the only fool willing to sell to ya! I owe the general my life; that I do."

"That too, dear Hermas."

Hermas grunted. "I'll get ya usual then."

Turning, he shuffled to gather a crusty bread loaf,

cheese round, and shiny green apple into a sack and pushed the bundle into Drakon's hands in exchange for the offered coins.

Hands resting once more on his ample hips, Hermas's gaze traveled Drakon's body. "Don't know how ya manage to stay the size of a horse eating like a peasant. I know you must have coin enough for meat." He shook his head as if Drakon was a puzzle he didn't have the energy to piece together. "It's none of my concern. Ya haven't died yet."

Hermas made a shooing motion. "Now, get. Ya scare away my customers!"

Drakon glanced from beneath his hood to where a group of women huddled, watching his and Hermas's exchange with a mixture of curiosity and mistrust. Annoyance rose hot in his breast, but he stamped it down. People always feared that which was different. He knew it well.

The last thing he wanted was to frighten away Hermas's business...no matter how the crotchety baker pretended Drakon's patronage annoyed him. Straightening, Drakon inclined his head to the older man, stuffed his purchases under an arm, and made his way down the winding street.

Drakon cut his way through the market, traveling deeper into the Commoner District. He no longer caught glimpses of the men trailing him, but the tingling sensation along his skin persisted. It would be simple to lose them in the slums where the unevenly stacked houses blotted out sunlight and moonlight.

He turned a corner and darted down an alley. Behind him there was a loud "oof," and a woman cried out. Drakon whirled about. An elderly woman lay on her back, sprawled on the dirty street, a spilled basket of turmeric coating herself and the ground.

Suddenly, two disembodied sets of footprints appeared in the yellow-coated road, heading after Drakon.

There was his invisible escort.

A spell hid their bodies from view, but it didn't conceal their interactions with the environment. Drakon tsked. Sloppy. Magic was a useful aid, but it could never replace common sense.

Sprinting off down the narrow alley, Drakon headed for what was said to be the most confusing intersection in the district. He glanced over his shoulder as he turned a bend. Water exploded from a puddle a few strides behind him, and the sound of sopping footsteps against the stone street pursued him. Apparently, the mages abandoned stealth in favor of speed.

He raced along on light and silent feet, thankful for the empty streets as the commoners would have long begun their daily work for the city's nobles. The intersection came into view like a tangle of ropes tied into a loose knot. Numerous alleys, streets, and overhead wooden bridges linking every section of the district came together in jumbled chaos.

Drakon dashed into the crossway and toward the adjacent wall. Using momentum, he placed a foot on the stone and bounded up the wall, hooking a handhold on the bridge above and hauling himself up and over.

He lay on his belly and angled his head to peer over the side to the street below. The sound of footsteps and heavy breathing entered a moment later.

"Did you...see...where he went?" Came a breathless, disembodied whisper.

"Of course not," answered an equally winded voice. There was a growl of frustration. "We must find him. Cast a location spell. There might be a chance to sense him before he moves out of the magic's reach."

The voices began to chant, and Drakon cursed inwardly. This day kept getting better and better. He lay still, closed his eyes, and turned his gaze inward, already beginning to feel the magic rising from the mages. The gift within him hummed dimly, but Drakon forced it out, wrapping himself in it like a blanket. The mages' spell crashed over him. It paused, a weight of impending doom. Drakon tensed and fell deeper into his power, reinforcing his magical cloak. Then the feeling lifted, and the surge rushed past.

"There is nothing," one of the mages said. "He must have moved too far out of range. Let us pick a direction and continue the search. Any action is better than remaining still."

Drakon waited until the sounds of their footsteps faded before dropping his shield. Fatigue washed over him, and he lay on the cobblestone for long moments, panting. After some time, he regained enough strength to stand and headed down a side street. Although his magic use drained him, Drakon walked for an hour, backtracking to ensure his trail wasn't rediscovered.

The graveyard rose from its dilapidated surroundings like the undead clawing its way from the dirt. Drakon ducked through a gap in the rusty wrought iron fence. The metallic tang of stone and newly turned earth mingled in the morning air. He dodged moss-covered graves, some leaning against each other like drunken friends, and wound farther into the maze of gray markers until he stopped in front of a raised tomb.

He spared a glance behind him. The graveyard was as still as the dead it housed. Turning back to his task, Drakon gripped the tomb's cold lid and shifted it to the side. The stone groaned, revealing an opening to a tunnel five feet below. Throwing his legs over the side, he dropped down and landed in a crouch in the narrow passage.

Shaking chalky dust from his clothing, Drakon retrieved a torch from a wall bracket, lit it, and pulled the tomb closed with the chain hanging from its base. Unable to stand in the low-ceiling space, he crab-walked a few paces before the ceiling climbed upward, and he could straighten to standing.

Water dripped from above and along the moss-covered walls to the dirt floor, creating a muddy soup that squished beneath his boots.

The network of passages had long been forgotten, but Drakon had found the layout tucked away in a rotted, dust-covered tome while searching one of his targets' belongings for magical trinkets. It took him over a month to memorize the underground system, and now he preferred the freedom and anonymity such travel allowed him.

He navigated the passageways and came to a familiar opening in the ceiling. Climbing up the hand and foot holds he had gouged into the wall, Drakon slid the covering open and peered out. The street above was clear, and twenty feet away, a two-story resident home stood in shadowed silence.

Drakon pulled himself up and out, hurriedly concealed the tunnel opening with debris, and entered the building. Trash littered the dim hallway, and the smell of scores of unwashed bodies turned his stomach, but he covered his mouth with a hand and hurried to his chamber. His room was sparse, with only a bed and a table, but he didn't need much. He had a dozen or more such dwellings hidden around the city, never liking to sleep somewhere for more than one night.

Drakon lit the candle on the table, stripped out of his cloak and tunic, and retrieved the waterskin hanging on the back of the door.

He produced a vial from a pocket before popping the cork on the waterskin and sprinkling a sand-like substance inside. He repeated the process with the items from Hermas. When neither food nor water glowed green, Drakon dropped on the bed. He ate quickly and then slid a jar of healing salve from beneath the bed, applying the thick cream to his arms and chest. As the magic soothed his aching muscles, he lay back with a groan.

His thoughts returned to his conversation with King Ewen. For the first time, he questioned the reasoning behind the murder. Ignorant commoner he might be, but he understood the High Priestess's duties were vital to the Glens' integrity and sustainability.

Could she so easily be replaced, as Ewen alluded? One could assume so. Many women had worn the mantle of High Priestess throughout the centuries...as many as there had been kings to reign.

Then why did doubt and worry pull and tear at him like strays with a strap of meat? The Glens might trap the wailers in with the Gathi, but it also protected them from the more significant threat. The Lim.

If the barrier was weakened, what would happen to the Kingdom then?

The more Drakon pondered Ewen's scheme, the less he was convinced it was the best option. Nolan and Ewen were powerful and dangerous. But were they mightier than a betrayed High Priestess with the backing of the land's archmages and nobles?

He didn't think so. The anxiety plaguing Drakon loosened its grip on his chest. If he played his cards right, he could reveal Ewen's plan and warn the priestess. *Yes.* He folded his arms behind his head and allowed a bit of hope to shine through the worry. How grateful would she be when he exposed Ewen and Nolan's treachery?

The High Priestess would be in no position to argue. She would either deny him and risk death or bestow him with the goddess's blessing for helping her. That would be his ultimatum.

Drakon's optimism slipped as he recalled Ewen's threat against Umgar. He would have to warn the general and make provisions to get the man safely from the city ahead of any blowback from Drakon's betrayal.

Drakon stared at the moldy ceiling, his mind racing with possibilities. He could die this night, but what was life without risk?

ॐ

Smoke coalesced in the large tavern as thick as morning fog. The glow of torchlight danced over the haze hanging in the air and off the worn faces of the people crowding the bar, giving them a ghostly countenance.

Umgar blew out a tendril of cigar smoke, adding to the saturated air. He glanced over the top of his cards at the men around the table. Crain, his captain and right-hand in the Royal Fighters, sat across the table with an impassive expression. *Good man.* Umgar had trained his card partner well. Their two opponents were commoner servants, one step above the slaves, whose threadbare garments looked ready to disintegrate from their bodies.

The man closest to Crain wiped the sweat from his brow. He bounced a curled knuckle on his lip and flicked a glance across the table at his partner, who looked like he swallowed hot coals and fidgeted in his seat. Guess the goddess hadn't blessed the pair with good card hands. *Pity.*

Umgar figured he should feel some guilt about taking the servants' meager earnings. He didn't. If they were foolish enough to bet their wages, he wouldn't deny them the opportunity to fill his coin purse. Blowing off steam with a hand of cards was every man's right and with the news he received tonight, Umgar had his own frustrations to exorcise.

"Quit stalling and play your hand," Crain said over the chatter. "The suspense is killing me."

Umgar smirked. "Yes, let's. I'm in the mood to relieve these fine gentlemen of their coin."

He laid his cards on the table and grinned—five golden dragons. Oaths and groans issued from his opponents.

Crain drummed the table and whooped. "Yes! Thank you." He tipped an imaginary hat at them. "It's been a wonderful evening." He leaned forward and divided up the winnings between himself and Umgar.

The older servant slumped in his chair, but his companion stormed from the table and shoved his way through the throng. The remaining man sat; his head hung. No doubt he had lost his family's daily, if not weekly, earnings. Cursed if a gnat of pity didn't nag Umgar. He sighed, put out his cigar on the table, and pocketed it. He rose and clapped the man on the shoulder. The contact jolted the man from his melancholy, and he glanced at Umgar in question.

"You see that beautiful lady over there?" Umgar motioned to where Romona poured rounds of mead at the swamped bar. "Tell her I told you I'd pay you a fair wage to clean up after closing."

The man stood and was nodding before Umgar completed his instructions. "Yes! Yes! Thank you, General!"

He hurried in the direction of Romona, his head held a bit higher.

Crain chuckled. "That was right charitable of you. The older you get, the sweeter you become. Another few years, and you'll be paying them to lose."

"Shut it or I'll pack you off to a Waystation."

Crain laughed again, and Umgar gathered his winnings into his coin purse. "I think I'll call it a night."

But first.

Umgar caught the hand of a shapely barmaid as she strode past. He searched for her name before recalling it. *Jasna.* Her father was one of his fighters. Her hair was thick black velvet, and her chocolate skin was smooth and unblemished. His gaze dropped to her bosom, which all but spilled from her low-cut dress. She smelled of flowers and cigar smoke. He wrapped an arm around her waist and pulled her closer.

She giggled and gave him a suggestive smile. "What can I do you for, boss?" Her rich brown eyes sparkled as she leaned her soft body against him.

"I'm sure I can find something—"

A prickle of awareness skittered up his neck, and he turned toward the open pub door. A shadowy figure slipped from view, merging into the night. He released his hold on Jasna, and she gave a huff of displeasure.

"Perhaps another time, sweetheart," he said and handed her a few coins from his purse.

She took the peace offering with a smile and sashayed into the crowd. Umgar glanced at Crain, whose hand hovered above the hilt of his sword. His eyes scanned the darkened street beyond.

"Everything all right, General?"

All jesting vanished from his voice. At a word from Umgar, Crain would investigate, but there was no need. Umgar had an inkling of who had come calling.

"Everything is fine. Stay here and enjoy the rest of your night."

Crain gave a curt nod and eased back into his seat. "I'll be here if you need anything."

They clasped forearms in farewell, and Umgar navigated through the card tables and pressed bodies. Music and muffled conversations lingered in the air as he climbed the stairs to his private quarters. As the owner, he elected to live above the tavern. Nothing deterred crime like knowing the general of the Kingdom's fighting force slept overhead.

The pub was one of many investments. A wise man never relied on one source of income. Especially when one of those incomes came from a mentally unhinged monarch.

Umgar paused at the top of the landing. His chamber door stood ajar. Flickering firelight from inside seeped onto the corridor floor. Only cleaning servants were allowed in his personal residence, and they knew to lock things up when they left. He crept closer and eased open the door. The hinges creaked, announcing his presence louder than any shout. He grimaced. He would have to oil them later.

He scanned the chamber—the fireplace cast dancing shadows on the walls and furniture. Nothing was out of place, although the darkened corners could hold any number of secrets.

Umgar strode inside, leaving the door open. He wouldn't cut off an escape without knowing for sure who lurked within. Moving to his desk, he picked up a bottle of ale and a glass, poured himself two fingers of amber liquid, and dropped down into a chair. He took a deep gulp from the glass, savoring the line of heat the drink traced to his belly. He peered over the rim of his glass at the towering outline next to his bed.

"Would it be too much to ask for you to come through the front door like a normal person? I've been looking for you all day, and you sneak in here when it's almost high moon?"

A shape detached itself, not from beside the bed, but from the wall nearest Umgar.

"Goddess!" Umgar started, spilling liquid on his hands and crotch. He swiped at his soiled clothes. "Are you trying to give me a heart attack?"

Drakon prowled into the flickering light, his stealth uncanny for a man his size. His stern face and hazel eyes revealed no mirth at Umgar's state. *Unsurprising.* The man had the sense of humor of a sour grape. Umgar couldn't tell what Drakon was thinking half the time.

A black cloak draped Drakon's broad shoulders and concealed what Umgar knew to be a lean frame. His dark hair was pulled into a leather tie, giving his angular face a rugged appearance. Drakon wasn't as muscular as pure-blooded commoner men, Umgar included, but his body was every inch a weapon. Umgar had made sure of it.

"I apologize for startling you," Drakon said. "I used the tunnels as far as I could before making my way here and came in through the second-story window leading to the hallway. I thought it better for business if no one saw me enter."

Umgar waved the words away. "Bah! If anyone has a problem with you, then they're not welcome here anyway." He placed his empty glass on the desk and motioned to the chair in front of him.

"Sit. Tell me why you're here so late."

Drakon arched a mocking eyebrow. "As if you don't already know, spymaster?"

"Indulge me. Who knows, my asset might have misheard."

Drakon passed the offered seat and closed the door. He rested a palm against the wood. Iridescent light shimmered from his hand like the sun through glass to cover the walls, floor, and ceiling. Energy danced about the chamber before absorbing into the wood.

An imperceptible weight seemed to round Drakon's shoulders with the exertion but only for a moment. No weariness hindered his movements as he eased into the seat across from Umgar. Drakon's rare ability still awed him, no matter how many times he witnessed it. The nobles said magic could only be achieved through Melika's blessing, a blessing reserved for those of noble birthright. Yet, Drakon's gift developed in leaps without any link to Melika. It made Umgar wonder, not for the first time, who supplied Drakon's power.

Umgar gestured to the door. "I assume we can speak freely now."

"Yes. No one can hear what's said between us."

"I thought we agreed you'd stop with the magic? Looks to me like you've gotten better, which only happens when you practice."

Drakon crossed powerful arms over a broad chest and leaned back into the chair. It was a stance Umgar saw all too often in the man's youth: a defensive posture.

"As I remember, our quote-on-quote agreement was you demanding I not use it, but I didn't agree to anything."

"Yeah? Well, you should. Ewen would kill you if he ever found out what you can do. I just want you to be safe. Using this—"

Umgar struggled for the right word. "*Gift* is dangerous."

"Your concern is noted but wholly unnecessary. I'm alive because I embraced my abilities. You need not worry about such things. My gift is no more or less dangerous than being an assassin, which is the position you aided me in securing."

An uncomfortable moment passed in the wake of Drakon's acknowledgment and dismissal of Umgar's concerns. Umgar thought of Drakon as a son. It didn't matter if only eight years separated their ages or that the man was as remote as a stranger. He didn't begrudge Drakon his intricate nature. The man had been to Targarius and back.

His gut twisted at the memory of the bloody and beaten

child who he had discovered on his doorstep. Umgar still didn't know the particulars which had led Drakon to him. Drakon rarely spoke of that night, and Umgar learned to stop asking.

Umgar sat forward, leaning on his desk and steepling his fingers. Suddenly, he was in no mood to play coy about the information he had received.

"I know what Ewen has commanded of you and about his threats toward me."

"I would've been disappointed if you didn't know. Yours is the art of finding and selling secrets."

"You make it sound distasteful, but information has saved my men and me countless times." Umgar tapped a finger on his chin, pretending to think. "As well as you if I recall correctly."

He leaned forward and lowered his voice although Drakon's magic ensured their privacy. "I don't overly concern myself with the nobles' religion, but I do concern myself with the natural checks and balances of the system. Killing the High Priestess would upset that system. We have no idea what would happen if the Glens collapsed, and no matter what the king believes, I'm not sure he nor Nolan truly understands the magic creating the barrier. If they did, they would have torn it down on their own. The Glens has been in place for millennia for a good reason. Whatever is out there must be worse than anything here. We shouldn't toy with it. Ewen is mad for suggesting it."

Drakon's eyes flickered with emotion. *Had he glimpsed eagerness backlight the young man's eyes?*

"I've thought long about Ewen's plan, and I have decided not to kill her," Drakon said as if commenting on something as trivial as the weather.

Disbelief stiffened Umgar's spine. "You have, have you? Then what in the Dark Realm do you—"

Drakon's raised hand stopped his rant. Umgar leaned back into his chair and waved for him to explain further.

"As I said, I have thought long and hard about this. I believe I might be in a position to make an alliance with the High Priestess. If I revealed Ewen's plan, I could barter for Melika's blessing. From what Ewen has in store for her, she'll have scant other options. The High Priestess and the other nobles will undoubtedly overthrow Ewen. With Melika's blessing and the magic that comes with it, I will be free of this life of servitude and feigned meekness. I can live the life I choose."

"And what life is that?"

Drakon shrugged. "It matters not. It only matters that it will be one of my choosing. King Ewen isn't such a loved ruler that he would be missed."

That much was true, but...

"You think to blackmail the High Priestess for Melika's blessing?" Umgar laughed despite himself. "What makes you think she won't smite you like an insect once whatever spell Ewen casts on her ends?"

Drakon's face darkened, but Umgar didn't care. He always knew of Drakon's lust for power, be it magical or intellectual, but he never believed him crazed until this moment.

"You don't have to do this. I have a contact in the Wild Gathi you can trust. You can go to the mountains and—"

Drakon's mouth drew up in a mocking smirk. "You think to hide me away with the king's worst enemies? The same people who go out of their way to raid any royal convoy that happens too close to their territory?" He let out a bark of laughter, lacking all humor. "I would surely go unnoticed there."

"Sarcasm doesn't become you, Drakon. Excuse me for trying to figure out a way to free you from Ewen and Nolan's game."

"I appreciate the thought, but let's not forget Ewen will kill you if I disappear. You should be praying this plan works in my favor."

"I'm not concerned about Ewen's threat," Umgar said, refilling his glass with ale and throwing back the shot in one gulp. The burn was a welcomed retreat. "I would know the moment he tried to make good on it."

"You place your faith in the whispers of nobles. It is foolhardy. They only seek to serve themselves. You know this is true."

"Actually, I don't, and neither do you. Your problem is you don't trust anyone. Not every noble is evil. Not all nobles are like the one who hurt you." The statement fell like a wet sandbag. Drakon stood abruptly, his chair skidding across the floor.

Umgar rose as well. "I'm sorry. I went too far," he said, striding around his desk and approaching Drakon. "I shouldn't have brought it up."

Drakon trembled, and his nostrils flared. At that moment, Umgar realized Drakon was more damaged than he could've ever imagined.

"Don't. Ever. Bring him up again." Drakon's skin was mottled red. His hands clenched and unclenched at his sides.

Umgar held up his hands in placation. "I won't. You have every right to feel—"

"You should leave Sura until all this is completed," Drakon cut in, clearly done with the conversation and once again in control of his emotions. "It might not be safe here no matter the outcome. There is no way to know."

Umgar's stomach sank. "What are you not telling me?"

Drakon raked a hand over his face and sighed. "Nolan tried to have me killed last night. Indirectly, of course. He omitted important information about the warden's manor on the chance I would be caught and killed. I imagine he'll come for you once I'm out of the way."

Umgar frowned. Nolan could be a problem. He was cunning and usually kept his own counsel. Getting information about the mage was like squeezing water from a turnip. He got nowhere. He would have to keep closer tabs on him.

"I'll handle it."

Drakon nodded. "So be it." He strode to the door and pulled it open.

"Wait."

Drakon turned his piercing gaze on him.

"If you are going to run toward disaster, I can offer a bit of help."

Umgar returned to his desk, pulled parchment and ink from a drawer, and wrote a name on it. He crossed to Drakon and held out the parchment. Drakon stared at it for a moment but took the offered slip.

"If anything goes wrong, Gordon is a good man. He lives about five miles east of Amberwell. Just tell him I sent you. He'll help you in any way he can."

Drakon stared down at the parchment again. He closed

his eyes for a long time and nodded.

"Thank you." He disappeared the slip into the folds of his cloak. "Don't underestimate Nolan or Ewen and be prepared to leave Sura."

Umgar's unease increase. He had the urge to embrace the man, but he knew any attempt to touch Drakon would trigger a wild and dangerous reaction. So, he clasped his hands at his back instead.

"May Melika be with you."

Drakon inclined his head. "And with you." He turned for the door and stopped, looking over his shoulder at Umgar. "I left my horse at the Waystation near Jenna—"

"I've sent for it."

A ghost of a smile touched Drakon's lips. Then he left and disappeared into the corridor.

Umgar stood there for a long moment, staring into the dim hall. Thinking. Planning. He turned back to his desk with purpose. New elements were at play.

He would prepare for the worst.

CHAPTER 6

Thunder rumbled overhead, and lightning slashed an angry streak across the night sky. Rain poured in diagonal sheets, drenching Drakon. He barely registered the storm, his mind preoccupied with the power he was on the verge of attaining. The allure of its promise drew him through the darkened, dilapidated Commoner District into the immaculate streets of the Noble District like a man into the arms of a faithful mistress.

He replayed his conversation with Umgar. The general couldn't understand the potential of Drakon's ploy. Umgar dealt with the status quo and was relatively free to do as he pleased, within reason. Although only Umgar and trusted Royal Fighters reaped the benefits of Umgar's station and influence, the rest of the commoners lived with constant abuse and subjugation.

Drakon's motives weren't entirely selfish. If he obtained Melika's blessing, millennia of deceit would unravel. The most prevalent lie being commoners were incapable of wielding magic. Exposing the falsehood would be worth any danger.

Lightning streaked across the sky, illuminating the palace gates ahead. Drakon swept back his hood and glanced up, revealing his face to the sentries and the deluge. An unintelligible shout came from the men, and the massive gate groaned upward to admit his passage. Drakon repositioned his hood and passed through. He continued across an empty courtyard to a storage building and slipped inside.

The door clanked shut behind him, muffling the storm. Orb light hovered overhead. He strode across the room to a doorway and an open stairway leading down. Orbs came to life, lighting a path as he descended until he reached the dirt-packed floor.

Down here, the air smelled of mold and damp earth. A warm glow shone from beneath a door. Drakon entered, and a petite figure in flowing robes whirled to face him at the sound of his approach.

The woman's alabaster skin and white hair glowed in the orb light. Her frost blue eyes and the tattoos covering her neck and exposed hands showcased her magical strength. Although she was not as paled as Nolan or King Ewen, the Archmage Fynna was, arguably, the second-most powerful mage in the Kingdom and, thus, not to be underestimated or trusted.

Drakon stalked farther into the room, his eyes sweeping the area. Barrels lined the walls from floor to ceiling and crowded into the center of the room, leaving the small space in which they stood. A large mirror adhered to the wall behind the archmage. Nolan was nowhere in sight.

"Nolan will be here shortly. He's handling some last-minute details."

Drakon scowled back at her. *Had she read his thoughts?* He didn't recall Fynna's magical abilities but would've remembered if telepathy was one of them.

The noblewoman leaned against a barrel and patted the air in a calming gesture. "Relax, Deathmark. The way you're glancing around, I don't have to be a genius to figure out you're wondering why I'm here instead of Nolan."

She pointed to the puddle forming beneath him from his drenched garments. "Would you like me to dry you while we wait?"

Drakon would shake hands with a wailer before he willingly allowed a mage to cast on him. Before he could say as much, she tipped back her head and laughed, the sound melodic. She only asked to irritate him.

"I'm not here for games, Fynna. Where is Nolan? The sooner he gets here, the sooner I can be on my way."

As if in response, the surface of the mirror rippled and stretched outward. A hand broke through the silver and gripped the mirror frame. A moment later, Nolan pulled himself free of the veil. His long robes settled to the floor as the portal closed with an implosion of energy.

Nolan's pale gaze fell on Drakon. "Good. You're here. Shall we then? I understand you aren't comfortable traveling via veils, but I'm sure you can put aside any minor discomfort you might feel to complete the task our king has set before you."

Nolan placed a hand on the mirror's wooden frame, and Drakon took in the mage's bedraggled appearance. Tendrils of hair escaped his bun, and a black smear stained the side of his nose. Drakon narrowed his eyes and inhaled. A hint of smoke lingered in the air.

What had Nolan been doing before coming here?

"All has been made ready." Nolan's words drew Drakon from his thoughts.

"You should have no problems reaching the High Priestess," Nolan said. The surface of the mirror liquefied and rippled like wind-blown water.

"Wait," Drakon said.

He didn't trust Nolan. The man tried to kill him only a day before. Targarius would freeze over before Drakon traveled through any veil the royal mage conjured.

Nolan dropped his hand from the frame, and the portal hardened back into the mirror's smooth silver surface. Nolan glanced at Drakon with a look of annoyed surprise. Drakon motioned to Fynna without taking his eyes from Nolan.

"I think we should let Fynna create the veil. I wouldn't want to end up in another realm by some unfortunate accident."

Nolan smirked but didn't refute the accusation. So, Drakon *was* wise in his distrust.

"Very well, Deathmark." Nolan stepped aside and allowed Fynna to take his place. Without question, she laid a hand on the mirror frame. Ripples moved across the surface. Their reflections faded into mist.

Fynna dropped her hand from the veil. "The High Priestess will be in the sacrificial chamber. I'll keep the veil open for an hour. Be on time."

Drakon didn't have to wonder what would happen if he was late. He crossed to the portal. An impenetrable murk fogged the interior, concealing the view to the other side. A twinge of doubt rose unbidden, and Umgar's warning came to the forefront of Drakon's mind. He forced away the disquiet. There was no room for doubt. His plan would work. It had to work. This would be the beginning of a new, better existence for him.

He stepped into the portal. The familiar sensation of displacement assaulted his senses, but unlike the passage

Ewen had forced him to traverse, he crossed instantly to the other side.

An agonized scream ripped through the night, and Drakon froze. A blanket of smoke stung his eyes and scorched his throat. The unmistakable scent of copper laced the air.

Blood. Lots of it.

Drakon pulled a handkerchief from a pocket and tied it over his nose and mouth, thankful the rain in Sura soaked him through. He inhaled filtered breaths through the wet material and took a cautious step forward. Moonlight was bright, but smoke reduced visibility to no more than ten feet. But he could see enough.

The torn remains of priestesses lay strewn across the ground. Remnants of white robes splattered with the dark liquid clung to tattered flesh. Dark puddles saturated the grass.

Dread pooled in his gut. Something was *very* wrong.

The compression of air at his back spun him in time to see the portal flicker closed.

He let out a colorful oath. It was a trap. He was stranded in goddess knew what. He clenched his hands into fists. As Melika was his witness, if he got out of this alive, he would kill both Nolan and Fynna.

A wet grunt turned his thoughts back to his current predicament. Two sets of disembodied amber eyes hovered in the haze. A second later, the large pale body materialized into view. A wailer, dark blood painting its mouth and chest in an awful tapestry, stalked forward. Too late, Drakon comprehended Ewen's plan and how the king ensured he would reach the High Priestess unencumbered.

Nolan had lifted the wards. Wailers were inside the

temple.

The creature plowed forward, maw stretched, and amber eyes ablaze with bloodlust.

Drakon managed to leap aside, narrowly avoiding being trampled. The wailer thundered past, a blur of pale flesh. It skidded, turned, and bore down on him again. Without thinking, Drakon drew his dagger and slashed a ribbon of crimson across his forearm. Blood welled and fell in fat droplets.

Chunks of soil flew as the beast's powerful legs dug into the ground, halting its frontal attack. Slit nostrils widened, and its vast chest expanded in a deep inhale. It issued a snort—

almost like a sneeze—shook its wrinkled head and retreated a step. *You don't like the smell of that.*

Unblinking, alien eyes regarded him. His heart rattled around his ribs like a caged animal. His innate flight response screamed for him to flee, to put as much distance between himself and the wailer as possible. His rational mind told him a retreat might trigger the creature's predatory instinct. In that case, he would need more than a dagger to dispatch the behemoth monster.

Drakon positioned his bloody arm toward the wailer. The creature hissed and retreated another step. An agonized whimper broke their stare-off. The wailer perked up, head whipping toward the sound. It stepped in the direction of the noise, glanced at Drakon, and then dashed into the haze.

Drakon released a breath he hadn't known he was holding. He shared no love for nobles, but he pitied the priestess. A moment later, the disembodied whimper transformed into screams that ended abruptly. Crunching and wet slurping followed. Drakon shuttered and blocked out the noises.

All around him, moans of the dying and grunts rose in a cacophony of slaughter. Flames flickered through the smoke like draped candlelight. The temple was burning. Drakon darted for the structure. The High Priestess might still be inside.

He took the steps two at a time and entered the entrance hall. Fire from torches lay overturned. Flames licked up curtained walls. Heat wafted like an oven. Again Drakon thanked the goddess for his soaked clothing.

Suddenly, a priestess stumbled into view from an adjoining corridor. Her white robes were stained scarlet and black with blood and soot. Three massive wailers clambered over each other to get to her. Her hands were raised as she muttered a frantic spell. The pursuing beasts stopped mid-run, paralyzed. Their oversized jaws continued to snap.

Her face went slack with relief a second before a fourth creature dropped from the ceiling onto her. She shrieked in surprise and pain and crumpled beneath its bulk. Released from the enchantment, the wailers converged on her, and she disappeared under a wave of pale flesh. Her screeches followed Drakon as he raced deeper into the building.

It was utter chaos. *Would the High Priestess still be alive when he found her, or would she be another body among the dead?*

Drakon kept to the shadows and searched the temple for the sacrificial chamber. Each room showcased the same scene—death and destruction. The few wailers he encountered sniffed, hissed, and gave him a wide berth. Finally, he arrived at a doorway beneath an archway. He explored nearly the entire structure. Either the High Priestess was beyond, or she escaped.

Making sure he wasn't seen, he slipped inside. The orb light illuminated a figure lying across the corridor floor. A widening pool of blood spread under the body like a blossoming rose. Drakon approached slowly.

Once white robes tacky with gore, pallid tattooed skin—it was another priestess. The woman sat propped against the wall, her eyes closed. She must have sought refuge in the corridor before dying. He moved to step over the body.

Blue eyes snapped open, focusing on Drakon. They were shocking in their alertness and clarity.

"Help. Me. Please." Her voice was faint, weak.

Drakon crouched beside the woman, cataloging her injuries: deep gashes across her narrow chest, right arm ripped away below the elbow. A hand gripped the stump, doing little to stem the blood spurting between the fingers. It was an arterial wound from the looks of it. She would bleed out soon. There was no help for her.

He stared into her heavy-lidded eyes. He had long hated the nobles—low-level, mage, priestess—it hadn't mattered. They were all the same. Selfish and entitled. Their disdain for commoners was evident.

Drakon dispatched his share of nobles in service to the king. There was a sense of justice in extinguishing their particular brand of evil, but, as he stared down at the dying woman, her cheeks rounded with the fat of youth, he felt uncharacteristic pity.

He pulled the sodden handkerchief from his mouth. The priestess's eyes flared in recognition, but she didn't speak.

"There's nothing I can do for your wounds," he said.

She coughed. Blood speckled her blue-tinged lips.

"You are… Assassin…. Please."

Understanding dawned. Hers was a plea for the release of death. Drakon gave a nod of comprehension. She gave a faint smile, a mere twitching of the mouth.

He lifted his dagger and cupped her head, tilting it forward and down. A swift movement and his blade slipped through the base of her skull. Her body stiffened and went slack. He withdrew the weapon and allowed the body to rest back against the wall. If her religion was to be believed, she was in a far better place than he.

Drakon straightened and continued along the passage. He could hear no screams or snarls. He let himself hope. Perhaps the High Priestess lived. Surely, she could withstand the monsters.

Heavy double doors loomed at the end of the corridor. Drakon crept closer. They were ajar. With a palm to the wood, he eased the doors open and slipped inside. Innumerable black candles burned along the walls, melting onto the stone floor in obsidian puddles.

At the chamber's center, a robed woman knelt within a chalk circle, her back to Drakon. The long robes engulfed a petite frame. Silver-white locks hung loose down a bent and bowed back. She rocked back and forth, her chanting the only sound in the quiet room. A yard away, another priestess lay on her back outside the circle. A sword protruded from her belly. Blood still leached from the corpse. A recent kill, but who had done it? Not a wailer. They preferred talons and teeth to man-made weapons.

A slight chill lifted the hair on the nape of his neck. A

tainted aura hung in the air, thick and suffocating. Instincts screamed for him to turn back, to get as far away from the temple as possible, but he resisted. He was on the cusp of life-changing power. He wouldn't turn away now, tail tucked between his legs.

He took cautious steps toward the woman, sheathing his dagger as he went. He needed to appear nonthreatening.

"High Priestess?"

He crossed the chalk. The woman didn't turn or stop her chanting.

"Are you all right?" No answer. "I have come to help you." He took another step and touched her shoulder.

She whirled to glower at him. He snatched his hand back and stumbled away. Inky orbs peered from the husk of a face. Shriveled skin was drawn tight over the skull. Oddly, the black tattoos of her station were missing from her flesh, and razor-sharp fangs framed an impossibly wide mouth.

Goddess. Her mouth. Someone moaned. Drakon realized he was making the sound and clamped his lips together.

The specter before him stood. Drakon scrambled back, wrenching the sword free from the corpse as he went. He leveled it at the demon.

"What have you done? What matter of dark magic is this?"

The priestess—no, *the creature* cocked its head to one side and blinked as if in recognition. The action was unnatural. Inhuman. Like an animal stared back at him.

"Nahum!" The word was hissed through fangs in the

grotesquely stretched mouth.

Drakon frowned. The strange word was familiar, but he didn't have the presence of mind to ponder it. His plan to receive Melika's blessing was slipping through his grasp. Perhaps the spell could be undone? He inspected the creature. It paced within the chalk circle. Viscous saliva dripped from its open maw and pattered on the stone floor. It roared.

Perhaps not.

Reversing the High Priestess's transformation wasn't an option. Still...the creature hadn't attacked. It didn't seem able to cross the barrier. There had to be a way to salvage things.

Movement from within the circle caused him to glance down. The transformed priestess knelt. It reached a malformed hand toward the chalk line. Light sparked as the ward repelled it back. Undeterred, it crept along, testing the ward with similar results.

Its attempts were futile. The enchantment was sound.

The creature scuttled forward, its stride uneven and jerky in the ill-fitting body. Stopping an inch from the barrier, it glanced down. Drakon's eyes followed its gaze to the chalk line...the scuffed and broken line.

Drakon replayed the past moments: Him stepping over the barrier. The High Priestess's face. Him scrambling back.

He cursed and glanced up into obsidian eyes a moment before the creature lunged across the barrier, taloned fingers curled, teeth bared.

Drakon called on muscle memory and his innate gift without conscious thought. The subsequent blast of energy he released slowed the creature's momentum but not before it sliced stripes across his chest. Pain seared through him, and he fell back, swinging the sword in a downward motion.

The steel severed the head with the ease of parting water. Instantaneously, power burst from the body like steam from a hot kettle. The force ripped across the chamber in a violent explosion. He flew across the room, collided with a wall, and sprawled on the ground.

Wheezing, his body battered, and fireflies lighting the backs of his closed eyelids, Drakon climbed to his hands and knees. The floor shook and rolled beneath him in a wave of stone. He struggled to his feet and fought to maintain his balance. Around him, wooden beams and gravel fell from the ceiling like deadly raindrops.

The surge had knocked him a few feet from the door, and he rushed for it, arms raised over his head and dodging the showering debris. Sprinting through the doorway, Drakon fled down the corridor. He chanced a glance over his shoulder. The room crumbled in on itself. The ceiling of the passage spider-webbed, micro-fissures spreading out and chasing him.

He doubled his pace, pushing past the sting of his lacerations and hurtling forward until the rumble of the collapse trickled to silence.

Drakon slumped against a wall. *Goddess, what had he done?*

He scrubbed an unsteady hand down his face. His body throbbed, and his tunic was sticky with warm blood. He had to retreat somewhere safe and treat his injuries. He pushed from the wall and glanced back. Dust drifted into a blue-black sky. The passage was gone. Rubble lay in its place like an open wound revealing the night.

Drakon eased forward and scanned the immediate area. He stilled, trying to make sense of the ravaged forest that lay bare before him. In the radius of the temple, trees lay broken and bent in an outward starburst of snapped trunks and limbs. Leaves and wood covered the ground in an organic blanket.

The surge—it plowed through the landscape, leaving devastation in its wake. *How much damage was done?*

A sorrowful wail rose from somewhere within the temple. Unfortunately, at least one wailer was spared. Drakon glanced around for the sword. It was nowhere in sight. He must have dropped it during his flight. All he had was a dagger, and although his blood seemed to repel the creatures, he didn't want to test his luck with the blade.

He needed warded shelter. The parchment Umgar gave him came to mind. He would find the man, Gordon. Then he would regroup and uncover what he unleashed in killing the priestess. Resolved, he slipped from the collapsed building and into the night.

∽∾∾

A shrieking, violent wind burst the windows of King Ewen's chamber. Shards of glass peppered the room like hail. Ewen startled awake, his hair and bedding whipped in the whirlwind. Debris rained from the ceiling, and tremors vibrated the floor, threatening to eject him from bed. He clutched the mattress with white-knuckled desperation.

Then the destructive wind was gone, and an uneasy quiet fell in the aftermath.

Ewen's heart pounded against the bars of his ribs. Cold sweat plastered his hair to his face and misted his body, gluing his linen sleeping gown to him like a second skin.

What in Melika's name happened? What could have created such awful power? His mind conjured the memory of his kill order for the High Priestess. No. No High Priestess's death caused any reaction in the past. Deathmark must have erred.

Ewen swore. Perhaps, it was time to rid himself of the troublesome half-blood? He had once been intrigued with the assassin's uniqueness and skill. Now, Deathmark's uncanny knack for escaping any situation unnerved him.

The assassin's cunning and resiliency could eventually develop into a threat. Deathmark was a decent servant, but like anything else, servants could be replaced. He would think more about it in the morning.

Ewen muttered an incantation. The shattered glass rose from the floor and mended back into the windows. Wooden furniture slid back into its rightful place. Fallen tomes returned themselves to the bookshelf. Now, he would summon Nolan. He would know the details of the High Priestess's demise and discover the cause of the power surge.

He threw the heavy coverlets aside, slipped from the bed, and hurried to his veil. The massive mirror encompassed the entirety of a wall. Its golden frame glittered with precious jewels, but Ewen didn't focus on their beauty. He uttered another spell. The portal misted as the enchantment called out to Nolan. Suddenly, the portal flickered and went dark. Ewen's eyebrows drew together in bafflement.

Surely...his magic hadn't—

A movement in the corner of the glass caught his eye.

Ewen narrowed his gaze, focusing on the figure. His mouth slackened, and his mind scrambled to comprehend the vision before him.

A woman garbed in flowing white glided from the darkness. Her unpigmented hair and robing billowed about her as if she was suspended in water. She came closer until he stared into her unnerving eyes. They were solid white, with no iris coloring or pupils.

Ewen raised a trembling hand to his mouth and shook his head. It couldn't be. But as he looked on, he knew it to be true. The smooth alabaster skin, colorless eyes, and beauty beyond human understanding—he saw this face all his life. It was depicted in every painting, sculpture, and spiritual tome. The goddess had come to him.

Melika.

He mouthed the name, his voice refusing to work, and dropped in supplication. His knees banged against the floor, but he didn't feel pain—only a rising sense of awe and completion.

Eyes lowered he tried his voice again. It wobbled like a prepubescent boy's, but he forced out the words in a rush. "Goddess, you have blessed me with your presence. How— What?" He clamped his mouth shut, unable to form his thoughts.

"Stand, Ewen, and gaze upon my face. You have ever been my faithful servant."

Her voice was like a song and called to him, soothing away his lingering fear.

He lifted his eyes. A radiance lit her from within and haloed her in the darkness surrounding her.

She was magnificent.

"I have chosen you to lead the Gathi in the upcoming trials, and make no mistake, trying times are ahead. Your power will be tested beyond imagination. I have watched your magic increase and mature. Of the kings and High Priestesses before you, you are the strongest in my essence. Every spell, every scripture you've learned will be called upon."

Her face darkened, but the expression disappeared so quickly Ewen wondered if he imagined it.

"This night, the Nahum has been revealed to me. The time for you to lead the Gathi from the Glens and take revenge on the Lim is at hand," she said.

A shudder slithered through him and tightened within his gut. The Nahum was the symbol of the last days. It was prophesied the man would usher in the Lim's return and the end of the Gathi and Melika. Eons ago, his people warred with the Lim. After years of war and death, the goddess erected the Glens with the drudges of her strength to protect them from the Lim and their false God. Even now, she hadn't recovered enough to remove the barrier.

Yet, her people grew in power during the tens of thousands of years within the barrier. Now, it was time for the Gathi's return to the land beyond the Glens, to reclaim their freedom and everything stolen from them.

Never had Ewen expected the prophecy to be fulfilled in his lifetime. His chest swelled with pride. He would be the one to lead the Gathi from their sanctuary and crush the Lim.

As if reading his thoughts, Melika smiled. "Yes, I have chosen you to guide our people in this last battle, but first, accept me into you. Receive me and all the power I offer to stand against the new threat of the Nahum and the ancient evil of the Lim." She held a pale hand out to him. "Your name will be known for generations as the redeemer of the Gathi."

Ewen nodded in breathless rapture. His hand rose toward the mirror of its own volition. "Anything you ask of me, I will do. I accept the power you give unto me."

The smile Melika gave him was like the sun, bright, warm, and comforting. "Your sacrifice shall cement your place in eternity."

Sacrifice?

Ewen's hand froze midway to the mirror, but Melika's slender fingers emerged from the veil and clamped around his. Pain erupted from the contact. Icy white agony licked up his arm and spread throughout his body like lava. He watched in helpless horror as the skin of his hand frosted in her grip.

He began to scream. The image of Melika burst into black mist, swept from the mirror, and forced herself into his mouth like a swarm of hornets down a funnel.

Ewen fell, clawing his neck, choking and kicking. A leg connected with a table. Glass shattered as something hit the floor. Darkness encroached on his vision. The absolute cold of malevolence filled him, consuming as it spread. For the first time, fear for his soul assailed him. He always thought his faith in the goddess would afford him eternal life.

How wrong he was. How wrong they had all been.

Within seconds, Melika's presence consumed the soul of the mightiest Gathi. King Ewen of the Kingdom of Somorrah ceased to be, and Melika blinked open her eyes into her new world.

CHAPTER 7

Dusk descended, offering the cloak of darkness. An unnatural warmth clung to the air. Drakon slipped into the murk between two merchant stalls and peered from beneath his hood at the hulking man, who glanced over his shoulder into the milling crowd of market patrons.

The man was Crain, captain of the Royal Fighters, and was at least a head taller than the surrounding commoners. Crain moved through the throng, unhurried but with purpose.

Drakon had been surveilling the man since his return to Sura from Melika's temple. Umgar's contact in Amberwell, Gordon, proved himself loyal to Umgar and provided Drakon with healing salve, a horse, and supplies for what turned out to be an arduous four-day journey back to the capital city.

While on the road, he overheard gossip of the Royal Assassin's rogue murder of the High Priestess and the hefty price King Ewen placed on his head. Five hundred thousand silks, to be exact.

Somehow defying reason, Ewen knew of his escape from the temple. *A pity*. Now the whole of Somorrah would gladly hand him over to the king for riches. As a result, he avoided cities and Waystations, braving nights within a warded circle, and entering the city via a long-forgotten tunnel system. Drakon also darkened his skin with ground torian root. He was certain his disguise would withstand a cursory glance.

Crain darted off the main street into an alley. Drakon waited a few moments, slipped back into the flow of bodies, and pursued. Maintaining a clandestine distance, he stalked the captain from the market into the more unkempt streets of the Commoner District, where light from the fading sun lit their paths. Cluttered merchant stalls and battered eateries gave way to lean-tos and clay and wooden huts with thatched roofs.

Crain stopped before a small shack. No light shone from its open doorway. Before entering, the man glanced back. His eyes slid past and returned to the place Drakon stood crouched in darkness. Drakon remained still, and after a long moment, Crain's gaze returned to search the empty street. Seeing no one, the captain disappeared inside.

After a beat, Drakon sprung from the shadows to the building. He slid his blade from its sheath. There was no indication anyone but he trailed Crain, but he would rather be cautious than dead.

He pressed against the outside of the structure, listening—no sounds issued from beyond. Drakon risked a look. The one-room hut was abandoned, and there was no sign of Crain. His gaze snagged on a heap of rags in the corner of the room. *Found him.*

He slipped inside and crossed to the pile. Dying daylight poured in through the windows and illuminated multiple boot tracks marring the dusty floor. He knelt, tracing a finger along the trails, which showed signs of many people coming and going from the door to the rags. The hut was obviously occupied.

He felt beneath the filthy garments until his fingers skimmed the rough fibers of a rope. He grasped it and hauled open the trap door. Stairs vanished into a well of darkness and torchlight flickered just out of sight. Drakon descended, careful not to make a sound on the wooden steps. At the bottom of the passage, his eyes adjusted. The space was more expansive than he remembered.

A shuffle at his rear sent him into a forward dive. Metal thudded on the soil floor behind him. Drakon rolled to his feet and whirled to face his attacker, dagger primed.

"Deathmark?"

Crain lowered his sword and squinted through the dim light. Only then did Drakon realize his hood had fallen back. He straightened from his crouch and sheathed his blade. Likewise, Crain returned his weapon to its scabbard.

Drakon inclined his head. "Captain. I'm impressed you noticed me tailing you."

"I didn't, but one can never be too careful these days. I held back to make sure no one followed."

"Indeed?" Goddess, happenstance had nearly gutted him. He needed to get his mind back into the game.

"Is Umgar here? I must speak with him."

"Yeah, he is. I'll take you to him."

Crain strode to Drakon's side and scanned his face. "Nice job with the torian root. You missed a few spots." Drakon scowled, and Crain continued, unperturbed. "We thought you might be dead. It's been days since news of the High Priestess's assassination reached us, and then that awful gale rolled through. It felled trees and buildings alike. Never seen anything like it."

He shook his head and set off down the tunnel, not expecting a reply. Drakon followed.

"Much has happened since you left."

"Such as?"

Crain glanced sidelong at Drakon but then cut his gaze back to the passage ahead. "I'll let Umgar fill in the details."

Drakon didn't push. He would find out soon enough. A door came into view, and Crain rapped a melody on the wood. A latch clicked, and the door swung in. A guard stepped back to allow them entry.

The chamber beyond had an earth floor and bare walls, cramped and sparsely furnished. The scent of unwashed bodies hung thick in the damp, stuffy air. Light from a single lantern danced across the down-turned faces of four figures, who loomed over a table with a map atop it.

"Crain. Did you bring any word from—"

Umgar glanced up and stopped speaking. His face was worn as if he hadn't slept in days. Once a testament to his lighthearted demeanor, laugh lines around his eyes now aged him. His eyes swept over Crain and then stilled on Drakon. The unkempt beard he sported did nothing to hide the wide grin splitting his face.

"I didn't believe you were dead for one minute! You've got more lives than a Sura alley cat, boy." He waved them over and addressed the other three men, who Drakon recognized as more Royal Fighter captains. "See that my instructions reach the cities and Waystations. Send word once it's done."

They voiced affirmatives and filed from the room. "Joah watch the tunnel entrance," Umgar said.

The man guarding the door grunted and accompanied

the others. The door clicked closed behind them. Umgar collapsed onto a stool, and it groaned beneath his weight. He rummaged in the folds of his tunic for a moment, brought out a cigar, and placed it between his lips but didn't light it.

"Have a seat." He motioned to the only other stool in the room. "Crain can make sure we aren't disturbed. You're late. The road from Amberwell must have been a long one."

Drakon crossed the room and lowered himself into the offered seat. He took in Umgar's tired appearance. The older man's countenance was as worn down as Drakon felt.

"I thought I told you to leave the city? I should've known I was wasting my breath."

"Now you understand how I felt all those years dealing with you." He shrugged his broad shoulders. "I stayed in case you managed to make it out alive. I'm not going to say I told you so but be aware I'm thinking it."

Drakon permitted a smirk. "Of course. For what it's worth, I regret not heeding your earlier warning."

"Your life would be easier if you would listen to me before the dung starts flying. Anyway, from everything my assets have told me, you need my help more than ever."

He did need Umgar. More apt, he needed the information he knew Umgar, as spymaster, possessed.

"The mission was a setup. The wards were lifted, and wailers overran the temple. As soon as I stepped through the veil, Nolan and Fynna stranded me, no doubt hoping the creatures would kill me as well as the High Priestess."

He told them about the decimated priestesses and his killing of the transformed priestess; however, he omitted her naming him Nahum. During his journey, Drakon recalled the meaning of the word and the accompanying prophecy. He was unsure how to explain the accusation and decided not to formulate any conjectures yet.

Umgar's frown deepened as he listened to Drakon's tale. After a long moment, he asked, "What do you mean she was possessed?"

"What I killed was her body but not her essence." Drakon paused, struggling to describe what he witnessed. To their credit, Umgar and Crain remained silent, waiting, and not asking the questions his words must have created.

"Her eyes were black. Soulless. The evil radiating from the creature was tangible. And it was a creature. There was nothing of the priestess left. I can't assume to know what it was, but it was no Gathi."

Umgar's skin went as gray as a stormy sky. He wiped a hand down his face as if to remove the visual from his mind.

"The night you departed for the temple a surge shook Sura. I mean, it blew out windows, toppled houses in the Commoner District. I'm told the entire Kingdom felt it. Not long after, this goddess forsaken heatwave started."

Drakon noticed the increased temperature the nearer to Sura he journeyed. He hadn't focused much on it, though. Staying hidden and making it back to the city occupied his thoughts.

"You believe the two are related?"

"I'm relaying events, though I'm not much for coincidences."

"I might have more information on the heatwave."

Crain spoke from where he leaned against the door. "One of our palace contacts says the king sent Prince Tobiah and a company of mages to Glensbrook to check the Glens. There are reports their crops have wilted and died due to the heat. It's believed it might be caused—"

He paused and shook his head as if not believing what he was about to say. "By a rupture in the barrier."

Drakon stiffened. It couldn't be...it was impossible.

Umgar swore. "Next time, start with that information! Is the asset certain this tear is why Ewen sent them?"

Crain had the decency to look chagrined. "Apologies, General. From what I could gather, she's convinced." Crain frowned, opened his mouth, and shut it again.

"Say it. Goddess knows it can't be any worse than what you've already told us," Umgar said.

"The asset also mentioned Ewen hasn't been himself. She said, and I quote, 'He's like another person.'" I didn't think much about it until Deathmark's tale. I still don't know if it's anything to be concerned about."

Every iota of Drakon's instincts screamed there was a connection between the two. He only needed to find out where they linked. His life depended on discovering Ewen's plans. Without the information, Drakon couldn't expose Ewen's treachery of the Gathi people and clear his own name. There would be no peace for him until he did.

"When did Tobiah and the mages leave for Glensbrook?"

"They left via veil before twilight."

This time, it was Drakon's turn to curse. Glensbrook was a two-day ride from Sura. The prince would be returning by the time they reached the city. As if reading his mind, Umgar stood and said, "I can get us there by morning. They won't begin any meaningful investigations until then. We have time to plan and gather previsions."

How did Umgar plan to get them to Glensbrook within

a few hours? The only way would be…

He locked eyes with Umgar, and the man grinned. "Don't look so disappointed. This is why it's good to be a spymaster. You never know when you'll need a low-level mage or two in your pocket. Many a mage will be all too eager to turn a blind eye and conjure a veil in exchange for my silence." He stood, rolled the map, and stuffed it beneath an arm.

"Crain, gather our fighters in the cities and Waystations. Once you're done, seek out the Wild Gathi. We're going to need their help."

Crain's head jerked back, his look incredulous. "Sir?"

"Yes. You heard correct."

"But the Wild Gathi? They never leave their mountain. What makes you think they will now?"

"Because they've been waiting for an opportunity to overthrow Ewen. You, Captain, are going to convince them now is the time, and the Royal Fighters are going to help them do it."

CHAPTER 8

Eza yanked the leathers up over her hips and crammed her gown into the satchel. The glittering circlet of precious stones adorning her head followed. She retrieved the fighting staff hidden behind a nearby stalagmite. A Lim princess couldn't be without her weapons.

She caressed the crystal hanging around her neck for comfort. All would be well. Resolved, she pulled the satchel's strap over her head and shoulder and hurried along the subterranean tunnel. Lichen and glowing moss grew within wet fissures of the surfaces surrounding her, providing a natural luminosity she found comforting in the silence of her underground home. Her bare feet made no sound on the uneven gravel as she went. Soon, she glimpsed a figure in the procession she followed.

No way would she stay behind playing court while a dozen of her Malachi warriors investigated the strange disturbance that shook their world. Eza had never seen her father so ill at ease. She needed to know what caused the quake. She would travel to the surface as well.

She crept closer. A few minutes more, and she would show herself. By then, they would have traveled too far from Natapa for Dagoti to turn her away. The overbearing leader of the Malachi would be incensed when he found out she trailed them. She could hear him now, *"The Zarea of the tribe cannot be risked. Go back home and knit rantoon skins like the other females."*

Her jaw clenched at the thought. She trained harder than any in Napata, males included. She would argue her skills surpassed many of the Malachi. She led hunting parties into the Darklands for food and protected her people against creatures that sometimes ventured too near the city. Her status as the Zar's daughter was of little consequence. She was no less a warrior.

Eza rounded a bend. The air grew noticeably warmer as they neared topside. She pressed against the knobby, damp cave wall, letting the moisture cool her. *Was the surface always so hot?*

"Eza! What are you doing here?" The disembodied voice came from above.

She let out a yip and swung her staff on reflex. A hand shot from the shadows and stopped her blow mid-swing.

Dagoti leaned into view from where he crouched atop a boulder. She tugged at his grip, adrenaline still tingling through her body from his sudden appearance. It irked her that she let him sneak up on her. Her focus was off. In the Darklands, a wandering mind could mean death.

He released her weapon and leaped down, landing in front of her like a graceful spider. He stood, laden with weapons and a pinched expression on his face. He folded strong arms over a broad chest. His long raven hair was gathered in a braid at his back. His onyx skin, like hers, nearly camouflaged with the backdrop. Dagoti was considered attractive. At least to those females who didn't know him. He was ever the pain in Eza's backside.

"You did that on purpose," she said. "How long have you

known I've been following you? Shouldn't you be at the front of the patrol?"

"I thought I heard something. Decided to check it out. I should've known you'd try something like this. You took the news of being left behind a little too well. You should be home waiting for Khell and the other tribal leaders." He grimaced, showing large fangs. "Now, I'll have to have someone escort you back. This isn't a game, Eza. I don't have time to babysit."

"One. Don't flash fang at me. It's rude. Two. Don't mention my betrothed. The thought of Khell makes my teeth ache. And last, let's not pretend I need your protection," she said, fighting the urge to throttle him with her staff. "I'm not going anywhere. You'll need every able warrior on this excursion of yours. Who knows what you're going to find on the surface."

Now that she had been discovered, there was no need for stealth. She shouldered past his bulk to catch up with the group.

"Eza. Stop."

She didn't slow her pace. An annoyed growl sounded behind her. She smirked, and soon Dagoti's heavy footfalls pursued.

"The way I see it, you should embrace my presence here," she said as he drew beside her.

"Should I now?"

Ignoring the evident sarcasm, she said, "Yes, you should. I'm the only healer left, which means I'm more precious to you than gems. It also means my body heals from injury faster. You and my father overlooked those facts in your need to keep me holed away for my own good."

"That wasn't my decision to make."

"But you didn't disagree, did you?"

His response was a huff. As they entered the ranks of the Malachi, the males and females of the elite group banged fists against their chests in respect. She returned the gesture as she passed. From her periphery, she could see Dagoti sulking. She gave him a placating pat on the forearm.

"There, there. Cheer up. I promise to follow orders like a good Malachi."

"That's the problem. I know you mean well, but you're not Malachi. You are the Zarea. No matter how many hunting parties you lead."

"Thanks for reminding me. I forgot," Eza said, her tone dry. She twirled her fighting staff in an expert maneuver, resting it back to the ground and giving a cocky wink. "Yet, here I am. One of the best fighters in the tribe."

Dagoti shook his head. "Your arrogance is infuriating. Be careful; it might get you in trouble one day. It's been years since I've been topside, but I remember it as a harsh and deadly place. You've never been to the surface. My job is to ensure your safety regardless of your capabilities."

"You cannot protect me at the cost of losing warriors who might need my healing. Plus," she placed two fingers into her mouth and whistled.

The shrill sound echoed along the passage and drew curious stares from the Malachi. A gargantuan shape scuttled down the wall face from where it had been stalking among the stalactites.

"I brought my own personal bodyguard."

Unease rippled through the group as the massive tobali settled at Eza's side. The closest warriors drew away and gave the creature sidelong glances. The lizard-like animals were usually solitary and violently territorial, but she raised Meko from an egg, and the creature was more baby than wild animal. An enormous baby with four-inch fangs able to tear anything apart threatening Eza.

Meko's muscles twitched under scaled, midnight skin. She nuzzled Eza's face with a giant maw. Eza patted Meko's neck and grinned at her.

"You won't let anything happen to Mommy, now would you, Meko?"

Dagoti cleared his throat. "Well, there's that."

Meko turned to nudge him with her snout, and he gave her an appeasing rub. "Fine. Let's get moving. We've lost enough time as it is. Have Meko follow from above though. She's making my people edgy."

Eza glanced to where the warriors huddled along the passage walls and away from the tobali. *Yes,* she thought, *that would be best.* She patted the creature's rough hide and pointed up toward the darkness.

"Up you go. I'll call if I need you." Meko gave her a parting nuzzle and disappeared back up the wall and out of sight.

Dagoti nodded and turned to the Malachi. "All right, let's get a move on. I want to make up time."

The warriors quickly fell into formation. Eza took up position beside Dagoti and began the hours-long trek to the surface. This was the farthest she had been from Napata. She couldn't ignore the burning coal of excitement building in her breast. They could be walking into danger, but it was new and different. She felt whatever they found would change them forever.

She prayed to Apalsi this wouldn't be to their detriment.

After what seemed an eternity, a pinprick of light appeared in the distance. It grew as their procession approached. The radiance wasn't the subtle luminance of the glowing moss of the Darklands. It was foreign. Their party had reached the opening to the surface.

The soft white glow irritated Eza's sensitive eyes. Not enough to cause pain, but she endured fleeting discomfort until her eyes adjusted.

She stood motionless, forgetting all else as she stared out into an alien land. Tall, unusual rock formations littered the landscape, and the ground under her feet was cracked and dry. An arid breeze blew up dust across the barren, wretched earth. An eerie stillness hovered in the atmosphere, unnatural in its quiet. No flora or fauna covered the darkened expanse. There was nothing.

Sweat dripped from Eza's brow and sprung up beneath her thin tunic and leathers. God, the heat was almost unbearable. This was indeed a cursed place.

"The Oracle believes the quake originated from the boundary," Dagoti said. "We'll go as far as we can tonight, but we'll need to take shelter within the caves before the large red orb replaces the cool silver one. The heat it emits leeches the strength and burns the eyes and body alike."

Eza glanced at the sphere floating in the night sky. At present, the temperature was higher than she was accustomed to. She couldn't imagine the climate worsening. She said a quick thanks to Apalsi for leading the Lim to the Darklands. Her people would've never survived such conditions.

A flicker to the west spurred her from her musings. She squinted into the distance, but nothing moved. Perhaps her eyes needed more time to adjust to the light. Dagoti moved to her side.

"What is it?" His deep voice was alert.

Eza shook her head, unsure of what she had seen. "I don't know. I thought I—"

The flicker came again. She pointed to a formation of rock. "There. Did you see it?"

She glanced at him. Dagoti stared in the direction she indicated for long moments, then his eyes flared, and he gave a slow, disbelieving shake of his head.

"Someone's moving out there. I think it's a Lim, and he appears wounded. What in God's name is he doing up here?"

Eza turned back. They couldn't stand and watch. They had to help him. A firm grip on her elbow stopped her before she realized she had taken a step forward.

"You, stay here."

"But I can assist." She tried to tug her arm from Dagoti's grasp.

"I'll bring him to you, but you will remain where you are. We don't know who or what attacked him or if he was followed."

His stern tone and flinty glare brooked no argument. Eza nodded. She had no desire to prolong the male's aid. Dagoti released her and turned to the nearest Malachi, a tall female with the sides of her head shaved and a long braid trailing down her back.

"Come with me."

They sprinted from cover toward the injured Lim. Their hands rested on their weapons and heads turning this way and that, sweeping the landscape for signs of hostiles.

Eza bit her lip, bouncing from foot to foot as she watched. She couldn't hear their words from this distance, but as Dagoti and the female approached, the male seemed to deflate, as if his strength sapped at the sign of rescue. Dagoti caught the male before he hit the ground.

They hoisted the male between them, one arm swung over each of their shoulders, and half carried, half dragged the man back toward the cave entrance. As they neared, Eza noticed a dark stain covered the male's torso from chest to crotch. The tatters of his tunic clung to the wound in a cakey mess of gore. His limp head lolled from side to side between his shoulders as he was hauled to safety.

She gestured to the ground. "Careful. Lay him here."

They eased him down and moved back as she knelt beside him to see the extent of his wounds. Horrific lacerations covered his torso. The skin was peeled back like caroon fruit, exposing the pink of muscle. His dark face was a canvas of bruises. His eyes rolled under closed lids and sweat drenched him. A low moan slipped from his cracked lips.

Eza folded back the shredded tunic, which was tacky with dried blood. She shuddered. Clay was packed into the lesions, and the wounds seeped foul-smelling pus. He must have stuffed the slashes to stem the bleeding. The desperate move saved his life in the short term but introduced an infection. She laid a hand on his forehead. The flesh was clammy and hot.

"Bring water. I need to clean his wounds," she said to no one in particular.

She didn't take her gaze from the male whose eyes twitched beneath his lids as if he was in the grip of a nightmare. She ran a hand through his sweat-dampened hair in an attempt to soothe him.

"Zarea, here's the water you requested." A male Malachi offered her a water skin.

She thanked him and took it. She needed to cleanse the wounds before healing the injuries. Dirt in a wound would cause complications during healing. She dug a clean cloth from her satchel and poured water over the slashes, loosening the clay and dried blood. She dabbed away the clumps, and the cuts bled freely.

The male gave a low groan, and she glanced down at his face. His countenance had grown even more ashen. She sped up her ministrations. When the lacerations were unsoiled, she laid a hand on the fevered skin of his chest. She closed her eyes in concentration, calling on her gift.

Inner warmth spread throughout her. She gathered it and forced it through her palm and into the prone male. Eza poured the energy out until the flesh beneath her hand cooled. She withdrew and stared down at her patient. His body haloed in an iridescent glow, which faded to reveal unblemished skin. Color returned to his sallow cheeks. Once chapped and bleeding lips were now smooth and plump.

Eza smiled as she looked into the male's alert and pain-free brown eyes. "What's your name, brother?"

He cleared a parched throat. "Koa. You saved my life. Thank you. You must be Zarea Eza. The healer."

"I am. Now, tell us what happened? Why are you traveling the surface alone? Where's your tribe?"

Her query drained the newfound vigor from him. He clasped her forearms in a vice-like grip, and she grimaced from the pain. Dagoti moved forward, but she shook her head.

Koa's eyes were bright, and his voice trembled when he next spoke.

"We went topside to check the boundary after the great trembling." He stared at Eza, not seeing her, lost in the awful memory. "They're all dead. Devoured."

Eza shared an intense glance with Dagoti. His face betrayed no sign of his thoughts, but she knew what he must be thinking—no creatures lived topside. The harsh climate wouldn't allow it. Koa's scouting party must have been attacked in the Darklands before reaching the surface.

"Did a Darklands creature kill your tribesmen? Before you left the tunnels?"

He was shaking his head before she finished. His hands clawed deeper into her skin, and she gritted her teeth so as not to cry out.

"No! The beasts came through the boundary. Pale abominations! Monsters! They came from the land of the Gathi. The boundary is broken."

CHAPTER 9

Heat gathered around Drakon like a wool blanket, stifling and oppressive. Beneath the shade of the forest canopy, he raked a sleeved arm across his brow, sopping up the rivulets of sweat dripping into his eyes.

He stared out at the inert city. Acres of wheat and corn crops swayed in the hot breeze. Glensbrook's open gates vomited forth no morning travelers as was customary for midmorning. The road was bereft of movement. No sentries stood watch atop the stone battlements. The lack of activity from the city settled in his gut like a tankard of spoiled milk.

"Something isn't right about this heatwave."

Umgar's voice drew his attention from his observations. The general leaned against a pine. Sweat rolled from his forehead into his thick beard and dropped on his tunic. Even the horses' coats glistened where they grazed beneath the trees.

"I don't know if the mounts would've made it this far had we not traveled by veil," said Umgar.

Drakon agreed. He didn't trust mages, but Umgar's mysterious asset had saved them from a strenuous journey. Only an hour before, he and Umgar stood in an abandoned storehouse on the outskirts of the Noble District, an active portal ready for use. The reach of Umgar's connections knew no bounds.

His attention drifted back to Glensbrook. "There's been no movement from the city in the past thirty minutes. I haven't seen one Royal Fighter at the gates, nor has anyone left to go out into the crops."

"I noticed, and I'm assuming you still want to have a look."

"Yes. Ewen's planning something. I want to know what it is. He must have ordered the inhabitants to stay inside for some reason. If we can find out what he's doing and tie him to the High Priestess's murder, it might be enough to turn scrutiny from me."

Umgar made a noncommittal sound. "We'll walk the rest of the way and leave the mounts here as a precaution. Even though we don't see any guards or mages, it doesn't mean they're not there. I don't want to announce our presence with the clopping of horse hooves. Going in on foot also ensures we'll be able to move covertly once inside. Keep your weapon at the ready."

Drakon's own weapon was a comforting weight at his hip. As an assassin, he favored the dagger, easily concealed and wielded, but the sword was much more effective in an open battle. Fortunately, he was a master of both.

They left their horses and crept forward under the cover of the forest until the woodlands ended a few yards from the gates.

A trickle of uncertainty pooled in Drakon's stomach as they neared. He withdrew his sword. The mimicking sound of metal sliding from leather signaled Umgar doing the same. They spread out, one on each side of the road, and padded through the gates.

An unnatural stillness greeted them. No person or

animal stirred along the main street. Carts and merchant stalls stood abandoned with merchandise untouched. With a hand signal, he motioned Umgar forward. They moved with caution, darting from side street to side street through the Commoner District and toward the city center. If Tobiah and his delegation of mages were still in Glensbrook, they would be there. It housed the temple.

As he passed a house, Drakon pushed open the door with the tip of his sword and peered inside. In the main chamber, a table was set. Untouched food lay on the plates. Flies swarmed, helping themselves to the abandoned spread. Nothing else stirred in the interior.

He leaned back outside and caught Umgar's expectant gaze. Drakon gave a slight shake of his head. He found the entire situation utterly perplexing, to say the least. Instincts told him to turn tail and flee. Nothing good would come from being here. Another, stronger emotion beckoned him forward, arguing something sinister lurked among the deserted streets, and he could better protect himself from the known than the unknown.

He led Umgar across another street, and the city center came into view. A temple to Melika stood at the core of the open space, a platform for public executions at its side. Two opposing structures. One offering eternal life through religion and the other the absolution of death. The Gathi way. Conform or die. Yet, the deadly stage wasn't what gripped and held his notice.

It was the hundreds of garments littering the ground around the temple.

"What in Targarius happened here?" Umgar's voice was a harsh whisper in the dead air.

Drakon didn't shift his eyes from the scene before him. He began to move in for closer inspection but observed a chalk line on the cobblestone. Kneeling, he traced a finger across the border. His gaze tracked it along the perimeter of the clearing. A circle ward.

The memory of a similar enchantment came to the forefront of his mind. One that held a possessed, transformed priestess. *Did these wards act as gateways of a sort? But for who or what?*

He studied the unfamiliar symbols outlining the chalk line but could make no sense of them. He might be missing critical clues to what might have happened in his ignorance.

A movement to his right drew him from his mounting frustration. Umgar stepped over the ward and crept to the closest mound of fabric, lifting it with the tip of his blade. Black powder poured from the garment like sand in an hourglass.

"These are all commoners and Royal Fighters. I don't see one noble robe among the lot." He dropped the garment back to the street and motioned to the mounds surrounding him. "It's like they were drained to dust."

Fingers of trepidation prickled Drakon's scalp. He clutched his sword. His eyes darted to the shadowed alleys and windows of the buildings lining the space, seeking any overlooked threats.

"I was wrong to come here. We need to leave now," Drakon said. His words were barely loud enough for Umgar to hear.

Suddenly, a screech echoed from within the city. Drakon stood from his crouch and turned in the direction of the sound. Hairs rose on the back of his neck and arms. His heart pounded in the cage of his ribs. That hadn't been a scream of pain or fear but one of unadulterated fury. He shared a quick glance with Umgar. His companion's lips were drawn in a straight line, his posture rigid as he clutched his weapon.

Another scream cut through the air. It was answered by another and another until a cacophony of screams and shrieks ricocheted off every surface.

A shape materialized at the mouth of an alley. It ambled into the clearing, head down, movements jerky and unsteady like a newborn calf. Flowing robes of the finest material draped over a contorted and hunched figure. Its bobbing head lifted. Stringy blond hair shifted, revealing obsidian eyes and a stretched maw with twin rows of teeth.

Drakon swallowed the bile climbing the back of his throat. "It would appear what happened to the High Priestess wasn't an isolated event," he said more to himself than to Umgar.

The possessed noble's mouth unhinged in a bloodcurdling screech. It rushed forward, crossing the distance in seconds. Drakon held his ground, thrusting his sword into the creature's sternum. The blade punched through the beast's back in a spray of black gore. Speared like a fish, it continued to thrash on the steel, teeth clacking and hands clawing for him.

Then its severed head was sailing through the air and tumbling to the cobblestone. Its body went slack, dragging down Drakon's sword. He glanced behind the creature. Umgar stood panting, his sword coated in onyx blood.

Drakon yanked his blade free, allowing the monstrosity

to sink to the street. "Thanks. We need to get moving before more of his friends arrive."

Umgar pointed with his weapon. "It's a little too late for that."

Drakon turned in time to spot another creature stumbling into the square from an alley at their rear. They back paddled farther into the city center, both scanning for other escape routes, but all plans of retreat disintegrated as morphed nobles spewed forth from surrounding alleys and buildings.

Drakon turned and fled for the only structure within the space. "We can make a stand at the temple!"

Motion flashed in his periphery. Drakon dropped into a crouch, sword angled up. One of the nobles made a dive for him. Its momentum carried it overhead, and Drakon's blade was nearly wrenched from his hands as it traced a line along the noble's belly. Innards baptized him from the gutted creature. He paused to wipe the gore from his face and leaped up to continue his flight.

Ahead, Umgar shouldered open the temple entrance and held it wide, waving Drakon on.

Drakon pumped his legs faster. Wild screams and snarls nipped at his heels. He didn't look back. He knew what followed—a tidal wave of death. The door was within reach.

A hand grasped the back of his tunic, but the fabric tore with an audible rip. Drakon was freed and thundered inside the sanctuary. Umgar slammed the door and wedged the locking bar into place. Bodies bombarded the barrier, and it quivered and bowed from the onslaught.

Drakon bent and gasped, trying to regain his breath.

There was a crash to his right, and he swore with the little air left in his lungs. Glancing over, he witnessed a creature pulling itself headfirst through a hole in a window. Serrated glass ripped through the robes and dug into its flesh. Oily blood dripped down the sill, but the monster didn't seem to notice.

Drakon darted forward, cleared a prayer bench, and made it to the noble as the beast gained its feet. He swung his blade, severing the head. By the time both head and body crashed to the floor, another creature was forcing its way inside. Drakon rammed his sword through its skull. He yanked the blade free, and the twitching body slid back through the breach and into the crowd.

He went to work chopping at groping hands until he cleared the window. He slammed and latched the interior shutters. Glass broke, and the pounding of scores of fists against the building thundered.

He glanced at Umgar, who, like him, was saturated with inky gore. "Any ideas?"

Umgar wiped his sword on his ruined leathers, which only served to smear more blood on the blade. He sighed and answered. "Matter of fact, I do. You're fortunate I decided to tag along on this fiasco."

He hurried down the aisle and disappeared behind the altar. Drakon's eyebrows furrowed in confusion, but he followed, curiosity taking over. The racket from outside nearly drowned out the sound of stone grating against stone.

As Drakon turned the corner, a wall gaped open. Inside, the floor sloped down into darkness. A smirk lifted his lips. If he never saw another dusty, darkened passage, it would be far too soon.

He glanced at Umgar and raised an eyebrow. His question clear.

Umgar shrugged a beefy shoulder. "I've known about the secret entrances into the temples for years. It's a part of the job. Apparently, when religion was first introduced, there were warring factions within the noble class. Attacks on temples were commonplace."

Drakon inclined his head. Umgar was invaluable.

Unlit torches hung in sconces on either side of the door. Drakon took one and handed the other to Umgar. He retrieved flint and steel from a basket near the altar and lit both torches. Behind them, wood continued to pop and groan from the wave of bodies pressed against the building. It was time to go.

He ducked into the passage and Umgar followed. There was a click, and the wall slid closed to seal them inside. The stale air smelled of wet stone and dirt. Their torches cast a small radius of light on stone walls and an uneven floor. Dust motes swirled in the torchlight. Drakon walked deeper. His shoulders scraped the narrow walls and gathered cobwebs as he went, but he was able to clear the worst of them with his sword.

Clearly, the passage had been unused for years. Perhaps since the religious unrest Umgar mentioned. The two men traveled in silence as they strained to hear sounds of pursuit. The entrance remained closed behind them, and the only noise was from their breathing and footfalls.

After long minutes of walking, the path began to angle upward in a sharp incline. *They must be nearing the exit point.* His hunch was proven as sunlight glared around a bend, signaling the end of the passage. He settled his torch in the sconce at the opening, thankful to be free of the confining space, and stepped into the sun.

A heatwave rolled over him and stole his breath. In an instant, sweat drew up from his pores. Everywhere dead, dry leaves and pine needles littered the ground. The few leaves clinging to the trees were brown and brittle.

Umgar halted at his side and mopped perspiration from his face. "Goddess, it's like we've stepped into flames." He squinted into the distance. His mouth fell open, and he shook his head. "Never thought I'd see the day."

Drakon followed Umgar's gaze. Beyond two fallen trees leaning drunkenly against one another, an iridescent shimmer rose into the sky. The Glens was created to protect Somorrah from the Lim, but few Gathi ever saw it in person. Enchantments normally rebounded trespassers. However, he and Umgar stood within yards of the magical boundary. Some part of him whispered this was not a positive development, but he ignored the voice, sheathed his sword, and strode closer.

Power radiated from the Glens and called to him. Underbrush grabbed at his clothing, but Drakon plowed forward until he reached the mystical barrier. He placed a hand reverently onto its surface. The fine hairs on his arms lifted. Energy pulsed through him, sending a tingling sensation to his feet. He pushed against the barrier and dragged his hand along its charged surface, not concerned over the increasing temperature around him. Something about the magic spoke to him. Felt familiar.

Abruptly, the resistance vanished, and his hand slipped through. Honed reflexes saved him from toppling face-first through the Glens. His breaths quickened. Fear locked his muscles. He stood motionless as a statue, gaping at the rippling line where his wrist disappeared into nothing.

Impossible.

"I must say, Deathmark. I am astonished to see you. I figured the beasties in the city would've finished you off. Yet, here you are. Alive. How unfortunate."

Drakon spun toward the voice. Prince Tobiah stood less than ten feet away; six pale-haired mages, three men and three women, fanned out on either side of him. Aquamarine robes bellowed around his petite frame in the light breeze. His olive skin was flushed and perspiration beaded along his hairline. Strands of his dirty blond hair stuck like leeches to his damp neck. His thin upper lip curled in a sneer.

Umgar sidled closer, his back to the boundary. He must have spotted Tobiah and the mages while Drakon was enthralled. Drakon admonished himself for letting down his guard. He allowed Tobiah of all Gathi to catch him unawares.

"What have you done to the people of Glensbrook?" Drakon inched a hand toward his dagger. "What kind of game is your father playing?"

Tobiah's smile tightened. His gaze shifted from Drakon. Uncertainty flashed in his eyes, but arrogance overrode it. He shrugged.

"They're new warriors for the coming war. Melika has shown my father the truth. You are the Nahum, and you will usher in an era of sorrow Somorrah has never seen." His expression appeared pained. "After all my father has done for you? Allowing you the freedom a smut like you didn't deserve. Do you deny it? Do you deny you're in league with the Lim?"

Drakon didn't speak. Denial wouldn't convince Tobiah of his innocence. The man's mind was made.

"You won't even try to deny it. You were always arrogant. A half-blood abomination sweeping through the palace as if you owned it. Father should've killed you as a babe, not elevated you from slave to a station of power. Mercy is a characteristic of the weak. You will see I'm not my father. I'll make sure you won't be fulfilling any doomsday prophecies."

Umgar moved to stand partially in front of Drakon, effectively shielding Tobiah from Drakon's aim. *Goddess, what was he doing?*

Umgar sheathed his sword and held up his hands, placating. "Wait. The decree was to bring Drakon alive. King Ewen wants him brought in for a public execution for the murder of the High Priestess. He will be beyond livid if you disobey his orders."

Tobiah's eyes narrowed as he regarded Umgar as if only now noticing his presence. His beady blue eyes shifted from Umgar to Drakon, took in Umgar's protective position in front of Drakon. A nasty grin spread across his face. A chill ran along Drakon's skin despite the sweltering heat.

"You're right, General. I am to bring in the assassin unharmed. Thank you so much for reminding me."

His fake smile dropped. "But you—I can kill." He nodded toward Umgar. "Kill him and incapacitate Deathmark. I want to be back in Sura before nightfall for the execution."

The mages began chanting, calling forth their awful magic. Beside him, Umgar jerked, caught in some unseen binding.

Drakon didn't think. He acted. Summoning his gift, he released a well of power, aiming the blast toward the nobles. The resulting surge was enough to send the seven nobles hurtling into the underbrush in an explosion of dried leaves and branches.

Before Tobiah or the mages could regain their footing, Drakon grabbed the back of Umgar's tunic and dove through the rent in the barrier, pitching them into the unknown.

CHAPTER 10

Drakon's head connected with the unyielding ground. Light erupted behind his closed eyelids in a constellation of stars. He groaned and lay motionless, spent from the energy expenditure, and fought down a wave of nausea.

After a moment, he prodded the tender spot where his head had smacked the earth. He winced. Tacky blood flowed from a cut above his temple. The wound was superficial at best. He inhaled a deep breath and nearly choked on the oppressive heat. Breathing was like sucking in sludge. The atmosphere leeched moisture from his body. A layer of perspiration materialized on his skin.

Goddess, had his actions sentenced them to a worse fate than a public execution? He rolled to his side, sharp rocks gouging into him. He opened his eyes.

Two blurry silver moons hovered above. Drakon blinked, and the moons merged into one as his vision cleared. Strange, towering rock formations sprouted sporadically in all directions like tufts of hairs in a splotchy beard. No trees, flowering plants, or even a stunted bush grew from the dry, cracked terrain.

Umgar groaned, and Drakon turned to see the man climb to his feet. Drakon pushed himself up on unsteady legs. Silence stretched as they took in the bleak environment. Umgar turned to the Glens shimmering behind them.

"Well, there's one bright spot in this situation. Tobiah hasn't come through after us yet, which means he can't or won't. I am grateful either way."

Drakon strode to the barrier and lifted a hand toward it.

"You sure you want to do that?"

"I'm only checking to see whether the tear remains. I won't step through. Tobiah and the other mages might still be waiting on the other side. I have no plans of being captured."

He rested his palm against the Glens. Solid resistance met his touch. As before, power lanced up his arm and through his body. Unlike before, his hand didn't slip through. Drakon walked the boundary for a few yards in both directions. It was as firm as a battlement.

"I don't believe it's possible to reenter from this side, and for some unknown reason, Tobiah and the mages cannot pass through." He let his hand drop, turned back to Umgar, and shrugged. "At least not the way we came."

"Why do you think they can't follow?"

"As much as Tobiah loathes me, he would've pursued me to the ends of the world. The only logical reason for him not doing so is he is physically unable to."

Umgar frowned. "It makes one wonder why we were able to get through."

Drakon pondered the same, but no answers revealed themselves. He chose to focus on the current problem facing them rather than ruminate on a puzzle of which the pieces were unknowable.

When he didn't offer a hypothesis but instead shrugged, Umgar let out an exasperated sigh.

"Your lack of curiosity is astounding." Hands on his hips, he surveyed their surroundings again. "Well, at least we're safe from the mages at the moment. I never imagined what might lay beyond the Glens. If I had, it wouldn't have been this wasteland. None of the stories of the war describe it as dry and barren. The change must have occurred after the boundary was established. However, the most pressing issue is we don't have supplies to survive in such an atmosphere. If night here is this torturous, then the day will be deadly."

He tilted his gaze to the brightening sky. "Even now, the day approaches."

As if to accentuate Umgar's point, an arid breeze rolled over them. Drakon stared into the predawn sky. They needed shelter and water. Their surroundings didn't offer the latter, but the former might be found.

He nodded toward the nearest outcrop of rock. "That's no more than a few miles away. We should find an over-hang or, better yet, a cave to shelter through the day. Then we can worry about finding water."

Umgar agreed, and they set off with haste across the flat expanse. Drakon took a few steps when a tingling sensation caressed the nape of his neck. Apprehension spread like cool water throughout his body, lifting fine hairs and tens-ing muscles as it went. He knew the feeling. Someone or something was watching them.

His eyes swiveled to log the landscape but registered only the rocky stacks in the distance. His gaze shifted from one to the other, seeking out the source of his unease.

"You sense that?" Umgar said.

His dark eyes flicked from side to side, also scanning.

His hands flexed at his sides and inched toward his sword.

Drakon gave a tight nod. He was acquainted with the sensation—the inkling of an unseen specter tracking every move, ready to deal a fatal blow. He recognized it in his victims when they turned and looked directly at him as if warned by a sixth sense. It never mattered in the end whether they knew their imminent fate. Death always came swiftly.

At present, there wasn't much he or Umgar could do until their pursuer showed his or herself, so they walked on. His gaze fell on Umgar's broad back, which was drenched in sweat. His former guardian was a warrior. Of all men he could be stranded with, the general and spymaster topped his list.

Still, his gut twisted at having placed Umgar in such a predicament. His constant desire for power, hatred for nobles, and disregard for Umgar's advice had blinded him to the real danger of Ewen's scheme. If he had listened...now, he was culpable in unleashing a malevolent force into the world and was labeled Nahum. Although commoners were without status in Gathi culture, they knew of the prophecy: Nahum would signal the end of the Gathi.

How? Drakon hadn't paid enough attention to the priestesses' ramblings in his youth to remember. He couldn't be such a person. Did he hate nobles? Yes, but he never aspired to control anything other than his own destiny.

"Don't look now, but I saw a glint from the Northeast."

The words pulled Drakon from the lake of his internal torment. He tensed, fingers tingling to draw his sword. "Did you see how many?"

"No. It was only a flicker of metal, but it was there long enough for me to know it wasn't a trick of the light."

"Unless whoever or whatever attacks, our objective hasn't changed. We still need to get to shelter," Drakon said after a brief consideration.

The formation loomed larger against the illuminating heavens. Less than a half a mile and they would be in relative safety.

"They'll follow us inside. I'll bet my life on it. We'll have a few minutes once we reach the rocks, and we'll know if they mean us harm."

"They could have attacked miles ago. Perhaps they're pursuing out of curiosity," said Drakon.

He honestly didn't believe the sentiment, but it was far preferable to another thought he didn't want to give credence to. Their stalkers could be hungry.

Minutes later, Drakon and Umgar stood in front of an imposing cave entrance. The yawning mouth opened like the maw of a titan and lay between two massive boulders. Drakon motioned for Umgar to fall back, entered, and swept the interior. The ground of the expansive cavity sloped downward and the air became markedly cooler the farther he traversed. Stalactites and stalagmites cropped up from the ceiling and floor like barbs and disappeared into the darkness.

Drakon scouted as far as he dared in the inky blackness. Finding nothing of concern, he retraced his steps and waved Umgar in. The men moved inside and wasted no time settling behind a towering stalagmite. The cave entrance was visible through a slither of space between the stalagmite and wall from their vantage. Drakon fell into a crouch to wait.

"I'll take first watch. Whoever is following us is patient. They shadowed us for miles without making themselves known. They're not in a rush to confront us. No need for exhaustion to overtake us both. I'll wake you if anything happens or when I need rest," said Drakon.

Umgar didn't argue. The general was in excellent physical condition, but he was also eight years Drakon's senior and accustomed to commanding from his headquarters, not the battlefield. Dark rings cradled his eyes, and his face was drawn with fatigue. Umgar slid down the wall with a groan, situating his blade over outstretched legs. Within minutes, his breathing became deep and rhythmic with sleep.

Drakon studied the cave's opening. No movement came from beyond. If their stalkers were still out there, they weren't in direct sight of the entry.

There was a scrape of displaced gravel, and the lightening sky backlit a head as it inched into view. The shadow paused at the entrance for a heartbeat and then scuttled forward.

Drakon cataloged the shape. Two arms and legs. Tall, even crouched as it was. He turned to nudge Umgar awake, but the spymaster's eyes were open, tracking the advancing wraith. The figure picked its way toward them. Its head cocked back and forth, scanning the cave but overlooking their hiding place.

Drakon inched to his full height and slunk behind the shape as it passed within arm's reach. In a swift movement, he drew an arm around the figure's neck and locked it into place with his forearm. His captive exploded with unbridled energy, bucking against the chokehold.

"Calm down. I only want to know why you're following us," he said close to its ear.

His response came in the form of a lightning-quick strike to the face.

ॐ

Tears sprang to Drakon's eyes. His grip wavered, and his attacker twisted free. He barely had enough time to lift his arms to deflect a strike intended for his solar plexus. His assailant spun and landed a kick in his exposed side.

Drakon crashed into a stalagmite like a man-sized boulder. An explosion of pain shot through his ribs. He gritted his teeth and pushed through the discomfort. The relentless figure pressed the attack, the absence of light seeming to have little effect on it. Drakon ducked a well-aimed swing. The strike passed close overhead, ruffling his hair.

From his crouch, he delivered two jabs to his attacker's gut in quick succession. An "oof" sounded from his adversary, and the specter folded. Drakon swept a leg under the person's feet. The body hit the unforgiving stone floor with a satisfying crack.

Drakon scrambled atop and straddled his supine prey, his muscular thighs pinning and immobilizing the arms. The figure grunted and bucked like a stallion beneath him until Drakon slipped the cold steel of his dagger against its neck. He leaned down and scrutinized the face in the scant light of the rising sun spilling through the cave mouth.

The woman's large, fervent eyes glared back at him. Absently, he mused that her eyes reminded him of the stray cats in Sura. Feral. Uncontrollable.

"Drakon. Don't. Move."

He stilled at the warning in Umgar's tone. What the…

Moisture slapped Drakon in the face like a wet rag. The reek of spoiled meat wafted over him on a menacing growl. He swallowed the knot in his throat with difficulty and slowly craned his head up.

Death crouched on a ledge above him. A gargantuan beast, probably over ten feet had it been standing, stared down at him with menace. In Drakon's stunned mind, he had the presence to think it resembled a lizard crossed with a horse... A colossal, mutant horse.

Golden serpentine eyes blinked two sets of eyelids as the creature regarded him. It snarled, lips curling back to exhibit dagger-length teeth within chomping distance of Drakon's head. Ropes of drool dripped from its mouth like the cave's stalactites. Its haunches twitched, ready to pounce.

Drakon gulped down the bile from his churning stomach. One wrong move and his head would be separated from his body. He forced a watery smile.

"Now, now, I wasn't going to hurt your friend."

His voice was low and pacifying as he inched the dagger away from the woman's throat and let it clatter to the cave floor. He loosened his thigh hold, and his attacker wiggled free to stand beneath the creature. Her back to the dawn, her peculiar features were again cast into mystery.

Drakon remained on his knees, hands raised. "Call off your beast. I didn't lie. It wasn't my intention to harm you. I only wanted to know why you were following us."

The woman laid a gentle hand on the animal's hideous face. It purred in response and nuzzled into her touch.

Drakon shuddered.

"Meko is not a beast. If she were, she would have ignored my previous orders not to kill anyone, and you would be dead. Why are you here?" Her voice held a strange accent, and Drakon had to pause for a moment to parse out her question before answering.

"Our sojourn here was an accident. Creatures attacked us, and our only escape was through the barrier to this place."

"Creatures?" The word was uttered with undisguised interest. "Tell me more about these creatures."

A sphere of sapphire light, reminiscent of Gathi orb light, flared to life in her palm and rose to bob above them. The muted glow melted shadows and revealed the cave in cool undertones.

Drakon frowned. She hadn't spoken any words of conjuring. *How had she created the orb without casting?* He began to ask when her pet climbed from its perch to settle beside her. Umgar whispered an oath, and Drakon agreed with the sentiment. Now looking somewhat docile, the beast towered over the woman, who was as alien as the creature.

She stood taller than most Gathi women and was only a few inches shorter than he. Toned muscles flexed beneath her obsidian skin. A brown sleeveless tunic stretched tight over her narrow chest. Her feet were bare, and a long black braid hung down her back. She could've been a commoner if not for her jet-black coloring, pointed ears, and unusually large black eyes.

Commoners were darker in complexion than nobles, but their brown tones could never compete with the intriguing shade of ebony of the woman. She had to be a Lim. It was the only explanation. He had not heard of any other race living beyond the Glens. Yet, she didn't seem like the blood-thirsty savage Gathi history depicted.

She flashed small fangs in a snarl. "Answer me, White One, or I'll let Meko eat you and your friend." She petted the beast for emphasis. "Were these creatures of yours pale with wrinkled skin? Describe them."

Drakon tried to ignore the animal's intimidating bulk and focused on the question. "The beasts you mentioned weren't the ones pursuing my companion and me, but I do know of the creatures you speak. We call them wailers. They hunt the forests of our land."

Her eyebrows furrowed, and she opened her mouth to reply. Suddenly, armed warriors swarmed the cave, and their presence dammed up her would-be response. She glanced back, gave an exaggerated sigh, and gazed upward to mutter something unintelligible. Drakon used the distraction to stand and put distance between himself and the advancing threat.

In moments, soldiers surrounded them. The newcomers were dressed similarly to the woman, in fitted brown tunics and leathers, and brandished all manner of sword, staff, and spear. An imposing man with rippling muscles and a grim expression broke from a contingent. His large hands held curved blades that were more machetes than daggers.

His dark gaze took in Drakon's and Umgar's measure as he approached his companion's side. "Eza, we'll speak later about your disregard for my orders."

She grimaced but didn't argue. The man was their

leader then. The stranger's deep-set eyes hadn't strayed from Drakon and Umgar as he spoke. Tension and animosity Drakon didn't understand rippled from him. Drakon's dagger hand clenched and released. As if sensing his intent, the warriors closed in, leading with the sharp ends of their weapons.

The man smirked and nodded to a female soldier. "Disarm them." She approached cautiously, and Drakon let himself be relieved of his sword. Umgar received the same treatment.

"We saw you come through the boundary from the land of the Gathi. Why are you here?" the leader said.

The woman, Eza, answered before Drakon or Umgar could reply. "They have information about the monsters that attacked our sister tribe. I believe they might be able to tell us the origins of the power surge as well. We should take them to father."

Drakon's face remained impassive at her mention of the surge, but he chanced a knowing glance at Umgar. The spymaster lifted a shoulder in an almost imperceptible shrug.

The leader huffed. "The Gathi cannot be trusted. We should kill them and be done with it."

Umgar tensed at Drakon's side, readying for a fight. Drakon surveyed the dozen or so men and women around them. Each stood with weapons leveled. He didn't doubt his or Umgar's fighting abilities, but it would be a short battle indeed. Fatigue and hunger already sapped at his strength reserves. He would be lucky to dispatch two fighters before being overwhelmed.

His gaze fell back to Eza, who worried her bottom lip, her eyes darting from Drakon to Umgar as she considered the man's recommendation. Of the two Lim, his best chance to forestall death lay with her.

"We indeed know the cause of the surge," he said, baiting. "It is the same force that damaged the boundary, which allowed the wailers through from our Kingdom into yours."

Eza's eyes narrowed. "Explain."

Drakon wanted to sag in relief. She was intrigued. He could leverage intrigue. He folded his arms deliberately across his chest. "I'd rather wait to speak to your father. You'll have to forgive me for not believing you'd keep us alive if I divulge all my secrets. This information is the only bargaining chip we have."

The man at her side took a menacing step forward, his blades lifted, fangs bared. "You dare bargain with us? I could kill you—"

Eza placed a restraining hand to the man's chest, halting him. The warrior clamped his mouth closed, his eyes still ablaze. Eza inclined her head.

"What Dagoti means is we won't allow unrestrained strangers into our home and risk endangering our people. You may speak with my father, but you'll come as our prisoners." She shrugged. "Once we know the truth, we'll decide your fates."

Drakon would take the reprieve. "I agree to those terms."

Dagoti's lips pressed into a thin slash. He motioned to the warriors who had relieved Drakon and Umgar of their weapons. "Restrain them."

Rough hands bound Drakon's arms behind his back. He wiggled his wrists, testing the bonds. They were unyielding. He wouldn't be escaping without his dagger. As if reading his thoughts, Eza stooped to pluck up the weapon and tucked it into her waist.

Dagoti signaled to the back of the cave, where contours disappeared into shadow, and spoke to the encircling Lim.

"We'll return to Napata through the Darklands. It will save time and, hopefully, help us avoid any of the wailer creatures." He turned to Eza with an intense glare and stabbed a finger in Drakon and Umgar's general direction. "You spared them. You guard them. If they kill anyone, it's on you."

He stormed off without a backward glance. Eza seemed to deflate. She sighed, saddled next to them, and jerked her head toward the procession marching farther into the cavern.

"Get moving, White One. For your sake, I pray you've not misled me, or I swear what you would've suffered at Dagoti's hands will be nothing compared to what I'll do to you."

CHAPTER 11

The man thrashed against the invisible hold crushing him against the pillar. His shrieks echoed off the walls of the silent throne room. His pale-blue eyes grayed and sank into his skull. Pasty skin shriveled like a grape left in the sun until the man's robes were but a billowing sack on his shrunken frame.

Strength infused Melika as she siphoned the last dregs of magic from the mage. Her rage ebbed minutely with the return of her power. She released her magical hold on the man. The body tumbled to the marbled floor to rest on its side beside five similar husks.

Melika glanced over the packed throne room. Mages and nobles from the city stood like upright corpses in a fear-induced hush.

"Let this be a warning to those who fail me," she said from Ewen's throne.

Her gaze traveled over the mage, Nolan, whose flinty eyes burned with a hint of outrage, but he dared not issue a word of dissent. Melika exhaled a calming breath and straightened the robes of her commandeered body. Apparently, the murder of mages, or any noble for that matter, was out of character for King Ewen. They would get used to it. She couldn't afford more failures. The capture of the Nahum was paramount.

Uncharacteristic fear threatened to overcome her. The assassin was the sole obstacle to her freedom and return to her former glory. Without the dormant power he possessed, she was but a shadow of herself.

She siphoned strength for herself and children from the Gathi, nobles and commoners alike, to sustain them in exile for eons. The nobles' continued reliance on her essence to create and use magic, amplified by the tattooed runes on their skin, supplied her with enough energy to escape the Dark Realm. It, however, wasn't sufficient to shatter the added barrier of the Glens.

Melika had buried knowledge of the Glens' true nature with deliberate lies and disinformation, which became ingrained into the Gathi religion. Likewise, she recast her identity as a goddess of life and magic, protector of women and children, healer of the sick. Their ignorance was a steady source of power.

However, the Nahum, a feeble assassin, threatened millennia of well-laid plotting. Rage dissolved her fear, and she clenched Ewen's too flat teeth. Had the High Priestess chosen more devoted priestesses to complete the summoning ritual, Melika would have been birthed into this realm in her proper form. The spineless fools had run at the sight of the transformation. As repayment for the betrayal, Melika managed to cut down one woman before she could escape. Still, it was little consolation at present.

She scowled down at the soft pale hands with their manicured nails and thin wrists. Her upper lip curled, a bitter tang in her mouth. If not for the concentrated power of this specimen, her condition would be unbearable.

"Father, I understand you are displeased."

The prince's whiny voice snapped Melika from her growing disgust. Tobiah paused as the weight of her glare fell on him. His wary gaze flicked to his mother, who sat on her throne worrying her bottom lip with her teeth and twisting her hands in her lap.

The undisguised uncertainty was nauseating. Perhaps she should have killed him, too. Weakness in any form was intolerable.

"Speak boldly. No wonder Deathmark eluded your pursuit. Such apprehension is unfitting of the Prince of Somorrah."

Tobiah's cheeks flamed pink, and his eyes flickered to the audience surrounding them. "I—I apologize, father. I was told the nobles from Glensbrook have disappeared into the nearby forest, but I'm certain we can retrieve them."

An unnatural silence stretched as Melika stared down the prince. Tobiah swallowed audibly but pressed on. "It has also come to my attention that Captain Crain and the city's contingent of Royal Fighters a—are missing."

Melika exploded to her feet with a scream of frustration. Everyone in the room shrank away from her like cowering dogs from an owner's stick.

"Must I do everything myself?" Her ire threatened another lapse in her control. You can't kill them all, she reminded herself. She needed them for the moment.

To prevent herself from killing anyone else, Melika stormed from the room and made her way to the king's quarters. Inside, she crossed to the large veil. A wave of her hand transformed the mirror into a portal, and she stepped through.

The decimated Temple of Melika lay in silence. Her

footsteps seemed muted as she traversed corridors streaked with rust-colored blood and bits of flesh. Arriving at the chamber she sought, she pushed open the heavy double doors.

Alabaster bodies turned in unison to face the door. Hundreds of amber eyes twinkled like fireflies in the dimness of the antechamber. Excited yips sounded from jagged mouths, and they jostled about, unable to remain still. Melika smiled, and a feeling of weightlessness filled her breast. She might wear another's skin, but children always recognized their mother.

She strode forward, hands outstretched to caress her offspring as they pressed closer, vying for her touch. One of her progenies stepped into her path. It huffed, demanding attention, and nuzzling her midriff. Melika paused, her smile growing wider. How she had missed these children, those who escaped into this realm long ago. She planted a gentle peck on its misshapen head. It mewled and closed its glittering eyes in bliss.

Melika moved on, wading through her brood, and continuing to pet velvety, wrinkled skin and doling out kisses as she went. She trod over torn, bloody robes littering the floors. The younglings had eaten well. *Good.* She hated leaving them alone while she played king to the Gathi. She consoled herself with the knowledge that it was a temporary necessity. One that would free her and her children.

Ahead, one of her offspring lay stretched across the bed. It was larger than the others—

an alpha. As an alpha, it possessed venom that poisoned the soul and the body. It lifted its head as she approached. Blazing eyes met hers.

"What news of the Nahum?"

It hissed and snarled its report. The Glens had weakened enough for a few younglings to cross the barrier. Unlike the Gathi nobles, her offspring didn't contain her essence and were without magic, which allowed their passage through the ruptured boundary. It would seem the damaged magic didn't sense them as a threat. They had been dispatched to find and return the Nahum.

Melika frowned as she paced before the bed. "I want him captured and returned before the Lim find him. If they haven't yet investigated the surge, they soon will."

Her teeth bared, and her fingers curled into claws at the mere thought of the Lim. Memories of failure and rejection rose like tentacles to coil themselves about her neck and drag her into a lake of misery.

Melika mouthed the name of the genesis of her hate. *Apalsi.* Her creator.

His blind love for the Lim led him to betray her—banishing Melika and her children unto the barren Dark Realm and imprisoning her Gathi army within the Glens. Yet, before sealing her away, Apalsi foretold of a child, one of new blood, who would have the power to undo all he had put into place but also to destroy her.

The Nahum. She spat. Tens of thousands of years roaming a black void, hungering, and searching for release taught her nothing if not patience. Decades passed before she realized some Gathi retained enough dregs of her essence for her to influence them from her prison.

A plan had formed. She had infiltrated their minds, eroding past events and amassing a devout following to provide sustenance and strength to her and her children for eons. It took more time and power to free a trivial number of her spawn from their prison into Somorrah. They fed and multiplied in the land, stripping it bare and pushing the Gathi further into her salvation. It was all an intricate game.

Soon, she would be untethered and able to exact the brunt of her vengeance. The power she gained from the Nahum, coupled with the energy she siphoned from the Gathi, would catapult her potency and permit her to break through the Glens. From the moment Melika saw Deathmark, she felt the uniqueness of his blood, the force he hid within.

Melika extracted herself from her thoughts. Trapped as she was, she was not without her charms. She would send more of her children to aid the hunt. The Nahum would stand before her by night's end, and then he would surrender his power and life to her.

She began to chant.

ৡᏅ

Melika stepped from the portal into the king's palace chambers. At once, a knock came at the door.

"Enter."

The prince slipped inside. His hair was unkempt, and his eyes shifted around the room, never settling on anything for too long. Melika concealed her annoyance with much difficulty. Killing the fool grew more appealing with each encounter.

"Pardon my intrusion, father, but I wanted to personally inform you that mages are combing the city for Captain Crain and the missing Royal Fighters. Nolan has instructions to execute the captain and his men on sight. Another group will round up the Glensbrook nobles in the morning. They'll also remove evidence of what happened to the commoners." He grimaced. "What did happen to them? We brought them into the summoning circle as instructed, but why were they not transformed?"

Melika considered if she should tell him the truth. But then what did it matter if he knew? She motioned for him to sit in a cushioned chair and settled into another before speaking.

"Commoners do not contain enough of the goddess's essence to withstand the siphoning. Unlike nobles, the little power they have is drawn out and reduces them to dust. Unfortunate but unavoidable."

As she spoke, he nodded his understanding and rubbed the back of his neck. He seemed agitated and changed the subject.

"Is there something else you wish to discuss? You seem preoccupied. Speak on it, and let's be done with the matter."

Tobiah leaned forward; his hands balled into fists atop his knees. "I'd like permission to apprehend the fugitive Deathmark. I've spoken to Nolan and a few high mages. They believe they can figure out a way to cross through the tear in the Glens, so I can pursue him."

Did they? No matter what the nobles told Tobiah, only she knew the way to escape the Glens. Apalsi created the barrier to entrap anything containing even the slightest trace of her essence. The prince's magic was weak, but he was still infused with her power.

However—her eyes perused his too dark hair, eyes, and skin—his frailty could be used to her advantage. It would be a trivial task to extract her essence from him. Then, like the younglings and the possessed nobles, he could pass through the tear. She gazed at his narrow chest, thin limbs, and meager stature. A soldier he was not. To have a chance against the Nahum, he would need to become more formidable. Fortunately, she could assist in that area. Melika smiled.

"Does that smile mean you'll grant me permission?" His face was buoyant.

"I'll give you more than consent. I'll give you aid. But first, a gift of power to make the trip possible."

Tobiah was on the edge of the seat, his eyes aglow. Melika leaned forward, offering her palm to him. He didn't hesitate. He grasped her hand like a drowning man to a bit of timber in a thrashing sea. She clamped down tight on the proffered appendage.

There was a moment of panic as pain and confusion crossed Tobiah's handsome face. He yanked his hand, attempting to break her hold.

"Father?" His lips and chin trembled. He leaned back and tugged harder. "Father, you're hurting me."

Melika held fast and allowed her true visage to flash across the mask of Ewen's face. Tobiah reared back and opened his mouth to scream. A casual wave of her hand stole his voice. He flopped about in the chair, jaws stretched and gasping like a fish on land.

With a curious detachment, Melika drained him of her essence and then went about the task of reforming. During her confinement, she perfected her aptitude for creation. She released her hold, looking on in satisfaction as the prince tumbled from the seat. His leg connected with the chair, sending it skidding across the floor to crash into a wall. Bones in his back, legs, arms popped and lengthened. Robes split to accommodate his expanding girth, and pale, wrinkled skin peeked through. Tobiah flipped over, arching his twisting back. His face bubbled like boiling stew beneath the flesh, and his mouth stretched wide in a silent scream, revealing twin rows of dagger-sharp fangs.

Once blue eyes burned amber.

Melika gazed tenderly at her creation. Birthing pains were of little consequence compared to the redemption of rebirth.

CHAPTER 12

The agonized screaming ended abruptly.

Crain watched the commoner woman drop to the cobblestone from his refuge twenty feet away. Her dark eyes stared sightless into the nothingness of death. Without conscious volition, his hand clasped his sword as uncontrollable tremors coursed through him. He stepped toward the door of the building, which housed the Royal Fighters' impromptu base of command.

A firm grasp on his arm jerked him to a stop. He turned to glower at the person who restrained him. Lieutenant Joah shook his head.

Joah's stern gaze flicked back to the scene taking place on the street. His lips thinned into a line, and he drew in a deep breath, resisting his own urge to intervene.

"We have our orders, Captain," he said after returning his attention to Crain. "You can't save anyone if you die today."

Joah was right, of course. Yet, inaction while innocents died went against everything Crain stood for as a fighter.

Outside, Nolan tsked and motioned to the still form lying inches from his sandaled feet.

"I truly take no pleasure in killing smuts, but I'll have no choice but to continue unless Captain Crain and the missing Royal Fighters return for sentencing. Like cowards, they have abandoned their posts. None of you should protect them as their abandonment puts public order and safety at risk." His icy blue eyes raked the crowd of onlookers, his tattooed face a mask of counterfeit sincerity. "If any of you have information on the captain's whereabouts, tell us now, and we can put this unpleasantness behind us."

A silence pollinated with fear stretched. Crain acknowledged it wasn't loyalty but ignorance holding the commoners' tongues. He and his fighters had made pains to move during the night to avoid curious eyes.

Nolan would get nothing from the Commoner District residents. As predicted, no information came from the multitude. The royal mage gave an exasperated sigh and addressed the mass of mages accompanying him.

"They weren't seen leaving the city. They're still here somewhere. Search the homes and kill whoever is hiding them."

The mob scattered into the surrounding structures. Individuals and families were dragged from their beds and out into the early morning light.

Crain glanced at the fighters who stood shoulder-to-shoulder behind him. More men and women were packed below in the underground corridor and chamber. Their grim faces were set with resolve. Many of their hands hovered over weapons, readying for the imminent battle. He muttered an oath. Their current plight was his fault. He had lingered too long in the city on the promise of information from the palace informant.

Melika curse his foolishness, he thought darkly.

A voice from outside yanked Crain back to the present a moment before the door was flung open. The mage stood frozen, seemingly stunned that the shack overflowed with the people he sought. The man recovered quickly but not fast enough to avoid Crain's blade.

The mage let out a squawk of agony and stumbled back into the street, casting the proverbial light on their hiding place.

"Don't allow them to cast!" Crain shouted as he burst from the doorway.

On the command, his fighters swarmed like hornets from a nest to sting with sword and spear, overtaking the nearest mages in their initial assault. From his vantage farther up the road, Nolan whirled toward them.

Crain and the nobleman locked stares. A slow, malevolent grin spread across Nolan's thin face. Crain watched in mounting horror as the man's lips began to move. The mage was casting. Nolan was casting, and Crain was too far away to stop him. With a sick feeling, he realized he would die before he could fulfill the charge Umgar had given him.

A sudden wall of energy raced along the ground like lit oil to encircle Crain and his fighters, obscuring his view of Nolan. The mages caught within the ring were blasted back and through the forcefield to vanish from sight. A ringlet of fire appeared before Crain, widening to the size of a doorway. A beautiful young woman, garbed in majestic azure robes, stepped from the portal.

His informant arrived.

He scowled. "Took your sweet time, didn't you? We were supposed to meet at dawn."

Fynna narrowed frosty blue eyes. "Let's not forget I don't work for you, Captain. I came as soon as I deemed it safe for me. At any rate, I needed a convincing reason why

I couldn't join Nolan on the hunt to find you. That said," she glanced at the glimmering boundary she erected and back to him. "I'll not be able to hold this enchantment much longer. We must go."

Before Crain could reply, she extended a delicate hand. The portal expanded to engulf them. In a blink, he stood in a quiet, wooded area with a dense canopy of trees above him.

Fighters milled about, bewildered and disoriented. Many of them never traveled via veil. It was a disconcerting experience when expected, but its effects were devastating when one was unprepared for the jolt. Two men vomited into shrubs. Others doubled over, hands on their knees and sucked in deep breaths. Crain swallowed down his own breakfast as it threatened a reappearance and sheathed his sword.

"You could've given a bit of notice before doing that, but thanks. Where are we?"

"There was no time for an explanation."

With an incantation and another wave of her hand, their horses and supply wagons appeared. Fynna tossed her white hair over her shoulder and gave him a smirk. "You're welcome. As for where you are, you're about thirty miles northeast of the city. The nearest Waystation should be a little over a half day's ride. I've cloaked you all to ensure no mage can track you."

He inclined his head. "We are in your debt."

"I know."

"What information did you bring, being we almost died waiting for it?"

"Take a walk with me, Captain."

Crain nodded and turned to Joah, who scowled at Fynna in open distrust.

"I'll be back. Make sure the horses and wagons are ready for the journey."

"You sure, Captain?"

"I'll be fine."

He turned away before Joah could object further and let Fynna lead him farther into the forest until they were out of earshot.

Fynna leaned against a tree and crossed her arms. She frowned, weighing her next words. Crain waited. He understood silence was better at pulling words from a person than questions. After a moment, she spoke.

"It's said that Deathmark and Umgar passed through the Glens into the Forsaken Lands. In a fit of rage, Ewen killed the mages who allowed them to escape."

Crain's mouth fell open. Of all the news he expected, this could not be.

"Impossible. No one can cross the Glens."

"There's talk of Deathmark being the Nahum. If this is true, then nothing is impossible. Whether he is or isn't, the king believes Deathmark is the Nahum." She shuddered. "Ewen is becoming more and more unhinged. For the sake of Somorrah, we need a ruler whose mind is stable."

"And who might that be? Tobiah? I dare say the prince wouldn't be an improvement."

The look she gave him was haughty and imperious, and a realization struck Crain. He reared back in incredulous disbelief.

"You? You think to siege power? What about Nolan? You think he's going to let you overthrow his master?"

She scoffed. "Nolan has been plotting to oust Ewen for years. He's been biding his time, waiting for the right moment. His procrastination is my gain. I'll handle the royal mage. Don't worry about him. Once Ewen and Tobiah are dead, I'll restore the Kingdom to sanity. I'll need Umgar and the Royal Fighters to hold the peace among the commoners. In return for your future service, I'll send word to your people in the cities and Waystations to meet you east of Senna City at the base of the Fetanian Mountains. Umgar and I agree the Wild Gathi could turn the tables in our favor. With the mages loyal to me, the Royal Fighters, and Wild Gathi on our side, we have a better chance at winning the approaching conflict."

Crain grimaced. If Umgar and Drakon had indeed crossed the Glens, command of the Royal Fighters fell to him. He would carry out Umgar's order and convince the Wild Gathi to join them against Ewen. Although, contrary to what Fynna believed, he had no intention of delivering his people into the hands of a new dictator. Before him was a rare opportunity to change the status quo.

If he had any say in the matter, neither Ewen nor any other noble would rule after the war.

ॐ

"We'll rest here for a cycle."

Dagoti's voice drifted over their procession to where Eza stood in the rear. She scanned the area and recognized the place. It was her tribe's routine stop when visiting the Coombe tribe. She had not realized how near the location was to the surface.

Their group moved toward the center of the cavern from a small tunnel, and multiple shafts led from the hollow. Massive stalagmites protruded from the ground as far as she could see. Water dripped from one side of the ceiling into a clear lake spanning the length of the space.

The Malachi spread out. A few warriors broke off to scout farther and the rest began unpacking supplies and unrolling sleeping mats. Her gaze fell on their strange prisoners. Ten feet separated the males after Dagoti had noticed them whispering minutes into the journey.

The Gathi were curious specimens. The older male had a thick beard covering most of his face, and his eye and skin coloring were closer to the ebony of her own people. However, the similarities stopped there. He was more muscular and bulkier than the sleek, muscled Lim. Both males lacked fangs, sported rounded ears, and suffered from poor eyesight.

Even with the aid of the Apalsi light sphere, their eyes strained in the darkness. From the histories passed down from the Oracle, Gathi had once been Lim. She pondered, not for the first time, what caused their mutations.

Her attention shifted to the younger, sallow-skinned Gathi. She found her intense curiosity toward him more difficult to conceal. Warring energies radiated from him, thrumming beneath his skin, and causing his aura to pulse like an erratic heartbeat.

It was intriguing. She had asked Dagoti if he detected the male's abnormal vibrations. Dagoti was of no help. He only frowned and said it was likely evil wafting off the Gathi. She rolled her eyes at the memory. She would visit the Oracle when they arrived in Napata. The ancient Lim would have the answers.

"You should see to your prisoners."

Eza broke from her musings to see Dagoti looking down at her. "They make the others uneasy. Everyone's anxiety is high because we must travel in the light to compensate for the Gathi's inferior sight. Any creature looking for a meal will spot us long before we see it."

"There's nothing to be done for it. Having the Gathi stumbling through the dark would also draw attention and slow our progress. I want to get home as quickly as possible."

"Eza," he said her name like a plea. "Everything in me is saying this is a bad idea. There are too many unknowns. I'm telling you; we shouldn't bring them back to Napata. They're Gathi, for Apalsi's sake! They're not to be trusted."

Eza understood his reluctance, but her father sent the Malachi to find answers. The males might have them. Beside her, Dagoti's frustration wafted from him in waves. She wouldn't change her mind about this and didn't want to argue.

"We can talk about this later," she said and then changed the subject. "I'll go tend to their wounds and offer them food."

Dagoti sliced a hand through the air. "You're not healing anyone."

She cocked her head to the side and folded her arms across her chest, staring him down as best she could, given he was a head taller. "I don't remember asking your permission. You might oversee the Malachi, but I'm still your Zarea. I'll do what I think is right for the tribe. At the moment, that is ensuring those males make it to Napata alive and unharmed."

A muscle worked in Dagoti's jaw like he was chewing a fistful of rawhide. His nostrils flared.

"Is that what you're doing?" He bent forward, not to be overheard. "Doing what's right for the tribe? If that was the case, you wouldn't be here at all. You would be mated and training to take over for your father, not running around pretending you're one of us."

The words momentarily stunned Eza. She opened her mouth to offer a retort, but her mind was wiped clean. She pressed her lips together and inwardly cursed the burning at the backs of her eyes. *Was that what Dagoti thought of her?* She trained harder than any warrior. Not long ago, she would have been expected to lead the Malachi as head of the tribe. That expectation changed with her mother's untimely death. Her father's coping mechanism was to remove the position from their duties. Now, she was supposed to be little more than a servant and bed warmer to a mate.

It wasn't going to happen. No matter what Dagoti or her father believed. She would be no one's subservient mate. Without comment, she turned and stalked toward the prisoners.

Dagoti muttered a curse. "Eza, wait. I didn't mean it."

Eza ignored him and kept walking. He had said exactly what he meant and what he thought wasn't her concern. She pulled a cloth from her satchel as she crossed to the younger male.

He was deposited a few feet away from his companion and reclined against a wall a few yards from the lake. His feet were crossed at the ankle, and his posture appeared lax, although sitting with his arms tied behind his back couldn't have been comfortable. His gaze flitted around the camp, tracking everyone and everything.

When Eza stopped before him, he glanced up at her expectantly. One eyebrow arched in an unspoken question. Intense eyes, which seemed to change from brown to green, glittered in the light, unreadable in their strangeness.

Unsettling.

For a fleeting moment, she debated getting as far away from the male as she could. He would bring her nothing but trouble. She stole a glance over her shoulder. Dagoti stood scowling and watching them with his massive arms crossed.

She turned away. No way was she running. Dagoti wouldn't let her live down the shame. She would chew rocks and enjoy it before she gave him that type of ammunition. She refocused on the Gathi. He regarded her with interest, and a thousand needles pricked her skin at his gaze. She cleared her throat and marshaled herself.

She motioned to the bruise above his left eye with her cloth. "That's developing into a pretty sizable lump."

Why had she said that? It wasn't like he couldn't feel it.

He gave her a closed-lipped smirk. "Nice of you to point it out." His tone was dry and heavy with sarcasm.

"Look, if you hadn't attacked me, I wouldn't have hurt you."

He snorted. "I'm sure. That beast you keep is quite a deterrent."

"I've told you before, Gathi. Meko isn't a beast. She's a companion. She was protecting me."

"You don't say?" He leaned his head against the rock and closed his eyes. "Also, my name isn't Gathi. It's Drakon."

Drakon, huh? She stared at him, with his tense muscles ready to strike, and thought it suited him.

"Are you going to tell me why you're here, Drakon?"

One side of his mouth turned up in something reminiscent of a smile, but not quite. He didn't open his eyes. "I'll tell my story to your father. Forgive me if I don't believe you won't kill me here and now if I were to divulge all my secrets."

He cracked an eye to stare at her. "Is there anything else you need?"

The eye shut again. Eza clenched the cloth in a fist. For someone asking questions, the male didn't appear interested in hearing the answers. She should leave him here with his lumpy head and deal with his companion. But no. It wouldn't do if he collapsed from a concussion later.

"I'm here to heal your wounds." She squatted, leaning forward to touch the swollen, red flesh.

His eyes snapped open, wide, and frantic. He twisted his body out of reach and pressed into the wall like a cornered animal.

"Don't touch me!"

The terror in the command startled Eza in its ferocity. She gasped and snatched her hand away. He blinked, her reaction snapping him out of his hysteria.

The haunted look in his eyes vanished, and he offered an apologetic smile. "Forgive me." He cleared his throat. "Thank you for your concern, but I need no tending."

Eza crouched, cloth in hand, breathless with her heart thundering within her breast. She never witnessed such raw fear in a person. Something genuinely horrible must have happened to him. She stared at Drakon for a long time until he began to fidget and look everywhere but at her. It was clear he wanted her to leave.

She straightened and rifled in her satchel for a bit of meat. At the least, she could offer him food. "If you're sure you don't need assistance, I'll be on my way. Here's some—"

A wail sliced off Eza's next words. The tiny hairs on the nape of her neck and along her arms stood alert. She glanced toward the sound. In the darkness beyond the reach of the camp's light, amber eyes blinked into existence. Answering shrieks and grunts accompanied the first in a frenzied cacophony.

Drakon was on his feet and towering over her before she registered his movement. His eyes darted to the enormous pale forms emerging from the inky shadows.

Then his blazing gaze landed on her.

"Cut me loose. You're going to need every able-bodied fighter if you wish to live."

The Lim stared at Drakon; indecision reflected in her dark gaze.

He began to demand she release him when her glare locked on something over his shoulder. Her eyes widened, and her breath hitched.

Instinctively, Drakon dropped into a roll and sprang to his feet. He spun in time to see a wailer plow through the space he had occupied. With a mid-air twist, the beast redirected itself and lunged for him again. The impact was like being crushed by a boulder. He crashed to the ground. Pain bloomed in his back and up his legs as the creature's weight settled on him.

He kicked out, using their combined momentum to

pitch it away. The beast sailed overhead and landed in the lake with a geyser of displaced water. It thrashed wildly before disappearing beneath the rippling surface.

A grip seized Drakon's shoulder. Too late, he realized his preoccupation with the drowning creature. A force yanked him across the uneven ground and lifted him. The wailer turned him in its grasp and roared. Ropes of saliva and foul breath peppered his face.

Then a staff crashed down on the creature's forearm, breaking bones, and its hold on him. The wailer dropped Drakon with an ear-piercing shriek. Another strike cracked against the base of its misshapen head. The beast stumbled to the ground. Eza pounced on its back and drove Drakon's dagger into an amber eye. The creature jerked and bucked, screaming and trying to dislodge her. She held onto the skin of its scruff with one hand, thighs clenched at its sides like she was taming a stallion.

Eza yanked the blade free and plunged the steel into the wailer's other eye.

The creature crashed to the ground, motionless. She hopped from the fallen monstrosity, picked up her discarded staff, and dashed toward Drakon.

"Turn around."

He did as instructed and offered up his bound wrists. With a tug, they fell away. Eza shoved the gore-covered dagger into his hand.

"Go cut your friend loose!"

He raced to Umgar's side without hesitation. At his approach, Umgar turned and offered his bindings.

"What are the odds of these wailers being here is a coincidence?" Umgar said as Drakon sliced through the rope.

"Not very likely."

"Figured as much."

Drakon craned his head, looking for—*Ah, there they were.* His and Umgar's swords lay, not five feet away, atop an unrolled sleeping mat. He hurried to the blades. Sheathing his dagger at his waist, he scooped up his sword and tossed Umgar's weapon to him.

The Lim warriors fell into a defensive circle with Drakon, Umgar, and Eza at the nucleus. Drakon sidled to Eza, his gaze never leaving the pale outlines closing in around them.

"If your people can buy me some time, I can create a blood ward to protect us."

"You can?"

The question hadn't come from Eza but from Umgar. The spymaster's eyebrows were arched toward his hairline as he glared at Drakon.

"It's not often I'm taken by surprise. What other talents have you been hiding?"

"This isn't the time."

Drakon turned from Umgar's answering frown. There was plenty he concealed from his former guardian, and there might never be a convenient occasion to confess them. At his side, Eza's focus hadn't shifted from the threat. She palmed the crystal pendant she wore in a tight grip for a moment and then spoke.

"Our help comes from a much more reliable source. We need no such aid from you." Her gazed darted to him and back to the stalking wailers. "If you stick close to me, however, I'll ensure your safety."

He would have laughed at the ridiculous statement had

a creature not taken that moment to charge their defenses. It leaped into the air to land talons first onto the chest of a Lim. The woman was knocked back into the circle. Before the flanking warriors could close the gap, a surge of wailers rushed the opening.

The defensive line collapsed under the battering tide of bodies like a bursting dam over sand. Soldiers disappeared under a wave of claws and teeth. Drakon braced to meet a galloping wailer. However, Eza stepped into view. She swept the creature's legs with a whirl of her staff. The beast flipped its tail overhead, kicking up a spray of gravel as it slid forward face-first. Drakon leaped aside to avoid the fleshy projectile and brought down his sword on its neck.

He pulled his blade free and glanced over to offer Eza a nod of thanks. A nearing grunt sounded at his rear. Drakon dropped to his knee and thrust his blade back. A body slammed into him. The weight nearly buckled his knees. The skewered wailer raked a taloned hand down his back, tearing the flesh into ribbons. Warmth spilled down Drakon's back and leathers. He shoved his sword deeper. The creature let out a gurgle and stilled, draped atop him like a grotesque blanket.

He heaved and dislodged the wailer. The body landed on its side, gore oozing from a wound in its gut. Drakon reached to touch his back. His hand came away coated in blood. His mind raced. The creatures had never attacked him. Fear of his blood always deterred them. Now, its scent did little to staunch the flow of their attacks. He didn't understand what changed, but it was clear his protection was gone.

A shadow eclipsed Drakon. He swung his sword toward

the new threat, but Eza batted his strike away. He glanced at her in confusion. She pointed.

"It's Meko."

The animal dropped from its perch. The ground quaked under its gigantic feet. Undeterred, three wailers raced forward in ambush. Meko whipped her tree-sized tail. It connected with the smaller beasts and pitched them into the darkness.

Meko whirled about with a speed Drakon would have thought impossible for its size and chomped down on the head of another creature, shaking it back and forth like a dog with a bone.

"Goddess, am I glad that thing is on our side," Umgar said as Meko dropped the mangled wailer and stomped down a crowd of the monsters.

Drakon had to agree. The onslaught was dying down, and the change could be attributed to Eza's companion. He allowed himself to hope. They would drive them back and win this battle.

Then he saw it—the largest wailer he had ever seen. Unlike its bald brethren, long dirty blond hair flowed from the beast's flat, wrinkled head.

It had hair. Recollection danced elusively on the outskirts of Drakon's mind but refused to come to the forefront. The gargantuan creature crouched at the rear of the action, unblinking and watching them.

No. That wasn't entirely accurate. Its amber eyes tracked Drakon.

Their eyes met over the melee. For an incomprehensible instant, the combat between the Lim and wailers faded, and there was only Drakon and the peculiar observer. Its fanged mouth hinged open, and it snarled a name.

"Deathmark."

It turned and fled.

A sudden cold plunged into Drakon's core. In all his encounters with the creatures, he had never known them to speak. Eliciting further confusion, was its recognition of him. He had to stop it from escaping and learn why it sought him out.

He took off in pursuit.

Eza called after him, but he didn't stop or slow. If he lost sight of the creature, he feared his chance for answers would be forfeited. The beast could talk, which meant Drakon could interrogate it to discover why the wailers were here and who sent them.

He slowed his breakneck speed to a jog. Away from the Lim's light source, the oily blackness of the strange underworld seemed a living entity. It swallowed the fleeing creature, and soon visibility eroded.

When he could see no farther than his sword tip, his error became apparent. The cunning fiend hadn't been running away. It was luring him from the group, and like a fool, he rushed straight into its trap. This new wailer was as intelligent as it was unusual. Drakon paused, listening, hoping his lack of sight would elevate his other senses.

A grunt and a shuffle sounded from somewhere in the dark. Drakon swiveled his body and blade toward the noise and waited for a repeat. And waited. It was as if the creature held its breath, aware Drakon listened for it.

"There you are! Why did you bolt like that? I wouldn't have pegged you for a coward, Gathi."

Drakon whirled at the sound of the voice. Orb light

bobbed over Eza. She stalked to him, clenching her staff and with fangs bared. He began to answer when movement from above caught his eye. The enormous, blond-haired wailer darted along the wall angling for them.

Eza turned, following his gaze.

Too late.

It launched at her. Both went down in a tangle of limbs. They came to a stop with the wailer on top. It snapped at Eza's face, but she shoved her staff between its gnashing jaws. It raised a claw to rake her unguarded stomach.

Drakon hurled his power out at the wailer's center mass. The crackling energy rushed from him like a shimmering wave, lifting the creature and sling-shotting it into a stalagmite.

Rocks exploded outward in a spray of granite. The weakened stalagmite let out a prolonged groan, trembled, and tilted. It remained precariously angled for a long moment before falling like a toppled tree, raking down a path of stalactites as it went.

Massive chunks rained from above. Eza scrambled to her feet and darted past Drakon.

"This way!" she said, wrapping arms over her head as if the feeble gesture would save her from the man-sized slabs exploding around them.

Her slender form slipped through an opening in the cave wall, and Drakon dove inside after her. A deafening roar reverberated behind them as the deadly shower continued. Dust shot into the tunnel, clouding the space with a choking cloud of debris.

Drakon scrambled farther up the passage behind Eza, fearing a collapse. Although after a few minutes, the sound trickled to silence.

From somewhere ahead, Eza coughed. Drakon sat up, tucked his nose in the crook of his arm, and waved a hand in a useless attempt to clear the air. He glanced behind them. Rock pressed into the opening, sealing them in.

"You have magic?"

Eza's awe-tinged voice floated to him through the grime. A light orb appeared, illuminating the shaft. Her wide eyes peered out of a face white with grit.

Who are you, really?"

Drakon started to explain that he was just a man. That he didn't understand his abilities any better than she, but the adrenaline, which propelled him during their flight to safety, chose that moment to dry up. Fatigue crashed over him like a tsunami and dragged him under its undertow.

He had time to register someone calling his name before unconsciousness overtook him.

CHAPTER 13

They were separated from the main group.

Hours had passed, or had it been days? Drakon couldn't be confident of time in this place of perpetual night.

Inky darkness stretched out around them in all directions. The faint radiance from Eza's orb light barely kept the encroaching shadows at bay.

The orb bobbed above and out front as they trekked through the honeycombed labyrinth Eza called the Darklands. Their forms and the surrounding environment were cast in a sapphire wash from the overhead orb. The tunnel ceiling was low, no more than ten feet high, and the walls glistened with dampness. It gave him the unsettling impression of walking through the innards of an immeasurable beast.

Drakon shuddered from the thought and the cool air, which decreased in temperature the farther they traveled. Goosebumps lifted the skin beneath his tunic, and the gouges striping his back were burning pains, draining his energy. Their meager rations of meat and bread had been exhausted long ago. There would be no surge of caloric strength to bolster him unless they killed and ate something soon.

Ahead, Eza led the way. She hadn't spoken much since his second refusal of her healing. Although his injuries pained him, they weren't as life-threatening as his growing hunger.

Eza went rigid. Her hand rose in the universal sign for "wait." Drakon stopped and watched as she cocked her head to the side, listening. He did the same but couldn't parse any sound from the silence.

She beckoned him forward. He crept to her side, followed the direction of her pointed finger, and squinted into the darkness. A tunnel, about the height of his chest and as wide as two men, opened into their shaft.

Eza leaned into him. The scent of earth and cinnamon accompanied the closeness. "It's a burvine burrow. They're venomous and lay in wait for an animal to pass, spring out and grab their prey, and then drag it back inside to eat. It's probably already scented us. The passage is too tight for us to maneuver when it attacks, and backtracking would add another cycle to our journey." She nodded as if convincing herself of her decision.

"We'll have to kill it. We can use its den for shelter while we rest. I'll go first. It'll strike once I'm in front of the opening. Kill it quickly when it reveals itself."

He nodded, slid his sword from its sheath, and edged alongside the burrow. Eza inched out along the opposite wall, placing her weapon between herself and the yawning hole. As she crossed before the burvine's lair, a large body shot out like a spring.

Eza planted her staff and vaulted above the creature's snapping jaws. Drakon brought his blade down on the exposed flesh. The steel cleaved the burvine like an executioner's ax. The clang of his sword on the cave floor was impossibly loud and echoed down the passage in either direction. The burvine's severed head separated in a spray of sour-smelling gore. Its mandibles clicked in spasmodic snaps and then stilled.

"Ugh."

Drakon shook blood as thick as coagulated honey from his boot. The dead burvine's body was translucent and re-sembled a giant grub. The organs that hadn't sloshed out on the ground were discernible through its parchment-thin skin.

Eza hurried to Drakon's side and used her staff to pry the rest of the burvine from its burrow. The body oozed out in a wave of moist flesh to join its other half.

"Get inside. The noise we made will no doubt draw more creatures our way, and this is the best shelter we have."

Drakon raised an eyebrow and glanced into the shaft. White mucus lubricated the interior and dripped from the ceiling in long ropes. A sickly-sweet funk wafted from within. He grimaced. Perhaps he would take his chances outside.

While he vacillated on whether being mauled to death was preferable to suffocating in an oversized worm's body juices, Eza made a sound of annoyance and disappeared in-side. He watched as the light vanished with her. Well, he couldn't stand out here in the dark. He sighed, returned his sword, and climbed in behind her.

The orb-lit the confines, and Drakon moved farther into the animal's den. Eza squeezed past and dragged the burvine's back end into the opening, sealing them inside.

"There." She stepped back, admiring her impromptu blockade and panting. "If anything comes to investigate, the stench will drive them away."

"Yet here we are...basking in it," Drakon said.

He was already getting a bit lightheaded from the stench. Although his less than stellar health could have resulted from blood loss, lack of food, or a combination of the two. He was running on the dregs of his energy, but he faced the rear of the hollow, needing to check their shelter for danger before he could truly relax.

"I'll make sure we're alone in here."

He didn't wait for a response before moving down the tunnel until it opened into a circular chamber where the ceiling was high enough for him to stand upright. The cramped nook sported a higher roof but was still a tight fit for two people. His head swimming, Drakon dropped to the damp floor. The burvine's greasy excretion squashed between his splayed fingers, but he forced himself to ignore the disgusting sensation.

He lowered his head to his chest and closed his eyes. If he breathed slow and steady, the smell was tolerable, but his sense of unbalance worsened with every passing moment. He struggled to lift his heavy lids. They wouldn't respond. The feeling of spinning increased, causing him to clutch his knees in fear he would topple and reminding him of his trips through veils.

Unease gripped him. This was precisely the disorientation he experienced when crossing through a portal. *But that was impossible.*

Drakon tried again to open his eyes. This time they obeyed, and to his astonishment, the stinking burrow didn't come into focus around him.

The sun shone in a crystal blue, cloudless sky, warming

his skin. Drakon blinked gritty eyes. He sat, expecting the aches and pains of his recent ordeal. Yet, no pain assaulted him. No scrapes, blood, or dust from the cave-in covered him. *Where was he, and how had he gotten here?*

A breeze drifted over him, bringing with it the overwhelming stench of rotting meat.

A shriveled gray hand lying next to his outstretched leg snagged his attention. His gaze followed the appendage to a mutilated corpse, swarming with flies that hopped over their gruesome meal. Laying atop the legs of the first carcass was another mangled body.

Drakon scrambled to his feet. He was on a hill. In the valley below, thousands of bodies lay strewn like discarded garments in a field, roasting under the midday sun.

His hand dropped to his hip to grope for his sword. The scabbard was empty. Drakon glanced down at himself and patted around for his dagger. It too was missing.

"I must say, I had doubts this would work."

Drakon looked up. Ewen stepped from a shimmering slit, which hovered a foot off the ground. As the king's slipper-covered feet touched down, the tear in the fabric of space knitted itself into a clear sky.

Ewen's scarlet robes billowed in the putrid breeze as he picked his way through the maze of dead.

"You see, with me not being at full strength and you being beyond the Glens, I worried I might not be able to draw you to me. I'm pleased I was wrong."

The king stopped within arm's reach. It was then Drakon glimpsed his eyes.

They were cold obsidian.

Recognition struck him like a jab to the solar plexus. He

took an instinctive step back, shaking his head.

"Impossible!"

He had seen the same malevolent, inhuman glare when he stared into the eyes of the possessed High Priestess. He understood then, as he did now, that some entity piloted the woman and now masqueraded in Ewen's body.

A slow grin crept across the impostor's lips, and a protrusion rippled beneath its skin, traveling from temple to collarbone and vanishing beneath the robing. The movement reminded Drakon of someone repositioning a too-snug tunic.

"You're what was released from the priestess. You placed the bounty on my head, not Ewen." Drakon's eyes widened as another realization dawned.

"The wailers. You're why they attack me, but why? You don't seem to have suffered since our last encounter. You've even managed to possess the most powerful Gathi in the Kingdom. What threat could I be to you?"

The poser cocked its head like a curious dog. Unblinking eyes bore into him.

"That is where you are wrong, Nahum. I've suffered for longer than you can fathom, but now my suffering is nearing its conclusion. Your existence will bring about my freedom or destruction, and I will not allow the latter. You are a child of light and dark. Inside you, simmers the power I require to liberate myself from the Glens and exact my revenge on my jailer. As your goddess, your sacrifice of your body and power is not only required but expected."

Drakon's mouth went slack as the entity's identity became clear. *It couldn't be.*

"Melika?"

The answering smile didn't reach the black eyes. "I'm much diminished in my current state, but yes. It is I." Ewen's face twisted into a pout. "Don't look so disappointed."

"But the goddess is good. Pure."

The denial sounded foolish even to Drakon's own ears. *How good could Melika be if she allowed the enslavement of the commoners and commanded monsters?*

Ewen laughed. "I assure you, I'm many things, but good and pure aren't attributes I can claim."

An incredulous laugh slipped from Drakon. "For eons, nobles have forced their religion on us, making us feel inferior, and all the while they've been worshipping a—"

He waved a hand in the direction of the creature wearing the king like a cloak.

"A demonic body snatcher?"

Melika's rebuke was swift and violent. The magical blow sent Drakon through the air, and the ground rose up to greet him. With a groan, he rolled to his side. Pain radiated from everywhere.

Then something clamped on his ankle. He looked down. A reanimated corpse pawed its way up his legs. Its purplish-black, swollen tongue dangled from an unhinged mouth, gray-filmed eyes stared lifelessly.

Drakon yanked back his leg and kicked it in the face, dislodging the creature. He tried to rise, but more hands fastened to his limbs, pinning him. Melika moved to stand above him.

"In this realm, between sleep and waking, I am all-powerful. There is nowhere you can run I won't be able to find you. There is no need to hunt you. I know where you are always, and if I possess your mind here, your body will follow."

Melika reached for him. Drakon strained against his restraints. He couldn't—wouldn't allow this monster to control and use him as a skeleton key to its freedom.

He bucked and twisted. The buzz of adrenaline hummed in his ears as he struggled. It grew into a rumbling roar until his body quaked from it.

Melika paused, hand outstretched, a look of bewilderment on Ewen's features.

At once, Ewen's form began to glow. Melika lifted her hands, turning them this way and that. A look of utter frustration and rage crossed her face a moment before light exploded from her, shattering her into glittering fragments.

Drakon squeezed his eyes shut against the detonation. Heat rushed over him, and the hands gripping him fell away. After a heartbeat, he cracked open his eyes.

A crystal pendant dangled over him. He blinked, and Eza came into view. She leaned over him, chanting, light radiating from her hands. Hands that cupped his face. As if feeling his scrutiny, she stopped, and the glow in her palms dimmed.

He took in the sensation of her warm, calloused hands on him and braced for the familiar emotions of disgust and terror to flood him. When they didn't surface, the tension bound in his muscles loosened. Then he realized he was lying on his back, gazing up at her like a halfwit. He brushed her hands away, sat up, and avoided her questioning stare.

He sucked in a deep breath of the burvine odor, and it was a comfort compared to his recent encounter with Melika.

"I don't know what you did, but you saved my life. Thank you."

"You went into a trance. I felt evil flowing around you, so I prayed for Apalsi to protect you. Where did you go?"

He had no idea, but he told her everything that happened. When he finished, her eyes were wide. A hand covered her mouth.

"Do you understand any of it?" he said.

She nodded. "The Lim have a prophecy of a male born of dark and light who will save my people and lead us back to the surface."

She stretched a trembling hand toward him and paused, unsure. Drakon went motionless, his breath tight in his chest. When he didn't flinch away, Eza cupped his face once more. Her eyes twinkled with something akin to reverence.

"Our savior is also called Nahum."

CHAPTER 14

Long shadows reached out from the surrounding forest like spectral fingers, ticking down the hours left before the sun dipped below the horizon. With nightfall came danger, and the responsibility for the encampment's defenses rested on Crain's weary shoulders.

He scrubbed a hand down his sweat-sodden face and leaned against a horse's stable. Mercifully, the heat was bearable here at the base of the mountains, but it was still abnormally warm. They had needed to rest and water the horses more often, which added two days to their initial seven-day journey.

Not that the temperature had been their only complication. Two skirmishes with Waystation mages and nightly run-ins with wailers had thinned their number. Although Fynna kept her word to convey Crain's instructions for reinforcements in the cities and Waystations to join him here, only a fraction of the force he expected had arrived in the past two days.

More disturbing, many of those men and women came with tales of onyx-eyed, fanged nobles roaming the forests and attacking any who crossed their paths. Like he needed more problems?

Crain sighed. He couldn't wait much longer for the stragglers. They would pack in the morning and trek up the mountain pass in search of the Wild Gathi. Umgar had given him the daunting task of persuading the ousted clan to join their fight against the king.

His mind drifted to his last interaction with the general. Umgar had pulled him aside before leaving for Glensbrook and entrusted him with a secret, which still stunned Crain when he thought about it. The mission's success was uncertain, but he would relay the information Umgar imparted to him. He prayed it would be the deciding factor of whether the Wild Gathi supported the rebellion.

He prayed enough of them still lived to make a difference in the coming conflict. They would need every man and woman in the battles ahead.

Around him, soldiers raced against the slave driver that was time, piling kindling into the deep trench encircling the camp and dousing it with oil. Fire was the only element the wailers feared. They learned that lesson the first night of their excursion when the beasts overran their wards without resistance. Apparently, following their insurrection, the mages had negated the power in their charms and wards. With no access to magic, Crain and his fighters were forced to employ primitive means of protection.

He ground his teeth at the memory. A quarter of the Sura regiment was dead before enough torches had been lit to drive the creatures away.

A whinny drew him from his dark thoughts and reminded him of his own task. He patted the flank of the horse that had stirred him from his reverie, and the chocolate gelding bumped its muzzle into his hand. After another pat, Crain retrieved a cotton hood from a sack and slipped it over the animal's head. He repeated the process with each mount. Blinding the horses would keep them calm when the wailers came. The last thing he needed was half the animals spooking and running to their deaths.

"Captain."

Crain turned to see Joah jogging toward him. The lieutenant's mouth was a tight line, and his eyebrows were drawn together in worry.

"A rider is approaching. Looks like one of ours from what the scouts can tell, but he's traveling alone."

"Alone? Which direction is he coming from?"

"The southwest."

Crain frowned. That was the direction of Sura. *Who would be arriving from the capital?* He left the stable and followed Joah to the perimeter, drawing curious stares as he passed. News of the traveler must have spread.

As Crain and Joah drew near, the rider dismounted and met them. He recognized the man immediately. Haran was one of Umgar's sleeper agents who worked in the palace kitchens. He hadn't seen or spoken to the man in at least a year. Their only contact had been letters hidden in designated drops around the city. If Haran was here, it meant whatever news he brought was worth shattering his cover. The situation in Sura must be dire indeed.

"Haran."

He clasped the man's forearm and clapped him on the back. Haran's hand trembled in his grasp. Sweat drenched the young man's face. His clothing was rumpled, and his lank hair stuck to his sweaty face. Dark rings hung like drapes beneath his eyes.

"Captain, I have urgent news from Sura. I request to speak with you," Haran's darting gaze flicked to Joah, whose frown deepened, "and the lieutenant as soon as possible."

Crain waved him forward. "You can brief us in my tent. You look like you could use a drink."

The three men hurried through the camp to Crain's quarters. Joah held open the tent flap, allowing Crain and Haran to duck inside and then followed.

"Sit," Crain said, sliding a stool toward Haran.

The man collapsed into the offered seat, his legs seeming to give out beneath him. Joah leaned against a post while Crain retrieved a jug of mead, poured a considerable amount into a cup, and handed it to Haran. He eased down in his own chair in front of the fighter, waiting with folded arms, as the young man guzzled down the liquid.

"Thank you, Captain," Haran said and clutched the cup in a tight grip.

Crain inclined his head. "Now. What's happening in Sura? It must be important if you thought you had no other choice but to leave your post and come here."

"After the Royal Fighters left the city, the king... He..."

Haran paused, and his Adam's Apple bobbed. "He's begun sacrificing commoners and nobles to the goddess. He says their sacrifice will help defeat the Nahum and free us from the Glens. He's already gone through most of the servants in the palace. I...I fled before it was too late."

Haran stopped once again. Tears formed in his dark eyes, and he dropped his gaze from Crain's stare, clearly ashamed of his actions.

"No one's judging you. You did what anyone would've done in your position. Now, I understand why Ewen would harness magic from nobles, but what did he seek to gain by sacrificing commoners? We've no power to exploit. It doesn't make sense."

Haran shrugged, at a loss. "I can find no reasoning behind it."

"Where are Fynna and Nolan? As the most powerful mages, I would think they'd be first on the list," Joah said.

"They've gone into hiding. Fynna met with me only once to say she and Nolan were amassing a group of mages to challenge the king. With everything happening, I don't know if there'll be many mages left." Haran twisted the cup in trembling hands and took a shuttering breath. "The wards no longer function for those who flee the city. I burned a high fire at night. The wailers came with nightfall, but none ventured near the blaze. I slept during the day and for only three or four hours. I've never been so afraid in my life."

With this confession, the strength holding the man together seeped away, and he sobbed. Crain placed a comforting hand on Haran's quivering shoulder.

"Fear is nothing to be ashamed of. Only a fool wouldn't have been afraid, but you didn't give in to your fright, and you've given us much-needed information. Many seasoned fighters wouldn't have been able to do what you did. You have shown more courage than most. Take pride in that."

Haran stared up at Crain, his face wet with tears, but his eyes glittered with determination. At that moment, Crain glimpsed a warrior in the making.

He allowed himself a smile. "That's it. Now, let's get you fed and find you a new job."

A loud murmur rose from outside. Crain shared a glance with Joah. "Stay here," he said to Haran.

He drew his sword and led his second from the tent. A few steps from the entrance, he froze. Figures emerged from the forest. Their skin was coated in brown and green pigment, which camouflaged them with the surrounding flora. Dark cloth, much like tree bark, covered their lean bodies.

Crain turned in a slow circle. Hundreds of men and women surrounded the encampment, their spears glinting in the evening light.

He wouldn't have to seek out the Wild Gathi after all. They had come to him.

༄༅

"It's only a matter of time before she comes for you again. Don't think I didn't realize that wailer lured you away during the attack. If it wanted to kill you outright, it wouldn't have needed to get you alone first."

In the compact burrow, Eza's large eyes reflected the orb light like a feline's as she stared at Drakon, her fingers twisting the crystal pendant at her throat, which was something he noticed she did when anxious. He agreed with her reasoning, and his empty stomach rolled with dread at the accuracy of her observations.

"We must get you to Napata as soon as possible. As the Nahum, my father will ensure your safety until we figure out what to do next."

"I'm not this Nahum or whoever the—"

He stopped himself before saying *goddess*. In no realm was the entity he faced godly. "I'm not who Melika or you think I am. I'm not born of light and dark unless you're taking into account the color of my parents' skin."

Eza's brow wrinkled. "I don't understand."

"In my homeland, Gathi nobles receive magic from Melika. The stronger their capabilities in sorcery, the paler their skin, hair, and eyes become. The most powerful nobles can become mages with utterly pallid appearances. It's a sign of great honor and prestige for noble families to pale. In contrast, commoners have no magical abilities, and our coloring remains nearly as pigmented as your own.

"My father was likely a mage and my mother a slave. I can't be sure because she died in childbirth, and the mage's identity was concealed from everyone. Although I've long suspected he was an influential man because he wasn't publicly punished for such an egregious crime. The man who came here with me, Umgar, rescued me from a life of slavery, trained me, and convinced the king I would make a worthwhile—"

He paused, not wanting to divulge to her his profession. The uncustomary hesitancy perplexed him. He had no reason to be ashamed of what he did. He never killed the innocent, but for reasons he couldn't explain, he didn't want her to be disappointed in him.

After a moment, he said, "Umgar convinced him I would be a competent servant."

"Umgar must be very special to you. I promise Dagoti won't contradict my orders. He'll take your friend to the tribe."

"He won't search for you?"

She frowned and stared at the dripping roof in thought. "I don't think he would, at least not yet. We were about a cycle and a half from Napata before our separation. Dagoti would return to apprise my father of the threats to our people and then come back to hunt for us. Although he wouldn't admit it, he knows I'm well-equipped to navigate back to the main passage leading to the city."

Drakon hoped she was right. If Melika was indeed deploying wailers to capture him, he wanted more than one woman, no matter how adept, at his side.

She refocused her intense gaze on him. "You say you're not the Nahum. Yet, you openly acknowledge commoners don't possess magic. You are a commoner, yes?"

The abrupt change in subject was difficult to follow, but he said, "I am."

"Then why do you have these special abilities?"

He shifted uncomfortably on the slippery floor. "I can't explain it. I assume it has something to do with my paternal lineage."

Eza chewed on the inside of her cheek, puzzling over his words. "Well—our lore says before the Great War, many Lim were deceived into serving a demon. This demon and your goddess are the same. During that time, all Lim had natural gifts, which Apalsi gave us at birth. Melika perverted our abilities with her essence and created the Gathi, specifically what you call nobles. If your parentage contains one-half noble blood, that innate corruption would account for one part of the prophecy—the dark. Your commoner, untainted blood, could explain the reference to the light."

Drakon wanted to deny her logic, to say no darkness resided within him, but he had always felt...tainted. If he was honest with himself, it was the impetus for his distrust of nobles and their religion. He saw his own potential for wickedness reflected in them.

Strange though Eza was, with her ebony skin, overlarge black eyes, and fangs, he discerned no evil or malice in her. She had no motive to lie about what she believed to be accurate. Perhaps Lim recollections of past events were indeed fact, and Melika had fabricated Gathi accounts. The more he thought about it, the more likely it seemed. What better way to keep a race of people subjugated than to re-write history to your specifications?

Melika believed he was the Nahum and pursued him as such. If he wanted to survive, he needed to hear the Lim version of the past.

"Tell me everything you know about the Gathi and Lim war," he said.

She shrugged. "I'm not a historian. I spent more time training than committing history to memory, but there are some facts all Lim were taught. One is that Melika was Apalsi's first creation. She was once his pride above others, but then Apalsi created the Lim. He fashioned a beautiful oasis for us to live in and bestowed on us many gifts. For example, I can heal with my hands. But there were Lim who could create flames, control earth or water."

Drakon's eyes widened. "There are Lim who can control fire?"

A pained expression crossed her face. "Not anymore. Over the millennia, our talents waned, and eventually, we lost them. I'm the last healer, and I fear my gift will die with me. But we're not talking about the Lim's bygone powers. I'm supposed to be telling you of the war."

Sensing her reluctance to continue on the sensitive topic, he nodded, and she returned to her tale.

"Melika grew jealous of Apalsi's affection for the Lim.

She wanted to taint our innocence, and she enticed many Lim with the promise of strength and riches. They accepted the magic she offered and began warring with the other Lim for control of the paradise. The name Gathi originates from the Lim word for lost. Many years of war passed before Apalsi intervened. He banished the Gathi beneath the barrier and Melika and her children to the Dark Realm. However, before Melika was exiled, she cursed our land. The rivers dried up, and every crop we planted rotted in the poisoned earth. Apalsi, too weakened by the battle, couldn't reverse the blight and hasn't been seen since. My people were forced to seek sanctuary from the punishing climate underground."

This was not the narrative he was taught. *How could everything he trusted with certainty be so flawed?* He leaned his head against the chamber wall, suddenly exhausted.

"I upset you. We should talk no more on the subject. Sleep. We'll resume our travel as soon as we're rested."

Slumber would be unlikely, not with Melika raiding his subconscious and attempting to possess him. "I don't believe sleeping would be wise for me. Letting my guard down in such a way might make me susceptible to another attack."

Eza's mouth formed an "O," and she shook her head. "Of course, I didn't think."

She scooted closer and reached for him. Drakon caught her wrists. When she touched him before, he had been in a trance and fighting an internal battle for his life. He was conscious now, and although her touch didn't elicit a fit of panic, he wasn't accustomed to another person freely touching him.

Her gaze flicked to his fingers wrapped around her wrists and back to his face.

"I can ensure your mind is protected. If you let me help you, you won't have to worry about the demon entering your subconscious again. Not sleeping isn't an option for either of us. Let me help you, please."

Drakon's gaze fixed on her eyes. The pitch-black irises were large, barely allowing space for the whites of her eyes. The odd feature should have made her appear fiendish, but her eyes held only sincerity. Trusting didn't come easily for him, yet this stranger wanted him to place his life in her hands?

For Eza's part, she waited, allowing him time to deliberate. Exhaustion weighed him down like stones tied around his feet. He hadn't had proper rest or food in days, and the deficiency was beginning to affect his concentration, making him a liability.

Decided, he released her wrists and jerked his head in a sharp nod. As if realizing how tentative his acceptance was, Eza placed her palms against his chest and closed her eyes. He tensed, awaiting the familiar manic dread to arise and consume his rational mind.

Nothing happened.

Actually, he did feel something. A comfortable warmth mushroomed from Eza's touch and spread throughout his body. The pain he endured from the wounds in his back eased and disappeared. Tension released from his muscles.

"What are you doing to me?"

She peeked up at him but didn't lift her hands. "I'm healing your injuries and infusing you with peace." She returned to her ministrations. "It'll shield your mind against

Melika and allow you to rest."

She leaned closer, her breath warm on his throat. He tensed despite the tranquility permeating through him, turned his face away, and closed his eyes, listening to their combined breathing.

"Slow your racing thoughts and let the peace wash over you. Your body is rejuvenated, and your mind is sheltered. Sleep." Eza's voice was soft and hypnotic.

A sense of comfort coursed through him, blotting out all other stimuli, and for the first time in his life, Drakon slept deeply.

CHAPTER 15

A guttural roar tore itself free from Melika's throat.

She swept an arm out toward the nearest object. The table flew across the chamber and exploded against a wall, sending a cascade of splinters in every direction. She paced the king's bedchamber, her feet eating the distance between the immense four-poster bed and the hanging veil. She wanted to kill something, to see blood.

Through the window, night crept forth, but Melika didn't summon orbs to illuminate the room.

She welcomed the darkness. It complemented her mood.

Once again, the Nahum eluded her. What was worse, a Lim had ripped him from her grasp. The she-devil. She almost had him. Another swipe sent a water basin arching through the air as she passed. Porcelain shattered into white shards on the floor.

The female thought to humiliate her? Keep her trapped within the Glens? Never. The ebony-skinned meddler would regret her interference. Pain registered in Melika's palms, and she glanced down. Blood dripped from her clutched fists. She uncurled her hands, drew in a calming breath, and knit the self-inflicted wounds in her hands.

This was but a minor setback. It had cost her copious energy to project herself into the assassin's mind, which she needed to replenish before she could set her next ploy into motion. She stopped, lowered herself into one of the few chairs that had escaped her rampage, and raked a hand through Ewen's luscious white hair. The Nahum's escape through the barrier was an unforeseen and worrisome complication.

Unease at her dwindling options caused her breath to catch in her chest and tension to coil in her stomach. Her opportunity for true freedom was slipping through her grasp like water through cupped hands. Memories of her and her children's hellish existence in the Dark Realm bubbled to the surface of her mind. Her fingers dug into the arms of the chair as she fought the bonds of the haunting images.

If the Nahum realized his potential, he could destroy all her efforts. The thought of returning to the abyss…

She shuddered. *No.* Failure wasn't an option. She would overcome this obstacle and make Apalsi and his precious creations pay for his treachery and abandonment.

A sharp knock sounded at the door a moment before it was thrown wide. Queen Opel stormed inside in a surge of silk rose-colored robes, and the door banged shut in her wake. Melika's eyes narrowed, and she crossed her arms. The self-importance and audacity of this particular mortal were more than she could bear at the moment.

"How dare you come here without being summoned!"

Opel's pale eyes flicked over the destroyed chamber, but she stiffened her back and continued forward. "What have you done with Tobiah? I haven't seen him in days. The last time I spoke to him, he was going to see you. With all you've been doing—I—I know you've done something to him." She stopped almost on top of Melika, her cheeks flushed from more than the heat. She pointed an accusing finger in Melika's face.

"I don't have the patience for a quarrel nor to entertain your accusations," Melika said. She made a shooing gesture. "Leave me."

Opel's thin nostrils flared in indignation. "You dare speak to me this way? I am your queen and—"

In a blur of movement, Melika stood to tower over Opel. The woman's following words choked off in a gasp, and she scrambled back. Her foot caught on a fragment of furniture, and she nearly tumbled. Her gaze darted around, only then realizing the danger she was in. When her eyes returned to Melika, gone was the anger and bluster. Her face was pallid, and her quick, panting breaths aroused Melika's innate predator.

Opel licked her lips. "Where's my son?" Her tone went from demanding to pleading.

Melika smiled, and the woman flinched away. "The prince asked if he could help capture and return the Nahum. I allowed him to do so."

"I don't believe you. You've been different since the ordeal with the High Priestess. I want to see Tobiah." Opel pushed her shoulder's back and set her jaw. "I'm not leaving until you show him to me."

Melika glowered down at the woman. She had given this Gathi the power flowing through her veins, and the fool dared make demands of her? She would siphon every iota of her essence from the ungrateful twit and leave Opel as hapless as the commoners the noblewoman despised.

"You come to me unannounced and uninvited and

make ultimatums?"

Opel shrank back from the verbal assault, her confidence ebbing once more. The sweet scent of fear bloomed from the woman and slid down Melika's throat like honey. Her stomach knotted in hunger.

The queen was not as potent in magic as Nolan or Fynna, but neither was she a low-level noble. Her power could serve as much of a purpose in Melika's plan as her son's fledgling energy.

Melika gripped Opel's slim shoulders. The woman tensed under Melika's palms, but she remained rooted to the spot. Something within her still trusted the person she believed to be her husband, even after witnessing the atrocities Melika committed using Ewen's body. The warring emotions kept Opel in indecision long enough for Melika to begin the process.

Queen Opel stiffened, her eyes widening in fear and confusion. "What?"

She reached up to pry Melika's hands loose, but they were welded in place. The woman began chanting a defensive spell. Melika chuckled at the meager attempt. Her own power couldn't harm her. Even now, the queen's struggles grew sluggish. Her face and eyes shriveled and darkened to brown. Her white hair thinned and shed like dandelion tufts as her borrowed magic drained from her.

Memories and events sped past in the dying woman's mind, bleeding into Melika's psyche. Melika ignored them. Such was typical when she fully reclaimed her strength from a Gathi. The recollections were a nuisance but would end.

A cluster of images flashed through Opel's thoughts.

Melika gasped, her head jerking back as if slapped.

She rifled through the memories like the pages of a tome. She shook her head with each scene she unearthed. Opel released a soft groan of pain, and Melika realized her fingers clawed through the woman's fine robing and into her flesh. She didn't care. Ewen and his queen were keeping a devastating secret from her.

Melika lifted the withered Opel, bringing her to eye level. The queen squirmed in her tight hold.

"I should thank you for being an insecure busybody. Without your snooping, your husband's efforts to hide his transgression would've been wiped clean using the same magic I bestowed on him. However, I'm not in a thankful mood, seeing that you remained a silent accessory for decades, and Ewen's actions have caused me unnecessary difficulty."

Opel's watery eyes widened. "But how?"

Melika allowed her true form to show through the facade of Ewen's skin. Queen Opel's eyes bulged, but her drained body could do little more than tremble. With a violent motion, Melika pulled her hands apart. Opel's shriveled body ripped from shoulder to groin like a grotesque wishbone. Gore and innards spilled to the floor in a wet mound, and Melika dropped the halves atop the mess.

Bathed in blood, Melika basked in the power pulsing through her and replenishing her. She stepped over the mangled corpse, strode to the veil, laid a palm on the cool frame, and focused on her offspring. However, she didn't summon those roaming the Kingdom. She employed her newly siphoned strength to slice through the membrane between worlds and beckoned to her younglings imprisoned in the Dark Realm.

The portal's surface rippled, revealing a vast void that threatened to engulf the gateway itself. Within the blackness, a dozen shadows undulated. They peeled from the darkness and slithered across the threshold. The portal closed behind them. They curled about Melika's limbs and darted around the chamber, tasting and learning.

Melika couldn't contain a satisfied grin. These were her first creations, and like their pale brethren, she had created them without her essence. They housed their own unique essences, which meant they could transverse the damaged Glens.

She held out a hand. One of her children returned to coil around her arm in a cold embrace.

"Retrieve the Nahum and bring him to me alive. Kill anything standing in your way."

Command received, they glided across the floor to the window and disappeared into the night. Melika gazed out after them. They wouldn't fail her. The assassin was as good as captured.

Melika waved a hand down her bloody robes. The garments reverted to pristine condition. Now, to other business. She needed to find Nolan, Fynna, and their defector group of archmages.

The queen only whetted her appetite. She was still feeling a bit peckish.

☙❧

The veil shut with a whoosh of expelled air, ruffling Fynna's hair and billowing her robes around her. Instantly, the unpleasant stench of decay assaulted her with a well-placed blow to her nasal cavity. Her stomach rolled in protest. She turned her nose and mouth into the crook of her arm and swallowed, forcing back bile clawing its way up her throat.

Dark stains and scattered bits of small, pink clumps speckled the grass and the temple's wide staircase ahead. It didn't take much intellect to infer this was all that remained of the Temple of Melika priestesses.

Goddess. When Fynna agreed with Nolan's plan to hide from Ewen at the decimated sanctuary, she couldn't have imagined the level of carnage the wailers had left behind.

This magnitude of mass destruction was outside her expertise. She excelled in strategy and subterfuge, not open warfare. It was much too primitive and bloody. She had trained to be a mage at the Kingdom's school of sorcery, which meant she was to orchestrate these events, not tread among them.

Naturally, she realized the result of Nolan's dismantling the High Priestess's wards would be the massacre of all within the temple. It was a necessary consequence of war. There could be no witnesses to the assassination. She and Nolan went along with Ewen's scheme, not because of Ewen's ambitions but for their own. If the High Priestess had remained alive, she would've installed that weak fool, Tobiah, as king once Fynna had removed Ewen and the royal mage. Thus, the woman's death was inevitable.

Yet knowing something transpired and trudging through the aftermath were two different things. She preferred her involvement in slaughter to be remote. *Thank you very much.*

"Fynna."

She jerked her gaze from the dried bloodstains. Nolan and twelve archmages, all whose houses were lower in power and status than the royal mage's and Fynna's own families but who were formidable in their own right, stood at the top of the stairs waiting for her. Nolan's pale cheeks were mottled red with heat and likely a bit of annoyance. He must have called for her more than once before breaking through her musings.

"Don't linger. The sun has set, and the wailers will be about soon if they aren't already. We need to locate a defensible position inside and charm it against the creatures. After which, we can focus on the Ewen problem," said Nolan.

Fynna nodded and hurried after the group into the building. Nothing moved in the darkened interior. Moonlight cast scant light on the evidence of a fire that stretched across the marble floor, walls, and ceiling.

Fynna strained to detect any noise in the unnerving silence. The only sounds were the shuffle of their footsteps. A coppery odor mixed with rot saturated the air. Fynna switched to breathing through her mouth and tugged her robes over her nose. Nolan and Kinar, a wizened but potent mage, conjured light orbs. As the illumination drifted upward, it cast a soft yellow glow over a ghastly scene and the source of the smell.

Blood coated every conceivable surface. Small amounts of flesh littered the floor, mingled with piles of excrement. Fynna lifted a foot. Tacky gore stuck to the sole of her shoe and the hem of her robes. Disgusting.

"Let's move. We don't want to be caught in the open," Nolan said. He led their procession deeper into the building.

Fynna's trepidation increased with every step they

took. Bundles of cloth were scattered along the corridors. She glanced down at one of the heaps as she passed. An indentation the size of a large body lay in the center, resembling a nest. Her stomach tightened with dread. Something was wrong. She padded to where Nolan crept in front of their group. His pale eyes shifted down an empty corridor and then to her.

"What is it?"

"I think the wailers are still here."

He lifted a single white eyebrow. "What makes you say that?"

"I'm fairly certain we just passed a nest."

Nolan glanced behind them at the bundle of rags and shook his head. "It can't be a nest. There's nothing left for them to eat here. Why would they remain?"

That was the question of the night, Fynna thought. Nolan stopped at a bisection of two hallways and peered around the corner. She stole a glance behind them again. Outside their sphere of orb light, her eyes couldn't penetrate the darkness, but her skin prickled with a sense they weren't alone. Curse Nolan, she was right, and she was going to make him listen.

"Nolan. I think we should find another place to hide," she said to Nolan's back as he disappeared around the corner.

He didn't acknowledge he heard her, and Fynna rushed after him, intent on yanking his arm. She rounded the corner, ran face-first into his back, and would have fallen had she not crashed into the next mage in line. Fynna righted herself and opened her mouth to hiss a reproof. Then shut it. Nolan had stopped mid-stride and peered unblinkingly into the blackness just outside the light's reach.

"Did you hear that?" he asked.

Fynna frowned, glaring into the shadows, listening. The sound came again—a scraping. *And was that a grunt?* With a wave of his hand, Nolan sent his orb farther down the corridor. It bobbed along, peeling back the layers of darkness inch by inch until it revealed what lurked within the pitch.

The passage pulsated with the pale bodies of wailers. Their wild eyes blazed, and they charged forward, some galloping on all fours and others scuttling from wall to ceiling.

"Melika, keep us," someone muttered behind Fynna.

Nolan uttered a spell. The blue flames flared to life in his palms, and he sent a fireball into the closest creature. It lit up like an oil-soaked torch. Its shrieks echoed through the corridors as it rolled around on the ground. The demise of their brethren slowed the remaining beasts but didn't stop them.

Fynna leaped aside to avoid a swipe. Claws slashed through her robes. A protection spell fell from her lips, and a force field engulfed her. When the wailer lunged again, it collided with the enchantment. Its massive body jerked from a current of electricity. It rebounded, plowed through a wall, and vanished beneath a shower of crumbling stone. Fynna summoned a flame and hurled it toward a leaping wailer. The enchanted fire struck the creature in its horrid face, and the beast crashed to the ground, sizzling and smoking.

Mages cloaked in magical shields welded fire all around her. However, even as one beast fell, three more took its place. If they didn't put distance between themselves in the fiends, they would fall beneath the wave of teeth and talons breaking against them.

As if sent from the Goddess, Fynna heard Nolan's voice. "In here!"

Nolan held open a door. She flung herself inside, followed by Kinar and a line of mages. Nolan slammed and locked the door behind them. He fell forward as a body rammed the wooden barrier. Muffled screeches and grunts filled the outside corridor.

"See if you can find anything we can use to ward the entrance or another way out of this room," Nolan said to no one in particular as he regained his footing.

His pale hair was in disarray, and perspiration dripped down his face. He looked like Fynna felt. Spent. She turned from the royal mage and surveyed the chamber. It was some sort of storage room. A few piled chairs and a rickety wardrobe towered in a corner.

She glanced back at her companions. A group of men and women flinched every time the door rattled, and the rest milled about; their glances darted around as if expecting one of the beasts to emerge from a darkened alcove.

Although Fynna's limbs shook, and she was dizzy with fear, she refused to give in to the emotion. Her future held more. She had a king to overthrow, a Kingdom to rule, and wouldn't end up a pile of wailer scat on the temple floor.

She stumbled over to the discarded furniture, which leaned against a far wall, and flopped down on a chair. It groaned under her slight weight. She drew in steadying breaths. Today was the first time she used her magic in a physical application. It was exhausting. She needed a moment to catch her breath, and then she would join the search for a way out.

A glint caught her eye. Fynna craned around to peer behind the tower of furnishings. A doorknob reflected the orb light. She leaped to her feet with a lightness in her chest and breathless with anticipation. This could be an exit. She squeezed behind the wardrobe, scooted to the door, and pushed it open.

An empty hallway lay ahead. Fynna clasped her hands in prayer. "Thank you, Goddess."

She stepped through the door and turned to call the group. Without warning, a brilliance materialized at the center of the room. Radiance poked through the spaces between the furniture, sprinkling Fynna with pinpricks of light. When the rays diminished, she bent forward to squint through a crack.

She nearly gasped aloud but stopped the sound before it could give away her position. King Ewen stood among the shocked mages. His alabaster gaze flicked to the closed doorway. It continued to issue bangs from the wailer assault. His eyes narrowed as if peering through to the other side. His jaw clenched, and he whirled on Nolan with bared teeth.

Fynna retreated a step into the corridor, unconscious of the movement.

"You murdered my children!"

"Are you mad? You morn those—those abominations? I should've killed you long ago. You're unfit to be king," Nolan said. The mages with the royal mage moved to encircle Ewen.

"Abominations?" Ewen said. He cocked his head, glancing from person to person. "If you believe you can kill me, you aren't as smart as I believed, Nolan."

With those words, the king roared and fell forward. Fynna's hand flew to her mouth. The king's skull elongated. Twin rows of fangs jutted from an extended, gaping maw. His extremities stretched. Claws sprouted from his fingers. His back and shoulders cracked and widened.

Ewen's ripping robes seemed to release Nolan from his paralysis, and he took a step back. He swung a hand toward the beast, an incantation falling from his lips.

Nothing happened.

A raspy chuckle came from the monster's throat. "I gave you your power. You cannot use my essence against me, and what I give, I can take away."

Fynna's head shake mirrored Nolan's denial. *Lies.* There was no way this creature was Melika. Yet, as the nobles spouted more impotent spells, her conviction crumbled. Only one force was powerful enough to nullify their magic.

"I see, I'll have to show you all the truth," Melika said.

The beast waved a hand. A white mist began to seep from the exposed skin of the mages. Horror-struck faces watched as their tattoos faded and vanished. Around the room, pale-blue eyes grayed. Flesh shriveled, bodies collapsed in on themselves, and corpses clattered to the floor like withered timber.

Within the passage, the traces of the curse were a physical blow. Fynna staggered against the wall and lifted her hands to her eyes. Mist seeped from her like fog over a lake. The dark runes tattooed on her flesh faded but didn't disappear. She had to escape before she ended up like the rest of the mages.

A moan from the chamber drew Fynna's attention from

her own plight. *Someone still lived?* Among the dead mages, Nolan twitched. He lay curled on the floor, seemingly untouched. The beast grabbed Nolan and lifted him. The man hung listlessly like a slack rope; no strength left in him.

Melika brought Nolan close to her hideous face. For a moment, Fynna thought the monstrosity would remove Nolan's head with a snap of her massive jaws, but instead, she spoke.

"Your people were bred for the day of my return and the reclaiming of my power. By accepting my essence into yourselves, you all became willing participants in your own demise. Yet, you, dear Nolan, may still play a role apart from the siphoning."

A portal appeared before the pair. Nolan's scream pierced the silence as Melika carried him through the veil. Before Fynna could digest Melika's words, wailers poured from the opening into the chamber.

She had seen enough. Fynna fled with a hand on the wall to guide her in the dark. She didn't dare summon orb light. Not only would it likely draw wailers to her, but she also feared the power inside her, no matter how reduced. Hisses and grunts sounded behind her. She ran faster, her mind whirling. She would escape and warn Crain.

He had no idea what they were up against.

CHAPTER 16

He was going to vomit.

Crain's inverted view of the world bobbed and blurred at a gut-twisting speed. After convincing the Wild Gathi his force hadn't sought a fight but, instead, wanted to parley, he had expected to be led into their stronghold.

Atop a horse.

He clenched his jaw against the bile climbing up his throat and squeezed his eyes shut. His stomach wedged itself in the vicinity of his chest, and the feeling of weightlessness worsened with the action.

Nope. He wasn't doing that. He popped his eyes open again and focused on the backside of the woman whose shoulder he was unceremoniously slung over like a large sack of potatoes. Crain wasn't a small man, but she carried his bulk with ease. If he wasn't nauseous, he would've been humiliated. Beside him, Joah suffered the same torture, draped over the shoulder of a man. Joah's inverted form bounced back and forth into Crain's view as their transporters dashed up the mountain trail.

Just when Crain thought he would lose the battle to keep his lunch from returning for a visit, they skidded to a stop. The woman bent and lowered him to the ground. He wobbled on unsteady legs like a newborn foal for a moment, trying to regain his bearings. Joah was deposited next to him, his brown face ashen. The dazed lieutenant shook his head and glanced around them.

Well, this was one way to locate the Wild Gathi village.

Night had fallen since their journey up the mountain. A full moon lit the settlement as brightly as any orb light. Houses made from wood, stone, clay, and animal hides surrounded pens filled with milling livestock. Flickering luminescence shone from around the cracks of doorways where furs hung. A few curious faces peeked from the gaps. Most noticeable, the uncommon heat hadn't penetrated this far up the peak. A cool breeze blew over Crain's drenched tunic, but the chill was welcomed compared to the miserable high temperature of the past few days.

Crain's hauler spoke in a hushed voice to her companion. The man nodded, strode to a large house, and disappeared through the flap. Concern for his safety warred with curiosity. No fires burned along the village's border. He glanced back down the trail, scanning for pale shapes shifting in the night. Nothing moved but swaying trees caught in a gentle wind. This short reprieve wouldn't last.

He cleared his throat. His guard's dark eyes narrowed as she glared down at him. At three inches over six feet, Crain wasn't accustomed to looking up at many people, let alone a woman. The giantess wore a fur-trimmed tunic and leathers. When he was a boy, his mother told him stories of enormous apes living in the mountains. Now, he wondered if the tales had started due to Wild Gathi sightings.

He motioned to the sheathed swords penned beneath her behemoth arm.

"You should return our weapons to us. The wailers could be here at any moment." At her blank stare, it registered to Crain that she had no idea what he meant.

"The pale creatures that attack at night," Joah said for clarification.

Comprehension flared in her eyes. "They won't tread on the mountain. You're safe." The "from them" was left unsaid.

How was that possible? Did the Wild Gathi have wards? Crain began to ask when Joah's transporter stuck his head out from the door flap of the house.

"You two can come inside."

He shared a quick glance with Joah and entered the house. The interior was warm and spacious. The space was narrow but deep, giving the illusion from outside of a smaller dwelling. Animal skins hung on the walls, and a table laden with an array of weaponry stood near the door. Across the chamber, a doorway led to what must be the sleeping quarters.

Seven people sat on floor pillows before a hearth. A pot bubbled over the fire. The smell of cooking meat reminded him he hadn't eaten since noon. A woman with onyx skin and salt and pepper hair glanced up as they neared. She had almond-shaped eyes and a full mouth. Although her hair was streaked with gray, no age lines marred her smooth face. She was beautiful. Her frown, however, wasn't.

Joah's guard strode to the woman and bent to whisper in her ear. Her head tilted to the side and her eyebrows furrowed as she listened. Her penetrating gaze shifted from Crain to Joah before returning to Crain. She gave a slow nod. The man finished his report and straightened beside her.

"Sit. You've come quite a long way to see us." She waved a slender hand toward two unoccupied pillows between herself and the six others, whose expressions were a mixture of curiosity, distrust, and agitation.

Crain and Joah did as directed. Crain folded his legs and shifted around on the pillow. Goddess, this was uncomfortable.

"I'm Taru, and I speak for the village. We're told you've come for help against your king."

A young woman with a pinched expression scoffed. Taru's glare silenced the outburst. "Why should we endanger ourselves and our way of life for you all? You commoners have happily served the nobles and received their protection for countless years. If they've turned against you, how is that our concern?"

"We haven't happily done anything. We are slaves," Crain said, trying his best not to grind his teeth.

"But you, Crain, are not. Jorc says you and your companion are Royal Fighters. You support the nobles' religion and maintain control of slave and merchant alike for your masters. Or has the purpose of the king's commoner army changed since last I ventured into a city?"

Crain squirmed under her intense scrutiny. Her assessment of the Royal Fighters was partially accurate. Yes, they had worked for the king, but they never lorded their station over other commoners, nor did they use force to maintain the law.

"Yes, we kept the peace, but we never killed commoners, and our Order has nothing to do with Gathi religion."

She leaned back on her cushion and raised an arched eyebrow. "Not anymore, you might not, but the original fighters did. We fled your cities because we refused to forget the past like the rest."

Joah stirred beside Crain, probably as uneasy with the turn of the conversation as Crain. Understanding the need to steer the discussion back to a safer topic, Crain said, "Now the future of the Kingdom is in danger, and I fear the reach of that peril won't stop at the foot of your mountain."

Taru scoffed. "How so? We'll live as we always have. Separate and free from a false goddess."

Crain felt his chance to garner their support slipping through his grasp. It was time to use the information Umgar had given him.

"Mersha's son needs your help," he said.

Speaking the name had the effect of an explosion. All at once, people began talking.

"Silence!" Taru's outburst hushed the others, whose gazes bore into Crain. "What do you know of my sister?"

"I know she traveled to Sura to recruit commoners from Melika and was captured. A nobleman impregnated her, and she died in childbirth. Were you aware of the child? Of Drakon?"

Taru's eyes glittered with unshed tears, but she jutted out her chin, refusing to let them fall. "I told Mersha she was a fool for attempting to open your eyes to the evil inside Melika." She shook her head, engulfed in a memory.

"She believed commoners deserved redemption and salvation. Her naivety got her killed. Yes. I knew of the child, but there was no way to safely extract him, and his blood is corrupted with Melika's essence. We couldn't risk bringing him here. He is lost to us."

Drakon had lived a life Crain wouldn't have wished on his worst enemy, and he wanted to condemn her for leaving the boy a slave, hated by the nobles, and feared by commoners. Crain was no fool, however. Speaking his mind wouldn't endear her to join their cause. Still, there was one question he couldn't stop himself from asking.

"Why do you believe Melika is evil? The goddess has provided protection from the wailers since they descended on the land."

"How can something that allows the enslavement and murder of the weak not be evil? When has Melika ever protected a commoner? The mages only created wards to protect themselves and their property. The slaves, servants, and even you, are property."

Crain sat without reply, ruminating on her words. Taru nodded as if his silence was answer enough. "So, I ask you again. Why should we help you?"

"I don't know if Melika is good or evil. I do know King Ewen is a threat to everyone in Somorrah in his current mindset. He's named Drakon the Nahum and—"

"The Nahum?" Her black eyes widened. Shocked gasps rippled through the group.

"Are you sure Ewen believes him to be the Nahum?" she said.

"Yes. He's placed a price on Drakon's head for his capture and return."

A slow smile spread across Taru's face, and she clasped her hands under her chin in a gesture of prayer.

"Thank Apalsi! It's time. Yes. We'll help you, but first, tell me about my sister's child."

PART II

CHAPTER 17

A violent shove sent Umgar, blindfolded and bound, stumbling forward into darkness. His foot caught on an uneven surface, and he did an awkward hop-skip to keep from face-planting. Straightening, he glared behind him to where he presumed Dagoti to be standing.

"Was that necessary?"

"Be silent and keep walking," came his jailor's voice.

Another shove propelled Umgar forward, and he clapped his teeth against an angry retort. His life depended on how this interaction went, after all. He wouldn't let a bit of irritability get him killed. A dead man would be of no use to Drakon.

Drakon.

Concern about his friend's well-being was a weighted vest around Umgar's chest. Tension curled and twisted in his gut. He had witnessed the conclusion of Drakon's battle with the peculiar wailer but was too far away to reach them before the collapse. When the debris settled, nothing but a wall of gravel remained.

Had Drakon survived?

Umgar squeezed his eyes shut as guilt rode him. He should have tried harder to convince Drakon to flee to the Wild Gathi. Perhaps then—

Fabric rustled behind him, drawing Umgar from his

spiraling thoughts of should-of and could-of and bringing him back to his current predicament.

A vice-like grip clamped down on his arm, and he was marched forward. The thick cloth over his eyes offered no hint of his surroundings. He focused on the sounds in the chamber. His and Dagoti's footsteps were all—

His ears perked. There were soft murmurs of conversation, the scrape of silverware against plates, and the aroma of meat and baked bread.

He was interrupting someone's meal. Great. Suddenly, the sounds stopped. The diners had noticed them then, Umgar surmised.

"Dagoti, what is the meaning of this? Who is this strange male?" The baritone voice was a mixture of curiosity and wariness. No hatred. *Yet.*

Beside Umgar, the Lim commander cleared his throat. "Zar Hazor, I'm sorry to disrupt you, but our patrol discovered this male and another at the barrier. They are Gathi who claim to have accidentally crossed into our lands."

The abrupt screech of a chair against the floor sounded, and Umgar was pulled to a halt. An uneven, shuffling gait neared.

"Remove his blindfold."

A violent jerk wrenched the covering from Umgar's face, and he blinked into the cool blue of Lim orblight. Glancing to his right, he sent Dagoti an annoyed scowl. The warrior smirked.

Umgar inhaled a calming breath and turned away. He wouldn't allow himself to be goaded into a confrontation. Instead, he assessed the chamber. There were no visible exits besides the one he had entered.

His gaze snagged at a table set for three, yet one meal was untouched. A frail hunched woman sat in front of her plate. Wisp-thin white hair did little to conceal the shape of a domed head and wobbly, pointed ears. Her long finger-nails tapped out a rhythm against the stone tabletop, and her milky eyes stared straight at him.

Unnerved, Umgar tore his gaze away from the old woman, noting various animal hides and weapons mounting the walls. A broken spear-stained brown with aged blood drew his attention.

"I killed the beast that took my eye and left me with this limp with that spear. I keep it as a reminder. No matter the size of an adversary, the Lim are always victorious."

The Zar stepped into Umgar's line of sight. He was tall and fit for someone Umgar assumed to be approaching seventy. The Lim's silver-gray hair was gathered at the nape of his thick neck and disappeared behind a set of broad shoulders. Dark skin gave him the appearance of a living shadow. A single, assessing eye stared from a stony face, taking in Umgar's measure with calculated efficiency.

"Who are you, and why have you come?"

Umgar shifted his weight from foot to foot, feeling more like a naughty teenager standing before a stern parent than a capable general. For the first time in a long time, he was uneasy in another's presence.

"I'm just a lost man who finds himself in a strange world," he answered. "I wish neither you nor your people any ill-will."

The Zar folded muscular arms over a barrel chest, a frown turning down the corners of his thick lips. "I will be the judge of that. Are you indeed Gathi?"

Umgar nodded. "My grumpy chaperone here stated the truth."

Dagoti hissed, but Umgar ignored him. A chuckle escaped the Lim leader. One corner of his mouth twitched before reverting into a scowl. His gaze flicked up and down Umgar's filthy clothing.

"I never imagined how a Gathi would look, but, had I done so, you would not have been it. You look much like us." The Zar shook his head. "Why, after all these millennia, have your kind decided to cross the barrier? How is it possible for you to do so?"

Hands tied at his back, Umgar managed an awkward shrug. "Our presence here is mere happenstance. An unavoidable accident. How we were able to pass through the magical barrier—"

He paused, searching for an explanation, and finding none. He gave another shrug. "There is no answer."

"I don't believe him," Dagoti said, drawing both the Zar's and Umgar's attention.

The warrior nodded in Umgar's direction. "On your word, I can lock him up on the lower level until we find out the truth and recover Eza."

At the mention of his daughter, the Zar's eye widened, and he seemed to brace himself—widening his stance and angling his body toward Dagoti.

"What do you mean by 'recover Eza?'" Why did she not return with you? The Malachi you sent back with the injured tribesman assured me Eza would be protected during the journey, which was the only reason I did not insist on her being brought back."

The younger man grimaced, unable to meet the Zar's

questioning gaze. Umgar held no warm feelings toward Dagoti, but he pitied the warrior. No soldier wanted to disappoint their commanding officer. Furthermore, from what Umgar witnessed of the commander and Eza's relationship, it was apparent Dagoti cared for the woman. Umgar's thoughts drifted back to Drakon. He could commiserate with the chest-crushing guilt that arose from failing to protect someone.

"I apologize for not keeping the Zarea safe. I should have done more to ensure her return," Dagoti said, finally lifting his eyes. He paused, indecision playing across his face, before continuing.

"However, Eza is a strong fighter. As capable as myself or any Malachi. She has braved the Darklands before and is not lost to us."

"She also has a formidable warrior at her side. Drakon wouldn't let anything happen to her," Umgar added.

When two skeptical gazes fell on him, Umgar raised his eyebrows in a "what?" gesture. "I thought that tidbit would be good to know."

"You would expect me to put my confidence in a male I have never met," the Zar asked.

"Drakon is in the same predicament as Eza. He doesn't know your Darklands or the dangers. He is not foolish enough to let harm come to the one person who can lead him out of there. You might not believe we wish your people no ill-will, but you will know the truth when Drakon ensures your daughter's safe return."

Umgar smiled, trying to project friendly, "trust me, I know what I'm talking about" energy and praying his words were convincing.

The Lim leader sighed, a sound holding the weight of the world, and squeezed his eye shut, letting his head fall back on his neck. At that moment, he appeared older and frail. "This is my fault," he said, his voice nearly a whisper.

Then he straightened and gripped Dagoti's shoulder, staring into the younger man's eyes. "I was wrong to blame you. Forgive me. Had I not attempted to prevent Eza from going with the patrol, she would have at least been better equipped for the journey. As a result, I doubt she packed enough rations in her haste. Now, tell me what happened."

Dagoti blinked rapidly before bowing. "Thank you, Zar. There is nothing to forgive. As for what happened, creatures set upon us as we traveled. During the battle, there was a partial cave collapse, but I saw Eza and the Gathi male escape through a side tunnel before debris sealed the opening."

"Were they the same pale monsters that massacred the Coombe tribe?" the Zar asked.

"I believe so. They were able to find us in the Darklands. The only explanation is that they are tracking these males."

The Zar focused a narrowed gaze on Umgar. "Is this true?"

Umgar shook his head. "I can't say with certainty the wailers didn't follow us, but I can say if they did, we are ignorant of it. In our homeland, we avoid or kill them. Although it seems some of the creatures crossed into your lands long before Drakon and I arrived."

The older man nodded, a thoughtful glint in his eye. "That is true. If your people fight these wailers, then you know the best way to kill them, correct?"

"Yes. You can kill them like anything else of flesh and

bone…with sharpened blades and superior tactics. They are not intelligent creatures, thankfully."

The sound of a chair scraping stone drew Umgar's gaze. The older woman stood. Picking up her cane from its perch against the table, she ambled forward, tapping the walking stick along the floor until she stopped in front of them.

Her cloudy eyes shifted from the two Lim and focused on Umgar. A sensation of vulnerability washed over him. It was like his inner thoughts were being sifted of their secrets. He rocked back on his heels, instinctively trying to place distance between himself and the unsettling invasion.

She smiled, showcasing her few teeth. "Pleased to meet you, General."

Umgar blinked. *Had he mentioned his rank?* He didn't believe so. Before he could sort the mystery, the old lady nudged the Zar in the side with her cane, hard enough to elicit a wince from the man, and motioned to Umgar.

"Why all this talk? At times, I wonder who is the fossil, you or me." She tsked. "Commune with Apalsi. He will reveal the inner workings of this male and the truth. You cannot discern the sincerity of his words through questions alone, but Apalsi will show you the content of his character."

Umgar frowned, glancing around the chamber for someone he might have overlooked. "Who is this Apalsi?"

The woman raised a set of white eyebrows and shook her head as if Umgar's question was too ridiculous to comprehend. She clicked her tongue and wagged a knobby-jointed finger at him.

"Apalsi is God. Who else would he be?"

God? Umgar groaned inwardly. With his luck, the Lim

would be as zealous as the Gathi nobility. Perhaps worse. When it came to religion, level-headed pacifists could turn murderous when their beliefs were questioned. He would have to tread lightly.

Keeping his face neutral, when he said, "Of course. I meant no disrespect and hope I have not insulted you." Her sightless eyes scanned his face. Once more, the penetration in that gaze discomforted him, and he fought the nervous urge to shift away from her.

"Your ignorance is nothing to be offended about. Would a parent discipline a child for not knowing how to walk or talk? What remains to be seen is whether, after learning the truth, you accept or continue in denial."

She tapped her cane against the floor to accentuate her point and turned to the Zar. "Do as you must."

The Lim nodded, closing his eyes, and seeming to retreat into himself. Umgar tensed. When the mages closed their eyes, a chant would follow. He had witnessed many public displays of discipline where a commoner was twisted and maimed or even killed with an uttered word. Panic rose. He could headbutt the man, but then what? Dagoti would run him through.

Umgar's racing thoughts stalled as an iridescent glow emanated from the Zar.

Without conscience thought, he retreated a step. Such magic was new to him—one that rose unbidden, with no need for voice or spell. Umgar waited, tense, for an attack.

Yet, the Lim leader remained still as stone, energy flickering around him in cool sapphire flames. His chest moved in steady breaths. Large hands hung loosely at his sides.

Unblinking, Umgar stood mesmerized as the flames

extended and reached toward him. A small inner voice shouted for him to run, to fight, but he didn't flinch from the power's approach. When it made contact, warmth and peace engulfed him. The tension he hadn't realized he held in his muscles loosened. Inexplicable tranquility filled him.

"W—what are you doing to me?" he asked, glancing down at his body, which was outlined in the blue fire that held no heat.

The Zar remained silent and still. Eyes closed—mouth in a firm line. Before long, the flames withdrew. Umgar felt their absence like a pail of cold water to his face. The power retreated into the Zar, shimmering on his tall frame and seeping beneath his ebony skin. The Lim opened his eye, stared at Umgar—

And smiled.

"You are a man true of heart. I found no deceit in you." He motioned to Dagoti. "Cut him loose."

Without a word of objection, the Lim commander moved behind Umgar. There was a tug, and Umgar's bindings fell away. Umgar rubbed his wrists and flexed his fingers to regain the feeling in his hands.

"Thank you," he said to the Zar.

The Lim inclined his head. "We are a warrior culture because the necessity of living in this dangerous underworld demands it, but I am always glad when battle skills are not needed."

Turning, the Zar shuffled back to the table and his deserted meal. He slid into his chair with a groan and gestured to the empty seat with the untouched bread and meat.

"Sit and eat. Your journey must have been a tiring one."

As if only now realizing its lack of nourishment,

Umgar's stomach rumbled. He smiled sheepishly and crossed the room to sit at the table. The old woman tapped back to her seat and resettled in one smooth movement.

Umgar frowned over at her. *How could one as frail as wet parchment and bent as a drawn bow execute such a graceful action? And without the groaning and popping of old joints?*

"Dagoti, please gather as many Malachi as needed to bring Eza back."

The command from the Zar distracted Umgar, and he turned to Dagoti, who remained standing near a draped doorway.

The commander nodded. "Yes, Zar Hazor. We can leave immedi—"

"The Zarea can find her way back herself," the woman said. A small, secret smile played across her lips as she picked up her fork and began shoveling her meal into her mouth.

Eza's father clenched his jaw. "And why is that, Oracle? You clearly know something."

The Oracle's eyes twinkled, but she took a long gulp from her cup, drawing out the silence. When it seemed the Zar would grind his teeth to powder, she lowered her drink and said, "Before the Zarea left, I gave her a gift from the Holies of Holies. It will keep her safe."

The Zar sucked in a breath, leaning forward, his former annoyance forgotten. "A gift from Apalsi? It has been centuries since such a thing happened. Why would you not tell me? What was it?"

Unfazed, she waved away the barrage of questions. "I do not tell you everything because you would attempt to control that which you cannot."

The Lim leader opened his mouth to argue, but the Oracle raised a withered hand, effectively silencing him. Umgar noted the interaction. The Zar might be her superior, but the woman wasn't without authority.

"What is done is done. Would you have rather I rejected a gift from God and leave Eza unprotected?"

The Zar slumped back in his seat. "Of course not."

She wagged a forkful of meat at him before popping it into her mouth. "I thought not," she said, around the mouthful. "It is the crystal pendant she wears."

Umgar's subconscious dug up the memory of the item and shoved it to the forefront of his mind. Eza had fiddled with the necklace numerous times during their journey through the caves.

"I've seen that pendant. Will it protect both her and Drakon?" he asked, not caring that he was interrupting. Hope that Drakon would be found unharmed outweighed politeness.

"I thought you said this Drakon would keep Eza safe? You do not sound so sure now," the Zar said, one salt and pepper eyebrow raised.

Umgar smirked. "I'm confident he will but having a bit of help is never bad."

The Lim inclined his head and returned his attention to the Oracle. "Well? Does it have enough power to ensure safe passage to Napata?"

The woman shrugged her thin shoulders, finished another bite, and rested her fork on her plate.

"Apalsi sent the gift, which, as you said, he rarely does. We can only trust that whatever it does, it will be sufficient to bring Eza and the male back."

"If vague were a person, it would be you," Umgar said beneath his breath, but the Oracle turned toward him and winked.

He drew back in surprise. "Are you sure you're blind?"

She cackled. "I am blind, not deaf."

As Umgar's neck and cheeks warmed with embarrassment, the Zar sighed, drawing her attention and freeing Umgar from his blunder.

"Dagoti will wait one cycle for Eza," the Zar said. Turning to address the commander, he said, "If she has not returned by then, retrieve her."

"Don't forget Drakon," Umgar said.

Dagoti leveled an annoyed glare at him. "Do I work for you now, Gathi?"

"Dagoti." The Zar cut in. "Please ensure the male is brought back as well. I would like to speak with him." He turned back to the Oracle. "I apologize, but she is my daughter. One cycle is all I can manage."

The Oracle nodded and took a sip from her cup, but it didn't hide the faint smile on her lined face. "One cycle will do."

The Zar gave Dagoti a subtle nod, and the man disappeared through the doorway. The Lim released a weary sigh and gestured again toward the meal in front of Umgar.

"Drink and eat. While you do, you can tell me your story and about the creatures. The other tribal leaders have gathered in Napata. They will have already heard of your presence and will want answers. I will hear your words first."

Umgar took a deep swallow from the cup. The liquid was thick and sweet but settled in his stomach like lead. He placed the cup on the table and met the Zar's gaze.

"I will tell you everything I know, and, hopefully, we can figure out what's going on and how to stop it."

$$\wp\curlyeqprec\mathcal{C}\wp$$

The subterranean river cut through the cavern and reflected the emerald gimmer of the moss covering the ceiling. Above, the plants twinkled like a blanket of gems and provided dim illumination. A rumbling waterfall dumped into the waterway a hundred yards from where Eza knelt on the riverbank.

She scooped a handful of the clear, chilly water and guzzled. Rivulets of the liquid spilled down her face and neck, but the majority drew an icy line down her dry throat to quench her thirst and fill her empty belly. Beside her, Drakon drank. Water dampened the front of his ragged tunic as he sipped from cupped hands.

Eza nibbled on her lip in thought. They should have reached Napata by now, but she had become disoriented. After cycles traversing the passages and caverns comprising the Darklands, the tunnels began to look identical. Fortunately, she realized her mistake, and they were able to backtrack without too much time lost.

Nevertheless, they had eaten the remainder of her rations cycles ago. Hunger twisted her gut, but all wasn't hopeless. She recognized this river and waterfall. They were less than a cycle from her home.

"Is that pendant of yours an heirloom? You touch it a lot when you're upset."

She glanced over at Drakon and then down to where

her hand gripped the crystal at her throat. She hadn't noticed taking it in her grasp. Pondering Drakon's question, her mind wandered back to the day she received the pendant.

Eza had visited the Oracle, an ancient Lim whose connection to Apalsi allowed her to glimpse the past and future. The patches of hair on the elderly woman's head were white, and the smile she had given Eza was missing most of its teeth. The Oracle's milky, sightless eyes stared into Eza as they sat across from one another sharing a meal, as though the older woman could see into Eza's soul.

She patted Eza's cheek with a gnarled hand, pressed the pendant into her hands, and said, "This is for you. I fear dark times are upon us, Zarea, and your role will be great among our people."

Dread had settled in her stomach, and her mouth was dry when she forced out her reply. "What is it for?"

The Oracle's response was cryptic and frustrating.

"It will be your light when shadows come."

A splash drew Eza's thoughts back to the present. "Are you well?" Drakon said. He squatted at her side, and his strange hazel eyes shifted over her as if checking for signs of injury.

"I'm fine."

She stood, dropped her hand from the crystal, and answered his initial question. "My pendant was a gift from a friend."

He nodded thoughtfully and then straightened. He waded calf-deep into the river's current and stared down into the rushing water with a hand on his sword hilt. His mahogany locks, uncommon among Lim, fell into his face, and he swept it back with an absent flick of his hand. The back of his tunic hung in tatters from the wailer attack, and the dark fabric was stiff with blood.

"We should try to catch something to eat. I assume there's some form of fish down here."

Eza shook her head even though he couldn't see the gesture. "The water is too clear near the river's edge. They would see us long before we could spear them."

"I'd rather try for a meal, nonetheless."

"Suit yourself, but there are more dangerous creatures than cave fish in there." He turned to her, and his gaze followed her pointed finger to where the clear water darkened to an impenetrable blue. "The water is deeper than it appears. You might not be the only thing seeking a meal."

She bent, retrieved her staff from the riverbank, and started down the river's edge. A few moments later, Drakon's quick footsteps followed. She gave him a smirk as he drew up beside her. The scowl he wore deepened.

"Don't worry. The green-glowing moss is edible, and I happen to know some grows behind the waterfall."

They covered the distance to the falls. Up close, mist sprayed from the crashing water, and a soft green radiance gleamed from behind the torrent.

"I'll climb up and gather the plant!" Drakon said, shouting to be heard above the thundering river.

Eza glanced down at his hard-soled foot coverings.

"My bare feet will grip the slick rocks better."

"Then I'll take off my boots."

"No need." She shoved her staff into his hands and started toward the damp rock face. "I'm already climbing."

He grumbled at her retreating back, but she kept going.

It was senseless to wait for him when she was likely the better climber anyway. Eza gripped the cool, slippery wall and pulled herself up and toward the underside of the falls. She moved briskly, finding hand- and footholds with ease. Mist soaked her, but within minutes, she was behind the spray and level with the moss. She heaved herself onto a ledge, began tearing thick patches of the luminous moss from the rocks, and stuffed it in her satchel. The clumps smelled of damp earth; nonetheless, her stomach grumbled in response. She would collect enough to fuel them for the remainder of their journey.

A muffled grunt sounded from below. Eza paused with a fistful of soft moss and turned to glance through the cascading curtain of water.

Below Drakon twirled his sword at...a shadow?

She leaned forward, squinting. What were those things? Formless shades slithered like slugs around Drakon. They moved in closer. He swung a blood-coated blade at them, and they shrunk back out of reach. *Did the phantoms fear the weapon or the blood?*

A shadowy tendril rose from the water behind Drakon.

"Drakon! Behind you!" Eza shouted.

Instead of turning toward the threat, Drakon glanced up at her. He had heard her voice but not her words. *Too late.* The tendril whipped around his neck and jerked him back. He made a choked gasp. His body smacked the river's surface in a geyser of displaced water. Metal glinted as the sword clattered to the riverbank. Then he vanished beneath the water.

Without thought, Eza dropped the plants and plunged into the churning water. The icy water was a shock to her senses. The river swirled her in its embrace, forcing her down toward the rocks below. She fought against the pounding current and struggled to orient herself in the dizzying spin. She glimpsed the faint glow of the moss and kicked toward it. Eza reached the surface, only pausing to fill her lungs before diving again.

Scanning the depths, she spotted Drakon. Shades coiled about his chest and arms. He writhed and thrashed against their hold but was steadily dragged deeper into the blue abyss. Eza pursued the tangled mass as fast as her limbs would propel her. The temperature plummeted as she went lower, and her body tingled and began to numb. Some part of her rational mind recognized the signs of hypothermia, but she couldn't turn around. She needed to free Drakon and get them out of the frigid water before they grew sluggish and lost coordination.

Suddenly, a ringlet of enchanted flames blinked into existence beneath them. The gateway's inky core stood out against cobalt surroundings like the gaping maw of an underwater beast. A chill separate from the water temperature settled in Eza's chest. If she didn't reach him, Drakon would be lost to her.

As if also understanding his worsening plight, Drakon's struggles redoubled. He managed to free an arm from the restraining shadows. Their tendrils whipped at him and blood spilled in dark clouds. A scream erupted from him in a release of bubbles.

Eza kicked harder. Faster. Her lungs burned with the need to breathe. She was almost there. Just a bit closer. But the phantoms moved with the speed of eels. They would reach the gateway first.

It was hopeless. It was…

In a moment of clarity, the Oracle's words came back to her.

"It will be your light when shadows come."

Eza clutched the pendant at her throat and channeled all her desperation into it. She didn't know what it would do but prayed it would make a difference. At once, brilliance exploded from the crystal and crashed over the shades like a tidal wave. Their smoky forms shattered in a spray of dark matter, and the gateway beyond winked out.

The crystal dimmed to a warm smolder. In the aftermath, only Drakon remained, floating limp, motionless. His hair floated around his head in an eerie black crown. Eza swam to him, seized his ruined tunic, and kicked for the surface.

She fixed her eyes upward toward the emerald light above. Still, she must be deep. The surrounding water was still dark and frigid.

She fought against the overwhelming urge to inhale. Her lungs burned, and her mind felt waterlogged. She focused on the motion of her legs. *Kick. Kick.* All too soon, her limbs began to seize with the effort. Drakon was like a sack of rocks dragging her down. Her shoulders and fingers ached from his weight. She kicked harder. She was starting to feel dizzy. The beckoning glow above grew clearer. Air was a few feet away…

She felt her head break the surface and sucked in an echoing inhale. She treaded water for a few seconds, dragging in cool air to feed her aching lungs. It didn't escape her notice that there were no gasping breaths from Drakon. She hauled her load to the bank and dragged him to the embankment.

Shivering with cold, Eza knelt beside him. His pale skin and lips were a bluish hue, and his eyes didn't flutter behind the shut lids. She placed a palm on his chest. It was still. She hung her head. A small moan escaped her.

Drakon was dead.

Her vision blurred, and tears splattered on his soaked tunic. The crystal pendulated in and out of view.

She froze. The crystal still pulsed with light. Perhaps it contained enough magic to save him. She snapped the pendant from the cord about her neck, placed it against Drakon's chest, and funneled her healing through the crystal into his body. Familiar heat rose from her palms. The crystal's shine intensified. The shimmer spread over Drakon's prone form until he gleamed. Yet, he didn't move or wake. Apalsi help her. She couldn't let the male die. If he was indeed the Nahum, the salvation of her people depended on him.

Eza fell into herself, picturing her healing life force as a pulsating sphere at her core—

full of Apalsi's spirit. She mentally severed a portion and willed it into Drakon. She then envisioned her shared power filling him and pushing the water from his lungs.

A hacking cough drew Eza from within herself, and she glanced down at Drakon. He coughed again. Water welled in his mouth. He gagged, and she hurriedly rolled him on his side. As he spewed water, she could only watch in wonder. No healer had ever brought a person back from death. Even now, she could feel a hollow where she had given of herself, but it had worked. He lived.

Drakon moved to sit up, and she guided him up with a

hand on his shoulder. He shivered, but his face had lost its pallid coloring. Other than mild hypothermia, he looked well.

She couldn't hide her wide grin.

Drakon stared at her, his expression unreadable. "I died."

Her smile faltered. "You did, but I brought you back."

"How?"

She glanced down to the crystal pendant, which lay on the ground, and Drakon's hazel gaze followed. It lay in the gravel, blackened and burned. Whatever power it had possessed was spent. Eza didn't understand how she had saved him but couldn't shake the feeling she had given this male more than a second chance at life.

She internally shook away the thought and rubbed her arms for warmth.

"Does it matter? You're alive, aren't you? I'd think gratitude would be the first words on your lips."

He frowned but nodded after a moment. "You're right. Thank you."

"You're welcome," she said.

Without another word, Drakon removed his boots. After a moment of confusion, where he began pulling his tunic over his head, Eza realized what he was doing. She whirled around, allowing him privacy.

"You should undress as well. Our clothing won't dry for some time without a fire, but we can at least take off the cold garments and wring them out. With any luck, the worst we get are bad colds. I've done enough dying for one day."

"Was that a joke?" Eza peeked over her shoulder.

Drakon was sliding out of his leathers. She turned away

again, her cheeks burning. He grunted in answer. Water pattering the ground sounded a second later, reminding Eza of her task. She stripped and began wringing water from her tunic and leathers.

"As soon as we're done, we ought to get dressed, gather our weapons, and keep moving. Stopping here was a mistake. I still have a bit of the moss in my satchel, so we can eat while we walk. If we make good time, we can reach Napata in half a cycle," she said.

"Then we should hurry," came his reply.

They left not long after. Eza led the way, but her thoughts remained in the cavern as she pondered how she had resurrected the male and what price she would pay for doing so.

CHAPTER 18

The tunnel mouth opened between two colossal statues. Sculpted from obsidian granite and chiseled into the wall, each sentry held spears in their stiff grips. Their faces were grim and unwelcoming, a warning to any who dared trespass. The strange, luminous moss coated every inch of the expanse and illuminated it in a subterranean version of day. A twenty-foot rampart, wedged amid stalagmites, blocked passage to the far end of the cavern.

Drakon walked alongside Eza as she hurried toward the Napata stronghold. A portion of the wall slid away and a dozen armed soldiers rushed out. Drakon's hand tingled to draw his sword. However, the situation called for tact and diplomacy, and drawing a weapon in their home wouldn't earn him any allies.

The Lim halted a few feet away, spears leveled at Drakon. Eza took a step forward, placing herself between him and the armed fighters.

"Eza?"

Dagoti broke from the line of Lim. He rushed to Eza and gathered her in a fierce hug, lifting and swinging her around before planting her back on the ground.

A spark of annoyance reared in Drakon's chest. Of course, she would be chummy with someone who wanted to kill him. To say the leader of the Malachi warriors wasn't one of his favorite people was an understatement.

As if hearing Drakon's thoughts, Dagoti shot him a scowl over Eza's head. "I see you made it here unscathed. Fortunate." He sounded as elated about the news as he would about having his fangs ripped out from the roots.

Drakon inclined his head anyway and said, "Where's Umgar?"

At the mention of Umgar, Eza stepped from Dagoti's embrace. "That's right. Where's the other Gathi? Is Meko well?"

Dagoti's gaze shifted back to Eza and softened. "Meko is fine. I sent a few Malachi searching for you and was on my way out with another party. Meko is with the others scouring the Darklands for you. She'll be happy to see you've returned."

He paused, his usual pinched expression returning. "The other Gathi informed the Zar and tribal leaders of the creatures but didn't reveal the cause of the power surge."

He leveled a sour look at Drakon. "I'm not convinced there's any truth to their claims."

"It's fortunate, then, that you aren't the person we need to convince." The words left Drakon's lips before he could think better of it.

Dagoti's black eyes narrowed, and he bared his fangs. He opened his mouth for what assuredly would be a threat, but Eza placed a restraining hand on his forearm.

"Please, Dagoti. There are enough problems facing us. I don't need you two at each other's throats. Tell me. Which tribes have arrived?"

The warrior continued to glower at Drakon for a long moment but then begrudgingly dragged his gaze back to

Eza. "All but the Hwen tribe, but your father never expected them to send aid. They believe if they don't get involved, they'll remain safe." He gave a disgusted snort. "They will soon learn that they can't hide forever. Ours is a shared fate. The other tribes arrived not long after we returned. Khell is here as the representative for the Gnehoon tribe. He's been worried about you."

At the mention of this Khell person, Eza rubbed her brow as if warding off a blooming headache. Her hand went up to toy with the ruined, blackened crystal pendant she had replaced around her neck.

"What happened to your pendant?" Dagoti eyed the crystal.

"What? Oh." She tucked the pendant into her tunic. "It's a long story, and we should hurry to my father. I'm sure he and the tribal leaders are waiting."

Dagoti, jaw set, gave her an evaluating glare. Then he nodded to the nearest warrior. "Blindfold him and take him to the council chamber."

Drakon stiffened and tensed to step away, but Eza intercepted the man as he started forward to carry out the order. With a hand lifted, she shook her head. "He won't be blindfolded. He isn't our enemy."

Dagoti let out an exasperated breath. "Eza, please. You don't know that, and I'd rather not have a stranger learning the layout of our city."

Eza didn't move. "I do know he isn't a threat. If he wanted to harm me, he could have done so during the cycles we were in the Darklands."

"But then he would've been lost in the dark. Your friend appears to be many things but a fool is not one of them."

Weary of the back and forth, Drakon spoke. "If it eases your mind, I will wear the blindfold. There are things I must discuss with the Zar and standing here bickering is wasting valuable time."

The soldier looked between Dagoti, Eza, and Drakon, unsure of how he should proceed. Finally, Dagoti shrugged. "Fine. You trust him. I won't say any more on the subject." He walked away and headed back toward the open gates. Without a backward glance, soldiers fell into formation and followed in his wake.

Drakon fell in stride beside Eza as she started forward. For reasons he dared not look too closely into, he wanted to thank her for being on his side and trusting him, but when he tried to catch her eye, she stared ahead, refusing to meet his gaze.

They passed through the towering gate, which was little more than a massive slab of stone. It slid shut with a rattling thud. The men and women guarding the rampart scattered to their posts, many casting backward glances at Drakon.

Dagoti, Eza, and Drakon continued on through a pair of gigantic granite doors. Then Drakon stared in awe. The street ahead shone in sapphire orb light, affixed to the ceiling, revealing an underground city of blue undertones. An intricate depiction of the sun, moon, and stars decorated the vaulted roof. Roughly cut doorways and windows sprouted alongside the alleyways in the stone walls. *Were these dwellings or businesses?* He couldn't be sure. Each was devoid of light.

Their footfalls echoed in silence. Nevertheless, pinpricks of awareness along the nape of his neck signaled to Drakon he was being watched. He glanced back at a darkened window he passed. The draping jerked closed but not before he glimpsed the large, frightened eyes of a woman. As he figured—the city wasn't as abandoned as it seemed. They must have evacuated the streets of the townspeople when they spotted them.

Their group turned down a dead-end road and stopped at an ornate door painted in deep blues and greens. Dagoti rapped on the door, and it groaned open. A woman, dressed in tunic and trousers with a sword strapped to her back, held open the door. She bowed low as Eza passed but stared in distrust at Drakon. He ignored her and followed Dagoti and Eza inside and down a staircase to the left of the doorway.

As they descended deeper into the earth's core, he was acutely aware of the hundreds of tons of granite atop him. How deep did the city go? He had an inkling that what he saw was only the surface of a collective nest, and the doorways on the streets above were much like the stems of a deep-rooted plant.

The staircase ended at three passages. Dagoti turned down the right shaft, and they continued along the orb-lit corridors, passing fabric-draped doors. Drakon even glimpsed a hot spring; its bubbling water and warm mist called to his aching muscles.

Before long, they entered a vast circular chamber. A massive orb pulsed in its towering ceiling. Row upon row of empty stone benches encircled the room, rising in levels. Four stairways divided the seating into sections, and a long table surrounded by many chairs stood at the chamber's center.

Four Lim sat around the table, speaking in low tones

with Umgar. His former guardian's gaze flicked to them, and his face split into a knowing smirk.

"I told them you'd be here soon enough."

Drakon nodded, glad Umgar was well and not a prisoner. Beside the general, an older man with a scarred face, weathered skin, and a silver beard stood. He wore a dark brown tunic and leathers, and a long braid hung down his broad back. His left socket was sunken where an eye was missing, but his remaining eye twinkled as he took in Eza.

He smiled, exposing large canines and deep crow's feet. He walked forward with open arms and a pronounced limp.

"Daughter."

Eza rushed to him, and he wrapped her in a hug. She pulled back and stared up at him sheepishly. "I'm sorry I left without saying anything. I—"

He shushed her. "We will speak on the topic later. I am overjoyed you are home safe." His gaze drifted to Drakon and grew earnest.

"Welcome to Napata, Gathi. Your companion has been accommodating in explaining to us the creatures invading our land—these *wailers*. What he has not told us, however, is how they and you, for that matter, came to be here."

A younger, lean man rose from the table and strode to stand beside Eza. He was attractive in the way of haughty nobility, with a long nose and prominent chin. Drakon disliked him instantly. The man placed a protective hand on her shoulder. Eza stiffened, and she shifted her weight away from the stranger. The Lim didn't seem to notice her discomfort. Although dressed in a tunic and leathers much like the Zar and Eza, his attire was the color of emeralds.

A glance at the remaining men and women at the table

revealed dark hues of cobalt and amethyst. Mr. Emerald narrowed his eyes at Drakon.

"I am Khell. The Zarea's intended."

Drakon felt an unidentifiable dip in his stomach at the news but didn't react or offer any congratulations.

Khell frowned and continued. "Zar Hazor is right. We should be told how these beasts crossed the barrier in the first place. How do we know you two didn't send them? We would be fools to trust anything from the mouths of Gathi."

Eza nudged Khell's ribs hard enough to make the man wince. "Stop it. Those creatures have attacked them, too. Drakon's not aligned with them."

"We had no part in sending the wailers to your land. Our presence here along with the appearance of the creatures is purely happenstance."

Eza's father stared at Drakon as if trying to deduce the truth from his eyes. "Dagoti says you claim to know what caused the power surge."

"I believe it resulted from the release of a powerful dark magic into our realm. The resulting blast damaged the barrier enough for the wailers, Umgar, and myself to cross; however, I was unable to regain entry to my land while on this side of the boundary."

"Are there anymore Gathi here?" The question came from Dagoti, who stood tense beside Drakon.

"I don't know."

"Convenient lies!" Khell said. "Neither he nor his silver-tongued friend can be trusted." He waved a hand toward Umgar, who shrugged, unfazed.

A tap sounded at the chamber's entrance. They all turned toward the noise. A hunched, old woman hobbled forward. Her brown robes rustled over the stone floor as she tapped her cane from side to side to guide her path. Her scant hair was white, and her huge, pointed ears wobbled as she walked. Milky, sightless eyes swept the room before pinning on Drakon. Her gaze emitted ancient knowledge and was somehow assessing. A distant sensation of recognition tickled the back of his mind. Did he know this woman? Impossible. But yet…

She gave him a smile and pointed a gnarled finger tipped with a long, yellowed nail at him.

"Welcome, Nahum."

Her intense, unseeing stare was unnerving. He felt all his secrets laid bare.

"You need not be ashamed of your past. It has made you into the man you are and has prepared you for the battles ahead," she said, appearing to read his thoughts. "The tomes say, 'they who sow in tears will reap in joy.'"

"Are you a thought reader then, old woman?" If she was, such power might be invaluable against Melika.

She gave a tut-tut of disapproval and wagged a bony finger at him. She shuffled closer and pointed to his chest. "Everything you need is in there."

"This is ridiculous," Khell said. "Oracle or not, you know well a Gathi cannot be the Nahum. Only a Lim can lead the Lim. That much is written."

The old woman continued to stare at Drakon. "The Zarea shared her life force with him. He is as much Lim as you or I." A collective gasp sounded from the Lim in the room.

"What does that mean?" Drakon said.

At the same time, Khell said, "Eza, is this true?"

Eza's large eyes widened. Her gaze flicked to Drakon

and back to the old woman. "We were attacked. H—he died. I didn't realize—it was the only way to bring him back."

Beside her, Khell released his hold on her shoulder as if scalded with boiling water.

"You did what was needed," said the Oracle.

"You knew. Was that why you gave me the pendant?" Eza placed a hand to her chest where the item in question lay beneath her tunic.

"I only knew you would need it. The whys and hows of our paths are always guided by free will and, therefore, unknowable. However, now your life forces are intertwined. Your union is more binding than that of a mating. Reversing something as absolute as death is not without cost, my dear girl. This is your payment. Only time will tell what effects it will have in the long term."

Shock and apprehension warred for control within Drakon. Had Eza truly not known what would happen? It was beside the point either way. She had saved him when he was too weakened to muster his power to save himself...and he had tried. Memories of his meager attempts to summon the energy to defend himself flashed across his mind's eye. He was forever in her debt. Even so, his gratitude didn't mean he would have to remain bonded to her.

"Can it be reversed?" he said.

"Preferably without him dropping dead afterward," Umgar said from his seat at the table. When Drakon shot him a narrow-eyed glare, he folded his arms and mouthed, *"What?"*

"It cannot be undone. Do not fret, however. Apalsi is vast, unfathomable, but he makes no mistakes. You are already stronger for it."

Intrigued despite himself, Drakon said, "What do you mean?"

"You can now use your gift without weariness. Also, Melika can no longer access your mind."

He hadn't used his power since the attack at the river, but he noticed his sleep had been unmolested. He assumed it was due to Eza's ministrations. Perhaps, in a way, it was.

The Oracle hobbled to a chair, sat with a grunt, and beckoned to him. "Come here."

Drakon didn't budge. At that moment, he wanted nothing more than to leave this place. The longer he stayed this side of the Glens, the more responsibilities that were thrust on his shoulders.

She beckoned to him again. "I promise, I do not bite. You would like to learn about Melika, yes? How she came to be? Her strengths? Her weaknesses? I can show you."

Her assurance of knowledge uprooted his feet. Knowledge was power. He crossed the distance and sunk onto his hunches in front of her.

"Give me your hand."

He hesitated again. He had grown to tolerate Eza's touch, but his tolerance did not extend to others. The Oracle gave him a knowing nod and spoke so only he could hear.

"I understand your distrust. If you allow it, your bond with the Zarea can be a refuge against the demons of your mind. The hurt of your past does not have to control your future."

Drakon gave a quick glance to Eza. A small part of him contemplated if such a thing was possible—to heal from the violations he had suffered. Perhaps...He shook himself mentally. What was he thinking? Only absolute power protected the weak. He knew this. Currently, that power was in the knowledge of what he was up against.

"I'm not seeking a bond or a relationship. I only want the information you promised."

He barely finished the statement before images bombarded his mind.

Melika stood with Apalsi, a being of light beyond Drakon's comprehension, as the God created the Lim from nothing. Then another image rushed forward. Melika raged with jealousy as the Lim were given power and basked in Apalsi's love. Yet another vision materialized. Now, Melika fashioned her own deformed creations in secret. More images blurred past, and he watched as Melika poisoned the minds and hearts of the Lim, turning them into the Gathi.

He was transported back to the field of corpses. The same place Melika had launched her mental attack against him. Only now, a battle raged between the Lim and Gathi. Apalsi appeared. He spoke words Drakon couldn't understand and banished the Gathi to the Glens and Melika and her children to the Dark Realm. Before being sucked through a veil, Melika cursed the paradise to wither to dust.

Drakon blinked away the visions. He was back in the chamber, his breaths coming in heavy gulps. The Oracle's milky gaze observed him. He swallowed, his Adam's Apple bobbing and his throat feeling gritty.

"Melika instigated a civil war because she resented the Lim. She has been leaching power from the Gathi for tens of thousands of years," he said to himself, working out what he had seen.

The old Lim nodded. "Melika retained a link to them through her magic. She distorted their memories and fed them lies to ensure they continued to worship her and provide her with a source of energy. Her essence in them drains their life forces and strengthens her. Anyone who relies on Melika's essence is tainted. Even those who merely live among the nobles."

"What did Apalsi say to her before he banished her?"

"He told her a child of new blood would be born and would hold the power to free her but also to destroy her. There is a reason you are one of a kind. Melika created checks and balances in Gathi law to outlaw the mingling of magical and nonmagical people to stop your birth. She assumed she could eventually discover a way to release herself. Still, Melika is not omniscient. She could not account for free will. People have a way of acting as they see fit."

The Oracle pointed to his skin. "You are the result of a union of dark and light. But light and darkness cannot coincide. Light is a poison to darkness. It will always shine a path through. You are a chosen son called to deliver your people and ours into a future out of Melika's shadow."

Drakon had no illusions about what he was. He had spent over two decades killing for the king. "There is no light in me."

"Your father is a nobleman, and your mother was not."

"I don't see why my lineage matters. The power I possess is nothing compared to the mages or a low-level noble."

"Some Gathi lost their connection to Melika over the eons. These became your commoners. Your mother was not a commoner, however. She was from a line of Gathi who repented for their past sins and fled Melika's influence altogether."

"The Wild Gathi," Drakon said in a whisper. She nodded

in understanding.

"These Gathi were forgiven and cleansed from their former misdeeds. You have inside you the potential for extreme evil or good. Your very nature battles itself, but you are called to lead in this last battle. You have but to answer the call to unlock your potential."

Any other time in his life, Drakon would have leaped at the opportunity for greater power. It was a constant pursuit. Yet, the sudden need to escape this woman and her weighty obligations was overwhelming. He straightened to his full height. He needed time to think.

He glanced around the chamber. Expectant looks met his gaze. Even Umgar stared back as if he expected a speech. Drakon had enough. He turned back to the little old woman, who sat with patience gifted to those of advanced age.

"I have much to think on, but I believe I've done enough soul-searching for today." His tone was harsher than intended, but it couldn't be helped. He was itching to leave.

She tapped her cane on the floor in thought and nodded. "I imagine my words have come as a shock. Take time to rest but not too long. The war has started and will continue whether you act or not."

Eza crossed to his side, bent, and kissed the old Lim's lined cheek. "Thank you, Oracle."

She motioned to Drakon but didn't meet his eyes. "I'll show you to your quarters."

No one attempted to waylay them as they left, not even Khell, who trembled with scarcely contained rage.

Drakon walk behind Eza in a state of semi-awareness. His body traversed the dim corridors, but he observed his surroundings as if from a distance. His thoughts whirled about his mind like leaves in a storm, making it impossible to pluck one musing from the jumble.

For her part, Eza didn't attempt to engage him in conversation. She stared straight ahead, seemingly as lost in her thoughts as he. In no time, they halted before a draped doorway. Eza pulled aside the fabric and ducked inside, and he followed. The interior was compact and sparse. A thin scaly hide covered a bed against the far wall and a chest sat at its foot. Dried meat, a pitcher of water, and flatbread were spread out on a table with two chairs. No other furnishings or decor adorned the room.

The sound of rustling came from behind him. He turned to see Eza slipping her staff from her back holster. She propped her weapon against a wall and began shrugging from the straps. As if feeling his stare, she glanced at him as she slung the item over a chair and sat.

"This is my chamber." She cleared her throat. A hand rose to toy with the ruined crystal, paused, and dropped to her lap. "It is customary for mates to dwell together."

A sudden headache bloomed at Drakon's temples and seeped along his forehead. "Eza, we aren't mates. You know this. I'm grateful to you for saving my life, but that is as far as my gratitude goes."

Hurt flashed in her onyx eyes so fast Drakon wondered if he imagined it. She busied herself with tearing free a piece of bread but didn't eat.

"I had no idea reviving you would bond us, but had I known, I would've still done so. The well-being of my people is more important than any inconvenience on my part. You could stand to be more concerned about the lives hanging in the balance and not your personal distaste about being bonded to me."

She stood suddenly, her chair skidding against the stone floor, and stormed from the room, leaving Drakon to stare at the fluttering door drape.

CHAPTER 19

Eza bolted from her chamber and hurried down the orb-lit corridor, her face, neck, and the tips of her ears felt impossibly hot. With no destination in mind, she placed as much distance as possible between herself and Drakon before she further embarrassed herself.

She replayed their short conversation in her mind's eye. Neither of them was overjoyed about the prospect of being bonded and subsequently mated to someone they hardly knew. The difference between herself and Drakon was that she would do anything, suffer anything for her people. *Was being coupled to her that abhorrent?* Of course not.

She made a right at the end of the hallway and slammed into something solid. She let out a surprised yelp, overbalancing and falling backward. Strong hands gripped her elbows and steadied her.

"Khell?" she said, squinting up into his handsome face. "What are you doing here? The tribal leader quarters are in the north wing, not here."

His cheeks flushed purple, and he looked abashed for a split second. Her eyes widened in realization.

"You followed us! What? Were you eavesdropping outside my door?"

He scowled, his nostrils flaring. Indignation replaced all his earlier chagrin. "I won't be guilted into feeling shame for wanting to ensure you aren't sullying our engagement with that male. I don't want you doing anything we both might regret when all this is over."

Eza gaped, mouth opening and closing as she processed the veiled accusation. Heat crept up her neck along with her rising temper. She began to speak but paused as two males turned down the hallway and approached them.

She shot an exasperated scowl at Khell before smiling and nodding to her passing brethren. They remained silent, the air practically crackling between them, until the two passersby disappeared around a bend.

Khell grabbed her elbow and dragged her to a nearby alcove, away from prying eyes. She snatched her arm from his grasp and shoved him against the wall.

"Don't you ever put your hands on me," she said through clenched teeth.

They stood there glaring at one another, both their chests heaving and Eza with balled fists, for long moments. Eza drew in a calming breath and spoke softly as if to a child.

"I understand you're upset about the mating, but there's nothing to be done about it."

"I don't believe that. We were betrothed since your birth. I am not going to allow some undeserving Gathi to swoop in and take what is mine. Did you consummate the mating?"

Eza's head jerked back as if slapped. "Excuse me?"

"You heard me. Did you two physically mate? If you haven't, this problem you've gotten us into isn't irreversible."

"That's none of your business!"

"The hell it's not. You're my intended. I have every right

to know if you've been unfaithful."

"The moment I bonded with Drakon, you lost any rights you might have held. As I said, I know the abrupt change in your status must be distressing, but coming here and demanding answers that are none of your concern is crossing the line."

Khell took a menacing step forward, but Eza remained still, not surrendering an ounce of ground. This was her home, and, although she understood his frustration, if not his disappointment in their canceled engagement, she wouldn't allow him to address her as if she was property up for dispute.

"What is the meaning of this?" They turned as her father entered the alcove from an adjacent passage.

The Zar's solitary eye narrowed in Khell's direction, and his lips lifted in a hard line displaying the tips of large fangs.

"If I ever hear you speaking to my daughter in such a manner again, I will gut you where you stand! Do you understand me?"

Khell's answering nod was immediate. "Yes, Zar Hazor!"

"The engagement is off and do not dare approach her about it again. Leave."

Khell, face drained of color, put on a tight, quivering smile. "At once, Zar Hazor." With a stiff bow, he fled down the nearest corridor and disappeared.

Eza turned to her father. He stared in the direction the male had gone, his wizened face unreadable. Then his gaze fell on her, and a smile softened his features.

He held out an arm to her. "Come. Walk with me a ways."

She leaned into his side, her arm going around his trim waist, and he wrapped a strong arm around her shoulders and kissed her forehead. His nose crinkled and he fanned a hand in front of his face.

"If you do not visit the springs before returning to your mate, Khell might get his wish after all. The young Gathi male will die from the stench."

She swatted him lightly in the stomach and let out a hearty guffaw. "Father! You're terrible!"

He chuckled and squeezed her to him. He steered them from the dim recess and back to the main corridor. The halls were empty save for a few warriors scurrying to and from their quarters with fresh garments or coverlets for the rest cycle, which began three hours before.

Her father's uneven gait was steady as they walked in companionable silence down two passages, up a flight of stairs, and through the arched doors of one of the many saruni harvest caverns.

Inside, rows of the giant pink ferns stretched toward the ceiling. Surging color undulated from the stalks to the leafy blades and back again like a rosy heartbeat. The sight of the gargantuan flora took her back to simpler times when she and Dagoti would play among the countless plants with the other children.

How she longed for the simplicity of youth.

Releasing her, her father paused beside one of the rippling plants, freed his dagger, and sliced away two long strips, offering a piece to her. She took it, biting into the fibrous leaf and chewing. She smiled as the sweet sap flooded her mouth.

"How is your mate? I cannot pretend to imagine how

stressful the news of today has been for him," the Zar said after swallowing his portion and moving farther into the towering crop.

Eza gulped down the saruni, which seemed to sour on the descent to her stomach. "He's managing as well as can be expected, which isn't well at all. I don't know what to do." She gave a helpless shrug. "The more I try to show my support and acceptance of our bonding, the more he pushes me away."

He nodded thoughtfully. "Consider how he must feel. Everything he knew as truth was revealed to be a lie. I do not know the male, his struggles, or his passions, but I have known many like him in my long life. An immense wrong was done to him. I can see it within the shadows in his eyes. Males like him do not trust easily, but you have an opportunity to help him overcome that inner darkness."

They cleared the saruni, and her father eased himself down on a boulder overlooking the crop. He motioned for her to sit beside him, and Eza propped herself on the hard stone to stare out at the beauty of the place.

She dropped her gaze and traced a finger through the fine grit atop the rock, not wanting to see his expression when she uttered her admission.

"Drakon doesn't want my help. He is very much against our joining."

Her father gave a heavy sigh. "He might not want it, but he needs it. As for the mating, give him time." He patted her hand, and she finally turned toward him. "Saving his life linked you both beyond what is typical. Some mated pairs go their entire existences without bonding."

His gaze went glassy, far away. He smiled, but it was

one of longing and sadness. "I loved your mother, but we never bonded. It is a connection unlike any other, or so it is said. You and this male are linked in a way that allows you to carry his burdens and him yours if you both take advantage of it."

Eza swallowed. He rarely spoke of her mother since the female's tragic death, the same event that had claimed his eye and crippled him. It was clear the loss, even a decade removed, continued to pain him. She decided to steer the conversation to more comfortable ground.

"How does being bonded help us build trust? I don't know much about it and never expected to bond with Khell."

He snorted. "Of course not. I realize now Khell lacks character and honor. You two would not have made a good match. Furthermore, bonding is rare. My parents never bonded. However, my paternal grandparents did, and their connection transcended the need for words. Fate has placed you with the Nahum. There is a purpose to all things. If he grants you permission, you can share memories. Doing so will reveal to you more about him and his past and help him win against Melika."

"But how is this memory sharing or mind-to-mind communication done?"

"From what I gather, it is as simple as how you and I are speaking. The only obstacles are you two. If you and the young male open up to one another, the link you share will do the rest."

Eza frowned. Drakon would need to hold a smidgen of trust in her for it to work. "What if he doesn't let me in?"

"You are the Zarea of Napata and your mother's

daughter. He will let you in, and once he does, he will come to love you as much as I do." He grinned. "Well...perhaps not as much as me."

She laughed. "Thank you, father."

He smiled and enveloped her in a hug. "You are welcome but do wash before you return to him. It will go a long way in aiding your cause."

They shared a laugh, and Eza felt more hope than she had since fleeing her chamber. She would help Drakon slay his own demons, and then they could get on with facing the one threatening their worlds.

CHAPTER 20

The banquet hall hummed with murmured conversations, and the delicious aromas of baked bread and meat wafted over the chamber as thick as chilled molasses. Crimson and black silk banners embroidered with the royal family crest hung from the vaulted ceiling and archways, rippling in the breeze from the open windows.

Men and women of various ages, dressed in vibrant, ornate robes, sat crammed at fifty tables. A sea of white-haired heads glinted beneath the orb light like newly fallen snow. Most of the assembly feigned interest in the elaborate feast laid out before them, but their plates and wine glasses remained untouched. Their pasted-on smiles trembled at the corners, and their gazes shifted to where Melika sat alone at the head banquet table—the queen's and prince's chairs noticeably vacant.

They likely wondered why they had been summoned but dared not ask.

Melika eyed the nobles with cold detachment, her mood stormy. The Nahum and the meddlesome Lim female had slaughtered more of her children. She wasn't certain of how the witch managed the feat, but Melika had felt the white-hot pain of their deaths two days earlier. The absolute void their destruction left in her breast gnawed away at her like wood rot.

Her vision blurred as unshed tears burned the backs of her eyes. Sorrow and rage battled within her, threatening to sear away the frail husk of the king she inhabited. She had enough of the pretending—the hiding—and she would repay her enemies tenfold.

But first, she needed these nobles, the strongest of their peers, to shore up her power and to be vessels for her formless offspring yet remaining in the Dark Realm.

Melika pushed back from the table and stood. Her chair scraped against the stone floor, drawing the attention of the crowd. The chamber fell silent in expectation, and every gaze rested on her.

She scanned their faces, varying from eager to curious to wary, for a moment before speaking.

"I know you all are wondering why I've summoned you this night." She rounded the table and stopped before a faint chalk line. The summoning circle encompassed the entirety of the chamber, hidden beneath embellished rugs and wall tapestries.

"The prophecy tells us that when the Nahum is made known, the time for us to leave the Glens and retake the Forsaken Lands is at hand. As the most powerful mages in the nobility, I will need your combined power to ensure we are victorious in the coming war."

A plump woman with a tattooed face stood; her sky-blue robes were damp with perspiration and swished as she wiggled her wide girth from her place at a table. She bowed to Melika.

"As the warden of Arrowford, you have my full support and that of the mages in my city." The men and women at her table, presumably the nobles she spoke of, nodded in agreement from their seats.

Melika inclined her head. The woman squeezed back into her chair with a pleased look on her round face. Melika let her gaze swing back over the chamber.

"Does anyone else share Arrowford's devotion and loyalty?"

They all rushed to their feet, murmuring meaningless words of allegiance. *Good.* Regaining her loaned essence didn't require their consent, but it was always better when they didn't resist. Before they deduced her intent, Melika connected to the power residing within each of them and began drawing it into herself.

At the nearest table, a wizened mage slumped, grabbing his chair to steady himself. He blinked and stared down at his hands. Mist rose from the skin. The tattooed runes on his flesh faded and disappeared.

That was when the screaming started.

Mages stumbled toward the doors and windows. A few souls crashed into tables; others tripped over abandoned chairs. Bodies slammed into tables, and the platters of food and wine goblets toppled to the floor. The stampede of fleeing nobles trampled those unlucky enough to fall.

At this rate, they would kill themselves before being of use, Melika mused. She waved a hand toward the crazed throng. The summoning circle activated. Blazing-white energy shot upward along the chamber's perimeter. A woman crossing the chalk line split from groin to shoulder in a spurt of gore. Her back half fell within the circle, and the other collapsed against the closed door, her outstretched arm and fingers twitching.

The trapped Gathi writhed. Their pale skin thinned to

parchment, and their brittle forms slumped to the floor. Melika hummed with the influx of power. Pure lightning coursed through her veins.

She stared out at the bodies littering the banquet hall. The mages still lived…for the moment. Her babies hadn't eaten in millennia. They would feast on the shriveled bit of soul within the husks.

Invoking her returned essence, Melika ripped a hole through the dimensional fabric into the Dark Realm. A familiar black, unchanging landscape stared back at her from the tear. Yet, there was movement in the darkness. Her children knew their mother, and they slithered forth into the chamber. Their insubstantial shapes moved like black smoke over the prone mages, seeping into them through noses, eyes, mouths, and ears to devour the withered souls within and fill the husks.

After a time, the bodies began to move. First, a finger twitched, or a leg spasmed, and then bodies flopped as bones broke and elongated. Robes ripped as they morphed. Claws sprang from fingernails and toenails. Teeth tinkled to the floor, and long, pointed fangs sprouted in their place. One by one, the forms climbed to unsteady feet. Obsidian eyes bore into Melika, awaiting instruction.

"Welcome, children. These bodies will allow you safe passage through this world, but before we can take back what is ours, we must capture the man who holds the key to our freedom. Even now, this man is hiding underground with our enemies. You will kill any Lim who stands in your way and bring the Nahum to me. I must have the power he holds to free us from our prison."

A chorus of grunts and hisses greeted her words. Melika

closed her eyes and projected her power outward, searching for the last known location of the Nahum. He was cloaked from her, which meant she could no longer pinpoint his exact position, but she didn't need precision. She only needed to get her children close enough to sniff him out.

With the majority of her essence returned, Melika parted her hands and created a portal. The ringlet of fire hovered a foot off the floor.

"Go. Find the Nahum and bring him back to me."

The horde ambled through the gateway to carry out her orders. Soon, she would be free of this land and able to exact her revenge on the Lim and Apalsi himself. But first, there was the matter of the husk she wore. The time for subterfuge was at an end. Melika stretched and flexed. The feeble flesh encasing her ripped and sloughed away to land around her taloned feet in bloody ribbons.

She whipped her serpentine tail, and her ebony carapace glistened in the orb light. Melika craned her head and roared. It was good to be back. She stalked through the destroyed banquet hall and to the corridor beyond. It was past time for the inhabitants of Sura to witness her in her true form and magnificent majesty.

The screams ringing out through the palace in her wake were music to her ears.

CHAPTER 21

Unfathomable how one's existence could change so irrevocably in such a short time but changed Drakon's had. The persistent attempts on his life and his recent bonding to Eza...his life had definitely taken a turn for the worse.

He paced the width of the chamber, as he had ever since Eza walked out on him. Drakon ran a hand through his untied hair and turned for another circuit of the room. Of the mounting problems he faced, his unexpected bonding bothered him the most. He didn't understand much about the mechanics, but the Oracle inferred the feasibility of his injury or death affecting Eza.

Unacceptable. Eza had acted on instinct to save him. He wouldn't repay her kindness with unnecessary harm or endangerment. He would inevitably be forced into a confrontation with Melika; he didn't want fear for Eza's safety to affect his response to the eventual threat.

There was a noise from the doorway, and Drakon turned to see the subject of his thoughts enter. Eza's hair was damp and unbraided and hung like an inky curtain down her back. She wore a clean tunic and leathers and carried a folded bundle in her hands. She met his gaze but looked away, strode to the bed, and placed the clothes in a neat pile atop it. She sat with a weary sigh.

"I thought you would be resting by now."

He stopped and turned to stare at her. "Do you wish I were?"

Eza lifted her eyes to the ceiling as if praying for patience. "Don't place words in my mouth. I understand your shock at the situation we find ourselves in, but I don't deserve your animosity. I did what was needed to save you, and knowing what I do now, I would do it again."

Drakon deflated at the reprimand. It was true. He was being unfair.

"I apologize. I find myself struggling with the weighty responsibilities and expectations thrust upon me."

"I understand, but all our lives have changed. I'd gladly undo all of this if I could, but life doesn't work that way."

She patted a spot next to her. "Sit with me."

When Drakon didn't move, Eza gave him a placating smile and said, "I promise not to touch you. I only did so before to heal your wounds."

"It's not that." In all honesty, he didn't understand his hesitation.

She patted the bed again and waited. Drakon sighed, strode to the bed, and settled beside her, more to prove proximity to her didn't affect him than anything else. The bed was soft, but he sat straight-backed and uncom-fortable, staring at where his sword and scabbard rested against the table. If Eza noticed his unease, she had the decency not to mention it.

"Please look at me." He did as she bade. Her large eyes appeared entirely black in the orb light, with only the corners of the sclera visible. They were alien but oddly beautiful.

"You might not believe this, but Apalsi has placed great power in you. You have but to acknowledge it."

He scoffed. "You're right. I don't believe it and forgive me if I'm a bit wary of gods and goddesses. I recently discovered mine is a demon bent on slaughtering me and wiping out an entire race of people. How do you know this Apalsi isn't the same? Where is he? Why doesn't he deal with the problem he caused?"

"I cannot begin to know how you must be feeling, but Apalsi's ways aren't ours to know. I understand if you are afraid. We all are."

"I'd rather not die, but I don't fear death. I have spent too many years in its company to fear the day it comes for me."

Eza frowned. "A bit of fear is healthy. Melika is becoming more desperate. She'll be keen to capture you before we mobilize and move against her. Also, my interest in your well-being goes beyond the prophecy. You and I are linked, possibly in life and death. I need you to have more care about your own mortality for my sake."

Drakon felt contrite at the reminder. *This was why it was essential to sever this bond between them,* he thought. He didn't know how to factor in another person's safety.

"I can promise I won't be careless with my life. I never am. But I cannot make promises of immortality. Regardless of what others might believe, I'm only a man."

Eza smiled, the gesture brightening her face and making her appear younger and carefree. For the first time, Drakon wondered how old she was.

"That's all I can ask. These are for you. "She picked up the bundle from between them and handed it to him. "They're clean clothing and should fit well enough. I borrowed them from Dagoti. I'll take you to get washed, so we can rest."

Drakon grimaced. "I'm sure Dagoti was delighted to spare a few items for me."

Mischief twinkled in her eyes, and the sides of her mouth twitched. "Well...I didn't exactly ask him."

Her admission shocked a short laugh from Drakon. It spurted out, rich and rumbling, and he snipped it off with an awkward clearing of his throat. Eza studied him with an intrigued purse to her lips.

"You don't laugh much, do you?"

Drakon shifted on the bed, suddenly self-conscious. "My life hasn't been much for humor."

"What do you mean—"

"Zarea Eza! The Dahi and Nadab tribes are here! I came as soon as I saw."

A young man, no older than seventeen, yanked back the door draping and stepped inside. His eyes widened when he saw Drakon and Eza seated on the bed. "It is true then? You mated the Nahum? I bet Khell is fit to be tied! I can't wait to see his face. I never liked him much anyway."

The boy paused to take a breath, but Eza cut in. "Thank you for letting me know, Pagon. Is there anything else you need? Drakon needs his rest."

Pagon gazed unblinkingly at Drakon. Drakon folded his arms and lifted a questioning brow. Perhaps the boy was a bit unhinged?

The teen blinked; his trance broken. "Are you really going to lead us against Melika? I heard there've been plenty of attacks already."

Pagon's gaze raked over Drakon, apparently seeking proof by way of wounds or blood. Drakon pondered the boy's question. He was the first person to ask Drakon if he would lead the Lim rather than assuming it a foregone conclusion. Was it a choice at this point?

After each assault against him, any hope of Melika losing interest was nonexistent. She would kill him, or he would kill her. He hadn't cowered, afraid and weak since childhood. Drakon wouldn't be a passive victim while Melika threatened him and the few people he cared about. And somehow, the Lim woman seated next to him had become part of that small number.

"I will," said Drakon at last.

The young man beamed, his grin taking up half his dark face. "Thank you! Thank you!" He bowed and nodded his way out of the room.

When he had gone, Eza turned to Drakon. "Did you mean what you said to him?"

"I wouldn't have said it if I didn't."

She grinned, and Melika be damned, Drakon felt an odd sense of gratification in knowing he pleased her. Instant annoyance flared in his chest. He wasn't taking on this responsibility for a boon. It was the right thing to do.

Her smile slipped. "You're frowning. Is everything all right?"

Drakon schooled his features into an emotionless mask. "Yes," he lied.

He stood with the bundle in hand and changed the subject. "However, I would feel better after I'm clean and have changed into something not torn and covered in blood."

She cocked her head and gave him an "I don't believe you, but I'm not going to press it" look.

"Fine. I'll show you to the springs. Perhaps the hot

water will loosen your tongue."

She strode to the door and held the draping open for him. Drakon followed, thinking he would rather face Melika and her horde before sharing his thoughts and confusing feelings with Eza.

⚭

Warm, moist air permeated the cavern housing the hot springs and provided a balm to the soul. A shroud of thick steam hung like a drape. Stalagmites sprouted alongside bubbling emerald pools free of bathers. Eza closed her eyes, inhaling the mild sulfuric scent. After traveling the Darklands, it was soothing to stand in the warmth and safety.

"Take as long as you would need. It's late in the sleep cycle, so no one will disturb you."

Drakon nodded and strode to the edge of a pool, where he deposited his bundle. He toed off his boots and was tugging his ruined tunic up before Eza remembered she should give him privacy. She lowered her gaze, only lifting her eyes when she heard him enter the water. He sat in the roiling water, which came up to his torso. Cupping water into his large hands, he began scrubbing his face. He moved methodically to his muscular arms and over a broad chest crisscrossed with scars. God, what had happened to this male?

"I'm in no need of a sentry. I don't plan to wander off, or is there another reason you stand gawking at me?"

At Drakon's clipped tone, Eza's eyes flew to his face. He had paused and was glaring at her through narrowed eyes, his lips in a tight line.

She had been staring, but how could she not? He was unlike anyone Eza had ever seen. His strangeness intrigued her. And, although Drakon commented on her apparent interest, her open perusal didn't seem to disturb him, which made her wonder.

"Why is it you don't like being touched?" The question slipped from her mouth before she realized the thought had formed.

His gaze dropped to the churning water. He gave a minute shake of his head and splashed water over his face. "You have the worst timing. This isn't something I wish to discuss. Especially now." He clamped his lips together as if to hold back any more words from slipping past.

Eza took in his pinched expression and clenched jaw and knew not to push the subject. She walked to the edge of the pool and sat with her legs folded beneath her.

"Tell me about your homeland then? I'd like to know more about the Gathi."

He exhaled a heavy sigh. "It's been a long few days. I just want to scrub the blood and dust away and sleep, if possible."

"We wouldn't have to talk. You can show me."

His eyebrows furrowed. "Show you how? By magic?"

"No, not exactly. Well, I don't completely understand the semantics, but as bonded mates, we can communicate mind-to-mind and share memories."

Drakon frowned and began to speak, but she rushed on, fearing he would deny the request. "We wouldn't have to touch. All you need to do is allow me in and think about an event or a place, and I'd experience it as you did. No talking or touching required."

Drakon pondered her words for a long time as he gazed into the water, and Eza feared he would refuse her, but then he glanced up and said, "I need only think of a place for you to see it?"

Eza wanted to sigh in relief. She nodded. "Close your eyes and focus."

When Drakon did as instructed, Eza continued. "Each person protects their psyche with their will and fears. Our bond enables us to bypass those barriers. Are you focusing on something you'd like to share?"

"Yes."

Eza closed her eyes and looked inward for their link. It rose from the haze between their minds like a golden thread. She focused on it and sent her incorporeal self down the tether to Drakon's mind. Immediately, a wall, solid and impenetrable, sprouted up to block her entrance. An intangible mist brought a chill that iced her to the soul. It swirled around her like a death shroud, gloomy and foreboding.

Let me through, please.

Placing her hand to the gray stone, Eza pushed. A section crumbled beneath her hand and toppled to the ground. Memories, like wisps of smoke, spilled from behind the barrier. A thin, wiry wisp drifted toward Eza. It flickered with an image of a vast, walled city shining under a yellow sun. This was the recollection Drakon wanted to show her.

Eza started toward it but stopped. Another memory wisp emerged. Eza craned her head to behold the colossal wisp. The memory drifted forward, casting all others in its shadow. Gray and flashing, the stormy wisp held her enthralled. She glanced at the sunny city, hovering an arm's length away.

She had asked about Drakon's homeland. Yet, a need to understand the man himself fueled her curiosity. She nibbled her lip in indecision. The turbulent wisp flickered, and Eza saw a boy with mocha skin, brown hair, and sorrowful hazel eyes. Decision made, she stepped into the memory...

Thunder clapped, and lightning flashed across a black sky. Fat raindrops beat down as two large palace guards escorted him through the downpour and into the stables. His tiny, emaciated form trembled as they entered the building.

Why had he been summoned? Surely, he hadn't offended the stable owner. Drakon trembled more. The two-day-old lashes across his back from when the prince had caught him eating a discarded apple core from the banquet floor and had him whipped burned at the thought of another beating so soon after the last.

The nobleman stood waiting before the doorway and sneered down at Drakon. The man was pale, with black runes etched across his exposed hands and neck. Moonbeam-colored hair sat neatly atop his head in a knot.

A guard nudged Drakon forward. "This is the lad you requested, Lord Layan. Are you certain you wouldn't want a larger slave to muck out the stalls?"

Layan's glare flicked over Drakon's head. He gave a disgusted snort. "If I wanted your opinion, I'd have asked for it."

His penetrating stare fell back on Drakon. "He's small because he works in the kitchens. Spending time in the stables will be good for him."

Lord Layan squeezed Drakon's arm hard enough to make him wince. "It will build muscle and ensure we get more out of him than bread making."

He waved a dismissive hand. "You two can leave."

The doors banged shut as they left. Layan stared down at Drakon with a gleam that made Drakon want to run back to the kitchens to the relative safety of Kina, the palace cook. She was a servant who sometimes watched out for him. She wasn't overly kind, but she was never cruel, which was more than he could say for most palace servants and slaves.

"I've watched you about, boy. How old are you now?" He continued to study Drakon, his pale-blue eyes unreadable. The nobleman fingered the collar of Drakon's wet, frayed, and soiled tunic. The digit trailed the skin beneath.

Drakon couldn't stop the shudder of fear lancing through him, but he didn't dare flinch away. "I'm nine, my lord. I'll be ten next month," he said, trying to hide the quiver in his voice.

He noticed the nobleman watching him numerous times during the past few months. Drakon had never said anything, only hurried along, seeing to his duties. But now, the man's cold eyes on him made Drakon afraid.

"Follow me then. I'll show you what I require from you."

Lord Layan turned in a flutter of lavender robes and strode away, Drakon at his heels. The stench of horse manure strengthened the farther into the stable they ventured and turned Drakon's empty stomach. The large animals eyed Drakon with dark, glassy stares as he passed. Soon, they entered a storage room stacked with bales of hay crowding the floor and piled against walls. *Was he to hall these to the horses,* Drakon wondered.

The door to the room closed with a thump, and Drakon whirled around. The nobleman stood in front of the door, blocking any escape.

And he was undressing.

Drakon backed away and bumped into a bale of hay. "M–my lord?"

The nobleman's eyes, which before were unreadable, sparkled with lust. A slow smile spread across the man's thin face as his robe fell away. Drakon turned to run, but the older man was faster and grabbed him by his tunic and slung him to the ground.

Drakon screamed as the man climbed atop him. Rain pounded the roof, and thunder drowned out Drakon's wails of pain and betrayal and the nobleman's grunts of pleasure.

Later, Drakon lay curled into a ball, his trousers around his ankles. His tears mingled with the dirt on the floor. Clothing rustled behind him. Then slipper-covered feet came into view, and Lord Layan knelt before him.

"Such a beautiful boy." He ran a hand through Drakon's dirty hair, and a whimper slipped from Drakon's lips. "A pity I must give you to the wailers, but I cannot risk anyone finding out what happened here."

Drakon sobbed and grabbed at the nobleman's robes, panic outweighing his pain and humiliation. "Please, My Lord! I'll not tell. Please, don't take me outside!"

Undeterred, Lord Layan yanked free of his desperate fumbling and began to chant. The room, hay bales, and the nobleman vanished into a void accompanied by a feeling of weightlessness and disorientation. A forest reformed around Drakon out of the darkness. Torrential rain beat his battered body as he lay in the sopping grass. He rose to his elbows, trying to peer through the storm into the shadowed foliage around him.

A shriek sounded nearby. Drakon held back a scream and rolled to his back, pulling up his ruined trousers. He had to find someplace to hide. Lightning flashed, illuminating hulking, pale bodies as they crept forward before the night darkened once more.

Drakon froze, terror seizing his muscles. The creatures stalked nearer, their mashed faces horrid. Their slit nostrils flexed, sniffing the air. The closest wailer inhaled, snorted, and stopped. It took a wary step back, shook its misshapen head, and huffed to clear its nose. Its companions had identical reactions. They hissed at Drakon but retreated into the trees. Then they turned and crashed away through the underbrush.

Drakon lay, afraid to move for long minutes, waiting for them to return and kill him. They didn't nor did any other wailers venture closer, although Drakon heard them stalking outside his line of sight. Understanding the Royal Fighters would never open the gates at night, he dragged himself to the base of a tree, pain racking his insides, and fell into a fitful sleep.

"Drakon!"

Drakon roused from slumber. He blinked at the sunlight shining through the forest canopy. He heard his name again and knew the voice. *Kina.* He tried to call out in answer, but his raw throat only managed a croak. He swallowed and called again.

"H—Here. I'm here!"

"Drakon?"

Rustling drew closer and, after a few minutes, Kina and a tall man, a Royal Fighter from his build and the sword he carried, appeared from the trees. The woman took one look at Drakon and began weeping. She removed her tattered cloak and draped it over him.

"You poor child. I knew the nobleman was lying when he told everyone you'd run off. I saw how he watched you." She shook her head, tears streaming down her plump face. "I went to the stables and saw the blood. Had I known—"

She trailed off. They both knew she would have been helpless to stop what had happened.

"I ran into this young man when I was searching the city for you. He suggested we check the forest for any sign of you. It's a miracle none of the wailers found you."

Drakon didn't correct her. He didn't know why the creatures hadn't attacked him. Perhaps it was the smell of his blood? Whatever the reason, he was grateful. Kina reached down to cup Drakon's face, but he turned away. He couldn't stand the pity reflected in her dark eyes. It made him cry anew. His tears and weakness made him all the more ashamed, and he sobbed into his hands.

Too battered to resist, Drakon allowed the man to gather him in his arms, but Drakon's silent tears continued to flow. The fighter shushed him as he would a babe. He blinked to stare at the man. An astute gaze seeming to search into Drakon's soul peered back. The man's dark eyes were ancient, knowing, and at odds with his youthful face. Unsettled, even in his pain and shame, Drakon looked away from the assessing glare.

"I am sorry this happened to you, little one," the fighter said. "But I know someone who will help you. He is a good man, and he will take care of you."

Gradually, mist wrapped around the figures in the memory, obscuring and reclaiming them. Eza was pried from the recollection and sent hurtling from Drakon's mind. Her eyes snapped open. Steam and the sulfuric scent of the hot springs returned.

Drakon stood, back to her, dressing and tying his leathers. Water beaded and rolled down his scarred back as he yanked on his boots with jerky movements.

"Drakon?"

He whirled around. Eza expected him to rage at her. To scream at her invasion, but the look on his face was far worse. It was blank, closed off.

"You had no right to that memory."

Eza's cheeks burned. He had trusted her, and she had invaded his privacy. Her snooping hurt him, no matter how he tried to hide it under a mask of dispassionate reserve. She climbed to her feet and took tentative steps toward him.

"I'm sorry. What I did was wrong, but I didn't suggest mind sharing to seek out that memory."

"No, but you found it all the same," he said, holding the clean tunic in a fist.

Eza reached out and took his free hand. He didn't snatch away as she feared, but he eyed her with a cautious glare that shredded her soul. This was not a male who easily trusted, yet he stood there letting her do something he would allow no other.

She turned his hand upward, seeking something she noticed during the memory. There it was—a brand seared into the flesh of his inner wrist. She knew if she were to glance at his other wrist, an identical brand would be there. She glanced from the brand into blazing hazel eyes.

Drakon gave a humorless smile. "Slave brands. They're a constant reminder of all I've suffered and that weakness cannot be tolerated."

Eza swallowed. "Who did the fighter take you to?"

Drakon smiled, and this time it was genuine. "Umgar." He pulled his hand from her grasp. "I take it you have no lingering questions."

It wasn't a question, but she shook her head anyway. It was a lie, however. Eza led Drakon back to their chambers in silence. Her mind swirled with questions about the male. As they lay in bed, him stiff with his back to her, she continued to wonder.

But she didn't sleep.

CHAPTER 22

Drakon broke the surface of wakefulness in confusion. He sat upright, gazing around the orb-lit chamber. Across the room, his sword rested against the table. Eza's staff leaned against a wall not too far away.

Eza. He glanced beside him at the rumpled, empty bed. She had slept there, a quiet and foreign presence at his back. He scrubbed a hand down his face, and his sleep-addled mind cleared. With clarity came flashes of the previous night. She had discovered his shameful secret. One he never disclosed the details of...even to Umgar.

Self-loathing and disgust washed over him, scalding his face with heat. The stain he carried was now as visible as the slave brands burned into his flesh. Drakon's heart raced, his chest tightened, and the chamber began to close in around him. He sucked in quick, shallow pants, his lungs unable to draw in enough air. He had to regain control. The nobleman was dead. He had seen to it himself.

Drakon shut his eyes and placed his head into his hands, forcing deep, calming breaths.

He's dead. You're not a child. You're not powerless any longer. He's dead.

He repeated the mantra until his breathing slowed and the tightness in his chest loosened. Drakon opened his eyes and lifted his head. He hadn't suffered a panic attack in many years.

"Good. You're awake."

Drakon startled and turned. Eza stood inside, her lengthy hair plaited down her back once again. She held back the draping and spoke to someone in the corridor.

"You can come in."

Umgar ducked into the chamber, a broad grin on his face. His gaze landed on Drakon, and his smile faltered.

"Did I come at a bad time? You seem odd."

Drakon swung his legs over the side of the bed and stood, only then realizing he had fallen asleep in his boots. "I am fine."

"Well, it doesn't seem—"

He shot Umgar a warning look. If he wanted to talk about what was bothering him, which he didn't, he wouldn't do it in front of Eza.

Umgar frowned but didn't push the topic. Instead, he strode to the table and plopped into a chair.

"I wanted to see how you were doing and update you on what transpired after you left the council chamber. As you might assume, the Oracle's assertion left the room in an uproar. However, other than a few tribal leaders, the rest are anxious to speak with you about what plans you might have as it concerns Melika."

He plucked up a sliver of dried meat from a platter, popped it into his mouth, and chewed with relish. Drakon seated himself in the remaining chair and began to eat as well. He thought for a moment and then asked, "Which leaders are hesitant about me?"

Umgar shrugged. "Well, Khell hates you, but you know as much. I also gather you understand why." Umgar's gaze flicked to where Eza stood, tugging on her back holster, and sliding her staff into place.

Drakon crossed his arms over his chest. "It can't be helped. And the others are?"

"The Pago tribe leader, Aros, is skeptical, but she isn't openly hostile like Khell. Probably needs a bit of convincing, is all."

"Khell is harmless," Eza said, cutting in. "He can be obnoxious, but after he's had time to adjust to the changes, he'll be a great ally." Her gaze flicked to Drakon, but he looked away, unable to meet her eyes.

Umgar cleared his throat, breaking the awkwardness of the moment. "Well, I hope that's the case, but I'll keep an eye on him all the same." He gave Eza a disarming smile. "Just a precaution, of course."

"Understood," she said.

"I also wanted to speak with you about the orders I gave Crain. About the Wild Gathi and who he is to meet," said Umgar, addressing Drakon again, his face serious.

Drakon's eyebrows farrowed. "Does it matter? As long as he can convince them to join us, I think whoever commands them is of little importance or am I missing something?"

Umgar twisted the hairs of his bushy beard in the following quiet. Drakon stopped eating and placed his bread on the platter.

"What didn't you tell me?"

Umgar shook his head as if coming to a decision. He gave a smile that didn't reach his eyes. "Nothing life-threatening. You're right. The main thing is to get them on our side. Everything else is inconsequential in the grand scheme. If necessary, we can speak later. For now, you're supposed to meet with the tribal leaders."

Drakon began to push further, but Eza said, "He is right. We should make our way back to the council room. Each tribe sent a representative and a contingent of warriors. They're waiting to hear from you."

Umgar stood, and Drakon did likewise. "Our conversation isn't over. I expect you to tell me the real reason you brought up the Wild Gathi."

Umgar grimaced. "I will."

Drakon snatched up his sword and scabbard, strapped them to his hip, and followed Eza and Umgar from the chamber. They traversed the labyrinth of corridors, and all too soon, they were reentering the familiar room.

The loud murmur of voices permeated the chamber, but it soon trickled to a hush as Drakon, Eza, and Umgar were noticed. Thousands of Lim filled rows upon rows of benches, which climbed the chamber walls. The weight of their gazes was oppressive as they tracked Drakon to the table and its waiting group.

The Zar sat at the head of the table with nine other Lim, including the Oracle and a scowling Khell. Dagoti stood behind and to the right of the Zar, his face pinched and his eyes flinty. A man stood behind Khell in the same position as Dagoti—perhaps Khell's commander? Next to Khell was a woman clothed in sapphire tunic and leathers. She inclined her head to Drakon but didn't smile. Standing at her right, a Lim man in matching colors nodded his acknowledgment of Drakon.

The last seated Lim were unreadable, a man donning amethyst garments and a woman in rust orange. Drakon glanced at the Lim watching from seats encircling the chamber. Their clothing reflected the hues around the center table: brown, sapphire, amethyst, ruby, emerald, and orange.

"Please sit." Eza's father motioned to two empty chairs nearest him.

Eza took the chair farthest from her father. Drakon frowned at this but sat in the remaining seat next to the Zar. Umgar took up guard at his back.

"The Oracle has shown you the history of the Lim and Gathi and the true nature of Melika. You now understand the demon's ultimate goal to use you and massacre the Lim. She will also destroy the Gathi on her unending crusade for vengeance. Knowing these truths, will you lead as the Nahum?"

The Zar spoke the question into the silent room.

Hearing the inquiry spoken so directly caused doubts to close in like storm clouds around Drakon. *Would he be enough to vanquish a demon? Could he effectively guide these people? He, an outcast, who never concerned himself with the lives of others?*

Beneath the table, Eza slipped her hand into his and squeezed. She gave him a nearly imperceptible nod. He drew strength from the physical reminder that he was no longer alone. He met the eyes of each Lim around the table and spoke.

"Yes, I will. Although I'll be honest in saying I don't know how I'm to make the difference in the coming war, I'll fight alongside you to ensure Melika doesn't destroy both our homes."

"The demon sent creatures into our lands because you

fled her. You brought this trouble to us." Khell's accusation fell like a mallet in the room.

Drakon turned to the Lim. "Had I stayed and been killed, you'd be facing Melika right now instead of sitting here, in relative safety, sulking about losing your chance at being the next Zar. Count your blessings."

Khell bared his fangs. "Watch your tongue, Gathi!"

The Lim standing at Khell's back laid a hand to the dagger at his hip, and Drakon felt Umgar shift behind him. A whack on the table drew every eye. The Oracle's cane rested atop the table where she had slammed it down.

"That is quite enough." Her milky gaze landed on Khell, and not for the first time, Drakon wondered if the ancient Lim's ability to see went beyond physical sight.

"No tribe will be forced to fight." Her glare left Khell and traveled to each seated Lim. "If anyone does not intend to follow the Nahum, make your intentions known. There is no room for discontent and insolence among ourselves."

Long silence answered the Oracle's words. Then the Zar stood. "The Oracle's visions are a gift from Apalsi. She speaks for him, and in my lifetime, I have not known her words to be false. I have also communed with Apalsi concerning the Gathi named Umgar, and there was no malice revealed within him. That is enough for me. Napata, as the Grand tribe, will follow the Nahum." He rapped his fist against his broad chest and gave Drakon a sidelong glance and a nod.

The woman dressed in sapphire rose, her intense almond eyes boring into Drakon. "I am Sage of the Hirane tribe. We will stand with the Zar and the Nahum. My warriors are yours to command." She banged her fist against her chest. The man standing behind her introduced himself as Vage, nodded, and rapped his chest in a salute.

The tribe leader clothed in amethyst stood with an eager smile on his dark face. "As will I, Zemket, of the Tow tribe." He gave another chest pound.

"And I, Doyna, of the Swabe tribe," said the woman in a ruby tunic and leathers. She stood and continued the ritual.

Khell and the woman in the rust-colored garments remained seated. *She must be Aros,* Drakon thought, recalling the name of the Lim Umgar had said was unsure of Drakon. She was older than the other leaders but decidedly younger than the Zar. Wrinkles lined a frowning mouth, but no gray hair streaked her ebony locks. An array of emotions flashed across her face before she eased to her feet.

"I, Aros, of the Pago tribe will follow the Zar and the Nahum." She rapped her fist on her chest.

Only the Oracle and Khell sat. Khell fidgeted, weighing his options, and not liking any, if his sour expression was an indicator. A small part of Drakon wanted Khell not to join them. He had enough enemies without enlisting another at his back.

Finally, Khell stood. "The Gnehoon tribe will stand with the Zar and fight for our people." He rapped a fist against his chest, and the guard at his back did the same.

It didn't go unnoticed that Khell pledged allegiance to the Zar and not Drakon. In the end, it didn't matter. Not if Khell's warriors fought against Melika. If the man became an issue in the future, Drakon would handle him then.

The Zar wore a forced smile when he next addressed the assembly. "The tribes have agreed. Now to begin planning and preparations—"

"Zar Hazor! Monsters have breached the gates!"

A lone guardsman stumbled into the chamber, his clothes in bloody tatters and his eyes bulging. His glossy stare bounced around the room, refusing to focus on one thing. A horrendous wound stretched the length of his hairline. It sizzled with yellow and red foam and spurted blood, painting his face in a crimson mask.

Immediately, the chamber exploded into motion with tribal leaders shouting commands to their soldiers. Warriors rushed from their seats and into the corridor, heading for the city entrance. Drakon hurried to the injured man, who crumpled to the floor, muttering incoherently. Dagoti was already there, kneeling beside him. He glanced at Eza as she knelt next to them.

"I can make no sense of what he says. His mind is shattered," he said.

"And he's been poisoned." Drakon motioned to the oozing gash.

Eza reached for the Lim. "Let me."

She placed hands on either side of the guard's head. A warm glow pulsed from her palms. The illumination surged beneath his skin toward the wound, and the yellow discharge weeping from the gash ran pale yellow and then red. Then the ragged edges of the slash reached toward each other and knitted into a puckered gray line.

Drakon uttered a soft curse, and a slow smile spread across his face. Eza's healing ability was awe-inspiring. He looked over at her. She wasn't smiling. On the contrary, her brow wrinkled, and she gasped. He returned his attention to the guardsman. Grayish-yellow tendrils spread out beneath the skin from the healed gash, disappearing into the man's hairline and advancing down his face and neck.

"I can't heal him." Eza stared down at her palms as if they had betrayed her. "I don't understand."

In a burst of energy, the man tore from Dagoti's grasp, his eyes wide and protruding. "White-skinned monsters. Black-eyed devils. I—"

He grimaced and collapsed back into Dagoti's arms with an agonized moan. "We need to get him somewhere safe," Dagoti said, his face drawn. He turned and shouted to two passing warriors, waving them over. He lifted the man toward them. "Take him to the infirmary."

Nodding, they hoisted the groaning guardsman between them and struck out at a hurried pace. Drakon shared a glance with Umgar. The man's outburst implied wailers *and* the possessed nobles were attacking. If a large enough number of the creatures attacked en masse, the Lim would need more than brute force to keep the beasts from overrunning the city.

☙❧

By the time Drakon arrived, the battle raged in a savage display. Grunts and shrieks rang out in the cavern. Ravaged Lim lay sprawled in spreading pools of blood atop the breached ramparts. Wailers and possessed nobles filled the courtyard. More creatures scaled over the walls to leap onto the people below. Others sprinted toward the city, where they collided with a line of warriors.

Eza's pet, Meko, stomped amid the melee, biting, and whipping her massive tail into the oncoming assault and hurtling pale bodies into rock. Still, more creatures spurted over the wall. Blood flowed, beast and Lim alike, its coppery tang coating the air.

"Don't let them reach the doors! Push them back and reclaim the lost ground!"

Dagoti yelled over the discord, and three dozen warriors dashed into the fray, weapons at the ready. Eza withdrew her staff and moved to follow, but Drakon snagged her elbow in a tight grip. She paused to glance at him.

Drakon gave a quick shake of his head. "It's too dangerous. Until we understand our bond more, you should stay back."

Eza yanked out of his grasp, her dark eyes narrowed, and her jaw jutted. "You assume I'd be the one injured or killed? You should worry more about your own safety. Between the two of us, you're the only one who's died."

He opened his mouth to retort, then clamped his lips shut.

Well. There was that.

But this was different. Their life forces hadn't been linked then. Now they were, and it changed everything.

"Look. I won't be able to ensure your safety."

"I didn't ask you to," she said through gritted teeth.

"We don't have time for this! She fights."

Umgar strode to them, unsheathing his sword and eyeing the chaos ahead. His frown deepened, and he met Drakon's gaze. "Every man and woman is going to count. Go. I'll shadow her."

Drakon clenched his jaw and nodded tightly. If he couldn't make her see reason, then Umgar as sentinel would have to suffice. "Fine," he said.

He turned his back on them before Eza could say

anything more. Obsessing over Eza's welfare would get him killed. He trusted Umgar to uphold his promise.

Drawing his weapon, he rushed toward the defensive line without a backward glance.

As Drakon approached, a man went down under the assault of two wailers. A possessed noble, a former woman in tattered gray robes, darted through the gap. It's crazed, onyx eyes homed in on Drakon. It shrieked, baring a blood-coated maw, and swiped a clawed hand at Drakon's belly.

He spun away. The overbalanced noble tilted forward. Drakon clamped the outstretched arm to the side and thrust his sword back and up. The blade punched into the creature's back and burst from its chest. He released his hold, turned, and yanked his weapon free. Another swing severed its head.

As the lifeless body collapsed, a force plowed into Drakon. He crashed to the ground. The breath exploded from his lungs, and he smacked his head against the unforgiving rock. Drakon wheezed, tiny black dots floating across his vision. A wailer rose over him, maw dripping with blood-tinged saliva. Its jaws opened, readying for the strike. Drakon struggled to lift his sword up in time, but it was too late.

The creature snapped steel-trap teeth at Drakon's face. Then a staff swung into view, thwacking against the beast's temple, and deflecting the bite. Another blow sent the animal sprawling. Eza stepped into sight and brought her stick down on the downed wailer's skull. The head shattered in a spray of crimson and gray gore.

She glanced down at Drakon, her eyebrows raised and a smirk on her lips. She reached a hand out to him. He took the offering, and she yanked him to his feet.

"Perhaps Umgar should guard you," she said. Then she turned and charged to the aid of two men battling a wave of nobles.

If Drakon wasn't so grateful to be alive, he might have been embarrassed. But, where was Umgar? He was supposed to be with Eza. Drakon scanned the battlefield.

He spotted the enormous wailer first. It stood behind the attacking creatures. Its presence itself wasn't what arrested Drakon's attention. Larger alphas mixed with their smaller brethren across the courtyard. However, this wailer was familiar...

An unusual mop of dirty blond hair hung across its face.

It was the wailer from the Darklands. The one that had spoken to him and led him into a trap. As if feeling his gaze, the creature turned and locked eyes with him across the melee. Its fevered, amber eyes flared. It bared its teeth. Yellow viscous liquid dripped from its fangs onto the struggling man pinned beneath it.

Drakon's eyes followed. Cold fingers of dread tightened around his chest. He was running before his mind could give conscious thought to the action.

Umgar. It had Umgar. Drakon elbowed through the defensive line, hacking and slashing creatures foolish enough to try to stop him. He was only a few steps away, but he couldn't move fast enough.

The wailer opened impossibly wide jaws and clamped down into Umgar's shoulder. Blood spurted. A scream drowned the sound of battle. Distantly, Drakon realized it was he who screamed, but the fact didn't linger long in his psyche. On reflex, he unleashed his power. The force raced forward, dislodging and launching the creature into a stalagmite.

The wailer rose on unsteady feet and shook its wrinkled head. Its eyes blazed, and it tensed to spring. Hand raised, Drakon sent another blast. It crashed back into the rock, pinned.

Drakon pushed with all the mental force he could muster. The beast bucked against the invisible restraints. Cracks formed in the rock around the struggling wailer's body. Drakon shoved. It screamed. The cracks spread in a spider web up the stalagmite as the creature sank another foot into the stone. Blood burbled from its open mouth and down its pale torso. Yet its evil eyes glared at Drakon.

Drakon released an additional pulse of power, rage fueling him. The stone groaned and crumbled. The wailer's chest caved. Its angry shriek cut off in a wet gurgle. Then its body disintegrated into a red mist that rained to the cavern floor.

Turning his attention back to the general, Drakon saw two warriors, one holding Umgar's shoulders and the other his legs, jogging back toward the city doors. Drakon raced after them, stopping only long enough to dispatch the creatures that got in his way. The Lim defensive line parted like a rushing river around a boulder, allowing Drakon to pass.

His gaze swept the surrounding area for Umgar. Drakon spotted him down the corridor, lying alongside a wall. Eza knelt over him, obscuring his face. Drakon sheathed his sword with trembling hands and hurried to them. Around him, the sounds of battle continued, and someone shouted for a retreat. The doors banged closed behind him, but the chaos fell away as Drakon weaved through the current of Lim toward his friend.

He focused on the prone body, his stomach rolling and his heartbeat sluggish as if it would stop at any moment. Drakon sank to his knees beside Eza and got his first view of the spymaster.

He groaned. Umgar's face was scrunched in pain with his eyes squeezed shut. Sweat beaded his brow. Blood spilled from punctures in his shoulder, painting the floor crimson beneath him and pooling around Eza's and Drakon's knees. Yellow pus bubbled and sizzled in the torn flesh—*venom*. Drakon had noticed it dripping from the alpha's mouth before it attacked.

Eza's hands glowed where they rested on Umgar's torso in a vain attempt to heal him; already, grayish-yellow tendrils snaked out from the wound. They spread under his flesh toward his neck and chest like earthworms through the soil.

Umgar's eyes opened into pained slits. His glossy gaze locked on Drakon.

"It was—"

A scream ripped from Umgar as pain undulated through him. His body stiffened, his back rose momentarily before collapsing back to the floor, listless.

Drakon squeezed Umgar's forearm. "Conserve your energy. I'm going to find help."

He looked at Eza. She removed her hands from Umgar and shook her head. Drakon didn't have to be a mind reader to understand. He could see for himself. The wounds no longer bled, and the pus had cleared, but the toxin continued to advance.

There had to be a way to save him. An antidote. *Something.*

A tug on the hem of his tunic drew his attention down. Umgar held a fistful of the fabric in his hand. Perspiration drenched his face, but his chestnut eyes were alert.

"It was Tobiah. The creature. Spoke to me."

Drakon didn't understand how it was possible. How had the Gathi prince become a wailer? However, now wasn't the time for questions. He nodded.

"I believe you. He's dead now. I killed him."

Umgar smiled, a gesture that was more of a grimace. Another wave of pain cut the action short. Umgar screamed until his voice cracked, and he finally, blessedly, lost consciousness.

An unfamiliar feeling of helplessness settled over Drakon, slumping his shoulders, and bowing his back. The person who had delivered him from slavery was dying an agonizing death.

He didn't know what he could do to stop it, but he owed it to Umgar to try.

"You," he said to a passing warrior garbed in the amethyst of the Tow tribe. "Guard him with your life."

To the woman's credit, she didn't balk at his command. She gave a sharp nod and took up guard beside Umgar, her dark eyes shifting from Umgar to the closed city entrance, where muffled grunts and huffs issued from the other side.

Drakon climbed to his feet, pulling Eza up with him. "Take me to the Oracle."

She hurried beside him. "Why? What're you planning?"

He strode down the corridor, not stopping as he spoke. "I'm not going to let him die. The old woman is going to tell me how to summon Apalsi."

CHAPTER 23

Their pounding footfalls and steady breathing echoed through the empty corridors as Drakon and Eza sprinted for the Oracle's chambers.

"We should go back. Dagoti and the others will need us if the creatures get through," Eza said as she led them down yet another identical passage.

"We are helping them. If you believe your God lives, then it can be reasoned he can be summoned. If Apalsi won't answer the call of his people in a time such as this, is he worth serving?"

Drakon glanced over at her. She was scowling, but she didn't respond. He wasn't a religious man, but he prayed the Oracle hadn't evacuated the city with the young and elderly.

"Are you sure the Oracle is still here?" he asked.

"She wouldn't abandon the tomes. She'd stay and try to hide everything she could. She'll be there."

He gave a short nod, taking the reassurance. They would know soon enough. They turned down a corridor, and an ornately carved door stood closed at the end of the hallway.

When they reached it, Eza banged a fist against the door. "Oracle! It's Eza. Open up. I need your help!"

They waited in tense silence. Perhaps the old woman

was forced to leave with the others? Then there was a click from behind the door, and it swung open with a groan of rusted hinges. The scent of fragrant incense and smoke spilled into the corridor. Gray wisps of hair poked out around a face like dried jerky. The Oracle quirked a white eyebrow and grunted.

"Took you two long enough." She opened the door wider, allowing them to enter. "I'll take you to the place you must seek Apalsi."

Eza's eyes widened, and she gave a slow, disbelieving shake of her head. "It's true? We have possessed the ability to contact Apalsi all this time, and you never told us?"

The ancient Lim waved the accusation away with a gnarled hand. "The option to do so is only for the Nahum, and even then, it is not certain he will succeed, which is the reason I remained here when the others left."

Although he knew of the woman's skill for foretelling, his heart began to race. She had known he would come. *Had she also seen Umgar's fate? Had she told him, Drakon could have commanded him to stay behind. He could have...*

"Do you truly believe you could have stopped him from fighting alongside you? Your guardian is a strong-willed man. He does what he believes is right."

Drakon blinked. The Oracle's milky gaze bore into him. *Had she...*

"I thought you said you couldn't read thoughts, old woman?"

She lifted and dropped a frail shoulder. "I cannot, Nahum. However, when a person feels strongly about something, he or she will project echoes of those things. You feel deep concern about your friend." She hobbled farther into the chamber, her cane clicking a path before her.

Drakon glanced at Eza, and she gave a helpless shrug and hurried after the woman. Rows of bookshelves crammed with tomes lined the walls. On a worktable, bottled herbs and liquids and a dried animal skin lay haphazardly.

A snort drew his attention. The Oracle stood before an archway with her frail arms folded over her thin chest.

"This passage leads to the Holy Place. The essence of Apalsi is greatest within the chamber. If you are to reach him, it will be there."

Drakon stared into the passage, which pulsed with the sapphire glow of the Lim's orb light but saw nothing.

Confusion mounting, he turned to the Oracle and said, "I don't understand. What's through there? I thought you were taking me to summon Apalsi?"

"Bah!" She clicked her tongue in dismissal. "This is something you must do alone. If you come to Apalsi, you must first believe he exists, and he is a rewarder of those who diligently seek him. He will search your heart. Then he will come to you. Or not. Being the Nahum gives you the possibility of summoning Apalsi, not a guarantee."

This was a test of his faith, then? Drakon pondered her words. He had little reason to believe in anyone or anything but his own might during his life.

Had his thoughts changed? Did he believe the God of the Lim existed? Melika and her monstrosities were indeed flesh and bone. Reasoning more than faith dictated her creator was also real. If that logic wasn't enough to convince him, his resurrection from the dead made him a believer. There was a being so mighty, it had loaned Eza the strength to defeat death. That same entity held the key to overcoming Melika and saving Umgar's life…a life that wouldn't be in peril if not for Drakon.

"I believe there must be something to counter the evil of this world." As Drakon spoke, he realized the conviction of the words.

A slow smile spread across the woman's dark face. She pointed to the archway with her cane. "There is more wisdom in you than you can fathom. I am confident Apalsi will find you worthy of the task set before you."

Drakon strode forward but glanced back at the threshold. Eza stood beside the elderly Lim, stroking her ruined pendant, and worrying her lip with her fangs. She offered him a smile that wobbled at the edges. The Oracle shooed him on.

Drakon nodded and stepped inside. The corridor was narrow, but the ceiling was high enough for him to walk without stooping. He followed the throbbing hypnotic light, which brightened as he neared until a small room came into sight.

The chamber was empty with bare stone walls, floor, and ceiling. Drakon cocked his head, letting his gaze sweep the area again. There was nothing, *but then…how was there light?*

"What?" Drakon said as he turned about, taking in his surroundings.

The luminescence seemed to come from the air itself. *What should he do?* Were there words he needed to speak? He hadn't asked the Oracle for instructions; however, given her leaning toward the vague, any words she might have given him would have been laced in mystique and riddle.

He waited for what felt like hours. Nothing happened. He released a breath. Apparently, Apalsi found him lacking. Perhaps there was another way to save Umgar—*maybe one of the many bottles he passed in the Oracle's chamber?* It was worth a try.

He began to turn. Something moved in his periphery. He whirled, curious as to what had caught his attention. At the chamber's center, an iridescent shimmer hovered and undulated a few feet off the floor. The translucent apparition glimmered with luminous colors, rifling through red, orange, yellow, green, indigo, and then violet as Drakon tried and failed to focus fully on it. Whenever he stared head-on at the spectacle, it shifted to the edges of his perception, as though it could be seen only from the peripheral.

Beyond the shimmer, a rainbow of wondrous color danced across the stone wall. Entranced, Drakon strayed closer, his outstretched hand reaching for the edge of the rippling presence. Would it be solid? Liquid? How would it feel against his skin?

An electrifying jolt zinged through his mind at the contact. A caressing shiver ran through his body, carrying along with it feelings of tenderness and weightlessness. The vastness of the entity was instantly apparent. It was unknowable and beyond any comprehension.

"You seek the means to overcome and heal. Noble pursuits both." The words weren't spoken aloud but in Drakon's mind.

After a moment's hesitation, he replied in kind. "Apalsi, I come to you because Melika threatens the Gathi and the Lim. Without the power to stop her, she will succeed in what she attempted many millennia ago."

The apparition took on a deep cobalt coloring. "I regret my neglect fueled Melika's jealousy and misdeeds. She was my first. A child of my heart."

Evident emotion rippled through their connection. Apalsi loved the demon. Loved her still, even after everything.

Responding to his thoughts, the deity said, "Melika is my creation, as are the Lim and Gathi. I cannot harm anything I love. For that reason, I give you this boon."

Before Drakon could respond, a tingling sensation shot up his extended hand, up his arm, and into his body. The feeling dispersed like scattered dust motes in the air of a sunlit room and settled deep into his marrow. He felt too large for his skin, as if this gift from the God expanded his body to the physical limit.

An identical iridescence haloed him. He lifted his hands, turning them this way and that, complete in his enrapture. He could feel the strength coursing through him.

Ever since he was a boy, Drakon dreamed of and pursued great magic. This power, humming through his veins, dwarfed his imaginings.

"I have abdicated a portion of my essence to you and amplified the strength of your blood magic. There is a unique force in you. This is why Melika's abominations would not draw your blood until she instructed them to do so. They sensed a force unlike any they knew and feared it."

Drakon shook his head. "If I've always had this ability, could I've killed Melika in the temple and put an end to this mess before it began?"

Shades of blue and violet flashed across the entity in a violent wave. "No. You had but a fragment of the power you now possess. Had you faced her, you would have been slaughtered. The gift you received cannot be taught in the Gathi wizardry schools or acquired like precious metals or rare jewels. It was given freely. Go. You have all you need."

The ethereal shimmer began to fade, and so too did the mental caress of the presence in Drakon's mind. Panic flared. He hadn't learned how to save Umgar.

"Wait," he said, stepping toward the dissipating haze as if he could physically stop a God from leaving. "My friend. He's been bitten and is dying. How do I save him?"

The apparition continued to wane. Drakon's gut twisted with fear. He had failed Umgar, his only family…

Apalsi's voice sounded across his psyche. "An alpha's venom is the corporeal manifestation of Melika's evil. When she no longer exists in this realm, those poisoned and who have not succumbed to the toxin will recover. Your friend's life is not surely forfeit."

Before Drakon could fully process Apalsi's words, the deity vanished.

The chamber continued to pulse with radiance, but the extraordinary presence that had filled the room was absent. Drakon glanced down at himself once more. He no longer shimmered. Yet, the feeling of fullness persisted.

He received what he came for. Now, there was the problem of killing a demon. For the first time since his journey began, it didn't seem like an impossible task.

ॐ

Laughter and smiles—the kind that bubbled up from true delight and peace of mind and burst from one's mouth—

were rare, foreign emotions to Drakon. Nonetheless, as he reentered the Oracle's quarters, the newfound hope welling within him spilled out into an uncharacteristic grin.

Eza, pacing near the door, dropped her tight grasp on her pendant. The furrow between her large dark eyes smoothed as she noticed him. An answering smile of her own spread across her face. She let out a loud whoop.

"Apalsi be praised!" She rushed to him, her eyes sparkling. "It's done? You summoned him?"

Drakon opened a hand, pooling power into his palm and shaping it with his mind. A sphere of pulsing blue energy materialized. The orb cascaded over itself, pouring down and maintaining its form in a constant cycle of motion and resorption.

He met her gaze. Tears slipped from her eyes, and wet tracks glittered on her cheeks, but her smile didn't falter. Suddenly uncomfortable, Drakon averted his gaze. He clenched his fist. The sphere vanished with a spark.

"I see he found you worthy. That is good."

For the first time since walking into the room, he looked past Eza. The Oracle sat on a stool near a wall. Her pointy chin rested on laced fingers, which gripped her cane. She gave him a wink.

"I never doubted you for a moment. Our God entrusted you with power beyond your imagining. Much is expected of you in return. I will look after Umgar while you do what needs doing. Worry not. He is in good hands."

Drakon didn't exactly have a plan, but he would figure it out. He nodded to the old woman and then hurried through the chamber to the door, Eza trailing him. He didn't know how long Umgar and the others poisoned with the alpha venom had before succumbing to the toxin, but the sooner he killed Melika, the better their chances of survival.

No matter how fast they ran, navigating the streets back to the main entrance would cost time, not to mention the energy they would need in the fight. An idea formed. *Did they have to return the way they had come?*

Melika and the Gathi utilized veils to travel great distances. If the demon's abilities stemmed from Apalsi, then Drakon might be able to generate his own portal.

Eza leaned into his line of vision, and her hand came to rest on his arm. He realized he stood motionless in front of the door.

"What is it?" she asked.

"I'm going to try something."

He placed a hand against the cool door and focused on the pulsating energy within him. The chamber around him fell away. A vision of the Napata gates formed in his mind, and he pushed toward it. Wind swept past him as a ring of fire blinked into existence in place of the door. Drakon smiled as the portal widened until it eclipsed the entirety of the wall.

Then his smile slipped. Unlike the Gathi veils, which were murky and obscured the other end of the connection, Drakon saw clearly to the other side. Wailers and nobles forced their way through the barricaded entrance. Lim fought shoulder to shoulder in the tight corridor. Bodies of enemy and friend littered the ground.

The strangled gasp from beside Drakon registered a second after Eza darted through the portal.

"Eza! Wait!"

It was already too late. She stopped only long enough to

free her staff from the holster on her back and strike a wailer perched on the back of a downed warrior.

Cursing, Drakon unsheathed his sword and followed.

The veil collapsed in his wake. A few strides ahead, Eza vaulted into a possessed noble, knocking it back into the courtyard where Meko's colossal jaws snapped it up. The massive animal launched it over her girth with a flick of her head. The creature shrieks faded as it soared over the rampart and out of view.

A blur of movement caught Drakon's attention. He brought up his sword in time to slice through the wrist of his attacker. The wailer's large pale hand flew free. Blood gushed from the stump. The beast fell with an ear-piercing bellow, clutching its bleeding arm to its chest. Drakon brought his blade down onto its short, thick neck. Its cries morphed into wet gurgles. Drakon swung again. The steel hacked through bone and flesh. The creature's gruesome head rolled to the ground, followed by the thwack of its body hitting stone.

Drakon turned from the corpse. The remaining Lim formed a line pushing the creatures back into the courtyard. He scanned the corridor for Umgar. The dead lay strewed about the floor.

Then he spotted the woman who he had tasked with guarding Umgar. She rested on her side, throat ripped out, eyes glossy in death. The general was nowhere in sight. Drakon's heart raced in the confines of his chest as he scanned the bodies for sign of him.

Dagoti stood ten feet away, shouting orders and slick with gore. Drakon jogged over to him.

"Have you seen Umgar?"

Dagoti spared him a quick glance. "I had him carried into the city when the doors failed. This is no place for the injured."

The release of tension in Drakon's muscles nearly took his legs from beneath him. No matter his feelings toward the man, he was forever in Dagoti's debt.

"Thank you."

Dagoti's lips press together in a tight grimace. "No thanks needed. He has grown on me."

Drakon smirked. "He has that effect on people."

Refocusing on the battle, he stared at the reinstated defensive line the united tribes struggled to maintain. The warriors pushed back claws and teeth with tall rectangular shields. Men and women behind them stabbed down over the human boundary with spears into a surging tide of monsters.

Many Lim remained uninjured and willing to fight, but they couldn't risk trading out with the soldiers comprising the line without fear of a breach. Fatigue would eventually crumble the defensive measure. It was only a matter of time before someone collapsed and the creatures surged forth again.

Drakon recalled how Eza had dispatched the river phantoms. *Could he do the same to these beasts?* It was worth a try. He summoned his power. It was the antithesis of these monstrosities. Light and goodness versus darkness and evil. More than adequate to repel and destroy. The energy's purity surrounded Drakon, begging for him to release it.

He obliged.

An explosion of energy burst from him, rushing

through the Lim, and crashing into the attacking creatures. Their screeches of agony echoed throughout the cavern. They crumpled and writhed as if fire engulfed them. And perhaps it was an accurate description.

Luminescence coated them, outlining the figures sprawled like Autumn leaves over the ground. Fumes rose, and the forms shrank in on themselves. The awful stench of burning meat caused him to gag, and he covered his nose and mouth in the crook of his arm.

Finally, the light waned. In the aftermath, smoking piles of sticky grayish-white substance spotted the cave floor in the place of the monsters.

A bark of laughter sounded beside Drakon. He turned to see Dagoti sheathing his sword, a broad grin on his face. The man lifted a large shoulder in a shrug.

"It seems you are the Nahum." He inclined his head to Drakon. "I stand corrected."

CHAPTER 24

Umgar's chest heaved in quick, shallow breaths in a fitful, unconscious rest. Sweat beaded his face and drenched his garments as if fighting the toxin wrung every ounce of moisture from his body. Grayish-yellow tendrils snaked over his exposed skin like poisonous vines sucking the life from him. Wrinkles Drakon never noticed before lined the general's face from the constant suffering.

Drakon shifted from his perch on a stool beside the bed. He took a cloth from the bedside table with trembling hands and wiped the man's face and neck. Returning it, he tugged the thin coverlet lower around Umgar's waist in a vain attempt to make him more comfortable.

How long did he have left to live? A few days? A week? If he didn't find and kill Melika soon, Umgar would die. Their force was to leave as soon as provisions and weapons were made ready. It wasn't soon enough.

He stared down at the man who was more a father to him than he had ever allowed himself to acknowledge or accept... Too afraid of the perceived weakness the emotions stirred in him.

Drakon always admired the man who had taken him in, paid for his freedom, and trained him to protect himself. Somehow, Umgar also convinced King Ewen to allow Drakon to enter the Royal Assassin competition after the previous assassin died. He smiled bitterly at the memory of how angry and betrayed he had been when he found out what Umgar had done. After years in Umgar's care, he began to feel, if not safe, content. He started to hope Umgar would let him stay.

Drakon let out a disgusted sigh. Foolish dreams. Umgar wasn't much older than himself. The general had done his best, even relaying information to Drakon to assist on many of his missions. He often pondered whether Umgar had developed his intricate spy ring for that reason.

A groan drew Drakon back to the present. Umgar's body tensed as tight as a bowstring, and he began to convulse. The coverlet spilled to the floor. Drakon grabbed the writhing man's wrists, pressing them into the bedding and pinning Umgar's flailing legs with one of his own. The cords in the man's neck tightened before he released a scream of utter agony.

Umgar tore his arm free and began clawing at the healed punctures in his shoulder as if trying to dig out the poison. Drakon recaptured the wrist and forced it back to Umgar's side.

Drakon turned his head and shouted toward the doorway. "I need help! And bring bindings!"

Seconds later, Eza entered with a length of white material in her hands.

"Hold his arms to the side of the bed. I'll bind him to the frame."

Drakon did as instructed. She laid across Umgar to still him enough to tie him, but she made quick work of securing his wrists and ankles. All the while, the man continued to scream, his large body thrashing and tugging against his bonds.

"Help him," Drakon said. His voice cracked. "Please."

Eza squeezed his hand and gave an understanding nod. Her tone was gentle when she spoke. "I'll do what I can to make him comfortable."

Umgar's head tossed against the pillow, but she gripped his face, holding it in place. He wailed louder still, his voice raspy and hoarse from the shrieking. The healing glow seeped from her palms into him like a full-body balm. The radiance haloed him before soaking into his skin.

Umgar released a ragged sigh and sagged into the bed. His breathing slowed and deepened, and he took on the impression of restful slumber. A quiet exhale escaped Drakon, and he briefly closed his eyes. It was nearly unbearable to watch the once-strong, vital man this way.

Eza straightened and turned to Drakon, her eyes alight with an emotion he couldn't name. Before he could comprehend her intent, she strode over and wrapped her arms around him. The tightness in his chest loosened at the contact. He hadn't known how much he needed comfort from another person until now.

He brought up stiff arms and returned her embrace, resting his chin atop her silky locks. How long they stayed there, holding each other at the bedside of his adoptive father, he didn't know, but when she broke away, the situation didn't seem entirely hopeless. And that development was as shocking as the hug.

Eza reached up and swiped a finger across his cheek. When her hand came away wet, Drakon blinked dumbfounded. He raised his own hand to his face.

He wiped more wetness away. Tears.

The last time he could remember crying was the morning he met Umgar. Drakon had stood, trembling and sobbing, before a younger version of the general. Umgar, massive in stature even then, had sat at a table, his morning meal spread before him. He had asked Drakon to join him, and although Drakon had been afraid, his empty stomach hadn't let him refuse the meal. They had eaten in silence until Drakon's stomach had become stretched with food for the first time in his life.

Drakon squeezed his eyes shut, pushing away the memory. More tears slipped free, and he quickly brushed them away.

He cleared his throat, feeling awkward, and didn't look at Eza as he said, "Thank you." He nodded toward the resting Umgar. "For everything."

"Of course. I'll always do what I can to help you." The *"because you are my mate"* remained unspoken, but he heard it all the same.

Their bond bothered him less than it had a few hours ago, and that alarmed him. He stepped around her and strode to Umgar's bedside. He stooped to retrieve the coverlet from where it had fallen and repositioned it over the sleeping man.

"Do you think he'll be all right here when we leave? Perhaps you should stay with him to ensure he and the others don't worsen."

She made a dismissive sound. "I know what you're trying to do. Don't. I'll be going with you. You're going to need me and every other able-bodied fighter. The Oracle can keep him comfortable until you do what needs to be done."

He glanced at her. "Surely, she isn't superior to the

healer?"

"No, but she's the best we have after myself, and since I'm going with you, she'll have to suffice. I can't heal him or any of the others. My gift and fighting skill will be better utilized on the battlefield."

He grunted in concession and refocused on Umgar. For the moment, Umgar was resting. They should do the same.

"We have but a handful of hours remaining before we attend the burials and I attempt to take our force through the Glens. We should rest," he said, leading her from the room.

Eza nodded grimly but didn't comment on the upcoming funeral ceremony. She was quiet and reserved on the subject, and Drakon didn't want to press.

They trekked through the corridors, coming across a handful of Lim, before Eza asked, "Will you create another portal? Do you believe you'll be able to get through?"

He gave her a sidelong look. Her face was cast in shadows from the orb light. "I can only try, but I think it will work. A man is awaiting us on the other side. If I focus on him, I'm certain I can open a veil to his location. We'll need him and the force he's gathered if we are to stand a chance against the demon."

Eza was silent for a long moment. Then she slid her hand into his and squeezed.

"If you believe it will work, then so do I, and Apalsi will be with us also," she said.

Drakon could still feel the power the deity had gifted him. Its thrumming presence was a constant reminder of his upcoming and inevitable clash with Melika. Furthermore, from his recent encounter with Apalsi, he suspected the God wouldn't be providing them with any more aid.

The rest, whether they triumphed or failed, was in their hands.

ॐ

Towering, obsidian statues lining the tunnel peered down at the silent funeral procession, their massive forms flickering in the sapphire orblight. Their sightless eyes followed the mourners as the group trudged down the cobblestone path, descending deeper into the catacombs.

Intricate carvings and sprawling murals decorated the walls and ceiling. Beauty surrounded them, but grief was a palpable weight around their necks, pulling faces toward the ground and bowing backs.

Everywhere Drakon looked, people stared down, focusing on their next step. Bandaged warriors, many held up on the shoulders of their brethren, hobbled along with stiff, pain-filled gaits.

There had been so much death, and there was no end in sight. The thought saddened Drakon. The Lim suffered enough in the savage netherworld they called the Darklands, but what was the alternative?

This was war. War was hell.

The shaft opened into a cavern with a ceiling disappearing into shadow. The procession filed inside, laying the dead—wrapped in white linen—in rows at the center of the chamber. Numerous tunnel entrances sprouted from the immense space, leading to what Drakon assumed were individual tombs. Each tribe branched off into formations with its leader at the helm. Zar Hazor, Eza, and the Oracle split from the Napata tribe and stood to face the assembly, leaving Dagoti with their people.

Most of the Lim remained at the gates to hold off further attacks and prepare for the journey to Somorrah; however, more than a hundred tear-streaked faces waited for the Zar to speak.

Drakon took up sentry against a wall, watching the overwhelming number of women, children, and elderly gathered.

Various symbols of their tribes were painted on their faces with a paste made from the luminescent moss. Drakon too was marked with such an emblem. The Napata tribe crest.

Glancing back up front, Drakon noticed the Zar scanning the crowd. *Who was he searching for?*

The man's gaze stopped on Drakon, and he gestured for Drakon to join them. Eyes widening, Drakon glanced at Eza. She gave a nearly imperceptible nod. He had his marching orders then. He pushed from the wall, aware of the eyes on him, and took up a position beside Eza.

Only then did the Zar speak, his deep voice carrying over the multitude and shifting their attention from Drakon.

"In this solemn time, we gather here to return our fallen brothers and sisters to the waters of eternity. Back to Apalsi's waiting embrace."

He nodded toward the rows of bodies between himself and the crowd. "During such times, when death comes and snatches away with quick efficiency, not the old and long-lived, but the young, we often wonder...Why? Why did they not have more time? Why the sacrifice and pain? I wish I could say with certainty the reason, but I do not have the answer."

He paused, allowing the weight of his gaze to travel over the throng. "However, there is one truth I hold in my heart. It is that we are not mere specks in this world, floating aimlessly on a breeze. Our essence is connected to and a part of something immensely bigger than our individuality. Apalsi is the tree, and we are the branches that sprout from him. We find comfort in knowing that when we are freed of our earthy bodies, we return to the creator, leaving behind our legacy and our energy to become nourishment to those remaining.

"As a people, we have suffered more than many could bear. A curse poisoned our land and forced us beneath the earth. Yet, we did not die as the enemy hoped. We persevered and eked out a life with our blood, sweat, and tears. We thrived in a world not made for us. And do you know why?"

His lone eye scanned the crowd again as if waiting for someone to answer the rhetorical question. "We flourished because of our unwavering faith in Apalsi and our stubborn audacity to survive! Our brothers and sisters gave their lives that we might do more than merely exist but have an opportunity for a better future."

His voice broke on the last word. He took a steadying inhalation, wiped moisture from his eye, and continued. "In life, there is a time for all things. There is a time to weep and a time to laugh. A time to mourn and a time to dance. A time to be born and a time to die. Although the time and place of our final breath are unknown, we know with certainty the day of our deaths is inevitable. Death is the great equalizer of all. No one, young or old, rich or poor, can escape its grasp.

"So, let us live a life worthy of the legacy we will eventually leave behind—one of selflessness, service, and unshakable faith that we are but pieces to a bigger whole. Because of the sacrifice of those laid out before us, we live. We will use the chance they have given us to fight the evil threatening our people."

Drakon listened, enraptured by the Zar's speech. Amid his evident pain, the Lim leader found the words to uplift and motivate his people. It was no less than inspiring.

Feeling a shift in the atmosphere, Drakon focused on the assembly. The crestfallen expressions were replaced with resolve and determination. Even the children, holding tight to their parents' hands with chubby fingers, stood shoulders back, chins held high with a sense of pride and purpose Drakon never witnessed among the Gathi.

The Lim had been victimized and banished, but despite it all, their culture displayed more humanity than Drakon's people, who were afforded the advantages of fertile land and sunlight. Even the way the Lim respected the dead was unheard of in Somorrah. To the Gathi, burial was a necessity to avoid the illnesses that spread when corpses rotted in the streets. Only those of the nobility received religious burials. Everyone else was dumped like waste into the overcrowded graveyards in the Commoner District.

Drakon doubted commoners believed anything other than oblivion awaited them after death. For his people, the end of this mortal existence promised a long-awaited rest from a lifetime of servitude. He always thought it would be enough. But hearing the Zar speak, for the first time in

Drakon's life, he longed for more. A connection to something greater...

Stealing a glance at Eza, he noted her rigid posture. She stared ahead, unblinking with her face set in an emotionless mask. Nevertheless, her large eyes glistened like black onyx with unshed tears, and a slight tremor ran down her arms into the fists held at her sides.

If Drakon learned nothing during their time in the Darklands, it was that Eza possessed a unique inner strength. Still, everyone had their breaking point. He feared she was nearing hers.

Without giving himself time to think, Drakon shifted closer and took her hand. She stiffened, and the heat from her gaze bore into the side of his face. He focused on the crowd, even as warmth climbed up his neck and crept over his cheeks. He couldn't look at her. If he did, he would pull away.

After what seemed like an eternity, she squeezed his hand and leaned into him. The silent acceptance of his awkward attempt at comfort made his unease bearable.

Suddenly, the Zar's voice rose in pitch and intensity, and Drakon's attention was drawn back to the proceedings.

"Now, our brethren will lend us their light," the Zar said, raising his hands. "As we send them back to Apalsi and thank them for their sacrifice."

Drakon watched with fascination as sapphire orbs lifted from the bodies and coalesced overhead in a sphere of pulsating energy. He shielded his eyes with a hand, enraptured by the sight, his lips parted, unable to look away.

Then the orb erupted in a silent explosion, sending the chamber into a whiteout. Drakon squeezed his eyes shut, tucking his face beneath a raised arm, retinas burning. Seconds passed before he blinked open stinging eyes. He lowered his arm.

Sparkling sapphire powder fell. Lifting a hand, he caught some of the curious substance in his palm. It illuminated the skin before sinking in and disappearing. *Wondrous.*

All around him, the dust haloed the Lim and was absorbed into their bodies. He glanced down at Eza, a question in his eyes, but she only gave him a faint smile and gestured toward her father, who peered over at Drakon.

"Energy cannot be destroyed. It merely changes form. Their strength now resides in us," the Lim leader said, answering Drakon's unvoiced inquiry.

Drakon nodded, understanding the sentiment, and the Zar turned back to address his people. "Now, let us lay our brothers and sisters to rest, each tribe for its members, and always remember death is but a portal to life eternal."

With that, warriors collected their dead and started down various tunnels, their leaders, and families in tow. Drakon released Eza's hand and started to follow the Napata tribe, but she grabbed his arm. He turned and regarded her with a raised eyebrow.

"Thank you." Her smile was soft and sincere. "I know comforting me couldn't have been easy for you, but you did it anyway. I want you to know I'm grateful."

A lump hardened in Drakon's stomach, and he gave a sharp nod before glancing at the disbursing crowd. "It was nothing. We should hurry after—"

His wandering gaze locked with a pair of eyes stretched wide enough for Drakon to see the whites around the irises from across the distance.

Khell stood before the dark mouth of a passage. Nostrils flaring, the tribal leader's clawed hand gripped the hilt of the sheathed dagger. Drakon followed the man's gaze to where Eza's hand rested on his arm. When he glanced back up, Khell had disappeared into the tunnel.

Umgar's warning about the jilted man resurged, carrying with it a fresh wave of hopelessness at his mentor's condition. Gentle pressure on his forearm pulled him from the depressing thoughts. Eza scanned his face with a furrowed brow.

"You look pained. I saw Khell as well. Try not to let him bother you," she said, misreading the extent of Drakon's worries. "I will speak with him."

Drakon shook his head. "No. It's nothing. I can handle Khell if the need arises."

Eza worried her bottom lip with a fang, clearly wanting to argue but then inclined her head and released him.

"If that's your wish. Wait for me for a moment? I want to check on Sage before we leave."

Drakon nodded, and she hurried over to where Sage stood over the body of her brother, Vage. Eza gathered the grim-faced woman in a tight embrace, rubbing her back and whispering in her ear. The tribal leader nodded blankly and stepped from Eza's arms, motioning for two warriors to lift the body before disappearing with her tribe down a tunnel.

"We are almost ready for the journey to Somorrah."

Drakon whirled around as Dagoti approached. "After the burials, I would like you to check the supplies to ensure we have everything needed for the surface," Dagoti added when he reached Drakon.

"Of course."

Dagoti frowned. "Are you sure you can get us through the barrier?"

Drakon watched Eza make her way back to him, her face solemn but hopeful. The question was one Drakon had pondered many times. He believed he could open a veil to Somorrah. There was no other option for him to save Umgar and both their worlds. He would get them through the Glens if it were the last thing he did.

"It won't be a problem," he said, hoping he hadn't lied.

CHAPTER 25

Two thousand warriors stood in formation outside the Napata City gates, supplies, and weapons in hand. They had gathered the bodies of their fallen comrades after the attack, and the soldiers had scrubbed away the mounds of wailer and possessed noble goo.

Still, hard-to-reach dried blood remained among the cracks of the courtyard as a reminder more death would follow.

Eza watched as four out of the five tribal leaders rallied their warriors for the journey.

Aros of the Pago tribe and Null, Khell's second-in-command, were in the infirmary healing from serious injuries sustained during the battle. She had tended to their many lacerations and bruises between visits to Umgar. Their injuries weren't life-threatening, thankfully, but they would need days of rest before recovering.

The same couldn't be said of Vage, twin brother to Sage of the Hirane tribe. A wailer had torn half his throat away, and he died in his sister's arms. Eza scanned the faces for the tribal leader. The female stood at the front of her warriors with drooping shoulders and a bowed spine. Her red and watery eyes stared from a distant, expressionless face. Eza wondered, not for the first time, whether it would be merciful to leave Sage behind. In her current state of mind, she might become a liability to herself and others on the battlefield.

"Daughter."

She turned to see her father striding toward her. He gripped her hands in one calloused palm. His face creased with worry as he stared down at her.

"What I would not give to be whole again, so I might see our people through the battles ahead. I do not know what lies past this point, but I know you are the best person to lead."

Eza flushed under his praise. "Thank you, father. I won't let you down. I'll guide the Malachi—"

He shook his head. "I do not only speak of our warriors."

She followed his gaze to where Drakon paced alone a distance off, a strained look on his face.

"He is unaccustomed to leading, but I raised you to take on such a role. This," her father waved a hand at the soldiers surrounding them. "Will be a challenge for him. You are in a unique position to guide him. Help him as only a bonded can."

"You know I'll do what I can."

"That is all I can ask."

He smiled and enveloped her in a hug. Eza clung to him, trying not to think about the possibility of this being the last time she saw him. She squeezed him harder. All too soon, he pulled away. His lone eye twinkled with unshed tears, and he cocked his head toward Drakon.

"You should go to him."

She nodded, gave her father a kiss, and strode over to Drakon. He stopped his pacing as she stepped into his path, his hazel eyes focusing on her.

"Everyone is ready?" he asked.

"Yes. We're waiting on you."

Drakon glanced over her shoulder at the males and females awaiting his orders.

"Then let us go—"

Suddenly, a pebble rained from above, bounced off the ground, and came to rest at Eza's feet. Before she could glance up, Meko landed beside them with an earth-shaking crash.

Eza groaned. She forgot to have the tobali lured into the Darklands while she left. The gargantuan animal strode toward her and nuzzled her shoulder.

"Apparently, she is also ready for the journey." Drakon's voice held a hint of a smile, although it didn't broadcast on his face.

"Well, she's not going." She pushed away Meko's giant maw as the tobali tried to lick her face.

Drakon eyed Meko with interest. "It will be useful to have her with us. She's a formidable fighter and ally. A pity we don't have a hundred more of her kind. Besides, I have a feeling she wouldn't take the news of being left well."

He was right, of course. In any case, she didn't have time to convince the strong-willed Meko to stay. The tobali could take care of herself, and Eza would feel safer with her companion near.

She stroked Meko's rough snout and glared into her golden serpentine eyes. "Fine. You can come, but don't eat anyone unless I tell you to."

Meko huffed as if offended and licked Eza's face. A moment later, they trailed Drakon back to the expectant Lim warriors.

Drakon cleared his throat and addressed the crowd. "I will open a portal to Somorrah. Doing so is the only way I believe we can cross the Glens. Once the connection is made, proceed through one tribe at a time. Napata will go first."

Without another word, he turned and raised his hands. Wind rushed through the cavern, whipping Eza's tunic about her. The fine hairs on her body lifted, and a ring of fire blinked into existence before them. A collective gasp rippled through the crowd like a rock tossed into a river. Images unlike anything Eza had seen came into focus on the other side.

Behind her, the Lim, able to see the sights, glanced around and fidgeted. Nervous energy began to spread from the front of the assembly to the rear. She had to act fast before fear took root. She did the only thing she could in the moment and marched past Drakon and through the portal into the unknown.

Light engulfed her, disorienting her. Eza shielded her eyes from the burning glare shining overhead. A warm breeze licked her skin, and she eased her hand down and forced her eyes open. Tears gathered and leaked down her cheeks. The pain was almost unbearable.

She turned her back to the bright sphere in the sky and took in her surroundings. Blurred olive and brown objects wavered into focus. Bizarre, tall ferns grew from the ground. She bent and traced a finger along a blade of peculiar green hair sprouting underfoot. Flexible. She tugged a piece free, smelled it, popped it in her mouth, and promptly spit it out. *That was foul.*

A gush of wind blew past, and she turned toward the portal. Meko, Dagoti, and the Malachi stepped from the gateway, ducking their heads, and shielding their eyes. More warriors came through and instantly repeated the gesture.

The Malachi leader made his way to her. His eyes squinted from either the light or anger. Probably both.

"Do you ever think before you act? What if more of those wailers were waiting here? You should've sent me ahead first."

"I do, and nothing was here. Therefore, we're not going to squabble over the hypothetical."

She ignored his muttered oath and surveyed their surroundings as best she could. They stood inside a topless cavern. A massive rock face, so tall Eza couldn't make out its peak, rose to their east. Brown staffs with mossy green tops towered above them.

"What a strange land," she said to herself. To Dagoti, she said, "Have the Malachi create a protective perimeter."

Although she knew he was still angry with her, he began relaying the command. After a few minutes, males and females from every tribe crowded the clearing. No one else came through.

Eza waited a few more moments for Drakon. When he didn't appear, she jogged back to the gateway before she could think about what she was doing. He should've come through already. She gazed into the opening, but from this side, it was like staring into a stream murky with stirred-up silt.

The gate began to shrink, pulling in on itself.

Panic gripped her. "Wait!" She raced toward the

shriveling ring of flame and slammed into a figure as it stepped out.

Drakon let out an "oof" as the air was knocked from him. His hand went to his sword, and his eyes scanned the area for a threat. Seeing none, he glanced down at her, a question in his eyes. Eza's face and the tips of her ears heated. Anyone within earshot had heard her shout and had seen her rush him.

She stepped back and gave a strained laugh. "I thought—maybe you were in trouble. You took longer than expected to come through."

He studied her as if trying to discern the truth through her pores. She fought the urge to squirm under his scrutiny.

Drakon finally released her from his intense glare and said, "I'm fine."

Mercifully, he changed the subject. "Crain is nearby. I used him as a focal point." He glared up toward the ball of radiate light in the sky, a line forming between his drawn brows. "The sun will set soon. We'll need fires along the perimeter to protect the camp from wailers. I don't know what effect, if any, the fire will have on the possessed nobles, however."

"Ho!"

The call echoed across the clearing, making its direction impossible to pinpoint. Eza pulled her staff free and searched for the source of the sound. Rocks skittered down the rock face, and she looked up.

A score of people stood along a ledge twenty feet above them. Paint covered their dark brown faces and bodies. Odd skins of fluffy material draped their frames, and they held an array of weapons. Then one of the figures laughed, the sound full of relief and mirth.

"Deathmark? Is that you?"

ಬಌ

Apparently, the portal had been visible from the village, and the Wild Gathi had come to investigate. The male, who Eza learned to be Captain Crain of the Royal Fighters, had been jovial and upbeat until Drakon shared news of Umgar's condition. From Crain's downcast features and reserve, his closeness with the man was unmistakable.

At present, she, Drakon, and Crain sat in a large house awaiting the Wild Gathi leader. A fire blazed in a hearth, combating the chilly night air, and providing lighting. Smoke rose and vanished through ventilation above the mantle. Eza ran a hand over the soft, fluffy skin cloak the Wild Gathi had given her—the temperature was much cooler in the mountains than in the valley. She lifted the garment and stroked it against her cheek. *Wondrous.* It was the softest material she ever felt. More of the peculiar fabric covered the pillow in which she sat.

"It's called fur."

Eza jerked the cloak away from her face like a child caught sneaking sweet bread. She glanced in the direction of the voice. Drakon stared at her. Sweat beaded his forehead, and dark smudges cradled his eyes, but his hazel gaze twinkled with inner mischief and the corner of his mouth twitched. *So, he was laughing at her?*

She smoothed the material back in place, pretending she hadn't been cuddling up to it mere seconds ago.

A tall and toned female ducked through the doorway.

The joviality vanished from Drakon's face, and he turned to the newcomer. She was older, perhaps in her late fifties, but her muscles were well-formed under her fur leggings. Her eyes scanned the room, searching for something. They widened when she spotted Drakon.

"You look so much like her." She took a few steps toward him but stopped when she noticed his rigid posture and scowl.

"Do I know you?"

"No." The female shook her head, the smile slipping from her face. She moved to a vacant spot and eased down on a pillow. "I am Taru. Your mother was my sister."

Drakon didn't blink at the revelation. His handsome face revealed no emotion. "Is that so?" His voice was low, cold.

The female appeared bewildered at his lack of reaction. A pained expression settled on her face. "Yes. I regret we could not bring you to our home."

"Regret changes nothing."

His words drained the blood from Taru's face, transforming her dark brown skin to a grayish hue. If Drakon noticed, he didn't show it. Instead, he continued speaking in an aloof manner.

"I care not of our familial ties. The only matter of import is whether the Wild Gathi will join us in ridding Somorrah of Melika's evil. All other matters can be left in the past."

Taru crossed arms over her chest and nodded slowly, her eyes no longer meeting Drakon's gaze. "I see. Well, in that case...Yes, we will join you. What is your plan?"

"We will head directly to Sura, which is the seat of Melika's power. Although I would prefer stealth, it will be impossible with a force of this size. The wailers and possessed nobles also roam the lands. They will notify Melika as soon as we're a few days from the city. Therefore, I suggest a frontal assault during the day when the wailers are unable to operate. That way, a good portion of her army will be neutralized. Any other—"

An uproar sounded outside. Taru leaped from her seat and hurried out the door. After a short glance at each other, Eza, Drakon, and Crain followed her into the crisp night. A group of Wild Gathi males stood speaking at once.

"Silence," Taru said. Everyone fell silent and stared sheepishly at her. She pointed at a broad male who was nearly as dark-skinned and tall as a Lim.

"What has happened?" she said.

"Erlik found a trespasser on the mountain. We were coming to inform you, but the guard wouldn't let us pass. He's on the way with her now."

As if in response, a male marched up the trail into the village. He dragged, half carried, a tiny, peculiar female with white hair and skin and faint tattoos covering her face. She was the strangest thing Eza had seen since arriving in Somorrah and reminded her of the blind fish that lived in the Darklands rivers and lakes.

Crain gasped. "Fynna?" He hurried to grab her from the male and steadied her.

Erlik wiped his hands on his leathers, a look of disgust on his face. He nodded toward the captain. "She's alive because she said she knew you. Is this the mage you told us about? The one who is supposed to help us defeat Melika? If so, she doesn't look like she's too long for this world, let alone up to a fight."

Fynna's unusual dark blue eyes landed on Eza and widened. Then her gaze traveled to Drakon, who stood silent and frowning down at the pale female.

Fynna gave a high-pitched, hysterical laugh. "You did it! You crossed the Glens." Tears streamed from her eyes, etching trails down her beautiful, grimy face. "Perhaps there's a chance for us after all."

At their mutual looks of confusion, she continued, "Ewen is dead. It's been Melika all along. She isn't the goddess we believed. She's a monster. A creature. She's killed the mages loyal to our cause and vanished with Nolan. I don't know if she can be destroyed, but perhaps it's possible with the Lim. We can but pray."

Then she dissolved into sobs.

CHAPTER 26

The stench of smoke and death drifted on the hot afternoon breeze. The blackened ruins of Senna reached up to the blue sky from scorched earth like broken, gnarled fingers. Drakon stared up at the crumbling gates, Lieutenant Joah at his side.

"This destruction is a few days old. Not even a smolder remains, and the blaze would've been visible for miles," Joah said.

He sank to his haunches, his keen eyes examining the road. He placed a hand in the dirt, running his fingers through it and likely noticing clues only an expert tracker could perceive.

"See these marks?" He pointed to indentations in the dirt. "Several people made it out on foot and headed west. Probably to the Waystation between Senna and Sura." He stood and wiped an arm across his sweaty forehead.

Drakon and Joah scouted ahead of the group, which had stopped to set up camp a few miles to the east. Initially, Drakon suggested he scout alone. In truth, he desired solitude from Taru's attentions, and he didn't trust himself around Fynna. She was culpable in Nolan's scheme to have him killed along with the High Priestess. It was inconceivable Fynna had been the mysterious contact within the palace.

For once, Umgar's intuition had failed. The spymaster

misplaced his hope in her ability to contribute to their cause. If she was to be believed, the evil they wished to confront had decimated the Kingdom's most powerful mages in mere seconds.

Joah waved a hand in front of Drakon's face, and he blinked from his inner ruminations and focused on the man.

"Did you hear what I said?" the lieutenant said. When Drakon didn't answer, he sighed. "I said I think the attack came from within."

He pointed to the symbols etched on the outer walls. "The wards are intact. There's no way the wailers got past them. But see there?" He wagged a finger at where the gate hung outward on rusted hinges.

"Scratches on the interior of the door," Drakon said, noticing scars on the stone but also longer, deeper gashes. Brown stains that could only be blood coated the inside of the doorway and ground as well.

"I think so. The people tried to escape the fire or something else." Joah shook his head. "I don't understand why no one opened the gates."

Memories of Glensbrook crept into Drakon's mind. *Had the people of this city suffered the same fate?* Any Commoners outside the summoning circle would have been food for Melika's growing army.

Dread pooled in his belly. His hand went to his sword. Keeping his head forward, he shot sidelong glances to the shifting shadows of the surrounding forest.

"Joah." His voice was a whisper. "We're going to walk calmly back to our horses and leave."

"Shouldn't we go inside to check for survivors?"

Sweat slipped down Drakon's spine, but it had little to do with the unbearable heat. His instincts were firing, and they were screaming at him to run.

"They're dead, and so will we be if we stay here."

He knew the instant the urgency in his voice registered. Joah stiffened, and his eyes darted from the city to the forest. When Drakon started for their horses, he followed at a clipped pace.

As they swung up into their saddles and steered their mounts around, the first figure bolted out from the cover of the trees. The noble—black eyes wild and hair matted—sprinted, covering the distance in seconds, and leaped for Drakon. He flattened against the horse's mane, allowing the creature to sail overhead and crash down on the other side. Dozens of the monsters poured from the tree line but also from the open city gates.

It was a trap.

Drakon urged his horse into a gallop, and the spooked animal sped away down the road, Joah close behind. He didn't look back, the angry shrieks and hisses of pursuit fading after a few minutes of hard riding. He slowed his mount to a trot but dared not slow further.

Joah rode alongside him. The man's dark face was ashen, and his voice was shrill as he said, "Is it me, or did those things coordinate a trap? I can't believe it."

Neither could Drakon. He had no doubt had they ventured inside Senna to investigate, the creatures would have crept in behind them, cutting off their exit.

"Let's get back to camp as quickly as possible and let the others know what we've seen. It goes without saying that we'll need another route to Sura."

The idea soured his gut. Two days had passed since leaving Umgar. A detour would cost time the spymaster might not have...if he still lived. Drakon pushed the depressing thought from his mind. He avoided using his new-found abilities within the Glens to prevent calling attention to himself, but perhaps it was time.

The ride to camp was silent and prolonged. They doubled back multiple times and traveled a distance in a shallow creek to conceal their trail, but neither saw nor heard any of the creatures. The sun leeched Drakon of strength, and he slumped in his saddle. It was cooler in the mountains, but the heat exacerbated the fatigue that dogged him since leaving Napata. A night of proper rest would help him recover.

Drakon and Joah arrived at the encampment as the sun began dipping behind the trees. They dismounted and handed their horses to a waiting fighter, who led the animals away. A soldier threw a torch into the perimeter trench behind them. The oil at the bottom flared to life and traced a crackling line around the camp, enclosing them until morning.

Drakon strode around the many campsites, heading for his tent. He passed Wild Gathi, Royal Fighters, and Lim eating and conversing in segregated clusters. With the addition of Taru's and Umgar's forces, their numbers swelled, but the three groups were far from united. If they wanted to defeat Melika, they had to work and fight as a unit. How he was to achieve such a goal, he didn't know.

He would ask Eza her opinion. He respected and valued her input on most subjects, and she was better equipped at dealing with personnel matters.

Arriving at his tent, Drakon turned to Joah. "Gather the Captain and tribal leaders and bring them here."

The lieutenant nodded and disappeared into the throng. Drakon parted the canvas flap and ducked inside. He crossed to a table and stared down at the map of Somorrah. With Senna compromised, they needed another route to Sura. Preferably one that didn't tack on another day or more to their journey.

He traced the lines indicating known roads. Detouring to the south around Crystal Lake would add another day and a half and heading north was out of the question. He cursed and slammed a fist against the table. There was no other choice. He would have to create a veil and hope Melika didn't notice the flare of magic and track it to their location. He wanted to confront the demon on his terms, and the element of surprise was an advantage he didn't want to relinquish until the last possible moment.

"I assume from your sour mood, you didn't return with good news."

Drakon looked up. Crain stalked inside. Doyna, Taru, Zemket, and Khell followed.

Khell wore his customary emerald garments and scowl. Drakon's fatigue magnified at the sight of him. God, he hated dealing with the Gnehoon tribe leader. If such a thing was possible, the man's attitude had worsened since leaving his second-in-command in Napata. If Drakon could have excluded the man from the meeting without backlash from Khell's contingent of warriors, he would have.

His gaze drifted to Taru. She gave him a tight smile. "I am glad to see you made it back safely," she said.

The older woman had been saying things of that

nature—nurturing words and showing concern over his person—since their first meeting. It was evident she wanted a more meaningful position in his life, but he couldn't focus on her or their possible familial reconciliation at the moment. Her obvious desire to connect with him did little to ease his discomfort, but he nodded, acknowledging her words, and looked toward the tent entrance. The person he sought was nowhere in sight.

"Where are the others? I'd like to speak with everyone at once. I don't want to repeat myself."

Crain came to stand next to him and glanced down at the map. He raised a questioning eyebrow but didn't voice his question.

"Eza took her odd creature to the lake for a drink and fishing. Thankfully, wailers don't swim and haven't devoured the fish population, or I shudder to think what her beast would eat if it got hungry enough."

Crain shivered, then continued, "Dagoti and the Lim woman, Sage, accompanied them. Joah found us in Fynna's tent. He went straight away to gather the others. They should be here shortly."

"Is the mage recovering?"

Crain frowned and shook his head. "She's getting worse. Fighting a fever and the sweats. Never seen anything like it. Your woman has been trying to heal her, but she says Fynna's strength continues to wane. Fynna might have escaped Melika's spell at the temple, but the demon is continuing to siphon power from her."

Drakon opened his mouth to correct the captain. Eza wasn't his. But at that moment, the remaining members of their group entered with Eza among them, and she hurried to his side.

"Joah said you all found something at Senna?"

"Yes. Do tell. We've been waiting patiently for the Nahum to let us in on his secret," Khell said from his post on the other side of the tent.

Drakon clenched his jaw. He would end up slipping his dagger between the man's ribs before long. Today, however, he pushed past his assassin instincts, ignored the quip, and answered Eza.

"Joah and I scouted north to Senna." He pointed to the area on the map. "The entire city is destroyed but not abandoned. Instead, dozens of the possessed nobles created a trap that, had we ventured inside, would've been disastrous."

Whispers rose within the group, but Drakon continued over the murmurs. "These creatures, unlike the wailers, can function in sunlight. I've searched for alternate routes to Sura. None of them work. They all add a day or more to our travel. Our only recourse is for me to summon another veil to a location near the capital and possibly tip off the demon to our presence."

He dragged his finger across the map to the location of their camp. "From here, I could create a portal within a rock-throwing distance of Sura. Of course, Melika would know we were there, but, at that point, it wouldn't matter. We would be at her doorstep."

Zemket, Taru, and Dagoti crowded around the small table and stared down at the map. Dagoti pointed at the symbol indicating Sura.

"The demon is here, you say?"

Drakon nodded, awaiting the warrior's input.

"Although using the portal would be faster and the best option, coming too close won't give us time for reconnaissance. I'd rather come in farther out and have time to survey the enemy's territory and find out what we're up against than to drop into the unknown," Dagoti said.

Khell huffed and marched over, clearly not pleased with being excluded from the decision-making.

"He's right. It won't matter if you dropped us on the demon's lap if we have no plans on how to get our people out alive. For you, this might be a suicide mission, but for the Gnehoon tribe, it's not."

Drakon's patience snapped like a tightly strung bow. "Never insinuate that I have anything but the best intentions for every person under my command. Nevertheless, only a fool enters a battle without the full awareness it could be his last, but I'm not surprised you're of such a mindset."

Khell swelled with indignation. "Call me what you will, but we all know you're rushing into this because your friend is dying back in Napata. His life is no more important than those we've already lost or any other soldier!"

Drakon's hand was at his dagger without conscious thought, but Eza's hand on his forearm stayed him. He glared at her, but her focus was on Khell.

"As we all know the reason you've been an insufferable brute since meeting Drakon. I was never fond of our match and am less inclined to join with you even if, by some miraculous event, I was free to do so. That said, I suggest you put your petty differences aside, or next time I won't stop him from running you through."

Sage snorted a laugh and covered her mouth with a

hand. If possible, Khell's ebony skin flushed. His fists clenched and unclenched at his sides. Drakon readied himself for the explosion sure to come. However, misfortune arrived and postponed the escalating confrontation.

A young woman, a Wild Gathi if her painted face and the skins draping her large frame were any indication, appeared at the tent's entrance. "Nahum, sorry to interrupt. There was an incident at the perimeter. A few of the creatures injured a woman and took a soldier. We need the healer!"

At once, the tent emptied. Drakon raced behind the soldier, his sword drawn. Night had fallen, and dozens of campfires dotted the encampment. At the edge of the camp, a Lim woman lay sprawled on the ground. Gashes across her chest gushed blood. Moans bubbled up from a bloody mouth. Eza knelt beside the woman, her hands aglow with her gift. In the distance, the screams of the captured man faded away with the snapping of twigs and guttural huffs.

"What happened?" Drakon asked the closest fighter. The man didn't react or appear to hear him. Instead, his bulging eyes stared into the darkness beyond the firelight.

Drakon stepped into the man's line of sight and raised his voice. "What happened?"

The shout jolted the fighter back to the present. He blinked and focused on Drakon with glossy eyes.

"We were patrolling and a group of those creatures... Not the wailers. The ones that were once nobles. They darted from the forest and reached across the flames." He motioned to the shallow trench of fire. "They grabbed Trent and me, but the Lim, she confronted the one that had hold of me. It struck her, dropped me, and ran. But they took

Trent." The man blinked rapidly, his eyes shining with tears.

Drakon turned to address the gathering crowd. "Stay away from the perimeter. They might attempt to grab someone else to draw us into the forest."

Worried faces met his announcement. Tonight would be a long night. He had hoped the blaze would be enough to deter the wailers and the possessed nobles. He had been wrong. It was apparent the creatures didn't have the absolute fear of fire as their brethren. There had to be a way to secure the camp.

Apalsi had gifted him with power. It was time to test his abilities. Drakon turned his mind inward to the force humming inside him. He visualized a barrier. One strong enough to protect them from the wailers and nobles. When the image was clear, he pushed it outward.

Energy burst forth, washing past the stunned onlookers, and encasing the camp in a pulsing indigo shield. Gathi and Lim alike gawked at the spectacle, then back to Drakon with a mixture of awe and adoration. At that moment, they were more united than in the days before.

He cleared his throat and turned. A wide-eyed Crain stared at him as if only now seeing him.

"Don't look at me like that," he said, suddenly exhausted.

The captain shook himself. "In my defense, I witnessed you create a miniature Glens without batting an eye. I'm allowed a moment of wonder."

"Yes. Well, your moment is over. I don't know the strength of the barrier. So, you should still set up a watch just in case."

"Consider it done." Crain turned and began gathering Lim and Gathi, speaking in hurried words.

Unable to withstand the stares, Drakon excused himself and escaped to his quarters. He lowered himself onto his mat with a groan. The nonstop travel of the past weeks was wearing on him. *How many days had passed since his misguided trip to Melika's temple?*

He let out a disgusted laugh. What an idiot he had been. He rolled to his back, watching the moonlight through the canvas, which rippled in a breeze. Sleeping in the heat was near impossible. He sat, removed his damp tunic, folded it, and stuffed it beneath his head as a makeshift pillow.

The entrance flap slapped open. Orb light rose to the tent's center, lighting the area and casting shadows on the thin walls. Eza strode to a basin atop a table, rinsed her bloodied hands, and dried them with a cloth. Inexplicable emotion danced in her eyes. Seeing the wounded Lim must have shaken her. She was a skilled fighter, but he didn't believe she had seen much death until now.

In previous days, she had watched comrades die and had killed creatures she never imagined existed. It was much to process. Eza crossed the space to him, her long muscled legs making short work of the distance. She squatted beside him, her face inches from his own.

Her ruined crystal, the one she had used to save his life and bond them as mates, dangled near enough to touch. A light sheen dotted her ebony skin. She rested her elbows on her bent knees. Her brow wrinkled as her eyes studied his exposed chest. Under her inspection, he felt wholly lacking, and although she had seen his scars and slave brands, they weren't things he wished to showcase. Unable to lie still under her scrutiny, he crossed his arms.

She blinked and met his gaze. "When were you going to tell me of your illness?"

He stiffened. "I'm not ill. I'm tired. That's all."

She clicked her tongue. "I touched your arm during your argument with Khell. I could feel the fever through your sleeve."

Drakon frowned, resisting the urge to feel his forehead to check. "I'll be better once I've rested. Don't worry over it."

Eza reached for him, the indicative glow of her gift spreading throughout her palm, but he captured her wrist.

Her eyes widened slightly. Drakon didn't understand the mechanics of her power, but he knew she recently healed a severe wound, not to mention the time she had spent attempting to cure Fynna.

He wouldn't take more from her. He placed her hand back on her knee.

"Save your strength. If I'm not better by morning, I promise to ask for your help."

He closed his eyes and rested back into his makeshift pillow, avoiding her searching gaze. Her presence lingered near him for long moments, until her footfalls announced her exit. With her departure, the orb light faded and disappeared from the backs of his eyelids, leaving him in darkness. He let out a deep sigh, opened his eyes, and resumed his stare at the ceiling, his mind ablaze with worries.

It was a long time before sleep overtook him.

CHAPTER 27

Melika plowed a path through the dense forest, crashing through the underbrush and snapping limbs. Her children kept pace, leaping from tree to tree or galloping alongside her, ready to protect her with their lives.

Two days ago, she had felt an almost imperceptible echo of Apalsi's essence. The jolt had flashed across her psyche in remembered pain and fear. It dissipated before she could pinpoint its exact position but lasted long enough for her to discern its direction. East.

She traveled via veil to the approximate location of the disturbance but had nearly turned back after days of searching with no other resurges.

But now...now she felt it.

Constant and intense, the creator's power pulsed as a blatant challenge. She sneered, her thin lips exposing jagged incisors. As she closed in on the source of her hatred, the more confident her conviction this new threat was indeed of Apalsi. And a threat it was. Anyone carrying even a remnant of his aura could be nothing but an adversary.

A pulsating dome came into view above the trees. Melika skidded to a halt within the shifting shadows of the tree line. In the clearing ahead, the glowing shield covered a large encampment. She tilted her head toward the familiar magnetic pull.

Yes. This was the source. Yet, she felt but a portion of Apalsi's essence. The only possibility would be if Apalsi abdicated power to the…

Melika stiffened. Impossible. He wouldn't do such a thing. *Would he?*

There was a movement to her right, and she turned toward it. Moonlight danced along the beautiful creamy skin of an enormous alpha as it darted toward the dome.

Before she could summon it back to her, it raised a taloned hand to the glimmering surface of the shield. An eruption sparked, blasting it away. The body landed in a smoking heap. A painful shock jolted Melika the moment its spirit blinked from existence.

A reflexive hiss escaped her lips, and she narrowed blazing eyes at the offending barrier. She would slaughter all under the Nahum's protection this night.

Eza stared in amazement at the charred corpse of the wailer lying on the opposite side of the dome. A few others witnessed the creature's demise and peered out for a closer look.

Smoke drifted from its blackened, flaky skin. Blood bubbled up from cracked and fried flesh, bringing with it the stench of fire-roasted rot. Her stomach churned. She held a sleeved arm to her nose, fighting an involuntary gag, and turned away.

Thank Apalsi for their protection. Even now, amber eyes lit up the forest around them like floating flames. If not for the barrier, they would be overrun. Eza squeezed past the onlookers, walking along the shield's perimeter. Her mind strayed to Drakon, as it had since leaving him to rest.

She noticed the change in him the day they left the mountains. At first, she attributed his ruddy, flushed appearance to the increasing heat. However, as days passed, his sallow, damp skin; the dark circles under his eyes; and his lethargy all pointed to a worsening illness.

His preference for suffering rather than accepting her aid baffled and infuriated her. As her mate, did he not realize his fate was her own? If she didn't know the horrors of his past, she would have Dagoti restrain him while she healed him anyway. But she did know his history, and she could never do that to him.

She sighed and pinched the bridge of her nose. Drakon was stubborn, but she was more so. She would give him until morning to come to his senses. That was as much patience as she could muster...

A sudden chill tickled along Eza's skin. Her scalp prickled, and the fine hairs at the back of her neck lifted. She stopped her amble and turned to stare into the forest. The faint grunts and huffs of wailers and the shrieks of the possessed nobles filled the night. Dozens of amber eyes stared back.

A figure shifted from a crouch and stood. Eza's heart raced. She gulped in breaths like a beached fish as she craned her head upward. A towering creature broke from the trees and crept toward her.

Its carapace was almost indistinguishable from the night cloaking it. Moonlight glinted off its obsidian body as it stopped before the barrier. A long-barbed tail flicked lazily behind it. Fangs the size of forearms protruded from a gaping maw, dripping with saliva. Its amber eyes narrowed, and it growled, the sound rattling through Eza's chest to her bare feet.

Nostril slits in its alien face flared: Once. Twice. A third time.

Was it smelling her?

Then the creature's eyes widened, and a taloned hand struck the barrier in front of her face. Sparks flew. Yet, there was no burned flesh, and the monster stood whole on the other side.

It glanced at its uninjured hand and back at Eza. It cocked its misshapen head and tapped a talon against the wall of power between them, igniting a new flare.

"I." *Tap. Spark.*

"Know." *Tap. Spark.*

"You." *Tap. Spark.*

"Lim." *Tap. Spark.*

The guttural, inhuman voice broke Eza from her paralysis.

"We're under attack! Someone wake Drakon!" she said, drawing her staff and backing away.

The behemoth pressed a hand to the dome, and the shield flared brightly. Squinting, she watched in growing horror as the pulsating energy retreated from the creature's hand, leaving a void that swiftly grew into a breach large enough for the monstrosity to step through. It grabbed for her in an explosion of motion.

She brought her staff down on its wrist. The beast bellowed and swiped again. She slid beneath the blow, coming up between its legs and delivering a strike to its inner thigh.

Eza managed to dive clear as the creature sank to a knee

with a shriek of fury.

"Eza! Watch out!"

Reflexively, she glanced toward the voice and instantly cursed her mistake. She tensed to leap away, but the tail lashed out like a whip, catching her in the side and sending her hurtling into a tent.

Eza groaned. Every inch of her body hurt. Warmth spread down her throbbing right arm. She glanced at it and bit back a moan. Flayed and bloody skin peeked out from her torn tunic. She wiggled her fingers. Pain flared like hot coal beneath her flesh, but, blessedly, she retained movement in the limb.

Shouts and the clanging of steel redirected her attention back to the present danger. Gritting her teeth against the agony, she struggled to her feet, untangled herself from the wreckage, and scanned the ground for her staff. It was nowhere to be found among the debris. She wasn't weaponless, however. She slid a dagger from a sheath at her hip.

Turning, Eza realized she had crashed far from the breach and the sounds of fighting. She broke into a hobbling jog and soon discovered the situation had deteriorated.

Dagoti now battled the behemoth. His sword glinted in the moonlight as he parried attacks, but he was on the defensive, backing toward the hole in the dome. Wailers crept inside and toward Dagoti's back.

Ignoring her pain, Eza placed the dagger between her teeth and charged forward. She planted a foot in a divot in the giant beast's carapace and scrambled up its broad back. It shrieked and shook back and forth to dislodge her. Fire-hot jolts lanced up her wounded arm, and blood slicked her hand, but she held on.

Pulling the blade free, she drove it in the creature's back repeatedly until it finally struck the flesh beneath the shell. It screeched and reared back, grabbing for her. Eza released her hold and attempted to slide out of reach, but its bony grasp plucked her from the air.

It squeezed. Eza screamed as a rib gave way under pressure. The creature lifted her before its face and gaping maw. It was going to bite her in half.

A massive weight landed on the arm gripping Eza. Eza turned to see Meko biting down with all her considerable power. There was a loud crack. Then the beast screamed, dropped Eza, and turned its attention to prying the tobali from its arm.

Eza hit the ground hard and rolled to her back, watching the continuing fight. Meko released the creature and climbed its back, biting and clawing at the shell.

"That's my girl," she said in a moment of pride.

A hand hooked under Eza's arm and hauled her to her feet. She let out a cry as her broken rib protested.

"I'm sorry, but I need to get you out of here."

Dagoti, bloodied and bruised, but looking far better than she felt, lifted her into his arms and hurried in the opposite direction of the raging melee. Sage, Khell, and Doyna jogged alongside, their spears and swords coated with blood. Around them, Gathi and Lim fought to stem the flow of wailers gushing through the breach.

"Once you're safe, Doyna and I will rejoin the battle. Khell and Sage will stay with you."

She began to argue, but an agonized cry drew her short. Dagoti stopped and turned. Eza's chest tightened.

No.

Time seemed to slow as the obsidian beast pinned Meko to the ground on her back and raked a taloned claw down the struggling tobali's belly. Innards spilled to the grass.

Eza watched in growing horror as Meko's golden eyes dimmed and her limp body was flung aside. A sudden cold chilled Eza's core, and her moan of grief swelled into full-fledged hysteria. Tears fell freely. She fought against the hands holding her, the loss washing over her in waves of nausea.

Then she was free and stumbling toward her fallen pet, but Meko's murderer stepped into her path and plucked her once more from the ground.

The demon glared down at her, blood weeping from a clawed eye. "Will the Nahum not save you?"

It turned for the barrier, batting Dagoti and Sage away as they tried to intercept it. Eza's vision blurred. The pain was overwhelming. She didn't know where Drakon was, but she prayed to Apalsi he didn't come.

഍ൠ

A sting catapulted Drakon from a dreamless sleep. Something came toward his face. He reached out, caught the hand, and twisted before the person could land another blow.

"Ah! Let go, man!"

Drakon blinked into complete consciousness. Above him, Crain's face scrunched in pain. He released the captain and rubbed his still tingling cheek.

"What are you doing? I might have killed you."

Crain waggled his injured hand, trying to regain the feeling. He scowled at Drakon. "I had to do something. You wouldn't wake. I tried everything else."

The man stood from his kneeling position next to the mat. He grabbed Drakon's sword from a table and dropped it on the ground beside the prone Drakon.

"Get up! If you hadn't noticed, there's a battle going on around you."

Those words did more to wipe the fatigue from Drakon's fogged mind than the slap. He bolted upright and yanked on his moist tunic. His sleep-muddled thoughts cleared. He felt no better for his rest, but he was exiting the tent, sword in hand, before Crain finished explaining.

Outside, chaos reigned. Campfires crackled, abandoned. Meals lay forgotten and trodden on the ground. Gathi and Lim darted in every direction. Some with weapons, some without. A few, much like Drakon, appeared to have recently been awakened and were in various stages of undress.

Adrenaline lent its energy, and Drakon hurried after Crain as the man dashed past rows of tents, heading toward the west side of the encampment. They ran, no evidence infiltrators made it farther into the camp in sight. His people must be holding them at bay. They might yet salvage the night.

Then they were in the fray. Drakon's eyes drifted over the pale wailers, the Gathi and Lim combating them, and snagged on the gargantuan creature towering over the throng. Its carapace glistened with dark, oily blood. Deep gouges marred its armored body. Cracks spiraled from its wounds like spider webs. Its powerful tail snapped forth, plowing through ally and foe alike.

As if sensing his presence, it turned its amber, malevolent glare on him. Recognition flared in its inhuman gaze. This beast knew him, and, on an elemental level, the power within Drakon discerned a corresponding tie to the creature.

With dawning horror, he realized this was Melika in her true form.

The demon raised a massive hand, and Drakon's heart stammered in his breast. A barely conscious Eza was clutched in its grasp. A skilled, imposing warrior in her own right, she appeared diminutive and delicate in the deadly grip. Her head lolled back on her neck. Ebony braids slid away, exposing a blood-coated and bruised face glistening with fresh tears. A ruined arm peeked from beneath the crimson tatters of her brown tunic.

Drakon swallowed, his throat dry and his sword suddenly too heavy for his numb fingers. He glanced away from the sight, careful to hide his mounting fear under a mask of indifference. He would be damned if he revealed even a hint of her value.

Melika made a huffing sound, and the surrounding wailers halted their attacks and retreated around her taloned feet.

"There he is. Apalsi's precious Chosen One." The demon's mocking tone was a dull blade against his eardrums. It wiggled Eza out toward him like a treat before a trained dog. "I have something belonging to you."

Drakon gritted his teeth but kept his voice flat, nonchalant. "She's no more mine than anyone here. Let her go, and we can finish this."

Melika cocked her head, the human gesture misplaced and awkward coming from the monstrous figure. "Lies." She shifted Eza to her slitted nostrils and inhaled. "Your stench radiates from her pores. What would you do to get her back, I wonder?"

He refused to look at Eza. Instead, he kept his gaze centered on his adversary's unblinking eyes. *What would he do?* Indecision warred within him. He could either save Eza and sacrifice himself or sacrifice her and save everyone else, including Umgar. No matter how gut-wrenching, the choice was simple.

Eza would agree no one person was more important than the mission. Yet, he hesitated to select the logical course and doom his mate to what he knew would be an awful death.

"She won't kill her."

The whisper-thin voice came from his rear. Fynna shuffled forward, a willowy arm draped around Doyna's shoulders for support. The mage glowered at the monster she once served, her cobalt gaze flinty.

"She won't destroy the only way to force you to surrender your power. That's the key to serving Melika. The siphoning must be from the willing." Fynna gave a humorless chuckle. "Unfortunately for us nobles, we unknowingly consented millennia ago. You must—"

"Silence!" Melika said. The roar echoed into the night.

Fynna cried out, hands clasping her head, and collapsed to the ground. White wisps drifted from her pale skin as the scant remains of her rune tattoos vanished. Her flesh tightened over her frame as if her skeleton fought to withdraw from its casing.

Melika was killing her. The information Fynna had could be the difference between life and death for them all. He had to stop the demon before she finished the mage.

Drakon spared a glance at Eza's still form. He wasn't a praying man, choosing to trust in his own strength and abilities, but he prayed Fynna was right about Melika's need to keep Eza alive. He was about to risk Eza's life on it.

He stretched a hand toward the demon and sent a blast toward her. The creature's eyes widened, her hideous features broadcasting surprise, a moment before the ensuing force launched her and the remaining wailers back through the breach like tumbleweeds. Before anyone could react, he willed the opening shut and reinforced it.

On the other side, Melika shook herself and climbed to her feet, Eza still in hand. The wailers fortunate enough not to be flattened beneath her massive body scattered into the darkness. The demon leveled her burning glare at him.

"Apalsi gave you much power. I'll have it by sunset tomorrow, or I'll begin carving pieces from this Lim until I do."

A veil blinked into existence behind her, and Drakon watched, mute, as the monster stepped through and disappeared.

CHAPTER 28

The punch snapped Drakon's head back. He stumbled back a step as fireflies fluttered in his vision. Khell advanced on him, his large canines bared and murder in his eyes.

"You spineless coward! You might as well have killed her yourself!" Curved daggers appeared in his hands.

In an instant, Crain and Joah moved to block the tribal leader's path. They drew their swords but angled the blades toward the ground.

"That's enough," Crain said, his voice calm but authoritative. "Fighting among ourselves won't change what happened or get her back. You heard what Fynna said; Melika needs her alive."

"I'm supposed to believe her? She's no better than the demon!" Khell said, jabbing a finger toward the collapsed mage.

Coppery blood filled Drakon's mouth, and he spat to clear the taste. Then, he leveled a murderous glare at the tribal leader.

"If you ever strike me again, I will kill you. I won't retaliate this time because I understand your anger." He took a calming breath and continued. "Had I attacked Melika, there would've been no way to ensure Eza's safety. As you heard, I have until sunset tomorrow to devise a plan to get her back. I won't waste another minute arguing my decision with you."

His gaze traveled from Khell to the Lim tribal leaders, all of whom wore varying levels of displeasure. "Or anyone else."

When no one spoke, he dropped his eyes, guilt making him unable to hold their gazes. He hadn't been entirely truthful. There was another reason for not challenging the demon. He was physically in no condition to do so.

Mysterious fatigue dogged him, sapping his energy. If he fought Melika, Drakon didn't know if he would come out the victor. He turned from their accusing stares. Regret was a dull ache in his chest. He would get Eza back safely, but first, he needed to know what Fynna knew.

He shouldered past the fuming Khell, not concerned about the Gnehoon leader attacking. If the man was foolish enough to try him while he was in this mood, Drakon would oblige him.

Suddenly, Dagoti stepped out in front of him, forcing Drakon to stop. Blood and sweat covered the Malachi commander's garments. Scrapes marred his stoic face, his eyes shone with suppressed emotion, and he held a staff in a tight grip.

It took Drakon a moment to realize it was Eza's weapon. She must have dropped it during the melee. Thickness formed in his throat, and another wave of self-loathing crashed over him. He waited for Dagoti to speak.

The warrior cleared his throat, his eyes glittering. "Eza trusted you. The Zarea is many things. A fool is not among them. No matter my feelings, I know she would want us to continue with the mission. I don't condemn you for your decision, but I do expect you to ensure we recover her alive."

Drakon gave him a tight nod, not trusting himself to speak, and the man stepped aside. Drakon continued to Fynna. She lay on the ground. Doyna knelt at her side, speaking in low tones. The mage's once lustrous, thick hair was now grayed and brittle. Her eyes were milky and clouded, and her skin was parchment-thin. She would soon die. For the first time, he felt no joy at the thought of a noble's death. Only a hollow spreading through his chest.

He turned to Doyna and motioned to the nearest tent. "Please take her inside and make her comfortable."

She nodded, gathered the fragile mage, and carried her away. Crain, the Lim tribal leaders, and Tura and the muscled Wild Gathi, Erlik, followed, but Drakon stopped Joah with a raised hand.

"I need you to gather a portion of the force to burn the creatures and bury our fallen. I also need a report of our remaining number and those injured."

"Of course. I'll find out who has any medical skills and set up a field infirmary to treat the wounded."

"Thank you."

Drakon paused and took in their surroundings. The metallic tang of blood was almost suffocating in the humid air. Gore painted the grass and tents in glistening splotches. Then his gaze snagged on Meko's mangled corpse.

Dagoti squatted beside the creature, silent tears streaming down his face as he stroked its massive head. Tightness squeezed Drakon's throat, and he cleared it before calling out to Joah's retreating back.

"Lieutenant?"

Joah turned; eyebrows raised in an unspoken question.

"Bury Eza's animal alongside our people. I don't care how long it takes."

Joah nodded, his face solemn, and moved into the crowd, issuing commands. Drakon turned and entered the tent, sweat beading his skin and soaking his tunic. Whatever information Fynna had, he needed it before his health declined further.

He strode to where Fynna lay on a mat, dragging a stool as he went and plopping it down beside her. He sat, elbows on knees, and stared down at her.

"Do you know what Melika's planning?"

Fynna's eyes fluttered beneath thin eyelids. "Death-mark—"

She paused to suck in a shuttering breath. "You always intrigued m…me. The only mixed b…blood allowed to live. I n…now realize your purpose w…was far greater than anyone knew." She opened her eyes and pinned him with her unsettling gaze. "I believe Nolan knew your potential. He hated you because you shouldn't have existed. He told me once. He knew your father."

Drakon frowned. Who sired him held no relevance then or now. He wanted answers, not to reminisce.

"Do you know what Melika is planning?" he said again, trying to get her to refocus. "You were sure she wouldn't harm Eza. Why is that?"

She sighed. "Before she cursed us, she said something. She told us, 'What I give, I can take away.' I believe. She cannot forcefully take a foreign power. If she could. She would've done so already. She needs you to abdicate."

Drakon wiped the sweat from his face. "That will never happen. She'll be expecting me tomorrow. However, if we arrive tonight, we can catch her unawares."

Even as he spoke, Drakon pondered whether he had enough energy to create another veil. He was no fool. Something was wrong with him, and he greatly regretted ignoring Eza's offer of aid.

As if reading his thoughts, Fynna said, "You will need your strength." She lowered her voice, so Drakon had to lean in to hear her. "I see your strain and the pale cast to your skin. No. There is enough magic in me to open a veil for a short time. Not large enough f...for your entire battlement but enough for a handful to get through. Consider it an apology f...for my selfish pursuits. I should have been more of an ally to the commoners. For that I am sorry."

Drakon surveyed the mage. She barely had enough strength to breathe, let alone conjure a portal.

"If you do this, you will surely deplete the remainder of your energy," he said matter-of-factly. "You will die."

She nodded. "I regret the part I have played. Once, I sat by while Nolan tried to kill you. I want to set things right." She raised her gnarled hand in a gesture of peace.

Drakon stared at the offering. She would sacrifice herself to assist them. *Could he trust her? More important, could he afford not to trust her?*

No, he couldn't.

Decision made, his large hand engulfed Fynna's as he gave it a firm, quick squeeze and released her before discomfort could set in. The ghost of a smile lifting her lips was one of relief.

"Thank you," he said. "I truly hope you find peace in death."

She closed her eyes. "Perhaps. Let me know when you

are ready."

Drakon turned and addressed the others in the tent. "As you heard, there has been a change of plans. We will travel to Sura tonight. We can't take our entire force, so stealth will be paramount. Crain, I want you with me."

A smile played on the captain's lips. "You couldn't have stopped me from accompanying you."

"I'm coming as well." Dagoti ducked inside, holding Eza's weapon. His eyes were red and puffy, but he wore a determined expression.

Drakon nodded to him. The Lim was a formidable fighter. His skills would be needed.

"We can't all disappear at once," Doyna said, her face thoughtful. "I'll stay behind with the main force. We'll continue toward the city on foot. We'll clear the wailers and possessed nobles we encounter and collect survivors as we go."

"Thank you," said Drakon. "Joah has proven himself capable. He will be a great help to you."

Near the entrance, Taru and her man spoke in hushed tones. Then she spoke, "Erlik and I will both will join you. My people have their orders and will obey them while I am away."

He nodded and stood. He glanced back at Fynna. "I believe we're ready."

The mage grunted and didn't open her eyes, but a ringlet of flame manifested within the tent. Drakon crossed to the portal and stepped through.

The last leg of his journey had begun.

৪৩

Fynna watched the last warrior step through the veil. She hoped they would succeed, and, perhaps, she would see the God the Lim served in the encroaching afterlife. Perhaps.

She smiled, exhaled her final breath, and surrendered to oblivion.

ॐ

Melika stepped from the portal; her vision hazed with fury. The Nahum had cast her, a superior being, from his camp as easily as one would swat a gnat. Her chest warmed with humiliation, and her hands tightened reflexively, aching to dig into his flesh.

A groan of pain drew Melika from her mounting rage. Glancing down at the battered figure in her hand, she fought the urge to squeeze tighter until bones broke and gore oozed between her clenched fingers. With a growl of disgust, she flung the unconscious female away. The body skidded across the floor, collided with the opposite wall, and came to a rest in a tangle of limbs. Another moan escaped the Lim's lips, but she didn't wake.

Ugh. Melika wanted to stamp out the wretched creature's life when she thought of the indignity. The shame pained her more than any of her physical injuries.

The ease in which the Nahum had evicted her awakened something she had not felt in millennia.

Doubt.

For the first time, uncertainty chiseled away at her confidence. *Was it possible her power wouldn't be enough to bend him to her will?*

A tentacle of fear slithered up her spine to wind around

her neck, threatening to choke and immobilize her. She shook her head, scattering the destructive thoughts. No. She was a mighty opponent in her own right. With her essence restored and the Nahum's female as leverage, her triumph was all but guaranteed.

Apalsi might have abdicated power to the male, but, in the end, it wouldn't be enough. The Gathi would require multiple lifetimes to comprehend and wield such strength. Time he didn't have, and she would ensure he never got, which placed the Nahum at a greater disadvantage. In contrast, she had prepared for this war since her banishment. Yet—doubt still clung to her like the stench of death on a corpse.

She could never be too cautious. Her life and the lives of her children lay in the balance. Arrogance wouldn't be her undoing. With a flick of her wrist, she tore open the fabric of space. A murky, crimson terrain rippled in the opening.

A small smile crept across Melika's face. It was time to check in on Nolan. After all, there were multiple roads to success.

૭০૩

Nolan's heavy breaths echoed in the dim, empty cave, which had become his only refuge. Coated in a layer of dried mud, he leaned against the cool wall. A branch trembled in his clammy palms, its roughness scoring bloody lines into his flesh. He took no notice, however, as he wiped sweat from his gritty face.

Too occupied was he with the land beyond the

throbbing ward line. A swamp hued in scarlet stretched out as far as he could see. In the sky, two ruby suns loomed overhead like twin giants, providing the alien world with an illumination but lacking warmth.

Nolan inched forward, hovering an unsteady hand over the defensive spell. Magical vibrations rose into his hand, and he exhaled slowly in relief. The magic still worked.

When he had regained consciousness, alone and powerless, he panicked and fled. It had been night, and a pink moon cast the marsh in shadow.

In retrospect, he knew had he awakened during daylight and seen the land in clarity, he wouldn't have ventured outside. However, it hadn't been day, and he had stumbled out in his ignorance.

A few paces into the mire, spiked vines whipped out from the brush, encircled his ankle, and snatched him into the air. An enormous maw, lined with needle-thin teeth, had opened between two trees. Dangling upside-down, he kicked and screamed as a plant the size of a small house hauled him toward it. His screams had drawn a bird-like creature to his struggle. It swooped down from the canopy, pecking at the killer vegetation and vying to claim him as its meal. Nolan was dropped in the ensuing melee and managed to retreat into the warded cave.

He rubbed absently at the crusted scar around his ankle and shuddered. He hadn't been out since. *That was how many days ago? Three? Four? A week?*

However much time had passed, thirst and hunger should have already stolen his strength. Nevertheless, he detected not a hint of the two. It would seem Melika's ward did more than keep the carnivorous locals at bay.

Seemingly summoned by his musings, a creature emerged from the maroon-colored water, the rosy sunlight glistening off its dark, slimy back. Large eyes, like banquet saucers, sat on stocks on either side of its narrow head. They rotated to stare in the direction of the cave before the beast disappeared under the surface in a ripple of waves. Nolan gripped his makeshift weapon tighter. Without his magic, sooner or later, the creatures or the fauna would make a meal of him.

He laughed bitterly. What a way for the royal mage to meet his end. It would have been better if Melika had killed him outright. *What did she gain from his continued suffering?*

A sudden flash whited out the landscape, and a shimmering slit materialized near the cave. A hulking, obsidian figure stepped from the tear, its coloring clashing with the alien surroundings like a fly in porridge. Huge, taloned feet sank into the red muck. Melika straightened as the gateway sealed. She strode forward, parting the high grass, her tail a thrashing overseer's whip behind her.

Nolan scrambled back, tripping in his haste. He went down hard and crashed into the far wall. Air exploded from his lungs in a "whoosh." He dragged in a breath and then another. Melika ducked inside and stood to her full height. Amber eyes appraised him, pausing at his injured leg. He thrust out the shaking branch toward her like a saber.

"Don't come any closer!"

Her massive head cocked to one side. A chuckle like grinding stone escaped her thin lips. "Put that away before you hurt yourself."

A motion from her taloned hand tore the stick from his

grasp and sent it hurtling from the cave to crash into the brush.

Nolan swallowed and met her soulless stare. She smiled, showcasing fangs that would have released his bowels if there was any food in him.

"That is better," she said and gestured to his ankle. "I see you tried to escape. I take it your attempt did not go well?"

She strode closer, her long legs eating the distance between them, and squatted. Her monstrous face hovered inches from his own. One of her eyelids drooped—the eye beneath wept black blood. Deep gouges marred her carapace. If possible, she was uglier than the last Nolan had seen her.

Terror traced an icy finger down his spine, and bile climbed the back of his throat, hot and acidic. Grimacing, he forced it back down.

Her lip curled in a snarl. "You dare look at me with disgust? You should remember it is I who controls whether you live or die. Does my true form frighten you so? Should I glamour myself back into your beautiful goddess? Will that make me more palatable?"

Nolan pressed farther against the wall as if the inch he gained would stop the demon from ripping his head from his shoulders if she chose to do so.

"W—what do you want from me?" he asked.

"Ah, that." Melika nodded. "Of course, there is a reason you still live. Once, you were second to the king in my blessing and power. You could say you hold a tender place in my heart."

Nolan couldn't help himself. He gaped. "Tender? Your

blessing was a curse to all who accepted it."

"But you did accept it. Did you not? You used your magic to serve me, whether you were aware of my true nature or not. Your compliance birthed this reality."

Nolan dropped his gaze, unable to face the truth. The bitter tang of self-loathing in his mouth.

"We did not know. We are not at fault—"

"What you tell yourself to cope with the realities is not my concern," Melika said. "It changes nothing. You will serve me again because it is the only reason I allow you to continue breathing."

The coolly spoken words brought Nolan's gaze back up in time to register a blur of movement. Melika's hands clasped his head and yanked him forward. He let out a shocked yip and tried to dig his heels into the ground. It was useless. Like an unwilling lover, Nolan was hauled into her embrace. Her mouth closed around his own in a gruesome kiss.

No...not a kiss. She exhaled. Something warm and viscous wormed into his mouth like a greasy slug, stretching his jaws painfully apart. His eyes bulged and watered as he gagged at the intrusion.

She lied. She was killing him.

Suddenly, the choking sensation passed, replaced with a coiling heaviness in his breast. Melika shoved him away, and he collapsed to the ground, clasping his chest.

"W—What? Did you do?"

Melika's fanged grin stuttered Nolan's racing heart. "You are now an important asset in this war. Be grateful."

"What—"

She waved a hand. Pain exploded in his torso, stealing

his breath, and curling him in on himself. Then, abruptly, he felt nothing. His mind disconnected from his body. The coolness of the cave floor vanished. Neither did he hear Melika's words, although her mouth moved as she bent over him. Blackness crept in around the corners of his perception.

This was the end, then? This was how he died.

His failing sight registered a veil appearing behind Melika. Nolan tried to reach out for it. To save himself. But his arms would not obey. Then his vision blinked out, and there was nothing.

CHAPTER 29

Most people went their entire lives unacquainted with the stench of death. Such a privilege eluded Drakon, however. Death was the familiar bedfellow of an assassin, and, as he stepped from the veil, the unmistakable, pungent odor tinged with the sickening sweetness of decomposition greeted him like a troublesome acquaintance.

He scanned his surroundings. They were in the Commoner District. Rubbish fluttered about his feet in a warm breeze. No firelight flickered from behind the curtained windows or around the door jams of the shacks. No sounds of life whispered through the barren streets.

Moonlight illuminated torn garments scattered in the street, glistening with dark stains. It seemed they arrived too late for many of the inhabitants, but Drakon hoped some had escaped the city. It would be dangerous surviving in the forest but not impossible. Given the state of Sura, the wilderness might be the safer of the two.

A compression of wind at his rear turned his gaze back toward the portal as it winked closed behind them. Gesturing to the nearest alley, he sprinted into its covering darkness, flattening himself against the flimsy wall of a lean-to.

Suddenly, a feeling of lightheadedness and weakness assaulted him. The sensation of spinning unbalanced him, his vision tunneled, and he blinked rapidly to clear his sight.

"Deathmark? You look one foot from the grave. Are you sure you're up to this?"

Drakon turned toward the whispered question. Crain stood glaring down at him. Someone conjured a small, dim orb light, and its sapphire tones danced off Crain's face, showing a wrinkled brow and deepening frown.

"I'm fine. I'll make it," Drakon said.

The fighter leaned closer so as not to be overheard. "You might think of me as the hired muscle, but I'm not stupid. You think I haven't noticed your declining health? I wonder if the curse Melika placed on the nobles is affecting you? You are half noble."

"I said I'm fine," Drakon said, his voice clipped.

Crain's lips pressed into a thin line, but the large man didn't contradict the obvious lie.

Unbeknownst to the captain, the same thought had crossed Drakon's mind—perhaps the siphoning affected the scant amount of noble blood in him. Nevertheless, nothing could be done about it now. His only option was to press on while he was able.

He addressed the group, which had begun to stare at their hushed conversation. "There's an underground tunnel system to the palace constructed as an escape contingency for the royal family. Their existence was secret; however, Umgar found out about them and told me. I've utilized them many times to travel unseen. The nearest entry is across the canal. If we can get into them, we should be able to travel unnoticed."

"How do you know those tunnels aren't overrun with the creatures?" Khell said, shouldering his way to the front of the group.

Drakon gritted his teeth. "I don't, but unless you have a better solution, then that's our plan."

The Lim gripped his spear, fangs bared, but didn't offer any suggestions as Drakon expected.

"I thought not," Drakon said, dismissing him and focusing on the other people huddled in the cramped alley. "I'll take point. Sage, Erlik, and Taru follow next. Then Zemket, Khell, and Dagoti. Captain, you'll bring up the rear."

He received nods from all but Khell and quickly led the procession through the darkened streets of the Commoner District. There were no signs of wailers or possessed nobles as they went. Their absence should have delighted him, but it only made him more tense. At last, the bridge leading to the Noble District came into view, and Drakon skidded to a stop and ducked back into a side street. His already queasy stomach plummeted.

"Why are we stopping?" someone whispered.

A ripple of unease traveled through their assembly as one by one each person peeked from cover to see what had halted Drakon. A host of wailers and nobles milled about on the bridge.

Crain peered from the alley again. He leaned back into the shadows and sighed. "We could double back to the east bridge." He rubbed his chin in contemplation. "Although the creatures seem to be guarding the crossing, which makes me think the other will be the same."

Drakon nodded. The action caused another wave of dizziness, and he steadied himself against the cool stone of the building at his back. When his vision cleared, he noticed Crain's furtive study of him.

Drakon averted his gaze from the captain's observant eyes and pointed to a boat docked beneath the bridge. "We can use that trading boat to get across. Extinguish the light. We'll go the remainder of the way by moonlight. Stick to the shadows and follow me. They won't see us unless they look down."

Partial darkness engulfed them as the orb light blinked out. He glanced once more at the crowd of beasts patrolling the bridge, making sure their passing wouldn't be detected. Then he sprinted across the street to where the craft bobbed in a docile current.

Drakon bent, loosened the rope tying the vessel to the dock and held the boat steady.

"There isn't enough room for everyone to cross in one trip," he said, his voice barely above a whisper. He glanced at Crain. "Take Sage, Khell, Zemket, and Taru across first. The rest of us will wait here for your return."

"Erlik will go. I will stay," Taru said. The Wild Gathi man shot her a narrowed-eyed glower, but she ignored him, choosing to level a defiant look on Drakon.

A tension headache wrapped around Drakon's skull and squeezed. He was confident her reasoning for wanting to remain behind had something to do with her misplaced guilt, but he didn't have time to argue the point. If she wanted to wait, he wouldn't stop her. His only concern was getting to the other side of the canal as soon as possible.

"Fine. Everyone else, load up."

It was a work of moments to fill the impromptu ferry, and Crain took up a paddle and sliced through the dark water toward the opposite shore. Drakon glanced up at the underside of the stone bridge. Huffs and grunts sounded every few seconds, but there were no cries of alarm.

We might make it across unnoticed after all.

The boat bumped into the bank in a manner of minutes. The Erlik and the tribal leaders climbed out and helped shove the vessel back into the current. Crain backtracked without incident. Drakon knelt and pulled the craft alongside the dock and waited until Taru and Dagoti scrambled inside before hopping in himself. Crain pushed off with the paddle and began the return trip.

Midway across the canal, a wail ripped across the night. Drakon startled, his hand going to the sword at his hip. Taru leaped to her feet, spear raised. The sudden movement unbalanced the craft. She tipped backward as if in slow motion, arms pinwheeling. Drakon made a grab for her but was too late. Her calves caught the gunwale, and she flipped over the starboard side of the boat with a yelp of surprise and a loud splash.

Above them, an awful chorus of grunts and snarls sounded. Drakon glanced up. Amber gazes and the shadowed faces of the nobles stared down at them from over the parapet. He cursed. So much for their covert crossing.

A body leaped from the bridge, crashing into the canal like a boulder. Another followed. And more still until bodies rained around them, sending water geysering around the small craft.

Drakon stripped his sword from his waist. "Keep going! I'm going after Taru!" he said to Crain before drawing his dagger and diving into the murky water.

The water was warmer than he expected. It instantly leached into his clothing, weighing him down. He spun around, searching, before spotting the hazy form of a noble.

Its tattered robing billowed out around it like a black shroud as it clawed toward Taru, who kicked wildly for the surface. However, Drakon was faster and made it to the beast before it could reach her.

He snagged the fabric of its robes and yanked it back. Then he buried his blade in its back. The creature opened its hideous mouth in a screech, releasing a stream of bubbles. It bucked in an attempt to escape, but he held on, stabbing until the water clouded with blood, and its struggles ceased.

Drakon released his hold, and the body sank, disappearing into the dark depth. He twisted, kicked upward, and broke the surface to a scene of chaos.

Dozens of possessed nobles littered the canal, and Taru headed for the shore. Crain and Dagoti were on the bank with the others, having abandoned the beached craft.

Drakon swam with waning strength, trying to distance himself from the beasts angling for him. He kept his eyes on the bank, expecting a taloned hand to clamp down in his shoulder at any moment. None did, however, and after a few minutes, he stumbled ashore, his wet clothes weighing him down like chains.

"Here!" Crain shoved Drakon's weapon into his hands.

Drakon took the blade and raced past the group as wailers poured down the embankment, and the first noble emerged from the water like something from a nightmare.

The tunnel entrance was close. *Only yards away.* He pushed himself forward, his vision narrowing and his head pounding as if a thousand drums beat within his skull. He spotted the flora concealing the opening and tore them away. Throwing the door open, he waved the others through and slammed the door closed. He shouldered the iron bar to lock the door.

It didn't budge.

He pushed again with the same result, and he could have screamed in frustration. The cacophony of shrieks and grunts grew louder. If the creatures got inside, there would be no way to outrun them.

"Out of the way!"

Drakon stepped back, and Dagoti shoved the bar with a broad shoulder. A clank sounded as the lock slid into place. A moment later, the door shuddered from multiple impacts. Claws raked iron, but the door held.

Drakon released a breath and sheathed his blade. He slid down to the floor. His adrenaline drained, and with it, his strength.

Orb light winked into existence, and Taru knelt beside him. Her chestnut eyes glistened. "Thank you for coming after me."

Drakon looked away but gave a tight nod. After a few moments and with a groan, he climbed to his feet. They must make haste...

"Look at him. He can barely stand." Khell's glaring face materialized before him. He waved a hand toward Drakon as if proving his point. "This is who we're following into the demon's lair? He's going to get us all killed. We should leave him here and find our own way into the palace."

"You can leave," Drakon said with an even voice, even though he wanted nothing more than to strangle the Lim. "No one is holding you here. Go on, see if you can find your way through this maze without me. You're an entitled, insecure child who has been lashing out because you didn't get what you thought was your due."

Drakon stepped closer, ensuring the tribal leader saw in his eyes the seriousness of his next words. "And if I have anything to say about it, you never will."

The attack came swiftly. Only years of honed reflexes saved Drakon from being skewered. He leaned back, and the spear sliced the air inches from his face. Before Khell could react, Drakon stepped inside the swing. His dagger hand came up in a violent arch.

Khell's eyes bulged, and his weapon clattered to the floor. A look of shock crossed his features as blood dribbled from between his parted lips. Drakon yanked free his blade from Khell's neck with a jet of crimson.

The Lim collapsed, gripping the wound, which gushed from between his fingers. Khell's mouth moved, but no words came out. Finally, his hand dropped away, and he stared sightless into space.

A stunned silence fell over the group. Drakon staggered to a wall, leaning a hand against it for support and panting. If any of the Lim wanted to avenge their brother, this was undoubtedly the time. He was in no condition to stop them.

"You had every right to repay his attack on your life in kind," Dagoti said after long last. "Had Khell succeeded, his actions would've doomed us all."

Zemket gave a long exhale and rubbed a hand down his weathered face. "Dagoti speaks the truth. Khell attacked you. You protected yourself. No one here blames you. Khell allowed his unchecked emotions to get the better of him. For that, I am saddened. However, we will stand witness to what happened here."

Sage, Taru, and Erlik gave sober nods of agreement.

"Dagoti. Help me with him. If we live through this, I will send his tribesmen to collect his body," Zemket said. He stooped over Khell and lifted him under the arms. Dagoti hefted his legs, and they moved the body to rest against the door.

Taru retrieved Khell's fallen spear, having lost her weapon in her dip in the canal. No one objected, and a few minutes later, their subdued group left Khell's corpse and began their trek through the labyrinth.

No one looked back.

෩෬

The putrid reek of rot and ammonia was first to welcome Eza back to consciousness. The second was an uncomfortable throbbing and itching in her side and shoulder.

Eyes shut, she kept her breathing slow and steady to mimic sleep and listened. Muffled grunts and huffing. The shuffling of feet from outside the room. She opened her eyes, but only the right side of the chamber blinked into focus. *What?* She raised a hand to her left eye and winced as her fingers touched swollen flesh.

She was in a deplorable state, and although her gift gave her the ability to heal faster than normal, she would require at least an entire cycle to reach fighting condition. One small mercy was the excruciating pain she suffered during her clash with Melika was gone.

Unbidden, Meko's brutal slaughter played back in her mind's eye. Her vision blurred. Warm tears slid from her eyes to her temples, but she blotted them away with a sleeve. She couldn't fall apart. There would be time to mourn later. Now, she needed to escape her current predicament.

She scanned the room. The spacious chamber was dark, but her night vision was excellent. Around her, broken bits of furniture and ripped fabric lay scattered on the...

The floor. That was where the pungent stench emanated. Eza studied the fabric littering the ground once more. Horror bloomed as she realized what she believed to be torn garments were, in fact, dried remnants of skin and flesh.

Her stomach roiled, threatening to empty its contents. She eased onto her elbows. Pain pinched her ribs and her shoulder, stealing her breath. She moaned through gritted teeth, her eyes squeezed shut against the sharp ache. She drew in slow breaths through her nose, easing them out through her mouth. She could do this. She would do this. A Malachi didn't wait to be rescued or killed. They fought.

She sat upright with a growl of pure willpower.

A scraping sound turned her toward the door. A form peeled from the shadows. She gasped. The vaulted ceiling had to be at least twenty feet high; still, the hideous figure of Melika hunched as the demon stalked forward. Scars etched her carapace, and her taloned feet clicked on the stone. She stopped to hover above Eza.

A blazing amber, malicious glare bored into her. In it was the promise of death. Had she been able, Eza would have run. Honor be damned.

"I had nearly forgotten the visage of a true Lim." Melika's voice warped around her four-inch fangs. Her icy stare traveled Eza's body. "Truly unremarkable. What Apalsi saw in you, I will never know."

Indignation flared, burning away caution, and Eza spoke before she could think better of it. "Only one of us is a drooling monster."

Melika snarled and bent to Eza, who fought the overwhelming urge to lean away. Instead, she sat motionless, the warm, sickly-sweet smell of the demon's breath moistening her face.

"Careful, Lim. Your God will not save you here."

Eza wisely bit back a retort. She had struck a chord when she insulted Melika's appearance. *It would be safer to change the subject.*

"What do you think to gain from holding me hostage?"

Melika snorted. "Let's not pretend to be obtuse. I know you hold value to the Nahum. You will convince him to abdicate Apalsi's power to me. Initially, I believed sacrificing him within the Glens would grant my freedom, but I now know my release lies in the abilities he has gained, not his mixed blood."

"I would never help you. You've already devastated the Gathi. Without the barrier to contain you, you'll do the same to my people." Eza shook her head in defiance. "No. I won't do it. You could've spent your banishment atoning for your sins against us. Yet you continued to let hatred and jealousy corrode within you. Apalsi would've forgiven you."

"Forgive?" Melika spat the word as if it were a lump of hot coal on her tongue. "It was he who betrayed me! He created the Lim. Coddling you, spending less time with his first and best creations, and placing you above all else. He banished me to a lightless void for tens of thousands of years. He should seek *my* forgiveness!"

The demon swung a massive hand to punctuate her

point, striking a nearby wardrobe and sending it careening into the wall. It exploded in a shower of splinters.

Eza flinched inwardly from the destruction. Her heart banged against the cage of her ribs, but she remained silent and still. Melika's volatile mood was unpredictable. One wrong word and the demon might kill her in a fit of rage.

Melika's breath came in huffing bursts. Her enormous chest heaved, and her serpentine tail whipped behind her in evident agitation. After long, tense moments, the demon settled. The fire within her glare now smothered to embers.

"You. Will. Convince. The. Nahum." She bit out the words with deteriorating restraint. Melika waved a hand, and a veil materialized before them.

"This is a portal to Natapa. I will offer you this bargain once." She placed a razor-sharp talon beneath Eza's chin, tilting her face upward. "He cares for you—"

Eza began to object, but Melika raised her voice and continued. "In those feelings lies his weakness. If you can convince him to abdicate to me, I will spare your tribe. Napata alone will be left in peace once I kill Apalsi and take my rightful place."

"If you fail," the demon paused to palm Eza's entire head. Claws pierced skin. Blood wept from shallow cuts in her scalp and dribbled down her face. "Your kinsmen will be the first I destroy, and I will take my time."

Eza swallowed, her throat thick. "How do I know you won't kill them anyway? Even if I do what you ask?"

"You don't. But rest assured, if you don't help me, your people will die this night. You can either have guaranteed death now or uncertain death later."

"Those are no choices."

Melika shrugged her prominent shoulder. "Yet those are the ones I offer. If I were you, I wouldn't place hope in a man who, the last time I saw him, looked near death. He will need a veil to reach Sura in the time frame I gave him. The effort and his declining health will drain the remainder of the fight from him."

For a moment, Eza stopped breathing. She hurried to cover the shock on her face. *Melika knew of Drakon's illness?*

"He isn't sick," she said, hoping Melika would let slip more information about what ailed Drakon.

The demon's smile was all fang and a hint of a secret. She shoved Eza's face away. "Of course, he is, you stupid child. Don't forget. He carries my essence within him. Therefore, he isn't immune to the siphoning."

Eza stilled. *So that was it?* The curse meant for the Gathi nobles was affecting Drakon as well. She wanted to kick herself for not figuring it out. *But what could she do?* She couldn't escape and warn him, not with her injuries.

A recollection of their memory sharing flashed to the forefront of her mind. Their bond allowed her to access his memories. The same could be done with thoughts. She immediately fell into herself, searching for the ever-present link between them.

There it was. Their link shone like a golden thread before her. Eza took hold of it and projected her thoughts, hoping and praying he received it.

Melika's curse is causing your illness. She's expecting you to drain your power by using a veil to arrive in time. Don't worry about me. Conserve your energy.

Hopefully, her message would reach him, but, for now,

she had to ensure her people lived long enough for Drakon to arrive. She blinked back to the present.

Melika stared intently at her but didn't appear to have noticed her mental withdrawal. She looked into Melika's emotionless eyes and lied.

"I'll take your deal. I'll do what you need me to do."

CHAPTER 30

The only description for the palace interior was utter destruction. Bodily waste and detritus created a layer of filth on the once-pristine floors, which clung to Drakon's boots. Unlike the Lim, who trudged along barefoot, he was grateful for the sliver of protection between himself and the muck.

His eyes watered, and his nose burned from the confined toxic fumes, which intensified his nausea and pounding head as their group crept, orb light overhead and weapons in hand, through the silent corridors toward Ewen's throne room.

"They've been using the place like a large privy," Crain said in a hushed voice, disgust evident in his tone. He walked beside Drakon in their small procession and shook a clump of feces from his boot with a pained expression. "One good thing is animals don't usually sleep where they relieve themselves, so it's unlikely we'll run into any wailers or possessed nobles."

Drakon thought the captain was being a bit too optimistic but didn't contradict the observation. Crain was right about the lack of run-ins with the creatures since entering through the tunnels, but their absence made Drakon more agitated. The group that had chased them into the passage knew of their presence. It wouldn't be long before they sounded the alarm.

Melika's curse is causing your illness. She's expecting you to drain your power by using a veil to arrive in time. Don't worry about me. Conserve your energy.

The urgent words invaded Drakon's psyche without warning. He paused mid-stride, his hand flying up to his head. *Eza?*

"What's wrong? Did you see something?" Crain said. He hoisted his sword higher, peering around to discover what had caused Drakon to falter.

Drakon steadied himself against a wall and shook his head. "I didn't see anything, but I heard something."

He turned and motioned for Dagoti, who crept forward from the rear. "I heard Eza." When the man frowned in confusion, he tapped a finger against his temple. "In here. Is it possible for Melika to infiltrate our connection and impersonate her?"

A slow smile spread across the Malachi leader's dark face, and he shook his head. "It's impossible. A mating bond is impenetrable. If you hear her voice, you can rest assured it is the real Eza. Bless Apalsi. What did she say?"

"She told me Melika is expecting us, but that's not surprising. Our plan hasn't changed. Once inside the throne room, we'll bar the door to prevent reinforcements," he said, deciding not to regurgitate the entirety of the warning. Illness or not, he wouldn't back down from this confrontation. "If Melika's not there, there's another entrance to the tunnels from the chamber adjacent to the dais."

Dagoti gave a determined nod, and Drakon was appreciative of the Lim's unwavering commitment to his Zarea. Yes, Eza's message troubled Drakon, but it didn't alter his resolve. The war would end this night in their favor or not. He, for one, was weary of being on the defensive and witnessing people moved about like pawns in the demon's game. If she planned to use his affliction against him, he could only hope his newly acquired power was sufficient to stop her.

He led them through the vacant corridors toward the throne room, his instincts firing and cautioning him that, although the building appeared deserted, Melika wouldn't leave her stronghold unguarded. Nevertheless, he pressed on, taking comfort in the fact the demon wouldn't anticipate a strike the same night as her attack. No doubt, she would expect him to, at the least, gather his force.

Drakon turned a corner, and the colossal doors to the throne room gaped open. Darkness concealed the chamber beyond. No noise issued from its depths, and the rank odor engulfing the palace dissipated.

"This doesn't feel right," Sage said. Her dark eyes darted to the blackness and then behind them. "No way it could be this easy."

Drakon agreed but moved forward, flattening himself against the wall beside the door. He glanced up at the towering door frame. The stone was free of etched wards or spells.

"Send the orb ahead. Let's see what's inside," he said.

As if on its own accord, the orb rounded the frame and floated into the room. Drakon peeked around the door, watching its progress. The sphere bobbed along several feet from the floor. The halo of light cast peeled away the shadows and revealed white marble columns, a vaulted ceiling, and tattered banners with the royal family's crest.

Benches lay broken and strewn about. Heavy draping covered the windows lining the walls, so not as much as a sliver of moonlight penetrated the oily dark. The outer ring of light displayed the dais, where the ornate thrones stood untouched.

What the orb didn't reveal was a single creature. *Strange,* Drakon thought. *Where in Targarius were they? Had Melika lied about where she had taken Eza, but to what purpose?*

No. The demon wanted him too badly. Melika was here...somewhere.

He pulled back into the corridor. Six pairs of expectant eyes stared back at him. "I don't see anything. I'll advance down the center aisle toward the dais. The rest of you pair up and move along the walls toward the front. Dagoti and Captain Crain, secure the doors."

When no one objected, Drakon took a fortifying breath, pushed from the wall, and dashed inside. The first thing he noticed was the light orb hovering in the center of the room, motionless.

Well...that wasn't entirely accurate. He slowed as he neared. The sphere moved forward but bounced back as if striking an invisible barrier.

A chill kissed the nape of Drakon's neck, and he glanced around for the others. Sage and Zemket dashed past the closed balcony doors on his right, drawing closer to the chamber's midway point. To the left, Erlik and Taru neared the same position. However, Drakon didn't hear the thud of footsteps, the rustle of clothing, nor the clank of the latching door. Then he noticed the absence of the stench permeating the palace. The air held an unnatural flatness, and he smelled nothing. Not the stink of waste or the dustiness of the decimated room.

It was as if his senses were muted or more like enchanted. At once, he realized why they hadn't crossed paths with any of the creatures.

They were all here. Concealed within the room.

Before Drakon could shout a warning, energy exploded from the chamber's center, sending them crashing to the floor. The illusion of an empty throne room flickered and disappeared, and countless wailers and nobles materialized in the space.

A foaming-mouthed noble charged Drakon, its jaws stretched impossibly wide and its taloned fingers reaching for him. He scrambled backward and kicked a bench toward the beast. The furniture skidded across the marble floor and crashed into the creature's legs, pinning it to a nearby column. Drakon jumped to his feet, sprinted to the noble before it could climb over the obstacle, and cleaved its head from its shoulders.

Drakon's vision swam, but as he turned, he caught sight of Dagoti collapsing under the weight of two wailers and started for him.

Suddenly, the door to the chamber adjoining the dais banged open. Melika unfolded from the doorway and stood at her monstrous height. Her blazing eyes met his over the battle and held. She uttered a word Drakon couldn't make out, and then he couldn't move.

He twisted and bucked within the magical hold, or at least he tried. He managed to blink. A force pried the hilt of his sword from his fingers, and it clattered to the floor. Unarmed, Drakon scanned the room, hoping the others had escaped. His stomach plummeted to his feet, however, as he saw each of his companions similarly incapacitated. The creatures halted their attack but circled, waiting for a signal to resume their assault.

"I admit, I figured it would take at least until morning for you to gather enough strength to make the journey." The demon stepped from the dais, and her minions parted before her like a breeze through wheat. Her long strides carried her to Drakon. She cocked her head to one side and chuckled. The sound was like snapping wood.

"You look unwell, Nahum. Is my magic not agreeing with you?"

Drakon forced his face into a neutral mask, although the truth was apparent in his waxen and sweat-drenched skin.

"What did you do to me?"

"I have done nothing. You're part Gathi noble, after all. No matter how much Apalsi tried to dilute it." A wicked smile inched across her hideous face, and Drakon went cold. "Which means half of you contains my essence, and that portion belongs to me."

If he could move, Drakon would have shaken his head in denial. He didn't belong to anyone, least of all, Melika.

It was true his father was of noble blood, but Drakon never studied or practiced Gathi magic. He hadn't paled, even though there once was a time when he craved to do so. In retrospect, he realized the error of coveting Melika's blessing and power. Such things had done what for the mages? Gotten them killed or transformed into beasts.

Melika was a mistress of lies, and her claim on him was nothing more than an attempt to fill him with hesitation and uncertainty. He tested the invisible restraints holding him once more. They held him tighter than a bowstring. He wasn't going anywhere until she deemed it. A wave of helplessness rode in on the knowledge and burned in his gut.

"I might be of mixed blood, but I no more belong to you than the Lim. I never pledged allegiance to you."

Melika gave a gruesome smile, all brutality and fang. "Is that so?"

She cupped his face in a massive hand, and a chill traveled over his fevered body. Cold settled into him, sinking into his marrow. He struggled to jerk away from her grip but couldn't. He was at her mercy.

She tilted his head, studying him. "I must admit, you do resemble your father. I can't believe I didn't notice the similarities before. Ewen did an admirable job hiding your existence from me and even himself. His deception was brilliant, really. He used a spell of forgetting on himself. There must have been a powerful incantation placed in the recesses of his mind to ensure he never outright killed you as well. Had I not gleaned the memories from that snooping queen, his secret would have died with him. Oh, you didn't know? Of course, you wouldn't have."

For the first time in his life, Drakon's emotions slipped past his studied mask of neutrality. His eyes widened in disbelief. Had he misheard? Ewen? King Ewen? The man at the core of every misfortune in his life couldn't be his father.

As if reading his thoughts, Melika chuckled. "Oh yes. It is true. Why do you think you lived when Ewen exterminated all other half-breeds? Your father fancied himself in love with your Wild Gathi mother. Although he hated the abomination he created, he honored her dying request that you be spared."

She stroked a thumb over his cheek. The gesture was tender, but gooseflesh sprung up in the wake of her touch. "Your father was one of my strongest conduits. My essence saturated him and transferred to you. You might deny it, but you can feel the truth of my words. I am as mingled within you as the portion of you that contains Apalsi's essence passed to you from your mother. We are alike, you and I. We are both products of selfish fathers. Mine banished me to a realm of darkness for daring to demand love and respect. Yours abandoned you to a life of servitude, misery, and degradation to preserve his image. Now Apalsi wishes to deceive you into fighting a war he began. While he is where? Doing what? If the mighty God cares so much for his creations, where is he now?"

"Your words would be more convincing had you not been attempting to murder me for weeks," Drakon said in a dry tone.

"My children were never to kill you, only return you to me."

"Clearly, you didn't specify the state in which they brought me to you."

Melika huffed. "You've been led to believe you must die to free me from the Glens, but you won't surely perish. You are my child, as are all the Gathi. Once you transfer Apalsi's power to me, I will possess the gift of creation. It would be within my ability to resurrect you."

Whether his rebirth was possible or not, she wouldn't do it. Melika didn't strike him as forgiving or benevolent. If she allowed him to live, he would always be a threat. She would do as he would in the situation: tie up the loose end.

She was only saying what she thought would help her achieve her goals. Once accomplished, she wouldn't hesitate to terminate his life. Moreover, it was prudent not to trust someone who tried to kill you multiple times.

"You still need a bit of convincing, I see," Melika said.

She released his face, straightened, and waved a hand. Eza appeared at her side in a moment. Eza frowned; one eye, the one not swollen shut, blinked rapidly as she glanced around as if in a daze. Her gaze widened as she noticed the others, and then she let out a long groan when she spotted him. He could practically see the *"I told you not to come"* in her glare.

The demon turned to her. "Your lover needs some convincing."

Drakon felt a tickle along their bond before Eza's voice echoed in his thoughts. *Melika's threatening to massacre my tribe if I don't convince you to abdicate, but you can't do it. She'll be unstoppable if she gains that power. If we fail, she will kill them anyway.*

That much was true. Before Eza could speak aloud, Drakon addressed Melika. "Nothing she could say would convince me to give you such power. Had Apalsi wanted you to have the abilities you long for, he would've entrusted them to you. However, he knew, as I do, that you are cruel and treacherous."

Amber sparks flashed in the demon's eyes. She showcased a fanged smiled full of menace and a promise of a torturous death. Gone was the false veneer of pretty lies.

She circled him. Drakon tensed, half expecting a fist to burst through his chest at any moment. He locked gazes with Eza.

When I give the word, you run.

Her eyes narrowed in defiance. *Free the others, and we'll fight alongside you. If we die, so be it. Malachi do not abandon their allies.*

Drakon cursed inwardly. With her injuries and reduced visibility, she would be more of a liability than an aide. He would have Dagoti carry her out slung over his shoulder if needed. He prodded the foreign energy thrumming below the surface of his skin, unfurling it and pulling at its tether until the power went taut.

Melika finished her perusal and came around to face him again. "Were you aware I was Apalsi's first creation?"

The abrupt change of subject startled Drakon, and he almost released his mental hold on his power.

The demon cocked her head and clucked her tongue. "Don't look so surprised, Nahum. I was there when he shaped my siblings and the Lim from the nothingness. Yet, when I secretly formed my children, they were monstrous. Crude. No matter how I tried, I could never replicate the perfection Apalsi achieved. I pleaded with him for the knowledge, but he denied me and commanded I destroy my own offspring!"

She waved toward the hideous wailers and deformed figures of the nobles, hunched and waiting with ravenous stares, to punctuate her outrage and disbelief. "But I couldn't kill the fruit of my hands. Instead, I loved and embraced them. I didn't shun them for their imperfections as Apalsi had me. You see, as my creator is a master craftsman, so am I."

A talon traced a line down Drakon's shoulder to his arm. A bitter tang filled his mouth, and his stomach heaved in revulsion, but he did not voice his disgust. He needed her talking a bit longer…

"My father passed his essence to you because he is too weak to face the spawn of his negligence. He sent you—"

Drakon let go. Power exploded from him. It blasted through the chamber, breaking the spell restraining them and incinerating the surrounding creatures. They burst into ash, which the gale whipped into the air and scattered about the room.

Drakon crashed to the marble floor and scrambled to retrieve his sword. "Dagoti, get Eza out of here!" he said, trusting the warrior would do as instructed, and rounded on Melika.

Stunned but unscathed, she shook her massive head to regain her wits. Drakon gathered the remainder of his strength and pounced, aiming at a fracture in her carapace and driving the blade to the hilt. The demon shrieked and fell to her back with a boom, shaking the building and nearly ripping the sword from his hands.

Drakon locked gazes with Melika as he rode her down to the ground, but rather than the shock and fear he expected to glimpse in her blazing eyes, he saw—triumph?

Her eyes flamed amber like a torch thrown on oil-soaked timber. An internal fire scorched through Drakon, and he collapsed to the floor, screaming and writhing. The pain was beyond imagining. All consuming.

His back arched in an awful contortion. A deafening crack sounded as the spine snapped. He continued to scream as more bones popped, realigned, and elongated beneath his skin. A shadow fell over him, and through his tears saw the demon looking down at him.

"No matter what Apalsi believed, I am ingrained into your very marrow. My essence will recreate you in my image, and you will serve me and only me. After I have you kill your lover, you will gladly abdicate to me. If not, we will return to this conversation once you finish using the others as rawhide."

Another bone snapped. Talons sprouted. Fangs jutted from bloody gums. Hair shed and pooled to the floor. Through it all, Drakon screamed.

ೞ�

Eza watched in mounting horror as Drakon's body contorted on the floor. Garments split at the seams. Exposed skin rippled as his skeleton rearranged and lengthened beneath the surface. The snapping of bones and his tortured screams echoed throughout the cavernous space while Melika stood by like a midwife overlooking a birth.

Eza had to do something. She started toward the demon, unsure of what she planned to do but determined to intervene.

A hand clasped her shoulder and whirled her around. "Oh no, you don't," Dagoti said, his fierce gaze shifted to Drakon and back to her. "He told me to get you out, and that's what I'm going to do."

"Let me go!"

Ignoring her protests and cries of pain, he jostled her toward the doors. Sage and Erlik were there, lifting the barricade bar. Zemket and Crain waited a few feet behind the pair, waving them forward.

Yet, Taru hesitated near the chamber's center, warring

emotions shifting across her face as she stood witness to Drakon's horrid transformation. Her gaze strayed to Eza's as Dagoti half hauled, half dragged her past. In an instant, an unspoken agreement crossed between them.

They wouldn't leave Drakon.

Taru stepped into their path. Eza twisted to the side in that moment, and the Wild Gathi slammed the blunt end of her spear into Dagoti's gut. He doubled over with an explosion of breath.

"Eza...stop!" he said between gasps, clutching his stomach.

But she was racing away. Melika stepped back from Drakon; her dark magic done. Only then did Eza notice Drakon no longer screamed. He lay in the fetal position with his back to her. His clothing hung in tatters from an uncharacteristically bulky frame. He sucked in deep, rattling breaths.

She slowed. "Drakon?"

No response.

She mentally reached for their bond. The golden thread disappeared into an impenetrable mist. Impossible. He was alive. She could see his chest rising and falling.

Then how...

She leveled a narrowed-eyed glare at Melika. "What did you do to him?"

Drakon rolled over at the sound of her voice, and Eza gasped and took an instinctual step back.

Apalsi, help me. His eyes.

Soulless, obsidian orbs stared at her with no hint of recognition. No spark of compassion. An unthinking husk.

His skin retained its mocha complexion, but his once handsome features were now sharp. Gaunt. The corner of his mouth quivered in a snarl, displaying blade-like incisors. He stood, and Eza craned her head to take in his towering form, which was now well over eight feet tall. She retreated another step. Talons hung from his fingers and shredded his boots. Muscles twitched beneath the tattered remains of his clothing.

"Nahum, he might be, but he is more like the Gathi nobles than Apalsi suspected," Melika said, coming to stand next to Drakon and stroke his cheek like a mother with a chubby-faced cherub. He didn't react to the touch, only continued his penetrating stare at Eza.

"His noble blood carries enough of my essence to allow me to reshape him." The demon laughed, a rumbling hacking noise that grated Eza's ears. "I order him to rip you apart and devour the pieces, and he would do so."

Dread filled her. Were Melika's words true? Could her dark magic override their mate bond?

Glancing at the creature Drakon had become, it was hard to glimpse the man he used to be. However, there was one thing Eza was convinced Melika couldn't command of him, even in his altered state.

"If you force him to harm or kill me, he'll never abdicate Apalsi's power to you," she said with more bravado than she felt.

"Is that so?"

"It is. We're bonded. Soul to soul. Harm me and lose any chance you have of freeing yourself and enacting your vengeance."

Melika frowned, considering the truth of her words. Then the expression morphed into a condescending smile. "If what you say is true, then he shouldn't be able to kill you.

No matter the coercion. Thus, I will call your bluff, Lim." A long, clawed finger unfurled to point at Eza.

"Kill her."

Drakon shot forward and lunged for her. A body barreled into his side, and the two figures tumbled in a heap, sending furniture debris flying and toppling a marble statue. When they came to a stop, Dagoti lay limp, blood spreading from his head.

Drakon pried himself from beneath shattered wood, and his head swiveled toward her, single-minded bloodlust in his jet-black eyes. He charged, cutting the distance in half before Eza could tense to run.

"Move it, Princess!"

With the command came the feeling of weightlessness and a stab of pain in her bruised ribs as Crain threw her over his shoulder. Her view of the rabid Drakon inverted.

Erlik, Sage, Zemket, and Taru swept in behind them to cut off his path. Drakon paused long enough to grab Erlik. He swung the large male as if he weighed as little as a doll and flung him away. He soared, arms and legs spread in an almost graceful arch...until he collided with an immovable pillar.

There was a sickening crunch as the Wild Gathi's head impacted. Its contents erupted in a crimson and gray spray. His body landed in an awkwardly bent mass.

Eza squeezed her eyes shut against the gruesome sight, but the image replayed on the backs of her eyelids. She feared it would be one she would never forget.

Sudden pain sliced through her shoulder. Her eyes popped open a moment before she was ripped from Crain's grasp. She crashed through a bench. Air exploded from her lungs as her head smacked against an unyielding floor. Stars burst behind her eyelids. Groaning, she tried to roll to her side. Sharp stings in her head and ribs laid her flat again.

Warm wetness coated her head and shoulder. As if from a distant tunnel, the sounds of battle continued around her. She blinked to clear her vision. Drakon dropped into view like a giant spider, his shuffling gait un-hurried.

He crouched over her. Mouth open in a snarl. Teeth smeared with blood. Onyx eyes seeing nothing.

She would die if she didn't reach him fast. In a final ef-fort, Eza envisioned their bond thread, yanked on it with all her might, and shouted.

Drakon! Don't do this! You promised to protect me!

He paused. Blinked. Once. Twice.

Tears escaped her eyes and pooled in her ears. *Drakon, please. Don't let Melika use you!*

As if burned, Drakon jerked away from her and stum-bled, clutching his head, and shrieking in agony.

She clenched her teeth and rolled to her side. *Fight it! You're stronger than this! Don't let her win!*

Suddenly, Drakon went silent, unnaturally still. Melika stalked toward him; her alien face impossible to read. Her amber gaze swung to Eza.

"It would seem you spoke the truth. Unfortunately—"

The attack was swift. Drakon sprang onto the demon. They crashed to the floor like dueling titans. A spider web of cracks snaked out from the point of impact. Drakon gouged his claws into the demon's armor. Bits of carapace flew free and clattered to the marble. Perched on Melika's chest, he bit into her shoulder and shook another fragment free. Melika shrieked in rage and agony.

A veil materialized on the floor beside the battling duo. Before Eza could shout a warning, Melika crushed Drakon to her in a violent embrace and rolled. They dropped through the portal, and it blinked out of existence.

"No!"

Eza crawled to the spot where they had vanished, fanning her hands over the cold marble, and frantically searching for a way to follow, but no evidence of their passage remained.

They were gone.

The throne room doors shuddered and exploded open behind her. Eza turned to see wailers and possessed nobles swarming the room, scuttling over each other like a living wave come to drown her. She struggled to her feet and fled.

Drakon was gone. Perhaps dead, and she might soon follow.

CHAPTER 31

Wind whipped Drakon's hair across his face in painful lashes as he somersaulted downward wrapped in Melika's crushing embrace. He clamped jaws into the soft, unprotected flesh of the demon's neck. Thick, putrid blood gushed into his mouth. He gagged and spat. Melika screeched. She wrenched him free and pitched him into a solo free fall. He fell for what seemed like hours through the darkness before slamming onto a surprisingly yielding surface. Air rushed from his lungs. He sank a few inches into the squishy terrain.

Groaning, he extricated himself from the ground, which shifted like wet clay beneath him. Mist hovered, obscuring his feet, and climbing up his thighs. The frigid air smelled of moist, rotting toadstools. His breath frosted in white wisps. The blood around his mouth and on his tunic iced as cold goosed his flesh and settled into his bones. *What was this place?* He glanced around. Only the mist deciphered land from sky. A featureless landscape of midnight blue glared back at him. Absolute desolation. No distinguishing landmarks. No man-made structures. No life. Nothing at all. Yet inexplicable shadows abounded, sprouting up as far as he could see. Suddenly, disembodied moans floated to him, coming from everywhere and nowhere he could pinpoint. A chill kissed the nape of his neck, and a memory bubbled to the surface of his mind. He had been here before. The day King Ewen demanded he travel to Sura via veil. The trip should have taken mere moments, but Ewen had forced him to travel through a shadowy realm. A large imposing shadow had approached him.

"I had no idea who or what you were, but I was drawn to you even then."

Drakon whirled toward the voice. Melika stood not twenty feet away, the alien sky silhouetting her massive frame.

"This is the Dark Realm then," he said, concealing the rising worry from his voice. "Why have you brought me here?"

He had scarcely finished the question when Melika vanished. He spun in the mist, his eyes raking the barren landscape for sign of her. Where had—

Melika materialized directly before him. With a blur of motion, she lifted and slammed him into the pliable earth. Before he could draw air back into his lungs, she straddled him. Her talons slowly dug into his flesh and grazed bone. He bucked and jerked like a half-trained stallion. A solid bulk jammed into his lower back, and he stilled. His dagger. Thank Apalsi for small favors. He inched a hand toward the weapon.

Melika lowered her gruesome face. Thick ropes of saliva snapped free from thin lips and dripped onto his face. Her eyes flared with amber light. "Admirable that, even with my essence flowing through you, you were able to break my control over your mind. Peculiar thing, the mate bond. Even so, here, my power is omnipotent."

She pressed her immense weight onto his chest. A rib

snapped like parched firewood. Drakon groaned through gritted teeth. She would ground his bones to dust if he didn't do something soon.

"...I could leave you here and allow you to watch me torture your bonded. A few days or weeks and you'll willingly abdicate the power that rightly belongs to me."

Drakon stiffened. He wouldn't let that happen.

The bottom of Melika's face split into a ghoulish grin. "As I'm sure you know, they're ways to torture a person without killing them. With all the power available to you, you lack the knowledge necessary to travel between realms. Least of all, the knowledge to locate your home realm among infinite possibilities. For eons, I possessed knowledge but lacked the power. You, on the other hand, will be trapped here with a power you cannot begin to understand. If you pass the power to me, I promise to grant you and your mate quick deaths."

Drakon wrapped fingers around the dagger hilt. "I would be a fool to take you at your word. I might never leave this place, but neither will you."

He ripped his arm free and rammed the dagger into her eye. The orb ruptured in a spray of ocular fluid. Melika reared back with a roar. Drakon staggered to his feet, fighting against the pain in his chest and arm. He released a blast. The shockwave struck Melika with significant force. She tumbled tail overhead across the landscape. Drakon hobbled forward, but the ground jolted and rolled under his feet like a sack of snakes. He lurched forward and fell to his knees.

A low maniacal laugh drew his attention to Melika. Wetness wept from her ruined eye. She stood, waiting as the land surged him toward her. "Did you really believe damage to this physical shell would be enough to kill me? I am eternal. Beyond your ability to fathom or destroy."

She raised her hands into the air. Around him, hands shot up through the mist to clutch his legs and arms. He hacked at the bodiless appendages and tore free. His struggles having displaced the mist, the ground was partially visible. He glanced down and wished he hadn't. Tortured faces and outstretched hands pressed up *through* the soil. Sightless eyes gazed upward, imploringly. Stretched mouths moaned, mournful and forsaken. The sound rose to a crescendo, saturating the atmosphere with desolation and despair. Drakon trudged forward, hands over his ears, but was dragged down. The groping hands wrapped around him, ensnaring him as securely as chains. Melika bent over him. Her tail whipped and slashed the air behind her.

"The souls of Gathi who've sacrificed their lives to me afford me power to command the land itself. I cannot be killed in this place. Yield and be granted the mercy of a swift death. Light cannot triumph in darkness."

Drakon struggled against his bonds. Long dormant feelings of helpless resurged. Panic tightened its grip on his throat, threatened to choke him. Power was supposed to protect him. Yet for the sake of power, he was tortured and the people he cared for most endangered. He had fought against the arrogant Gathi nobles and now Melika and her creatures, all the while growing more powerful, and that power had failed him.

Exhaustion washed over him. He felt ancient. For the first time, he wondered what it would feel like not to have to fight. If he let go of this power—this light entrusted to him? His heart stuttered. A memory crystallized of the Oracle's words to him back in Napata.

"Light and darkness cannot coincide. Light is a poison to darkness. It will always shine a path through."

That was it. He was always meant to relinquish this power to Melika. It could only achieve its potential in his surrendering it. Peace rose and beat back the panic and weariness weighing him down.

He stared into Melika's injured gaze. "I'll abdicate."

Melika's black tongue snaked out to wet thin lips. "Will the power to me. Just a thought and all will be done."

He nodded and focused on the power swelling within him, gathering it and pushing outward. Iridescent wisps lifted from his skin, reaching for Melika, and pressing into the armor of her carapace. A faint luminosity radiated from her and brightened as Drakon willed every drop of power from his body to hers. Melika tilted her head back and moaned in rapture. Her once obsidian eyes blazed with iridescent fireflies. Pure, untainted light. Poison to her darkness.

Melika's sounds of pleasure cut off with a gasp. She blinked rapidly. The radiance emanating from her began to smolder. Vapors of smoke billowed from her frame. She reared back with an agonized shriek and collapsed into convulsions, her limbs beating a dull rhythm against the tortured ground. Flesh bubbled and sloughed away. The light within her intensified, and Drakon had to look away. In a violent flash, Melika erupted. Iridescent dust rained down. His restraints vanished. The ever-present moans ceased. Drakon slumped forward onto his hands and knees. He closed his eyes, listening to the steady beat of his heart.

It was over.

"You've done well, Nahum."

Drakon slit open an eye. Then both eyes widened. Before him in majestic radiance stood the Oracle of Napata, the Royal Fighter who had taken him to Umgar as a child, and the young slave girl he had rescued from Jenna City.

Each stared at him with identical, familiar gazes…ancient and assessing as if they could see into the core of him. Suddenly, everything made sense—the tickles of recognition and unease he felt when he met the girl and the Oracle. On a subconscious level, his psyche had linked them to the fighter from his past.

The Oracle approached, her thin white hair and robes blowing in a wind with no origin. Her milky eyes twinkled, and her mouth curved into a smile.

"I have always been with you. Guiding you. Thank you for doing what I could not," all three of the forms spoke in a deep, rolling voice.

"Apalsi?"

"Yes."

Drakon blinked in stunned silence as the Apalsi Oracle lowered a hand to his brow. Warmth and renewed vigor flowed through him like liquid sunlight. He shrank. Talons retracted and morphed into nails. Unlike his initial, painful transformation, Apalsi's ministrations were a warm caress. The Apalsi Oracle offered her hand. He took it and allowed himself to be pulled to his feet.

"Thank you."

She nodded. "For your sacrifice, I have cleansed Melika's essence from you and restored your power. You will need it as you unite the Gathi and Lim to destroy the remnants of Melika's taint in your world," said the three forms.

Drakon frowned. "Melika is dead. Isn't she?"

"Ones such as Melika and I can never die in the way of men. Nonetheless, her essence has been rendered inert. The nobles who weren't transformed have lost their magic, but the other abominations remain free."

"Can't you banish them back to the Dark Realm?"

"I will not directly intervene. I did once to save the Lim from Melika and paid the price. It is not our way. I've given you all you need. Now, return to your place and people."

What price had Apalsi paid? Drakon opened his mouth to speak, but, in an instant, he stood blinking into the bright light of the Somorrah morning. Someone gasped. He turned toward the sound and was nearly knocked from his feet as Eza catapulted herself at him, wrapping her uninjured arm around his waist in a fierce hug.

Eza smiled up at him, her large eyes shimmering. "I thought I'd lost you." His hand went up to rub the back of his flushing neck. He cleared his throat.

"What of Melika?" came a familiar voice, saving Drakon from his discomfort.

Drakon glanced over Eza's shoulder. Dagoti, bloodied and bruised, stood alongside equally battered Sage, Zemket, Taru, and Crain. At once, Drakon detected Erlik's absence and the tear tracks tracing clean lines down Taru's grimy face. There were losses on both sides this day.

He glanced back at Dagoti. "She's gone. We'll have to track down and kill the remaining wailers and possessed nobles. We can regroup—"

There was a thunderous crack overhead. Every eye

swiveled upward. The sky rumbled. Iridescent light shimmered, casting the heavens in an array of colors before an explosion rippled outward and disappeared into the distance. Immediately, a cool breeze ruffled Drakon's hair and tattered clothing.

"I don't believe it," Crain said, awe lacing his voice as he stared into the sky. "I think the Glens just exploded."

If the Glens was destroyed, it meant Melika was indeed gone, and her curse on the Forsaken Lands was lifted. Drakon shared a glance with Eza. A slow grin spread across her face. From this day forward, there would be no separation between the two lands.

Both their people were truly free.

EPILOGUE

Eza leaned over the wooden fence, its rough surface digging into her bare forearms, but she didn't notice. All her focus remained on the formation of recruits in the training yard.

"One!"

"One!" their echoing voices rumbled through the dewy morning air and brought a smile to Eza's lips.

The males and females varied in complexion, from pale to ebony. They counted through maneuvers, mimicking Dagoti's thrusts and twirls with their practice spears.

It was the second training day for this particular group, and their form was nonexistent. Many held their elbows too high, resulting in their weapons angling toward the ground. Others spread their feet too far apart or too narrowly—mistakes that would be corrected during the months-long program.

At the edge of the assembly, a petite, fair-haired female, who appeared no older than twenty, wiped sweat-drenched hair from a flushed face. Her bright blue eyes held determination as she struggled to twirl a spear that was ill-matched for her size.

Eza pursed her lips and shook her head. An unsuited weapon could be as detrimental to a fighter in a battle as being unarmed. Tomorrow, she would restate the importance of selecting the correct size weapon for one's stature.

Such was a common problem for recruits from the former nobility. Their smaller bodies required additional combat strategies to compensate for their size disadvantage. However, Taru turned out to be a skilled instructor and had developed fighting techniques to negate the issue.

Since Melika's defeat, the program Eza, Taru, and Dagoti had created and implemented showed positive results. More than one hundred trainees had graduated to join the cities' defense patrols. However, it would still be months before the graduates tested their competence in the hunting parties.

"At this rate, they would be wailer food in ten seconds flat. They look horrid."

Eza glanced over her shoulder toward the raspy voice she hadn't heard in weeks. Aros stood, a hand shading her eyes from the sun, and frowned out at the trainees.

With stroll tucked beneath an arm and ink staining her tunic, forehead, and nose, the female looked like a quill had attacked her. Large dark rings cradled her eyes, and her cheeks sunk in a little too much for Eza's liking.

Eza leaned against the fence and shrugged. "If they were already warriors, we wouldn't need to teach them. They desire to fight, which makes all the difference. As a warrior, you can understand the dedication needed to train. They do their best. That's all we ask. We won't be sending them out on hunts anytime soon, but I believe they will improve for even that task."

Then she trailed her gaze down Aros's form and met the tribal leader's eyes. "You look exhausted and too thin. Take better care of yourself. I don't need you falling ill. Now, why are you here when you obviously should be resting?"

The female nibbled her bottom lip with a fang, indecision flashing across her worn features.

Curiosity piqued, Eza leaned forward and raised an eyebrow in question. "Well? Will you leave me to wonder? You have had your nose in tomes since we relocated, and I've barely seen you for meals or patrols. Your news must be important for you to suffer sunlight."

Aros pulled a face, her hand still propped at her brow, blocking her sensitive eyes from the sun's rays. "How you all bear this God-awful light is beyond me."

Eza smirked. "You would adapt if you spent more than a few minutes outside every few days." She tugged the female's hand down from her face.

Aros hissed and squeezed her eyes into slits, but her hands remained at her sides. "Was that necessary?"

"Probably not," Eza said with a shrug.

They shared a laugh, but then Aros released a heavy sigh through pursed lips. "You are right. There is something I wish to share with you."

The gravity in Aros's tone had Eza schooling her expression. "Go on."

"Remember what Drakon told us about his encounter with Apalsi? After Melika was destroyed?"

Confused, Eza shook her head. "He said many things—"

Aros waved her words away and began to pace. "So he did. However, the part that intrigues me is when Apalsi mentioned that meddling in our affairs was not their way. Remember? Yet he was the quiet, guiding force, orchestrating events that eventually helped us defeat Melika."

Eza dropped her gaze to the ground to dig a boot into the loose soil. Yes, she remembered. How could she not?

The implications of the words bothered her more than she would admit.

Glancing up to meet Aros's eyes, she asked, "You've figured out what Apalsi meant?"

The tribal leader paused her pacing and shrugged. "It is all speculation and conjecture at this point, but I do not believe he is the only of his kind."

Eza's mouth went slack. She blinked once, twice, a third time. "But how?"

Aros raised her hands in a *"beats me"* gesture. "I do not know, but his words prove he is one of a group, not a solitary and unique being." Aros's eyes widened, sparkled, and a broad smile spread across her face. "If there are more like him, who, for some unknown reason, do not condone intervening in our affairs, it would explain why Apalsi used multiple forms to aid us covertly."

Eza frowned. She didn't know what to think. "Is there any evidence to support your theory? It's a lot to assume with nothing to back it up."

Smile faltering, Aros said, "No, not exactly, but I have read tome after tome from the Lim archives about our original magic. I have also contemplated Apalsi's words." She ran a finger absently along the scroll tucked beneath her arm.

"I am not saying Apalsi is not our creator. I firmly believe that is accurate, but I wonder about his current absence. What if his people found out about his interference? Perhaps, that is why he has not reached out to us." Aros ended with a helpless shrug.

It was true. No one, not even Drakon, had seen the God or any of his forms since Melika's defeat, the destruction of the Glens, and the Gathi's loss of magic.

"Have you shared your concerns with anyone else?" Eza said at length.

"Of course not. I wanted to share my thoughts because I knew you had lingering questions about Apalsi's disappearance."

"I appreciate your coming to me, and, considering the elders can no longer commune with Apalsi, I'm inclined to believe your suspicions."

Aros nodded. "I will continue to search the Gathi historical records and the Lim scrolls for clues about our original magic. Perhaps, I will discover answers to Apalsi's origin in the process."

Eza toyed with the ruined crystal pendant around her neck. It was a reminder of Apalsi's favor. The possibility of others like him was difficult to fathom. Even so, what did she know about the deity? Or about Melika, for that matter...

"What theories do you have about what happened to Melika?" Eza asked, focusing on another mystery that haunted her. "If the demon cannot die like mortals, where does that leave us? Could she regain strength as she did before? Is our reprieve only temporary?"

Aros rubbed at the back of her neck, her eyes focusing inward as she pondered the questions. "I have not found anything in the Gathi archives," she began slowly. She met Eza's gaze. "But that means little, however. It is not as if Melika would have allowed evidence to remain that would have exposed her deceit."

She stroked her chin with a long finger. "My working theory is that because Drakon destroyed Melika's body and

Apalsi severed her parasitic link to the Gathi, she cannot regain strength to regenerate her physical form or return to this realm." Aros shrugged. "Although she left her abominations for us to deal with, Melika herself is not a threat."

Eza grunted, and the knot in her stomach loosened. Turning to stare out at the training yard, she noticed the lesson had concluded, and the recruits were dispersing for a morning break. "I'm glad to hear it," she said and turned back to Aros. "Our number of skilled fighters is increasing, and there is also the magic Apalsi left with Drakon. That will be enough. For now."

It was Aros's turn to raise an eyebrow in question.

"I don't think I'll ever feel safe knowing Melika, weakened or not, is alive. I want you to look for a way we might regain our original magic. We can never be too prepared," Eza said.

A smile split Aros's face, and she swatted Eza's shoulder with her scroll. "We had the same thought. I am already looking into it."

Eza hugged the female. "Thank you."

Aros winked and then hurried away down the narrow path leading to the gardens and disappeared through an archway.

"Haven't seen that one in a while. We could use her expertise on the training field."

Eza startled and whirled around. Dagoti loomed over her, a frown on his face as he leaned against the fence, watching the place Aros had vanished.

"Gah! Don't sneak up on me," Eza said, elbowing him in the ribs.

He didn't register the blow, but he glanced down at her.

Sweat dewed his ebony skin, and a goofy smirk lifted the corner of his mouth. "I didn't creep up on you. You were distracted. Drakon should let you out on more patrols to keep your skills sharp."

Eza cocked her head to one side and propped a hand on her hip. "Excuse me? Drakon doesn't decide what I do or don't do."

The smirk became a toothy grin. "Doesn't he?"

She scowled and moved to punch him, but Dagoti raised his palms in a placating gesture. "I'm only teasing. No need for violence." Then he motioned toward the gardens with a hand. "I thought Aros had taken up residence in the library. She always tells me no when I try to get her outside. What did she want?"

The last thing she needed was Dagoti getting wind of her request to Aros. Although the warrior accepted her healing and Drakon's powers, he was closed-minded toward most magic. It was all questionable in his view.

Eza shrugged as nonchalantly as she could manage. "She was sharing her findings about Gathi histories and her theories of how their occult rituals evolved over—"

Dagoti groaned and cut a hand through the air to stop her. "Never mind. I feel my eyelids growing heavy. Aros is an excellent fighter. I wish I could convince her to help train these poor souls."

Eza punched him then.

"Ouch!" He rubbed his arm and frowned at her. "What was that for?"

"Don't call them that. They might overhear you, and they aren't poor souls. Not with you training them. Those males and females have endless potential. I'm sure they will improve as time goes on."

He grunted. "Well, they aren't as bad as the first batch. I thought most of them would accidentally kill themselves or us!"

Eza laughed, remembering their first group of trainees. Poor form had been the least of their worries. Three months passed before the former Gathi nobility and commoners spoke to one another, let alone worked as a cohesive unit. The Lim trainers had instituted strict oversight to build good faith between the two factions. Although distrust wasn't completely gone, trust was developing as more groups passed through the program.

"If we could whip that group into shape, everything that follows is a simple feat," she said.

Dagoti nodded. "Still, these recruits need at least eight months of instruction before I'm comfortable assigning them to their posts."

"Captain, come have midday meal with me!"

Dagoti tensed and cursed. Raising an eyebrow, Eza glanced around him. A raven-haired female waved from across the training field.

Eza squinted. "That's Joah's younger sister? Kata, right?"

"Don't remind me," Dagoti said, closing his eyes and pinching the bridge of his nose. When he opened his eyes, he appeared weighed down with exhaustion. "She is a nuisance, always late, won't focus, and doesn't take direction. It's like trying to train a toddler. I caught her drawing stick figures in the dirt the other day with her practice sword!"

Eza concealed her bark of laughter with a cough, and Dagoti pinned her with an incredulous glare. "Is that so?"

she said and bit down on her lips to hide her smile.

"It's not funny. The only reason I put up with her is because of her brother. I wouldn't let her within ten feet of any weapon if it weren't for him."

Eza placed a fist to her mouth, trying to appear concerned when all she wanted to do was laugh. She didn't know Kata well, but the female got under Dagoti's skin. She liked her for it.

Dropping her hand to reveal her smile, Eza winked at Dagoti. "Well, are you going to eat midday meal with her?"

His face soured. "Don't be absurd. Of course, I'm not."

"Why not? She seems nice, and she's cute—"

"I don't socialize with recruits," he said, the words clipped. "Especially not odd, scatterbrained ones."

"She doesn't seem that bad. All she needs is a little guidance."

Dagoti snorted and pushed away from the fence, turning to stride back across the field. "Then you give it to her," he called over his shoulder.

He marched passed the female without as much as an acknowledging glance. Kata's wide smile never faltered as she fell in behind him, her rapid-fire words unintelligible across the distance.

"That's an interesting pair," Eza said, turning away.

It would be best if she too ate and cleaned up. Perhaps, she would find Drakon and share a meal with him.

Should she tell him about Aros's suspicions? No. Drakon had enough worries. She wouldn't add another to his growing list. Nodding to herself, Eza hurried along the path toward the palace, her thoughts anxious but hopeful for the future.

ॐ

Drakon reclined to the right of the throne in one of the nine council seats, in which he was a member. Behind him, a drapery hung emblazoned with a crest depicting a shield with three intertwined hands. Each hand represented one of the factions intricate in defeating Melika: the Gathi, Wild Gathi, and the Lim.

Three months had passed since his battle with the demon and Apalsi's disappearance, in all his forms, and Drakon bore witness to wondrous changes. The effects of Melika's curse on the Forsaken Lands had collapsed. As a result, the Lim were venturing back to the surface world. Rivers flowed unencumbered from Somorrah into once dry riverbeds. Nutrient-rich plant life dotted the dusty orange landscape like a young man's fledgling beard.

The Wild Gathi, with Taru's leadership, rejoined society as well, relocating to the cities and assisting in their restoration. Those nobles not transformed during Melika's siphoning—entirely men, women, and children of weaker, lower-level families—had lost their dark magic and station. There were no longer noble and commoner distinctions.

Or slaves.

He rubbed absently at the slave brands burned into his wrists. The abolishment of slavery had been his personal highlight of the changes. The Gathi were now one tribe united with the Wild Gathi and Lim. Nevertheless, memories ran long, and it would take lifetimes to heal the wounds left from years of prejudice, elitism, and hatred. Still, he marveled at how far they had come.

"Drakon?"

He blinked, realizing from the annoyance in the tone, the speaker had addressed him more than once.

"Are you sure about this?" the man said.

Drakon sighed and focused on Umgar, who sat on a plush, high-backed throne. The former general leaned forward, elbows on his knees. His chocolate skin glowed with health in the light streaming through the open windows. A breeze ruffled his lavender robes.

"When will you cease asking me this every time you see me?" Drakon said. "I have never been surer about anything in my life. You're better suited to politics than I. I trust you to guide the Umun into a new, prosperous era."

Umgar smiled. "I do like the name the people have chosen for themselves."

Drakon nodded. Umun was the old Gathi word for solidarity. It fit.

"They would prefer you lead."

"They do, but I don't. The people support the council's decision to appoint you as Supreme Leader over our joint lands and people. I'm content with my position."

Umgar chuckled, his eyes twinkling with mischief. "Right. General Deathmark of the Umun armed forces. The people would settle for nothing less. How goes the search and destroy missions?"

Drakon's good mood dampened, and he sat a bit straighter in his seat. "There has been little wailer and possessed noble sightings around the cities and Waystations. We believe the majority escaped into the Forsaken Lands and the Darklands tunnels beneath. Captains Crain, Taru, Doyna, Null, and Sage are heading the initiative to clear and secure Somorrah. Captains Dagoti, Aros, Eza, and I will organize squadrons to hunt and destroy the remaining creatures that fled the Kingdom."

He paused; aware his following words would draw questions. "But first, we will be visiting Napata. Eza hasn't seen her father since we left the Lim city and wants to assist her tribe's relocation to the surface. Of course, we'll clear out any creatures we encounter on our journey but will return with a larger contingent to thoroughly sweep the passages."

Umgar raised an eyebrow. "You won't be traveling by veil?"

"No. The Umun already see me as a—"

"Savior?" Umgar said, clamping his lips together to hide his spreading grin.

Drakon scowled. "Which is why I use my powers only when necessary. I desire no additional attention."

"Ah, yes," Umgar said, beginning to tap out a beat on his thigh and sing.

"The mighty Drakon. Slayer of demons and evil minions.
In his trail, a spray of crimson.
He battled a wretch and delivered the Kingdom."

Drakon groaned, his face and ears burning. He pushed to his feet and hurried down the dais' steps. "I see it's time I left. If you need me, I'll be preparing for my journey."

A belly laugh followed him down the aisle, and he smiled despite himself.

"Why didn't you tell me you were leaving?"

Umgar stifled his guffawing as Taru strode through the throne room's open doors. When she reached Drakon, she stood on her tiptoes to give him a quick peck on the cheek. The first time she had done this, he hadn't registered her intent until the deed was finished. When no feelings of overwhelming disgust or shame came, he recognized and welcomed the internal shift. That particular, debilitating demon had been vanquished as well. However, physical touch wasn't yet something he was comfortable with in general, but he had come to appreciate the closeness from those in his inner circle.

He smirked at her. "I didn't tell you because you're not going." She opened her mouth to argue, but he held up a hand, silencing her reply. "I need you here to help the others clear the Kingdom. Don't worry. I'm taking a capable force and Dagoti with me."

She folded her arms over her chest and grunted. "Well, I see you have everything planned. Come and see me before you leave, though."

"I will."

She squeezed his forearm and then turned, dismissing him.

"I need to speak with you about the permanent settlement of my people," she said to Umgar, going into the reason for her visit.

Drakon nodded to Umgar, who now wore an earnest expression as Taru continued speaking and took his leave.

He exited the chamber and traversed the now-pristine corridors, which had taken a small army and dogged determination to detach the hardened layers of gore and excrement from the floor and walls.

Former nobles, their alabaster skin free of protective runes, worked beside their one-time servants and slaves to paint and restore the palace's grandeur. They paused in their work to wave or offer tentative smiles as he passed.

Drakon returned them all.

Then he stood before his chamber. He slipped inside and closed the door quietly behind him.

Eza's voice called out to him. "Drakon?"

He strode through the spacious antechamber, decorated in royal blue and gold, and into an equally vast bedchamber. "It's me."

He glanced about. Remains of a meal lay on a table and Eza's staff rested against the enormous four-poster bed, but the woman herself was nowhere in sight.

"Where are you?"

"I'm outside," came her voice.

Drakon crossed the room and parted the sheer curtains to step out on the balcony. Eza leaned against the wall with her arms folded over her stomach and a foot propped up. She gazed down into the courtyard.

Her smooth ebony skin glistened in the sunlight, and the dark curtain of her unbraided hair billowed around her face on a gentle wind. Her leathers melded to lean legs, and she wore a crimson tunic with a ring of fur at the cuffs, even though the temperature never dipped low enough for pelt during the day. He found her curious infatuation with the material endearing.

High-pitched giggling drew his gaze downward. Six children played a game with an air-filled bladder in the yard. Their contrasting coloring showed they were Lim and former nobles. It was nice to see such a sight considering a few of the declassed nobles lamented their loss of magic and status.

As far as Drakon knew, they couldn't even summon orb light. Although the vast majority accepted the new leadership and way of life, unsettling numbers chose to leave Sura and the surrounding cities for the abandoned settlements near the mountains. More than he would have liked.

"Are you well? You're frowning at the children."

The question pulled Drakon from his darkening thoughts, and he glanced back at Eza. Her large black eyes swept his person as if searching for injuries. Initially, such displays of concern made him self-conscious. However, he had grown fond of having someone to worry over him. They had cultivated a more profound emotional relationship during the past months.

She was his closest companion and biggest enigma. They fought together and slept side by side each night. Even so, he continued to stop himself from crossing a line that, in his mind, kept them from truly being mates.

Staring into her caring eyes and beautiful face, he wondered why he held himself back. Suddenly, her eyes widened, and she glanced away and tucked her hair behind a pointed ear.

Apparently, his thoughts were transparent.

"Are you going to answer my question?"

Drakon strode over to the balustrade and leaned against it, facing her. "I apologize. I didn't mean to make you uncomfortable. And I'm fine. I was only thinking about the portion of our paler population who have retreated to distant cities. It worries me. It is difficult to trust after so many years, however hard I try."

Now, he was referring to much more than his sentiments about the derelict nobles.

Eza eyed him intently and then nodded. "I understand. Give them the benefit of the doubt. If they continue to live harmoniously with us, then they should be free to reside where they please." She pushed from the wall and came to stand before him. "Have all the arrangements for our travel to Napata been finalized?"

"Yes."

"When do we leave?"

"Three days. It will take that long to gather provisions for the force."

She stepped into him, her arms encircling his waist and her head tucked under his chin. She squeezed him. He returned the embrace, inhaling her unique scent of earth and cinnamon. His breast swelled with an emotion he couldn't quite grasp or comprehend. He only knew it felt right. He would cherish this woman for as long as she let him.

"Thank you," she said into his chest. "I know the journey won't be without danger."

He smiled and squeezed her tighter. "After all we've seen and done, I believe we can handle a jaunt to Napata."

ॐ

Consciousness returned to the man in degrees.

He was instantly aware of the heaviness of his limbs as if two-thousand-pound weights hung from them. He blinked. Or, at least, he tried to, but his eyelids remained motionless. The well of darkness encased him completely.

Unease slithered down his spine and coiled into his gut. Heartbeat thrashing in his ears, he attempted once more to move. Anything. A finger. His foot.

Nothing happened.

Again and again, he struggled until his breaths escaped him in gasps, and he trembled from the exertion. He sucked in a deep breath and exhaled slowly, and the action calmed the mounting terror clawing at him. He focused on his surroundings to glean information about his whereabouts.

No sounds aside from his steady breathing greeted him. No smells, faint or otherwise. He couldn't even feel the tactile presence of the surface on which he lay. Nothing. Not the soft give of a bed nor the unyielding resistance of a floor. He was adrift in a void.

Unbidden, the clammy hand of panic reached out of the emptiness for him. *Where was he? How did he get here?*

His frantic thoughts stuttered and ceased as something unfurled, twitched in the recesses of his mind. It wiggled, seeming to gain awareness as the man had only moments before. Then it spoke in a weakened voice much like gravel crunched beneath a boot but undeniable and familiar.

My dear Nolan. It would appear I require your services after all.

There was no tamping the unfettered terror escaping him. Nolan opened his mouth and, this time, his body obeyed his command.

A wretched scream of absolute despair and hopelessness tore from him and vanished into the abyss.

END

ABOUT THE AUTHOR

D.T. Stubblefield is an unashamed bibliophile, former editor, wife, mother of three beautiful girls, and servant to a fur baby! She can usually be found with her nose stuck in a book, listening to an audiobook, or typing away on her next novel.

If you enjoyed this book, please consider leaving a review. Every review helps spread the word. For more information, visit her website at www.dtstubblefield.com.